Praise for *The Foundling Boy*:

"I loved this book for the way, in its particularities and its casual narration, it admitted me to a world I knew nothing about and the many ways it made me care. It is not just a glimpse into the past, but the study of the heart of a man and his times." Paul Theroux

"The Foundling Boy is a legitimate, if not yet fully grown, heir to the great line of storytellers running from Fielding to Giono." *Le Figaro*

"This is a book to devour, savouring every last mouthful." Pierre Moustiers

The Foundling Boy

by Michel Déon

translated from the French
by Julian Evans

Gallic Books
London

This book has been selected to receive financial assistance from English PEN's 'PEN Translates!' programme, supported by Arts Council England. English PEN exists to promote literature and our understanding of it, to uphold writers' freedoms around the world, to campaign against the persecution and imprisonment of writers for stating their views, and to promote the friendly co-operation of writers and the free exchange of ideas.

A Gallic Book

First published in France as Le jeune homme vert by Éditions Gallimard, 1975

Copyright © Éditions Gallimard, Paris, 1975

English translation copyright © Julian Evans, 2013

First published in Great Britain in 2013 by Gallic Books, 59 Ebury Street, London, SW1W 0NZ

A CIP record for this book is available from the British Library
ISBN 978-1-908313-56-0

Typeset in Fournier MT by Gallic Books
Printed in the UK by CPI Group (UK) Ltd, Croydon, CR0 4YY

2 4 6 8 10 9 7 5 3 1

Jeanne could not find a way through the hawthorn hedge. The stiff branches slashed at her face and arms. She ran along the path in the hope of finding an opening, but the hostile, aggressive hedge was impenetrable. Clasping her large barren bosom with both hands to stop it bouncing, she felt her heart's panic-stricken thumping as a sharp pain under her left palm. But she could not give up. Behind the hedge, in the young birch forest, a child was wailing, and its fitful cries, carried on the evening air, were calling for her help. She badly wanted to rescue the baby lost in the wood, but her heavy legs felt glued to the earth and her lungs were failing her. She gasped for breath. If she did not hurry up, the child would die and Albert would never forgive her. What made her panic most was that, although she must have run the best part of a kilometre to try to find a way through, the cries were as close as ever, as if the baby was following her behind the hawthorns. Then she realised that the path must go in a circle around the wood, whose dappled foliage was rustling in the fading light. The wailing broke off, and Jeanne stopped, paralysed by fear, with such a lump in her throat that when she tried to call out, only a croak passed her lips.

'What's the matter?' Albert said.

A strong hand, with its calloused palm, squeezed her arm, and Jeanne's anxiety vanished. She opened her eyes onto the darkness of the bedroom, made out its shape and the position of the window, saw the curtains stir in the breeze. Albert's thumb stroked her forearm with a reassuring gentleness.

'There's a baby crying,' she said.

'No there isn't, it's nothing ... go back to sleep.'

9

'There is, there is, I promise you. Listen.'

They stopped talking and heard nothing, and then there was a wail from somewhere close by, weaker than in Jeanne's dream, a last exhausted whimper.

'Oh,' Albert said. 'You're right! It sounds like an injured hare.'

'I'm sure it's a baby.'

'At this hour ... outside our window?'

He had a literal mind that had no room for anything unexpected. Jeanne sat up in bed, listening intently. There was another plaintive, desperate wail.

'Maybe it's Old Souillet's crow. It imitates anything that moves.'

'I'm going to see,' Jeanne said, stretching out her hand to grope for the sulphur matches on the bedside table.

The Pigeon lamp gave out a gloomy, yellowish glow that shed almost no light. Jeanne adjusted the wick, put a dressing gown on over her nightdress, and went down the wooden staircase. The house had two entrances, one opening into the park, the other onto the road. Without hesitation, Jeanne went to the door to the road and opened it. A wicker basket sat in the middle of the steps, festooned with ribbons. Her hand made contact with a wool blanket. Bringing the Pigeon lamp closer, she saw a minuscule face screwed up against its glimmer. The baby gave a weak cry and its mouth twisted up.

'Jesus! Mary! It is a child! Come down quick, Albert.'

She forgot that Albert could not come down quickly. He had only one good leg and needed time to strap on the other wooden one, pull on a pair of trousers and grip the banister, step by step.

'Are you sure?' she heard him shout from upstairs.

'Am I sure? Listen to you!'

'Bring it up then, and we'll see. Is it just one?'

Only then did she think to look up and down the road, but the dark night only revealed what she knew already: a bend to the right, another to the left, the hawthorn hedge opposite. A light, almost warm breeze caressed the shapes of the shadows. A few stars twinkled in the sky. The moon was not yet up. On windy nights you could hear distinctly the waves buffeting the cliffs, but tonight the sea was calm and far away, as if blotted out by the summer night. Jeanne cautiously picked up the basket and carried it to the bedroom. Albert was waiting in his nightshirt, sitting on the edge of the bed with one leg dangling, holding a paraffin lamp.

'So you were right. It is a baby,' he said, stroking his thick moustache.

'He can't be more than a week old.'

She lifted the baby out of the basket and brought him closer to the lamp. A warm blue shawl tied with ribbons enveloped him. Next to him someone had placed a full bottle, a hairbrush, a tin of talcum powder and a sealed envelope that Albert opened. 'I was born on 16 August. I don't have a name. You can find one for me if you want me to stay with you.'

'The bottle's cold. You look after him while I warm it up,' Jeanne said, with the decisiveness that characterised her at important moments.

She placed the baby in Albert's arms. Never having held a child in his life before, he was petrified, and he remained sitting on the edge of the bed, his good leg sticking out, bare, hairy and muscular. He had not moved an inch when Jeanne came back and relieved him of his burden.

'He's a nice boy, anyway,' he said.

The baby's mouth opened wide and clamped shut on the teat. Air bubbles rose in the bottle as its level dropped. Twice Jeanne gently took the bottle away from him to burp him by patting him on the back. Albert, bending over him, received a blast of sour milk smell full in his face. In a cupboard Jeanne found some baby clothes that had been used nineteen years before, for Geneviève. She undressed the baby, washed, talced and re-dressed him.

'He's a handsome boy,' she said, with an approving nod, referring to what she had just uncovered and covered up again, as though long experience and many patient measurements entitled her to identify a promising future.

He was hardly wrapped up again before he fell asleep, his fists closed, as two anxious faces bent over him: Jeanne's round and moon-like, with small grey eyes marked with crow's feet and a chin adorned with a small polyp, Albert's long and hollow-cheeked, eyes yellowed by caporal tobacco smoke and calvados fumes, and a thick greying moustache as stiff as a brush.

These loving, anxious faces were the first to imprint themselves on the visual memory of the small boy who was christened Jean and took the name of his adoptive parents: Arnaud. Exactly as in a fairy tale, Albert and Jeanne placed gifts in his basket-cradle, the only possessions in which they were rich: courage and goodness, uprightness and charity, all the qualities that were largely responsible for Jean's later misadventures and for the opinion, partly false, that he formed of the rest of humanity. I say 'partly false' because from his childhood onwards he also met with spite, hypocrisy and mistrust, of which wiser fairies might have thought to inculcate an instinctive recognition in him. But we know that evil always surprises, and it is trust's task to be disappointed. Jean opened his eyes onto a marvellous world, filling his lungs with the air of peace and freedom, a world where the brave were rewarded and the guilty pardoned. A great epoch was dawning. There would no longer be need of soldiers: Albert, along with many other veterans, was seeing to it, and of all the politicians who held forth in those years he listened to, and read, with most warmth and emotion those who promised an end to those wars for which men departed joyously, flowers in their rifle barrels, and from which they returned with a wooden leg where their left leg had been. I forgot to mention that Jean was born in the year of the treaty of Versailles, 1919; that since our first sentence we have been in Normandy – the hawthorns, the sound of sea against cliffs; and that Albert's leg was left behind in the mud at Verdun in the course of one of those futile attacks that some generals seem to have a knack for. Among the other faces that offered themselves to Jean's wide-eyed surprise, let us note immediately:

Monsieur du Courseau, owner of La Sauveté, of which Albert and Jeanne were the caretakers; Madame du Courseau, née Mangepain, who, the morning after the boy first appeared, had returned from a journey to Menton where her daughter Geneviève, nineteen years of age, was being treated for her lungs; Antoinette du Courseau, four years old (a home leave of Monsieur du Courseau's after the battle of Les Éparges); Michel du Courseau, two years old (another leave of Monsieur du Courseau's, before embarking for Salonika); Captain Duclou, Jeanne's uncle and one of the last Cape Horners; Monsieur Cliquet, retired railway employee, Albert's cousin; and last but not least Monsieur the abbé Le Couec, parish priest of Grangeville, a Breton exiled to Normandy by higher authorities nervous of his separatist fancies. This was not, we must acknowledge, a particularly large universe, but Jean could have fared worse, knowing only – until he finally left for military service – narrow-minded parents, an imbecilic schoolmaster, a numbingly dull priest, and a country house made gloomy by constipated proprietors. There are, actually, a couple of truly constipated characters lurking in this list. It will be clear who I mean in time. I prefer not to be specific, because it is after all possible that their attitudes will not seem constipated to readers of this story and may even be applauded by a silent majority. I am happy nevertheless to reveal that I am not talking about Monsieur du Courseau, whom Jeanne ran to inform as soon as it was light, pushing the baby into Albert's arms and leaving him both paralysed by his responsibilities and furious at being forbidden to smoke his pipe in any room where little Jean was.

*

At about five o'clock in the morning, winter and summer, it was Monsieur du Courseau's habit to get up, go down to the kitchen and make himself a large bowl of coffee, which he drank standing up in his dressing gown before going to his library where he closeted himself until eight. He was a tall, native Norman, ruddy-complexioned, blue-eyed, with a muscular neck and hands the shaped like paddles. Since being demobilised, he had put on weight around his waist but was unworried and even satisfied to note the reappearance of noble curves that the mud of the trenches and the diseases of the Army of the Orient[1] had banished for a time. Nor did he worry about his baldness, which revealed a splendid skull, shining, smooth and emphasised by a corolla of greying hair. No one having ever seen a new book cross the threshold of his private library, it had to be assumed that he spent his time there rereading the same books, notably a complete Dickens in orange-red soft covers, a set of Balzac bound in shagreen, the works of Voltaire in the thirty-two-volume 1818 edition, and twenty or so biographies of William the Conqueror, his hero and the only man he admired, because he had defeated the English. Nothing of Antoine du Courseau's reading ever surfaced in his conversation. When he was not eating, he liked to talk about food (when he was eating he was not talkative at all, being occupied with the sensations of eating and their analysis), about flowers (but only with Albert), about women (but only with the abbé Le Couec, who wasn't afraid of them), about cars (but only with Ettore Bugatti whom once a year he visited at Molsheim to buy a new car), and about politics with nobody, having given up being outraged by anything. He had in fact ignored all political matters since his youth, when he had inherited La Sauveté from his mother and a fleet of trawlers from his father. Madame du Courseau was quite comfortably off too, being descended from three generations of millers who had long ago hung up their white jackets, the Mangepains of Caen. Yes, I know, how aptly named! But I can do nothing about that. The war had passed by without greatly troubling them, unlike many others whom it had

14

enriched or ruined. Only two shadows darkened this happy picture: in Serbia Antoine had been wounded in the shoulder by a piece of shrapnel, and there was no question of his ever hunting again; and in 1917 Geneviève had begun to cough blood. Since then she had been living at Menton. Earlier in the summer they had feared for her future, but Madame du Courseau, who had rushed to her bedside, then announced that she was returning, Geneviève being out of danger …

Jeanne did not find Monsieur du Courseau in the kitchen, where his bowl still stood on the table next to the calvados bottle and the warm coffee pot, confirming that he had been there recently. Though fully aware of the instruction that he was not to be disturbed in his library, Jeanne did not hesitate and, instinctively understanding that there was no point in timidity, she opened the door sharply. A paraffin lamp lit the book-lined room and the desk, on which a china tobacco jar gleamed along with some other copper or silver objects. From a corner of the room there came a muffled cry, and a figure sat up. Monsieur du Courseau, for it was he, tidied himself, while on the day bed a black shape went on wriggling. Jeanne recognised Joséphine Roudou, a twenty-five-year-old from Martinique who, since Easter, had been looking after Michel and Antoinette in Madame du Courseau's absence. In a gesture of modesty Joséphine pulled her nightdress up over her face, offering the charming sight of her brown belly and a sex darker than anything else in the library.

'What is it that is so serious, my dear Jeanne?' Antoine asked in an untroubled voice, since he was one of those men whom pleasure never left distracted for longer than two or three seconds.

'We found a child on our doorstep in the night.'

'Which one? Antoinette or Michel?'

'No, somebody else's child!'

15

'But how very interesting. And what is his name?'

'He doesn't have a name. He's about a week old.'

'Goodness me! It must be some sort of joke …'

'Who would dare to make a joke like that?'

'Very true … Madame du Courseau is coming back today. She'll know what to do. While we're waiting, Joséphine can take care of it.'

'Joséphine! Her? Never.'

There was a clucking from underneath the nightdress, and Monsieur du Courseau turned round as though he had just discovered a third person between Jeanne and himself. The sight of her belly still twitching with gentle spasms reminded him what had just happened.

'Put that away now, Joséphine, please, come along.'

She lowered her nightdress and her face appeared, wild-looking, with the whites of her eyes showing. Without the madras headscarf that usually covered her head, her thickly corkscrewed hair gave her a Gorgon's head that was frightening enough to make Jeanne shiver.

'You can go back to your room,' Monsieur du Courseau said.

Jeanne barely saw her dart out of the library, run down the hall and upstairs, leaving behind a scent of peppery skin and a trail of luxuriant free-and-easiness which could, very evidently, turn a man's head, but which Jeanne herself, immune to such charms, judged particularly harshly.

'Where is this child?' Monsieur du Courseau asked.

'With Albert. Albert adores babies.'

'In that case he couldn't be in better hands. Without doubt the best thing to do is to inform Monsieur the abbé Le Couec. Now I need to read …'

Jeanne left the library, disappointed at not having been able to share her excitement with Monsieur du Courseau, although she knew him well enough to be aware of his character and unresponsiveness. And he had given her good advice. The abbé Le Couec was exactly the man she needed. Her bosom swelled with hope, and her generous imagination was already hatching a thousand plans. At last providence

16

was answering her prayers, just when age was forcing her to give up what she had wished for so much: a child. She would keep him, he belonged to her; she made the resolution as she crossed the park, its colours awakening in the early morning with its yellow-tinged dawn and ragged grey strips of cloud. A delicious scented freshness was rising from the earth, from the long bluffs of rhododendrons and the beds of dahlias, begonias, roses and marigolds. Jeanne knew that she had never been as happy as she was at this minute. She forgot the scene she had just witnessed, which should have outraged her, but which later she would relate in detail to her husband, leaving him unable to stop thinking about the story, which took him back to an African woman in a brothel behind the lines, a week before he lost his leg. Her breasts had been like watermelons and he had experienced the most intense pleasure between her strong thighs, nothing like the honest conjugal embraces in which Jeanne had become less and less interested after she had stopped hoping for a child. When Jeanne told him about Joséphine they both swore discretion, but their vow was futile, for soon everyone in the district knew and admitted that Monsieur du Courseau had a partiality to dark skin. Captain Duclou explained that sailors who had tasted such charms remained spellbound for life. Antoine must have picked up bad habits in the Army of the Orient, and since that date there had always been black women at La Sauveté. Each year, at around the same time as he changed his Bugatti, Antoine paid off the Martiniquan or the Guadeloupean he had employed the year before and requested another, who would arrive on one of those banana boats out of Dieppe, fresh, plump and brightly dressed, with gold rings in her ears. I shall not say much more about Joséphine Roudou, whom everyone disapproved of and then rather missed after she exchanged La Sauveté for a fleeting fame in Montmartre before one of those unpleasant maladies that women catch from men of little hygiene carried her off in the space of a few weeks.

Madame du Courseau – I also forgot to mention that her first name was Marie-Thérèse – arrived back at Grangeville the same morning that Jean was settling in with his adoptive parents. After she had kissed Antoinette – largely indifferent – and Michel – who clung to her desperately – Marie-Thérèse hurried to Jeanne's to see the baby. Events would almost certainly have taken a different turn if Monsieur the abbé Le Couec had not been present. That excellent man was in the kitchen, in the middle of an elaborate Cartesian discourse.

'Religion,' he was saying to Jeanne and Albert, 'is shared more easily in this world than anything else. If this child has already been baptised, a second baptism will do him no harm at all. You must not hesitate. A good Christian cannot live properly without the succour of a patron saint. Let us put him on the right track, as Monsieur Cliquet would say. There will always be locomotives to pull him, and if he stays in a siding at least he will be relieved of his original sin. Albert, I know you have no religion, but the most profound sceptics can't be against whatever it is, without contradicting themselves. Give the child a chance, I mean an extra chance, given that he already seems to have been so fortunate in the choice of his adoptive parents ... Ah, Madame du Courseau, greetings. How is our Geneviève?'

'Better, much better, Father. But what's this news, Jeanne? A baby has fallen from the sky at La Sauveté? Where is he?'

'He's asleep, Madame.'

'He's just been fed,' Albert added.

The priest had stood up after putting down his glass of calvados on the waxed cloth of the kitchen table. He was fearless in the face of his parishioners' hospitality. His complexion, which was on the ruddy side, owed much to the visits he made after mass each morning, but his robust constitution allowed him these excesses. He had strength to spare, even after four years of carrying wounded men and digging the graves of the dead in the mud of the trenches. On his return he had put his old, worn cassock back on with its greenish and violet tints, his only vanity being to pin to it the ribbon of his Croix de

Guerre. The presence of that decoration caused Albert to forgive the priest for still being a priest, and although he still had a number of quarrels with him on points of theology, these were little more than annoyances between the two men, rapidly erased by the evocation of the ordeals they had both undergone. Jeanne listened to them open-mouthed, her faith blind and immovable, unlike Madame du Courseau, who would have preferred a priest of greater worldliness at Grangeville, one with a fine speaking voice and more aptitude for the harmonium than apple-based spirits.

'I'll go up and see him,' Madame du Courseau said, in a tone of great firmness.

'You'll wake him up!' Jeanne moved to block her way.

'Jeanne, don't be ridiculous ... It's perfectly clear that you haven't had children. A baby doesn't wake up just because you bend over his cradle.'

'Perhaps I haven't had children, but I have had Geneviève. For long enough that she calls me "Maman Jeanne".'

'I haven't forgotten, I haven't forgotten ... But—'

The discussion would have gone on indefinitely, and harsh words doubtless been exchanged, if Jean had not at that moment had the good sense to cry out. The two women went upstairs. In his Moses basket, fists clenched, the baby was yelling at the top of his lungs. Jeanne picked him up and calmed him immediately. Madame du Courseau wanted to rock him, but when she held him, he started howling again.

'You see,' Jeanne said proudly.

'He's certainly sweet. We shall look after him. I've given it some thought, and we'll put him in Michel's room. Michel can go to Geneviève's.'

'No,' Jeanne said, 'he's staying here.'

'Goodness me, dear Jeanne, what can you be thinking? You have neither the time nor the means to take care of a child.'

'I'll find the time and the means. This baby was put outside my front door. God wills me to have him.'

'I rather suspect that in her guilty haste the mother got the wrong door. Quite clearly she wanted to leave him at ours.'

'With suppositions like that you can remake the whole world. This little boy – Albert and I have decided to call him Jean – belongs to us.'

'His future—' Madame du Courseau began.

'He shall have a future. Money doesn't buy you happiness. We'll teach him to work hard and to love his parents.'

'He's a little young for that, don't you think?'

'We'll wait.'

If Marie-Thérèse du Courseau thought she would find an ally in the priest, she was seriously mistaken. The abbé Le Couec sided with the Arnauds, and nothing would induce him to change his mind, even when the mistress of La Sauveté quite unscrupulously raised the subject of Albert's atheism and anticlericalism.

'Madame,' the abbé said, 'to state the matter briefly, God knows how to identify those among his lost or straying sheep who have Christian virtues and sometimes a charity greatly superior to those who go to mass regularly. Even as a freemason who subscribes to *L'œuvre*, Albert is an example to many.'

'I doubt that your bishop would be of the same opinion,' she answered in a tone with an undercurrent of menace.

President of a ladies' workroom at Dieppe, Marie-Thérèse du Courseau possessed some modest access to the see. They listened to her, flattered her, and she considered as great favours the self-interested kindnesses of the hierarchy. But the abbé Le Couec cared nothing for the hierarchy. He feared neither its reprimands, being bereft of pride, nor its threats of transfer, feeling himself in any case to be a stranger everywhere outside Brittany. Madame du Courseau continued to exert pressure from every angle, but the Arnauds stood their ground. It must be said that she was also fighting a lone battle, her husband taking no interest in the affair. All of her ingenuity was rebuffed by Jeanne's blinkered stubbornness, a stubbornness all the fiercer because the caretaker sensed, on two or three occasions, that some dark plot was threatening her possession. The plot finally failed, thanks to the sergeant at the gendarmerie, the mayor and the primary school teacher, who came down on the side of the Arnauds. Jean had found refuge with them. He would stay there, and no Joséphine Roudou or Marie-Thérèse du Courseau would be allowed to dote on him.

Madame du Courseau still refused to surrender, but continued her campaign in such a way as not to make an enemy of the boy's adoptive mother, and if she had any regrets she nevertheless rapidly understood, in the wake of two incidents that could have ended in tragedy, that the foundling's place was not at La Sauveté. On the first occasion little Michel, just two years old, was found standing next to Jean's cradle, trying to stab him. The baby was asleep in the sun in front of the lodge when Jeanne heard a scream. She dashed outside to glimpse Michel, his fist clutching the handle of a kitchen knife, struggling with Joséphine Roudou. In his cradle, Jean's blood was running onto the pillow from a long gash on his left cheek. If Joséphine had not been there, Michel would have put his eyes out. On another occasion it was Antoinette who ran to warn Jeanne that her brother had stolen the rat poison and was trying to make the baby swallow it, although from that episode he suffered nothing worse than an attack of vomiting.

Have I said anything yet about the physical appearance in which Madame du Courseau, née Marie-Thérèse de Mangepain, offered herself? No, because to me it seems that it goes without saying, but a person reading over my shoulder is worrying me somewhat by describing her as in her forties, ugly, simultaneously authoritarian and sickly-sweet, dressed like those ladies of good works who seem constantly to be watching out for the sins of others. Let us not allow free rein to anyone else's imagination, apart from my own. At the time this story begins, Marie-Thérèse de Courseau is thirty-eight years old. In three years' time she will cut her hair short, which will save her from too harsh a transition to her forties. She drives herself to mass in her own trap, swims in the Channel during the three summer months, cooks very admirably when necessary, teaches the Gospels to the children of the village and, as we have seen, presides over her workroom at Dieppe. Dressed by Lanvin, there is no trace in her of the provincial lady in her Sunday best. No one has ever seen her faint at a trifle. In fact, you could say that she is a woman with a strong head, although the head, in her case, is misleading: an expression of sweetness, a voice of honey, a kindness that is only withdrawn whenever she encounters an object in the way of her desires — as for example when Jeanne decided to adopt little Jean. The ambiguity of her character is apparent in her relations with her children. She was never interested in Geneviève until her daughter started coughing. She more or less ignores Antoinette, but repeatedly reveals her adoration of little Michel. If asked the question, 'Do you have children?' she will answer, 'Yes, I have one child, Michel, and two daughters too.' To go a step further and pierce the veil of intimacy, she fulfils her conjugal obligations without appetite, as a dutiful woman does. Antoine's misdemeanours caused her pain at first, but now she is indifferent to them. She has not been insensitive to the 'du' that precedes Courseau, and is no less proud of having been born a Mangepain, the more so now that a brother of hers is a deputy, elected on a right-wing platform in Calvados. She knows perfectly well, however, that if the 'du' Courseaus have one or two pretensions, they do not feature in any directory of the nobility. Sometimes people address her as 'baronne', and she does not always correct those who do. Thus are titles forged, over a generation or two. I come back to that expression of sweetness that one can usually see on her face. It has not always been there: as a young girl Marie-Thérèse had a lovely complexion, fresh and pink, that made people forget a certain sourness in her features: thin lips, a sharp nose. As she has got older her complexion has faded, and her sweet expression has corrected the loss. Almost everyone is taken in, except, probably, the abbé Le Couec, whose own sweetness is not on the surface and who, by dint of hearing the confessions of Norman farmers, is more than a little sceptical of the innate goodness of humankind.

So Jean stayed with the Arnauds. I shall not recount his early childhood, which was composed above all of little needs and great appetites, illnesses he had to catch, tears, laughter, cries and the smiles his adoptive mother was always looking out for on his lips. To Jeanne's profound annoyance, Madame du Courseau insisted on interfering with the baby's education, which had the result of exacerbating Michel's jealousy. It was a strange thing to see this child of two years old, nearly three, grow pale with anger whenever Jean's name was mentioned. It amused Michel's sister Antoinette to provoke him. Perhaps it was to irritate him even more that she conceived a passion for Jean. Escaping from Joséphine, then from her successor, Victoire Sanpeur, she ran to hide in the lodge. Jeanne had no more faithful ally than this five-year-old child. Keeping a lookout at the kitchen window, as soon as Antoinette saw her mother approaching she would shout, 'Watch out, it's her!' whereupon Jeanne would throw herself into some frenetic task – waxing the floor, polishing her copper pans – to justify her monosyllabic responses to Madame du Courseau.

As for Albert, he continued to grumble. For him, peace would truly have meant peace if his employers had found him a couple of assistant gardeners and some decent fertiliser. His grumbles met with no response from Antoine du Courseau, who, up until the war, had taken little or no pleasure in analysing his own feelings, and in his private moments was frightened to discover in himself a kind of unease for which he could not find a name. He would have been amazed to learn that the feeling in question was one of boredom. Boredom that he banished in his own way by straddling whichever Martiniquaise was working at La Sauveté at the time or by reversing his Bugatti out of the garage to race the country roads using every one of its thirty horsepower, scattering hens, dogs, cats and dawdling flocks of sheep as he went. It was thus that, one afternoon in the summer of 1920, at the wheel of his sports car, he reached Rouen, crossed the River Seine and, having sent a telegram back to La Sauveté telling them not to wait, continued via Bernay and Évreux deep into an agricultural Normandy that was foreign to him. France seemed terrifically exotic to him, so full was his mind's eye still with the memory of landscapes burnt by the sun, cracked by cold or glowing with poppies that he had encountered in southern Serbia and Macedonia. This was a France he did not know, unless he had forgotten it, and it worked its way back into his mind via neat villages full of flowers, hundreds of delicate churches, and a countryside drawn in firm and well-finished lines and softly coloured in grey, green, and red brick. The war had not passed this way, and to see the parish priests out walking, mopping their brows with big checked handkerchiefs, the postmen on bicycles in their straw hats, the children mounted atop hay carts bringing in the second cutting, you would have thought the whole conflict merely a bad dream born of men's unhinged imaginations.

The greedy Bugatti gobbled up the kilometres, trailing a plume of ochre dust behind it, its engine burbling with a joyful gravity that communicated itself to the driver. The indefinable malaise Antoine suffered from was left far behind, at La Sauveté. At petrol depots he stopped to stretch his legs and answer the questions of mechanics who walked respectfully around the car, examining it. The same model, a Type 22 driven by Louis Charavel, had recently won the Boulogne Grand Prix, and the automotive world was beginning to talk about

Ettore Bugatti and his little racing cars that were beginning to eat away at the supremacy of the monsters made by Delage, Sunbeam, Peugeot and Fiat.

Antoine felt so relaxed that he stopped to have dinner at Chartres, after changing his tyres and four spark plugs and filling up with petrol. Afterwards he drove straight out of the city and into the night. His headlamps lit no more than a few metres of the road ahead and he had to ease back on the throttle, driving inside a small, tight circle of light that threw trees up as he passed and pierced the thick shadows of sleeping villages. Two or three times on the outskirts of a town he almost drove into an unlit farmer's cart. He felt as if he was playing Russian roulette and stepped on the accelerator once more, drinking in deep draughts of the cool night as dense as a mass of black water rolling over him. At about two o'clock in the morning, apparitions began rearing up at the roadside. He was driving in a trance that was close to drunkenness: columns of soldiers in sky-blue uniforms were marching northwards, followed by towed artillery, 75-mm guns that paused to fire between the trees. Each shot pierced the night with a burst of red and yellow. He passed a convoy of ambulances coming towards him that left a long trail of blood on the road, then floated to the surface of a lake that muffled the noise of the engine and the screech of the tyres. Here he felt marvellously well for a moment, but then was buffeted by waves and the bodywork groaned and the muffled engine stopped with a hiccup. He fell asleep on the steering wheel, waking up at the first rays of the morning sun in a ploughed field, soaked in dew. The engine fired straight off, and he bumped back to the road. Day was breaking over the Bourbonnais, with its white villages and pretty cool-smelling woods. He carried on to Lyon, where he arrived shortly before lunch after following the banks of the sluggish Saône. He was thirsty and hungry and stopped at a roadhouse by the Rhône. He was served with a jug of Beaujolais, saucisson and butter, while children and gawpers surrounded the Bugatti, parked at the kerb. It had suffered during the night. Squashed mosquitoes and moths dirtied its fine blue bodywork, and its spoked wheels bore traces of its trip across the field. But even as it was, it still looked like a thoroughbred at rest, its neck proudly tensed, its round rump with its cylindrical petrol tank. Antoine arranged for it to be washed at a garage and only then thought of himself. His hardy woollen suit was holding out, but his soiled shirt and day-old beard did not suit the owner of a thoroughbred. He bought a shirt and changed into it at the barber's after the barber, a small, catty man he could not bring himself to speak to, had shaved him. He was in a hurry to get started, to feel the warm wind stroking his face once more and hear the engine's happy purring. Lyon's deserted streets surprised him. Not a single passer-by, not a tram, the curtains all drawn and shutters shut, café terraces empty without a gloomy waiter in sight, the Rhône unfurling its bluish cold waters between banks of pebbles, Fourvière on the hill blurred in a heat haze that smothered even the sound of its bells. The Bugatti, rolling between gleaming tram tracks down cobbled streets, tried vainly to dislodge this strange torpor by the clamour of its four cylinders. Lyon was at lunch.

By mid-afternoon he had reached Valence. Another France began here, on the road out of town, in the pale green and grey of its olive trees. A violent surge of happiness filled Antoine. He knew now where he was heading. The road led all the way down to his daughter Geneviève. It had all been planned for a long time, and he hadn't known. There was no hurry any more. He dropped his speed and drove more carefully. On the way out of Montélimar the next morning, he bought clean underwear and filled the Bugatti with nougat. Now and again he urged it to a gallop, and the plane trees flashed past in splashes of sunlight through the foliage. The Provençal landscape, so harmonious and beautiful – the loveliest in the world – sparkled before him like a mirage with its walls of black cypresses, its roofs of curved ochre-coloured tiles, its peaceful, blessed farms and pale sky.

At Aix he stopped at a garage to have the oil changed, and a mechanic addressed him as 'captain'. Antoine recognised him: Charles Ventadour, tall and emaciated with a gypsy's complexion, a driver in his company who had driven his truck all over the potholed and cratered roads of Macedonia. Aix was one place it was worth giving up some time for. He knew his destination from here, so there was no hurry. He dined with Charles Ventadour, who reminisced about Serbia, the Turks, the roads where the Army of the Orient had got stuck, gone down with diarrhoea, shivered with malaria. He exaggerated, but in the overblown colours of his recollections there was the beauty of a shared memory, and both men suddenly felt a brotherhood so close that a friendship was born, a friendship that could never have existed in the army. After dinner they slumped in armchairs on a café terrace on the Cours Mirabeau. Why didn't all of France live here? Shed its ambition, and let happy days roll past around a fountain bubbling with foam, watching pretty girls with passionate eyebrows and hourglass waists. Antoine thought fleetingly of Victoire Sanpeur. Even with her springy, curly sex, she didn't make the grade.

He set out again next morning, and when the sun was nearly at its highest drove through a little port full of green, lateen-rigged tartanes with crude patched sails. On the dock a few conscientious artists had set up their easels and were painting, dripping with sweat in the heat. On the road out of the village he stopped at an open-air café at the edge of a beach and got out. He was lent a black swimming costume with shoulder straps that was too big for him. A pretty girl with brown hair, pink cheeks and thick eyebrows brought him half a baguette split in two and stuffed with tomatoes, anchovies, onions and garlic, over which she drizzled olive oil from a large glass. Sitting on the sand, for once he ate distractedly, his eyes fixed instead on the sea's incandescent blue. Tartanes slipped across his field of vision, halfway to the horizon. From time to time he turned round to look at his Bugatti, which glittered in the sun like the sea. Passers-by placed their hands on its panels, stroked it, squatted down to get a better look at its transmission, its brakes, its rear axle. Someone mentioned that the place was called Saint-Tropez. Antoine decided that when his children had all left home and he was widowed – in his mind the plan had no snags – he would sell La Sauveté and settle here. At the same moment he made the mistake of looking down at his paunchy stomach and white Celtic skin and running his fingers across his bald head, trickling with sweat. He did not like what he saw and felt. The passing years had turned him into this heavy, clumsy man, who only felt unconstrained behind the wheel of his car. The swimming costume he wore was ridiculous, and in a mirror at the café he had glimpsed his face and seen his eyes ringed with white circles from his mica goggles.

Perched on the corner of a table, the girl who had served him swung her shapely leg back and forth, exposing a tanned knee. She was talking to a boy her own age, and their singsong accents mingled. For the pleasure of seeing her up close again, and to separate her from the interloper, he asked for another 'pan bania' and a bottle of Var rosé. As she squatted to place the tray on the sand he saw her knee again and, looking up, found himself staring into a face full of warmth and innocence and smelling a scent of nectarine, lightly spiced with garlic. She was lovely, she was simple, she was not for him. As he left, he presented her with a big box of nougat that she accepted with exclamations of pleasure. Her name was Marie-Dévote.

The road through the Esterel wound deep into the red rock and through pine forests whose scent washed over him in great gusts. The car responded joyfully to the effort Antoine demanded from it. Its tyres squealed in the bends and it leapt up the hills and grumbled on the descents with that sweet musical sound that only a Bugatti makes. Behind it trailed aerial pools of castor oil-scented air. Antoine drove through Cannes and Nice without stopping. They were towns for winter visitors, deserted during the summer. Beyond the port at Villefranche, signposts indicated Menton and the high corniche road. He slowed down. Night was falling on Mont Boron. At altitude and this time of evening, the Bugatti's engine was at its best and would take off at the slightest pressure of his foot, but Antoine was no longer in any haste. In three days, time and space had lost their meaning. After he had seen Geneviève he might go on to China. This admirable machine, so precise and eager, would never develop a fault. At La Turbie he stopped near the Trophy of Augustus to look down at the coast, where the yellow lights trembled and twinkled along the sea like a rosary. A bit further on, at Roquebrune, he noticed at the roadside a little restaurant whose terrace overlooked a slope sown thickly with plum tomato plants. The patron stood at the door in a singlet and linen trousers. An enormous, still-pink scar cut across his face like a stripe, deforming his mouth. He spoke with difficulty. Antoine sampled *soupe au pistou*, stuffed *fleurs de courgettes* and fried anchovies. The man served him with a weary casualness. In the kitchen, behind a bead curtain, two women were moving around busily: they could not be seen, but their shrill voices were audible, one young, one old. They did not appear, and once dinner was over they slipped away without passing through the restaurant. Antoine requested a *digestif*. The patron brought a bottle of Italian grappa and two glasses and sat down opposite him.

'So you travel like that, eh?' he said. 'Leave us poor devils standing.'

Raising a hairy hand, he stroked the awful scar on his face with his fingertips, sighed, and gulped down his glassful.

'What about you? What did you get?'

'Oh, practically nothing. A few splinters in my right shoulder. Six months ago another piece came out. I'm not complaining.'

'Except for hunting …'

'Except for hunting.'

'Where did you get to?'

'Army of the Orient. What about you?'

'Verdun. Douaumont. Do you like this grappa?'

'Not bad. A bit young. I'm from Normandy, calvados is my drink.'

'I wouldn't say no. They used to give us a glass before we went over the top.'

They drank for a while, silent, then carefully exchanging a few words that let each place the other. Antoine would willingly have finished the bottle, but there were still a few kilometres to go, and the smashed face in front of him depressed him terribly. So many soldiers went to war with the idea of sacrificing their life, or possibly their left arm, but not one imagined that they might as easily come back with their face a pulp, and look like a monster for the rest of their days. He was conscious of his own cowardice, but without cowardice, as without lies, life was impossible. It looked as if there was a night of reminiscing ahead, scenes and stories spilling out in bulk across the tablecloth, stoked by the warmth of the grappa.

'Were you an officer?' the man asked, his expression wary.

Antoine felt sorry for him. He had no desire to leave a bad impression, or deepen the certain bitterness of this defeated man.

'No,' he said, 'corporal. Finished as a sergeant.'

'Like me. Stay a bit longer.'

'I need to get to Menton.'

'She'll wait for you …'

'It's my daughter.'

'Ah! I understand. Well, come by again one day. We don't stick together enough. My name is Léon Cece.'

Antoine got back into the car and freewheeled down to Menton. The cicadas sang in the pine woods and tomato fields. The town was already deeply asleep. It felt like the sleep of a sick person, so respectful was the silence of the deserted streets. The fragrance of lemon trees in blossom and the dimmed glow of the streetlights were redolent of hospitals. The houses were hidden deep in jungly gardens, walled behind high gates. Not a fishing boat moved in the dock. Antoine drove cautiously along the Promenade and eventually found a passer-by who told him the way to the clinic, a large turn-of-the-century detached house deep inside a silent park. The windows were shuttered and the doors locked. He switched off the engine, turned up the collar of his jacket, rested his head and arms on his steering wheel, and went to sleep.

It was not the dawn that woke him, but the sound of a pair of shutters opening on the balcony above his head. Geneviève appeared in a white nightdress with a ribbon in her hair. She seemed terribly thin to him, and pale, but more beautiful than before, a creature so fragile that the morning breeze or a shaft of sunlight might kill her.

'It's you, Papa!' she said. 'I thought it was. I was sure I heard the sound of a Bugatti last night. Is it the new one?'

'Well, it's the new one for now, the Type 22, four cylinders. Bugatti's planning to replace it soon with the 28, which is apparently a marvel.'

'I already like that one!'

Antoine puffed himself up. 'Do you want to go for a spin?'

'It's difficult so early. The door's still locked. A bit later, if you like.'

'I'll go and have a coffee. Look, I've brought you some nougat.'

He tossed two boxes up to the balcony, and Geneviève retrieved them.

'Thank you! It's so sweet of you to think of spoiling me. I adore nougat. When you come back, could you be really kind and bring me cigarettes and matches?'

'You smoke? That's not good.'

'Nothing is good from where I'm standing.'

'Really? I thought you felt better. You're worrying me.'

From her pout he recognised his daughter from several years before, his little girl whom he had kissed on the doorstep of La Sauveté on the morning in August 1914 when he had left to join his unit. She had changed quite suddenly: now she was this frail young woman with an oval face and loose blond hair, who made him feel shy and intimidated.

'Don't worry,' she said.

'But you won't get better!'

'Do we get better?'

He realised that he wasn't sure enough of the answer to be able to convince her. He could only think of distractions.

'Do you need perfume?'

'Well, if you can find something fairly modern … '

'I'll try.'

A figure in pyjamas appeared on the next balcony, a dishevelled man who began to gesticulate, showering them with insults.

'What the hell is going on? Are you mad? There are people asleep here, sick people, and you don't give a damn!'

'Calm down, Piquemal,' Geneviève said in a gentle voice. 'It's my father. We haven't seen each other for five years. Anyway, he's going. He'll come back later.'

'Your father, your father!' Piquemal shouted, but said no more as he was choked by a fit of coughing.

'You know you mustn't get angry. It's very bad for you.'

Piquemal, doubled up with coughing, retreated into his room.

Geneviève leant down to her father.

'Don't be offended. He's half mad. In any case he hasn't got much longer.'

'I'll be back soon,' Antoine said.

'See you very soon, Papa.'

The sloping drive allowed him to roll the Bugatti back to the gate, where he dropped the clutch and had the satisfaction of hearing the engine fire immediately. Menton was waking up in a golden dawn, an oblique light that slid across the oily sea and stroked the trees in the gardens. On the quay fishermen in straw hats were untangling their nets. He eventually found a barber, who shaved him and let him wash. He bought a new shirt and discarded the one he was wearing. Throughout his journey he had not burdened himself with anything: shirts, socks, undershorts, toothbrushes marked his route, tossed in ditches or available rubbish bins. It was harder to find somewhere to buy perfume at this early hour, but he came across a shop that advertised 'goods from Paris'. Lacking in expertise, he relied on the saleswoman's advice, then looked for a florist's and ordered an enormous bouquet of white roses. The thought of burdening his Bugatti with roses threw him for a moment.

'Would you like me to have them delivered?' asked the florist, a small brown-haired woman with a downy upper lip.

'That's not a bad idea. With this package, if you don't mind. Be careful, it's perfume.'

'Do you have a card?'

He found one in his wallet and wrote carefully and legibly,

> *My little Geneviève, these flowers will express all my affection much better than I could do it myself. Here also is the perfume you asked for. If you don't care for it you can exchange it; I've left the name of the shop on the packet. Your papa, who kisses you.*

Feeling much calmer, he headed west once more and drove as far as the outskirts of Roquebrune, to the restaurant where he had stopped the previous evening. On a chair outside, still dressed in his grubby singlet, the patron was plucking a chicken.

'Hello!' Antoine said, without getting out of the car.

'All right? So, your daughter is well?'

'Much better, thanks.'

'Are you eating with us?'

'It's a bit early and I've a long way to go. Another time. I'll be back.'

'Always in a hurry. Like a fart in a fan factory, you are.'

'That's life!' said Antoine, who would never have thought he could slip so easily into this sort of badinage.

'With a puss like mine, I don't know that there's any more life to be had. But you're right to make the most of it. On your way ... see you again, and try not to have to scrape yourself off the road in that thing!'

'Don't worry, I'm a careful driver.'

He let in the clutch and the Bugatti leapt westwards down the coast, only stopping when it reached the outskirts of Saint-Tropez and the open-air café. Lounging in a wicker armchair, Marie-Dévote was reading a magazine with a cat on her lap. She turned her head and smiled.

'Back already? Did you get bored?'

'I'm hungry.'

'It's not really lunchtime yet. Will you be happy with a bowl of bouillabaisse?'

'I'm sure I will.'

He sat down under the arbour, facing the beach, while she disappeared into the kitchen. A light breeze was blowing, raising ripples that expired on the white sand. He would happily have gone for a swim but the memory of his white, unappealing body disgusted him. Marie-Dévote put a steaming bowl and a carafe of Var wine in front of him.

'It's quiet here,' he said.

'On Sundays it gets busy.'

'What day is it today?'

'Friday. What are you doing that's so interesting you can't remember what day it is?'

'Nothing,' Antoine admitted.

'Doesn't your wife say anything?'

'No.'

He wanted to ask her to sit on the corner of the table the way she had the day before, and swing her leg and show him her knee, but standing in front of him, hands on hips and feet apart, she seemed much stronger and more solid than he remembered her. Good health, sunshine, the men she had to serve and whose jokes she tolerated, had made her grown-up at twenty. But it was more than that: she had ripened, she was ripe like a luscious Provençal fruit, with that directness of expression and rough candour that women from the Midi have. When she laughed she revealed strong teeth solidly planted in a hungry mouth. Marie-Dévote was as far away as it was possible to be from those girls of good Norman families to whom he had been introduced and from whom, out of boredom and lack of critical sense, he had chosen Marie-Thérèse Mangepain.

'Are you always on your own here?' he asked.

'Cheeky! I can't half see you coming! No, I'm not on my own. Maman's here. She never leaves the kitchen.'

'And your father?'

'My father's dead. In the war. Like everybody.'

'Not me.'

'I saw you on the beach yesterday. Your shoulder's all kersnaffled.'

Antoine didn't know the expression, but there was no need. Marie-Dévote's speech communicated above all by its musicality, her sentences that began sharply and finished smoothly, with an internal sensuous and lush music that he could have listened to for hours without trying to untangle its sense. But her attention had shifted from Antoine. A fishing boat was being rowed onto the sand. A tall tanned boy leapt out of it, his trousers rolled up to his knees, a bucket in his hand.

'It's Théo!' she said delightedly. 'He's bringing the fish.'

She ran towards him in her bare feet. Antoine was eaten up with jealousy, and as he became aware of it he felt glad to experience the feeling. Something was moving inside him. A barrier was crumbling. He belonged to the world of the living, the world of Théo arriving with a bucket of fish, of Marie-Dévote running towards the young man with ill-concealed pleasure. Théo handed her the bucket and walked off, and Marie-Dévote lost her sparkle for a moment, became suddenly dull and lifeless, but the decline was brief. Antoine finished his carafe of rosé and asked for another, merely for the pleasure of seeing her get up, walk the length of the arbour and return with her light, swinging step, as if she were walking on the tips of her toes. Instinct demanded that he leave there and then, to nurse his appetite to return.

That evening he stopped again outside Charles's garage at Aix. His work finished, Charles had his head under a tap of cold water.

'All right, Captain? How's the beast?'

'Perfect, Charles. Are you free this evening?'

They had dinner together on a bistro terrace, talking naturally about the war they had shared together in the Balkans, a thankless and miserable episode but one that Charles, with a southerner's talent for storytelling, had an ability to wrap in unexpected colours. Antoine, who remembered only mud, dysentery, thirst, hunger and wretchedness, listened with childlike attention as Charles crossed the Vardar on 22 September 1918, resupplied the Serbs at Gradsko two days later, raced in his truck to Prilep after the Bulgarians had set it on fire, and charged into Skopje alongside Colonel Gaspereau's Chasseurs d'Afrique. Punctuated with a regular 'crash, bang, wallop!' that shook the table, his irresistible account attracted both waiters and patron to their table, making them briefly oblivious to the other diners. To Antoine Charles's war was unrecognisable, as he juggled with entire divisions and possessed an incredible gift of ubiquity. But what did it matter? The former driver elevated the squalid, organised the disordered, gave reason to absurdity. When he at last sat down with the Bulgarian government to sign the armistice, the restaurant was in near rapture. The patron shook their hands, his eyes welling with tears.

'You're truly brave men,' he said in a long sigh of garlic. 'We owe you a great debt!'

A little unsteadily, drunk on stories and red wine, Antoine found a hotel room and slept a dreamless sleep.

Next morning Charles inspected the Bugatti, changed its tyres and spark plugs, and retimed the ignition. When the engine fired up, his mechanic's eyes shone with pleasure. Back at the wheel, Antoine had one desire: to get back to La Sauveté, which he did at the astounding average of seventy kilometres an hour, seeing nothing but the road ahead, the dust, the bends, the trees that whistled past his ears.

La Sauveté had survived his absence. Driving through the gates, he saw Albert limping in front of a wheelbarrow being pushed by one of the village boys. Victoire Sanpeur was strolling hand in hand with Michel and Antoinette through the rose walks. Antoinette ran to her father and climbed up to sit next to him. They did a lap of the park and pulled up at the steps of the house as Jeanne was coming out with Jean in her arms. Marie-Thérèse showed her surprise in an offended frostiness.

'Where were you?' she said.

'I went to see Geneviève.'

'I see.'

'Do you object?'

'Not at all. I assume you're joking.'

Antoine bent over Jean, who stared at him with wide eyes, and gently squeezed his cheek. The baby smiled and held out his arms.

'Extraordinary!' Marie-Thérèse said. 'Such a difficult child, and look at him smiling at you.'

'He's not difficult,' Jeanne countered. 'He just doesn't like everybody.'

'He's not wrong!' Antoine said.

Marie-Thérèse flinched, and said with feigned gentleness, 'I thought that children could always sense whether you really love them or not.'

Antoinette drew herself up, her eyes thunderous.

'But Papa does love children!'

Tears welled in her eyes.

'Don't you?' she said.

'Yes,' Antoine answered, distracted by the appearance of Victoire dragging Michel behind her. He succeeded in wriggling out of her grip and ran to bury himself in his mother's skirts.

'Maman!' he yelled, trembling with fright. 'I don't want *him* to take you away in his car.'

'There's no danger of that, my darling. No danger at all!'

'What an idiot,' Antoinette said.

Antoine caught the Martiniquan's gaze. She lowered her eyelids, fringed with long, curly lashes. It was a yes, but he would have to wait until tomorrow morning, at five o'clock, after his bowl of coffee laced with calvados, on the hard day bed in the library. He sighed.

I mention 1920 only as a reminder. It no longer interests us. But let us touch briefly on the things that were bothering Albert at that time. Paul Deschanel, preferred to Clemenceau by both the Chamber of Deputies and the Senate as president of the victorious French Republic, was found wandering in his nightshirt at a level crossing after the official train had passed by. He was suspected of being a delusional lunatic and unfortunately the suspicions proved correct. Forced to resign, he was replaced by Alexandre Millerand. In the United States, matters were no better: the president had disappeared. Intoxicated by the ovations he had received and his own verbal incontinence, Woodrow Wilson shut himself in his room and refused to see even members of his administration. His wife served as intermediary, deciding world affairs between two rubbers of bridge. The League of Nations – upon which, despite the United States' refusal to join, Albert had pinned his hopes – did not prevent the Soviets from invading Poland, the Greeks from attacking Turkey, or the French from 'pacifying' the Rif. Albert lived from one disappointment to the next. When he held young Jean in his arms he sang to him, as a lullaby,

> *And all you poor girls*
> *who love your young men*
> *if they reward you with children*
> *break their arms, break their legs*
> *so they can never be infantrymen*
> *so they can never be infantrymen.*

Jean would never be a soldier. It was a promise, made on oath.

We jump forward then, to August 1923, three years later, to find ourselves again at La Sauveté, one fine afternoon when the sun sparkled on the sea that was visible from the first-floor windows. Monsieur du Courseau had lifted the edge of the lace curtain to admire his garden. Seated in a tub armchair, he kept his leg, encased in its plaster cast, up on a stool. A month earlier, as he had tried to avoid a cyclist without lights in the middle of the night on the waterlogged Tôtes road, he had slid off the carriageway and hit a fence that, fortunately, was made of wood. The car – the new Type 28 Bugatti, three litres, eight cylinders – had not been badly damaged (punctured radiator, bent front axle), but Antoine's left knee, which was less sturdy, had shattered on contact with the dashboard. At the factory at Molsheim the car was being repaired, and would be delivered back to Antoine at the beginning of September. Even though there was no question of his driving anywhere in the near future, he was suffering from not having his baby in its garage, a loose box adapted for the purpose. He liked to know it was there, even when it was quiet, and he loved its sudden gleam whenever he pulled back the garage's sliding door to let in the daylight. The bodywork shone a beautiful blue, the chrome flashed in the sunlight. Stuck in bed, then in an armchair, Antoine, deprived of his thoroughbred, felt his loneliness painfully acutely as he faced convalescent hours of desperate slowness. For at least another month there was no question of his being able to escape from his agonising melancholy and take to the road again.

The lifted lace curtain revealed a corner of the park where, at that moment, Albert was watering with an apron around his waist and a straw hat on his head. Sitting in a garden chair a few steps behind him, Adèle Louverture was dozing, her chin tipped forward. Behind her, Michel du Courseau (six years old) was carefully cutting with a pair of scissors the knot of the cotton scarf that held back the girl's thick hair. When she woke up, her scarf would fall, and her hair would tumble free. From behind the du Courseau boy, Jean Arnaud (four years old) watched him with his hands behind his back and his head on one side. After he had finished cutting the knot, Michel moved over to Albert's hosepipe. Still armed with his scissors, he stabbed quickly, several times, into the rubber of the hose and ran off, handing the scissors to Jean as he did so. Albert's flow of water dwindled to a trickle. Turning round, he saw jets of water spraying from the punctured hose and his son holding the scissors. Jean made no attempt even to draw back, taking the two slaps without complaint and running away to cry, pursued by Albert's curses. Adèle, awakened, raised her head and her scarf fell off.

She saw at once that it had been cut with scissors.

Antoine rang a bell that had been placed there for the purpose. Marie-Thérèse came in. Ever since her husband's accident, she had lived in a state of devotion and goodness. The tenderness with which she spoke to her friends about 'poor Antoine' had left many thinking that he was dying. The more anxious of them came to visit and were reassured: the dying man was doing well, in spite of his immobility. He kept a box of cigars and a bottle of calvados next to his armchair. He still looked fresh. After a period of eating very little, before the accident, he had regained his appetite, although it was an appetite that baffled the Normans who knew him: he ate bread rubbed with garlic, requested bouillabaisses, demanded aïoli with his cod, and chewed olives while drinking a yellow liquid which a few drops of water transformed into a whitish solution with a flavour of aniseed. In short, he was not in Normandy but elsewhere, living in an unknown world of lovers of spicy food. Marie-Thérèse understood perfectly well that he was being unfaithful to her. Her pride would have suffered if she had not been able to console herself that she was hardly the only victim of his infidelity: Joséphine Roudou, Victoire Sanpeur, and now Adèle Louverture had all found themselves in a similar position.

'Are you feeling unwell?' she asked, without much hope that he would say yes.

41

'No, my dear. Unfortunately I'm not feeling unwell, but I should like to say something to my son.'

'Michel?'

'Do I have another?'

She acknowledged that, at La Sauveté at least, he could only mean Michel.

'I'll send him to you, but … '

'But what?'

'You're always so hard on him.'

'Have you ever seen me hit him?'

'No. You're worse. Either you don't speak to him, or you look at him with astonishment, as if he were a stranger.'

'He is a stranger. He's the only person in the world who looks at me with terror in his eyes, and occasionally even something close to hate.'

'He's a wild boy. You need to make a bond with him.'

'I'll try.'

He turned his head impassively and lifted the curtain again. Albert was repairing his hosepipe with some rags and string. A few steps away, Jean was watching with his hand on his cheek. The slight movement of his shoulders gave away his stifled sobbing. Antoine's silence conveyed to Marie-Thérèse that she should now do as he had asked.

He waited calmly, followed with an attentive ear the discussion between mother and son at the bottom of the stairs and their slow approach to the first floor, then listened, without attempting to work out their sense, to the excited whisperings on the other side of the door. Finally Marie-Thérèse must have managed to convince him, for Michel entered alone into the room with his father. He stood with his back against the closed door, his legs together, his head high. They exchanged a look and Antoine was glad to see that his son did not lower his eyes. They sized each other up for a moment in silence,

42

the father almost startled to find his son good-looking – this boy he knew so little of – the son surprised that his father did not vent his anger straight away.

'You're really quite a handsome little chap!' Antoine said.

It was true. At six years old Michel, slim and with long, well-muscled legs, square shoulders, a long neck, a well-defined profile and pale blond hair, was a beautiful child. Antoine felt he was seeing him for the first time. What sort of incomprehension had kept them apart for so long? He mused on this for a moment, distracted at first, then suddenly conscious of what was happening on the other side of the door, of a mute and fearful presence. He waited; there was plenty of time. It was Marie-Thérèse who, unable to bear the silence any longer, knocked, tentatively opened the door and put her head around it. Antoine smiled.

'Don't worry. I haven't eaten him.'

'But you're not talking.'

'We are communicating to each other matters that cannot be spoken aloud.'

Barely reassured, Marie-Thérèse retreated. Antoine listened to the sound of her feet going away downstairs and, without allowing vexation or irritation into his voice, said, 'Aren't we, Michel?'

'What?'

'I think you know what I'd like to talk to you about.'

'No.'

'Something about a headscarf and a hosepipe punctured with scissors.'

Michel breathed deeply, like a diver about to disappear underwater.

'Don't punish Jean,' he said. 'He's only four.'

'Because he did it.'

'Yes.'

'He's very precocious, isn't he? But I appreciate you taking his side. You're a good-hearted boy.'

'He's a servant's son.'

'Jeanne is not a servant. I don't like to hear you say that word. Jeanne is our caretaker and her husband is my friend.'

'How can he be your friend? He's a gardener.'

'I prefer a gardener to many of the people your mother makes me entertain in this house.'

'Anyway, Jean doesn't know what he's doing.'

'Are you sure he did it?'

'Yes.'

Antoine remained silent. He was discovering who his son was, and the discovery interested him. In one sense he was proud that the boy was sticking to his lie, knowing that his father knew. He allowed that he had courage, and a deep scorn for the truth.

'I want to be sure that Jean won't be punished, so I would like Albert to come up and see me. Would you be very kind and tell him?'

Michel's hand was already on the doorknob.

'Wait. Don't be in such a hurry. Give me a kiss.'

'Why?'

'Because it will give me pleasure.'

Michel let go of the knob, walked over to his father, and gave him a cold kiss on the cheek.

'Thank you,' Antoine said. 'Now you can go.'

He watched Michel run out and go to the gardener. Albert put down the nozzle of his hose, dried his hands on his thick blue canvas apron and limped up the avenue, trousers flapping around his wooden leg. He kept his back straight, and no one watching him would have felt under any obligation to show him charity or pity. He was a deeply accepting man, who offered his suffering to the cause of peace about which he spoke so often, with the fervour of a visionary. Antoine was very fond of him and discreetly let him know that he was, as is proper between men.

'I'm interrupting your work,' he said when Albert entered.

'I'd finished, Captain.'

'Captain' had replaced the 'sir' of before the war. They had met in uniform, on leave, and from that moment on, master-servant relations had become impossible. Better to substitute their military ranks, which at least reminded them in a soulless peacetime that men might come together in a brotherhood of respect, without servility.

'Have a chair. A small glass of something?'

'I wouldn't say no.'

Albert filled his pipe and lit it. The pungent smell of caporal tobacco spread around the room. He took the offered glass, which was not small, and dipped his moustache in it.

'The 1920,' he said.

'Mm. The last carafe.'

'It's good.'

Antoine swallowed a mouthful. 'Yes. Good, but no more. It hasn't learnt how to age.'

'You don't ask that from calvados.'

'Yes, I know. Albert, I asked you to come up because you slapped Jean this afternoon.'

'He deserved it. The hosepipe's buggered. I'll have to get a new one.'

'No, don't. I'll have it replaced.'

'I said I'll do it!' Albert said bad-temperedly.

'From the window here I saw Michel cut Adèle's scarf and then puncture your hosepipe. He gave the scissors to Jean to hold and ran away.'

'Are you sure?'

'I'm sorry.'

'Then I've made a bad mistake.'

'Did Jean protest?'

'No, Captain. The little fool!'

Antoine saw Albert's discomfiture, which was not due to his remorse at having smacked his child but to the idea that an all-powerful Justice had been offended against. He would have liked to find a way to reassure his friend: all-powerful Justice was doing perfectly well (in men's minds at any rate), despite the daily offences showered upon her. It was a pity that Albert didn't possess a more relative sense of the great moral principles: he was storing up sad days for himself, disappointments and rages that would not be good for his health.

'He didn't say anything to me, he didn't even try to defend himself!'

'He's still a very small boy. I'd like you to send him to me. I want to talk to him, but don't tell him what it's about. Let me deal with it.'

Albert downed his glass and left, looking thoughtful. A short time later Antoine heard a faint tapping at the door and called to Jean to come in. The boy entered, looking serious. His shorts were too long and covered his knees, and Jeanne, in her economical way, had studded his boots so that he slipped on the polished floorboards. He came to Antoine's armchair and kissed him on the cheek.

'Hello, Monsieur.'

'I know who stabbed the hosepipe and cut Adèle's scarf.'

'Oh, you know!' Jean repeated, smiling.

'But I don't understand why you didn't say it was Michel who did it.'

'If I had, he would have hit me, and anyway nobody would believe me. He's your son.'

Antoine felt a gulf opening up in front of him. This small, sweet, discreet boy was showing him a world far more complicated than the one in which the du Courseaus lived so complacently. He grasped Jean's hand and squeezed it in his own.

'You see ... I didn't know any of that, and I'm very grateful to you for telling me. Do you like secrets?'

'What's a secret?'

'Something you only share with one person.'

'Yes.'

'All right ... you and I are going to have a secret. Michel won't be

46

punished for his naughtiness, but you and I will be friends for ever. We'll never argue. We'll tell each other everything, and when one of us has a sadness he'll tell the other one, who'll cheer him up.'

Jean watched Antoine, concentrating carefully. He did not understand everything he was saying, but the friendly sound of his voice made enough of an impression on him that afterwards this scene never left his memory, and nor did Antoine's affectionate hug that accompanied it and smelt of cigars, calvados and embrocation. As Jean was leaving, Antoine called him back.

'Let me look at you again. You remind me of someone, but I don't know who.'

'Someone?'

'Yes, we'll try and find out who. Goodbye, Jean. Come up and see me when you get bored. We'll talk.'

In September, from his bedroom, Antoine followed the days' rhythm. The rose bushes faded to make way for autumn flowers. One morning, the last horse they kept in the stables, which took Marie-Thérèse in her tilbury to church at Grangeville on Sundays, was led away on a long rein behind a knacker's cart. A few minutes later, Madame du Courseau appeared at the gates at the wheel of a Model T Ford, in which she turned two circles in the drive before parking in the loose box belonging to the Bugatti. Antoine rang his bell. Marie-Thérèse appeared, her cheeks pink, a little out of breath.

'Did you see?' she said.

'I saw, and you have three minutes to take your heap of junk out of my Bugatti's garage and put it somewhere else.'

'But the Bugatti's not there!'

'All the more reason. Would I put another woman in your bed when you're not there?'

'I must say I think you're being extremely fussy to include a car in your respect for the conventions.'

'Then you respect them too!'

'I knew you were attached to your car ... but to such an extent ... more than to your wife, more than to your children ... '

'Have I ever specified the degrees of my passion? No. So stop making things up and go and get the woodshed behind the outhouse cleared out. You can park your dinosaur there.'

Marie-Thérèse did as she was told, and the Model T Ford did not cohabit with the Bugatti, which returned from Molsheim one afternoon with a mechanic in white overalls at the wheel. Antoine, who had been brought down to the ground floor on a chair, studied his car, its engine still ticking from the road and its bodywork spattered with squashed mosquitoes. He had it washed as he sat there, with a sponge, warm water and hose. The blue paintwork and spoked wheels gleamed in the warm afternoon light. Everyone came to watch: Adèle, Jeanne, Marie-Thérèse, Albert, Jean, Michel, Antoinette and two other servants, whose names I shan't bother with because they were only casual staff. Hands caressed the bodywork, the chrome and the oak steering wheel, felt the still-warm bonnet secured with a leather strap, the gear lever and oil pump lever. Antoine managed to squeeze himself into the passenger seat, and the mechanic took the wheel again. They did a lap of the park to the sound of eight cylinders firing like organ pipes, raising a delicate cloud of white dust behind them. When they arrived back at the front steps, the abbé Le Couec was waiting, a handkerchief in the neck of his cassock.

'The golden calf!' he said in his rich, gravelly voice. 'How we love the golden calf! And the sinners they do increase ... Pity the heavens as they empty!'

He nevertheless helped Antoine to extricate himself from the cockpit and get back upstairs to his room, where they remained alone with the carafe of calvados and the box of cigars. A strong smell rose from the abbé, who did not always take great care of his cassock. Domestic matters did not preoccupy him. He lived in one room of the rectory, which functioned simultaneously as bedroom, library and kitchen and which, very occasionally, he allowed a female parishioner to sweep and dust. But as a former infantryman, trained by the *Manuel d'infanterie*, he paid very particular attention to the health of his feet. The faithful souls who visited him often found him sitting in a chair and reading his breviary with his cassock hitched up to his knees, revealing his sturdy legs and hiker's calves and his feet soaking in a bowl full of water, in which he had dissolved coarse salt collected from the hollows of the rocks. Grangeville's parish priest needed this treatment: he walked a great deal. To walk to Dieppe and back did not trouble him in the slightest. He had walked to Rouen in twelve hours once, to answer a summons from his bishop, and returned the following day at the same pace, relieved of a number of bitter feelings after a stormy audience.

Antoine, whose nose was sensitive, offered the abbé a cigar, which the priest lit after clearing his throat.

'Not bad! So how goes it? I'm not talking about your knee, naturally.'

'Another fortnight and I'll be as nimble as a deer,' Antoine responded, pretending not to understand.

'It's been two months, hasn't it?'

'Yes, two months.'

'Two months without sin! Some people up there will be very interested in your soul.'

'How very kind of them.'

Antoine recounted the story of Jean and Michel, of the punctured hosepipe and the cut-up headscarf. The abbé listened less than attentively. The first glass of calvados, drunk a little too quickly because he had been thirsty, distracted his attention. He would have liked to know its vintage, but when Antoine began to think aloud he was not to be interrupted.

'I'm very drawn to Jean. If you could see how serious he is, how closely he looks at you, if you could read his thoughts as they pass across his face, you'd be asking yourself the same question as I do: where does he come from? And it is doubly frustrating that when I look at him, I say to myself every time: I know that face, I've seen it somewhere before. In a dream? In the real world? Impossible to tell. Will we ever know?'

The abbé maintained a prudent silence. He knew, but no one would make him betray a confidence. Or possibly later, if circumstances demanded it. He poured himself another glass of calvados and sipped.

'One thing at a time. Don't get too interested in Jean Arnaud. Your son has priority, and he needs it. Jean, on the other hand, has all sorts of advantages: a mother of admirable virtue, a father who is both a hero and an idealist … '

'You're suggesting that Michel doesn't have those advantages?'

'I'm not suggesting anything. By the way, how are matters at Saint-Tropez?'

'Excellent,' Antoine replied, put out and instantly withdrawing into himself in the wake of his rebuff. Quite understandably, he did not hold with a priest reminding him, in conversation, of things said in the confessional. But the abbé Le Couec, a man of excessive integrity, could not forget words murmured in an unguarded moment. Antoine's life, both internal and external, belonged to him, and he intended to maintain his right to oversee it outside the church as well as inside.

'You're fortunate,' the abbé said. 'You might have been a lot less lucky.'

'I'm obliged to you!' Antoine said drily.

'As a matter of fact, I have never understood what drove you away from Madame du Courseau.'

'If only I knew myself!'

'She has great qualities.'

'I shan't contradict you on that point.'

'She's an excellent mother.'

'Without a doubt.'

'She is beyond reproach.'

'Who would dare say anything to the contrary?'

'So?'

'She bores me,' Antoine said wearily.

The abbé did not know what boredom was, and supposed it to be some sort of illness that a healthy man would fight with prayers, calvados and long, strenuous walks. Perhaps Antoine's illness was the result of him never going out without his Bugatti.

'When your leg's out of plaster, we'll take some exercise together.'

'I had a sufficient dose of that to last me a lifetime between '14 and '18.'

'The doctor will most certainly prescribe another one.'

'The park will be quite enough for me.'

Shouts and laughter came from outside. Antoine lifted the curtain. Antoinette was chasing Jean, who was running away from her with all the speed his legs could muster, round and round some armchairs and a bench. Finally she cornered him and threw her arms around him to kiss him. He wriggled out of her grasp and kept running, looking behind him and paying no attention to Michel who, as he ran past, stuck out his foot. Jean went sprawling, but made no sound, and got up again with knees, hands and chin covered in blood. Grabbing a stick, he launched himself at Michel, but Adèle, who had come running, took the stick from him and let Michel run away. Antoine heard snatches of his daughter vehemently arguing, accusing Michel. Madame du Courseau and Adèle took Jean inside to clean him up and paint him with iodine.

'Did you see that?'

'Yes. Strange. Very strange. I'm surprised at Michel. At Sunday school he's a very attentive and devout little boy. A good Christian in the making. He's very talented, you know. On Sunday he sang a solo in church, in a marvellous soprano. I would have given him absolution without confessing him. If you give him modelling clay,

51

he'll sculpt you miniature saints that are little masterpieces. I intend to ask him to make the Nativity models for me at Christmas.'

'An artist in the family? That's all we need. Where does he get it from? I have nothing to hide. Not a creative bone in my body. Generations of unambiguous Normans going back as far as you like. I'm the first of my line who's even dreamt in his sleep. Nothing on the Mangepain side either. Not a glimmer of sensitivity anywhere.'

'Let's not make too much of Pasteurian inevitability. It's a perfect case of spontaneous generation. We should wait ... all children are gifted. It's afterwards that it goes wrong.'

They carried on talking as the dusk fell, one of those long conversations containing many overtones, peppered with Antoine's occasional acid and cynical remarks and the abbé's stolid common sense. When the latter stood up to go, the house swayed a little around him. The room stank of cold cigar smoke. The carafe was empty. On the stairs the abbé missed his footing and travelled the rest of the way on his bottom, laughing like a lunatic. Marie-Thérèse offered to drive him back to the rectory.

'No, thank you, my dear. I've filled my tank and I need to burn it off.'

'You talk like my husband, Father. Like a mechanic.'

'They don't yet have their saint, but they will. They deserve him. If need be, I shall go to Rome personally to petition His Holiness Pius XI. Actually, you've hit on something, I shall go and make my request this instant.'

He caught his foot on the doormat inside the front door and nearly fell over again.

'Father!' Marie-Thérèse said in a voice full of reproach.

'My dear penitent, one does not dictate his conduct to a priest such as myself. I have certainly overdone the calvados in your husband's company, but it is when the spirit elevates itself and is released from material contingencies that ideas come in their multitudes. On which note, the Lord bless you and keep you.'

Taking down his wide-brimmed hat from the coat hook, he placed it on his head with an energetic gesture and strode out into the darkening night. She watched him until he was past the gates and was surprised to hear him, just as he presumably thought himself out of earshot, let go two crisp and substantial farts that rippled through the evening air. But with what circumlocutions could she report that to his superiors, especially when the abbé couldn't care less? He had two more calls to make, before returning to the rectory and a dinner of cold potatoes and a bowl of curd cheese.

The purchase of her Model T Ford changed Marie-Thérèse's life profoundly, and even her appearance. She abandoned her Lanvin for a more sporty look, exchanged high heels for flats, bobbed her hair and started smoking two packs of caporal cigarettes a day. Her stubbed-out butts filled the ashtrays at La Sauveté, and when she spoke her breath, laden with cold, sour smoke, hit you in the face. She drove prudently and without haste along the region's narrow roads, venturing twenty-five or thirty kilometres from Grangeville but never overstepping the confines of her self-imposed kingdom. She often took the children with her, including Jean, to show them churches and ruined abbeys and the châteaux of friends, where they were invited in to nibble snacks in large, gloomy rooms that smelt of furniture polish and old ladies. The château that fascinated Jean Arnaud the most was the Malemorts': an elegant residence in red brick, flanked by two turrets and a pretty dovecote. The Marquis de Malemort, who had recently turned thirty, was struggling valiantly against the hard times. He had razed three-quarters of his parkland to turn it into fields and taken back his two tenanted farms to run them himself. Each year this solid Norman with his highly coloured complexion lost a little more of his aristocratic manner and looked a little more like a peasant, but on Sundays, dressed in grey and wearing white gloves with a carnation in his buttonhole, at the reins of his trap, in which sat the marquise and their daughter, Chantal, he still possessed a definite style. People bowed low to him not from servility, but as befitted a proud picture of the past in an era without pity.

You will be saying: what is all that doing in here? Why don't you tell us about Antoine's road trips instead, about Marie-Dévote and Théo, about Charles Ventadour, about the man with the mangled face at Roquebrune, about Geneviève? My answer is to beg you, please, to allow me a little time. This is a long story and the Malemorts have their place in it, especially Chantal, who is exactly Jean's age and a ravishing child, with black hair and eyes of forget-me-not blue. At four years old Jean would willingly stand in front of her and just adore her, or if he could would stroke her porcelain cheeks and her long and graceful neck; but the Malemorts were intimidatingly grand, and Chantal was a shy child who spoke in a quiet though not affected voice. Marie-Thérèse, of course, occasionally daydreamed of marrying into the family, and with her tendency to long-range calculation had already mentioned it to Michel.

'What a gorgeous girl she'll be! And how well you'll get on together! Next time you ought to bring her one of your little sculptures. They have a piano. I'll accompany you and you can sing "*Auprès de ma blonde*" …'

'But her hair's black!'

Madame du Courseau was not so easily discouraged.

Albert hated 'lending' Jean and consented reluctantly, under pressure from Jeanne who said, over and over, 'Our little boy needs to see the world.'

The 'little boy' had already decided to see it. The closed universe behind La Sauveté's high walls made him feel uncomfortable. At every step he encountered either the traps Michel set or Madame du Courseau's smothering affection, and if it was neither of those it was the haughty disdain of the governess who, like clockwork, a fortnight after taking up her post, turned into the biggest snob in the house. At least when they were in the car Michel felt car-sick as soon as they started moving and spent the best part of the journey throwing up out of the window, and the black woman was never invited. And sometimes out on the road they would see the blue Bugatti overtake them or pass them going the other way, and for a split second they would make out Monsieur du Courseau at the steering wheel, his cap back to front and his big mica goggles shielding his eyes from the wind and dust. As soon as his plaster cast came off he had started training again, criss crossing the country to get back into condition. One day, on a bend he was deliberately taking as tightly as he could, he nearly collided with the Ford. Wrenching the wheel over to avoid him, Marie-Thérèse put her nearside wheels into the ditch. Antoine reversed back to her.

'Nothing broken?' he asked, not getting out of the car.

Antoinette was crying with laughter, Michel was moaning. Madame du Courseau, pale and furious, snapped, 'No!'

'I'll ask them to send the oxen then.'

An hour later a farm worker hauled the Ford out of the ditch, but that evening Antoine was not to be found at La Sauveté. He had left for the Midi.

For three years his route had not changed by a kilometre. The only difference was that he now followed it less madly, no longer sleeping in ploughed fields, stopping instead to rest at Montargis before pushing on to Lyon where, at the same bistro each time, a sausage and a jug of Beaujolais were waiting for him. At Montélimar he stocked up on nougat, and at Aix he stopped to have dinner with Charles and listen to his stories of an imaginary war so much more glorious and heroic than the one they had lived through that it was almost a pleasure to recollect it. Charles's skill lay in never merely going off into fables of his own heroism, but instead weaving Antoine into them with such conviction that Antoine let himself be carried away, involuntarily holding himself straighter, looking for the stripes on his sleeve, covering his ears when the crash-bang-wallops of his former driver rang out, marvelling at his own cheek towards his colonel, and at the offhand way he treated the liaison officers dispatched by headquarters. He protested mildly at Charles's story of how he had picked him up at the roadside, wounded in the buttock by a Bulgarian cavalryman's lance, but Charles – who, like every good storyteller, brooked no interruptions – stuck to his version and refused to back down, even when Antoine, by now rather tipsy, jumped up and began to drop his trousers to prove that his buttocks bore no trace of the alleged shameful gash. The restaurant owner halted this affront to public decency just in time, and Antoine resigned himself to accepting that the shrapnel wound in his right shoulder had metamorphosed into a less dignified laceration as the result of a heroic confrontation with a moustachioed horseman who had the yellow-tinged face of a Tatar and had been terrorising and violating the gentle Serbian peasant women in the countryside all around. In fact, Charles's conviction was so strong that Antoine surprised himself on his return to his hotel by contorting himself in front of his wardrobe mirror to try to verify the mechanic's words. All he could see was his slightly fat, fairly white and very ordinary bottom, and he went to bed nursing a pang of regret that he had not really had a truly heroic Balkan war.

Antoine's appreciation of Charles Ventadour had grown at each meeting since their first in 1920. He was particularly grateful for Charles's substitution of his own appalling and pitiful memories by an epic of men's valour, an adventure in which Justice advanced in triumph at the head of armies marching to drive out the oppressors and restore the happiness of the oppressed. Alas, there remained the memory of Les Éparges, from which a man could not free himself so easily, and often at night Antoine woke up covered in an icy sweat, the taste of earth in his mouth, his temples thumping as if a mortar had just exploded, face to face with that colossus with the black, mud-covered head who had erupted in front of him in the small hours one morning leading a shrieking horde behind him, and whom he had had the good luck to kill with a single pistol shot to the heart. Who could transform the memory of such panic-stricken terror and cowardly slaughter into a knights' joust, in which French elegance would crush Teutonic brutality? No one, sadly, and Antoine, sedated every three or four months by Charles on his way through Aix, found himself exposed afresh to the obsessive images of his nightmare as soon as he returned to La Sauveté. But Provence offered remission, and it would have been excessively ungrateful of him to complain. A new life began there, and whenever the Bugatti, singing down the route des Maures, rolled into Grimaud to the buzz of cicadas, the resin smell of pines, and the perfume of thyme and lavender, whenever a first bend suddenly disclosed the glittering Mediterranean, the roofs of Cogolin and Ramatuelle, and the small port of Saint-Tropez cluttered with tartanes and smaller boats, Antoine's heart swelled with an inexpressible happiness. Often he would pull up to gaze at the view and delay the pleasure to come, to relish for a moment longer that wonderful 'before', so full of the promises of Marie-Dévote, of grilled fish on an open fire, of olives kept for him in oil and vinegar, of dried figs in winter or melting in the mouth in September, of Var rosé and glasses of pastis distilled secretly by Théo, drunk in the evening in the open air, bare feet on the table, chewing langoustines. Those people knew how to live.

It was lunchtime when he parked in front of the hotel, whose handsome sign could be seen from a long way off: Chez Antoine. To the beach café of 1920 had been added a pretty building finished in ochre plaster, whose bedrooms overlooked the beach. Marie-Dévote and Théo lived on the ground floor and rented the first, to painters mostly. Maman still ran the kitchen, invisibly but noisily, fanning the flames with her curses. Antoine had not seen her more than four or five times in three years, one such occasion being the marriage of Marie-Dévote, at which she had appeared swathed in black and wearing a wide-brimmed hat from which floated a veil held in place by a pair of jade pins. Of the face he caught a glimpse of that day, he could only remember a red nose and striking black eyes like Marie-Dévote's.

Yes, Marie-Dévote was married. I have not had time to say so until now, or perhaps it was so obvious I did not take the trouble to make it clear. In any case, no marriage was more natural than hers, for she had been sleeping with Théo since she was fifteen and he was handsome and lazy, which makes it much easier to keep a man at home, have him all to yourself, not share him with his work, and keep him fresh for bed at night. There is an interesting philosophy at work here, which I have no leisure to develop because time presses, but which deserves some reflection by the reader. It will have its defenders and its critics. Some will judge it impracticable, others will point out that it can only thrive in sunny places, where a man can live on very little: an olive, a chunk of bread, figs off the tree, and bunches of grapes hanging from the arbour. The admirable thing is that this philosophy was an instinctive reflex for the happy young couple, who did not go round in circles analysing the situation. They simply lived the way their feelings took them, and, young but already wise, congratulated themselves on such a perfect success.

Théo helped by possessing great understanding. He had no better friend than Antoine, and on the days Antoine was there he went fishing at dawn and returned, noisily, in the small hours. The little hotel adjoining the beach café, and a fine new boat that was soon to be equipped with an outboard motor, justified this sacrifice. And when their benefactor had gone Marie-Dévote came back to him more tender than ever, and as though her appetite had merely been whetted.

*

Théo appeared first at the sound of the Bugatti's engine revving for the last time before Antoine switched off. Antoine pulled off his helmet and goggles. The sight of his face reddened by the air, with a white line across his forehead and pale circles around his eyes, made Théo buckle with laughter.

'Saints! You should see your face, old friend. You look like a watermelon. Come on, get out if you can. If not I'll fetch the corkscrew.'

Antoine, ordinarily rather thin-skinned, put up with Théo's jokes. He felt he owed it to the man whose wife he was sleeping with so openly. At least that was how he saw it, although from his point of view Théo was convinced that it was he, the husband, who was cuckolding the lover. As a result they were both full of sympathy for one another, and incapable of hurting each other.

Marie-Dévote was on the beach, at the water's edge, her skirt hitched up to her thighs, showing off her beautiful long brown legs as she washed the catch she had just gutted.

'Really, Antoine, it looks like you smelt there was going to be bouillabaisse today.'

'My sense of smell is acute.'

He kissed her on both cheeks. She smelt of fish, and as he closed his eyes for an instant she changed in his imagination into a sea creature, a siren come to warm herself in the sun. He would happily have laid her down on the beach and wriggled beneath her skirt there and then, but Théo was standing a few steps away, his hands on his hips and his brown face lit by a wide smile.

'I'm hungry!' Antoine said to conceal his agitation.

And he was hungry for Marie-Dévote. She was one of those women that one wants to bite and eat, whose skin tastes of herbs and conjures up the pleasures of food as much as those between the sheets. He kissed her again on the neck and she squealed, 'Hey! I'm not a radish, just because I've got a sprinkling of salt on me. Leave a bit of me for Théo. He needs feeding too.'

Unluckily, the sea's blue suddenly darkened, violent gusts whipped across its surface, and a warm drizzle stained the sand. Eating under the arbour was out of the question. Marie-Dévote laid the tables in the dining room, one for Antoine, Théo and herself, another for the two painters living on the first floor, who came down soon afterwards.

Antoine regarded them with suspicion. He distrusted artists, though he had never seen any at close quarters and all his knowledge of them was from books. These two looked reasonable, however. Properly dressed in corduroy and suntanned, they conversed normally without raising their voices, ate with knives and forks, and drank in moderation. One was well-built and had a thick neck, the other was slim and distinguished-looking. Marie-Dévote served them but so gracefully, unobtrusively and rapidly that she never seemed to leave her place at the table between her two men, both in a cheerful mood after drinking several glasses of pastis. Antoine watched her from the corner of his eye as she crossed the room, flitting from one table to the other. Then he saw one of the painters studying her, and his heart sank.

'Come on, Papa, don't be jealous!' Théo, leaning over, muttered to him. 'They're not going to steal her from under your nose.'

Of all Théo's jokes 'Papa' was the only one that irritated Antoine, especially in front of Marie-Dévote.

'If you call me "Papa" again, I'll break a bottle over your head.'

'Keep calm, Antoine, I didn't mean to upset you. You're "Papa" because I think of you as part of the family.'

Turning to the two painters, who had stopped talking at the commotion, he added, 'Antoine is a friend. Our great, great friend. He's not from round here. He comes from the north where it's cold and it rains a lot.'

'I should like to point out,' Antoine said, 'that it is likewise raining here.'

The deluge was streaming noisily down the windows and obscuring the view of the beach. The sea was only thirty metres away, but it was impossible even to make it out.

'We need the weather,' Théo said. 'Without it the plants, they all die, and it's a desert. Even the cold. It kills the germs, otherwise you walk round knee-deep in them and pretty soon you die.'

His self-assurance had grown since his marriage, and Antoine suspected that he might even be reading the odd newspaper and picking up some basic facts there that he then passed off as his own knowledge. But Antoine's problem was rather more pressing than the irritation he felt towards Théo. Inactive since his accident on the Tôtes road, reduced to the furtive kindnesses requested and received from Adèle Louverture in his room, where there was always the danger of being disturbed, and with his blood now warmed by pastis, rosé wine and Bénédictine, Antoine battled against the arousing effect of Marie-Dévote's skipping around the room. From the corner of his eye he followed her bottom and legs as she moved rapidly between the kitchen and tables; he miserably failed to resist the temptation offered by the neckline of her blouse, and would have given anything to be the little gold crucifix that swung between her breasts on a black velvet ribbon and caressed each of them with every movement. Théo was not so accommodating as all that, and would certainly not have given up his siesta with his wife without a number of expansionary projects that had been evolving over recent months, all of them requiring Antoine's patronage. Having left his friend in lengthy nail-biting anticipation, Théo suddenly announced that he was summoned to Saint-Raphaël and stepped outside to catch the bus that stopped in front of the hotel. The two painters, giving up hope of a break in the clouds, started a game of *jacquet*, and Antoine, successfully trapping Marie-Dévote in the hallway behind the door, at last placed her hand where she could measure the length of his admiration.

'And who'll do the dishes?' she asked, in entirely token resistance.

'Bugger the dishes.'

It is true that there are moments when the dishes are no longer of the slightest importance. Marie-Dévote did not need a great deal of persuading. And so they spent the afternoon together in bed, and I shall stop there, because this story already has many longueurs, and note merely that it was highly successful.

They slept for a time, and were woken by the sound of hooting as the bus returned from Saint-Raphaël. Marie-Dévote sprang out of bed and dressed in the twinkling of an eye to go and meet her Théo. Antoine's mouth felt furry and his eyes swollen. He too got out of bed, walked down the beach, jumped into the sea, splashed around like a seal and came out breathless but rejuvenated. It had stopped raining, and one of the painters had set up his easel on the beach and was finishing a picture of Théo's boat, beached on the sand. A soft orange-washed light spread from the horizon into a sky that was free of clouds. Antoine walked behind the painter and felt a shiver of delight. He knew nothing of modern art, but this painting, laden with primitive colours and an ample, sensuous reality conveyed in reds and blues, charmed him instantly.

'Do you sell your work?' he said awkwardly, not knowing how to go about such questions with an artist, without offending him.

'From time to time,' the painter said, cleaning a brush.

'I mean: that picture.'

'Who are you?'

'Antoine du Courseau. But the picture will be for Marie-Dévote and Théo. They haven't got anything for the walls of their dining room.'

'Ah!'

The painter tidied his palette away and, folding up his easel, offered the canvas to Antoine.

'Take it now. If you don't I'll change my mind. I'll glaze it for you when it's dry.'

'But … I need to give you something for it.'

'Of course … write to my dealer. I'll give you his card. He'll tell you how much. That's his business.'

Antoine stayed standing alone on the beach, the canvas in his hand, like a stray object he had discovered on the sand. Dusk was falling. A cool onshore breeze began to blow and he shivered.

'Saints! What's up, Antoine? Are you dreaming?' Théo shouted. 'Come and have a pastis.'

He walked back to the terrace. The bottle was waiting next to the carafe of cold water. Théo poured pastis, then water. Antoine placed the painting on the table and drank standing up.

'Do you like it?'

'I suppose so. Hey … it really looks like it.'

'To decorate your dining room.'

'Nice. The boat looks as if it's about ready to go.'

'Are you fishing tonight?'

'I'm thinking about it.'

It was part of the game. Antoine played with ill grace, and Théo brought it to an end by giving in, but only after enjoying Antoine's discomfort. He left to go fishing with his lamp, and Antoine remained in the dining room with Marie-Dévote and the two painters, who acknowledged his shy nod with a smile. Marie-Dévote had rings around her eyes and the slightly too languorous and feline look of a woman who has spent the afternoon satisfying herself fully. Antoine still wanted her, but more calmly and deliberately this time, and as he sipped her *soupe au pistou*, served steaming in big blue china dishes, he felt to an extreme extent – to the point of oppression – the fear of loving and of experiencing an impossible passion for a woman who could never be his. It was a bewildering feeling, a feeling that, for all its desire, revealed the bitterness of a wasted life. He wished he had never met Marie-Dévote, and he cursed the appointment with fate that had driven him, on an August afternoon three years earlier, to this beach café where a young girl sat sunning her brown knees on the terrace. At the same time he was forced to admit that, in the absence of Marie-Dévote, these last three years would have been pitiful, without any grace, joy or happiness. Without any happiness at all. He looked up.

'What's the matter?' Marie-Dévote said. 'Your eyes are watering.'

'The soup's hot. I burnt myself.'

'Oh good. I'm glad it's nothing worse!'

She left to help her mother with the dishes and he turned to the painters, who were also finishing dinner, and raised his glass.

'Why don't you join us?' the one who had sold him the picture said.

'I'd be delighted.'

They questioned him diplomatically, and he answered without bending the truth. One of the two men knew Grangeville.

'I was up that way last year. I rented a little place near the cemetery. Very soft light. Grey gravestones, white cliffs, the sea. One of those places you wouldn't mind dying in. I came back with a dozen seascapes, but that's not what the dealers want. The only thing they can sell is the sun. Isn't that true, André?'

'Yes. And we'll give them as much as they can handle, blue skies, blue seas, red sails, green boats. I know it like the back of my hand by now, I could go and paint it all in a cellar in Paris with a bare bulb over my head. This is the future, the Midi; people are going to make fortunes here ... '

They discussed their respective dealers with a scorn and aggressiveness that startled Antoine. He had been expecting revelations about art, some explanation of heaven knows what, and all he got instead was talk about money, names, exhibition dates and moaning about critics who only cared about official art, that great producer of war memorials. Antoine had never questioned whether these memorials were beautiful or ugly. In the course of his excursions he had seen them going up in every village, allegories in exaggerated drapery shielding a wounded soldier with a tender hand, proud bronze infantrymen watching over tearful women and children. They seemed unhealthy to him, full of dishonest symbolism, but the thought of judging their beauty or ugliness would never have occurred to him without the two artists' sarcastic commentary. He felt ashamed of his ignorance, and left them to go to his room. Here, a little later, Marie-Dévote followed him.

'Would you like it again?'

'Of course, it's all I've got. I don't give a damn about all the rest.'

And it was true: about all the rest he didn't give a damn, and there was no pain, no sorrow, but when he pressed Marie-Dévote against him or, daydreaming, stroked her pretty breasts and their brown tips, something else existed: his pleasure. He stayed at Saint-Tropez for three days, his limit, which he never exceeded, so that he could be sure of leaving with a trace of animal regret on his lips that provided him with the certainty that he existed. The route des Maures, then the high corniche road to Nice, took him down to Roquebrune, where he stopped. Léon Cece, recognising the note of the Bugatti's engine, appeared at his door in linen trousers and torn white singlet. Far from fading, his facial scars had deepened, splitting the soft tissue of his cheek, twisting his mouth, and attacking one eye, its bloodshot white beginning to bulge out of its orbit. His restaurant was doing badly. In the egotism of peacetime, diners were not willing to put up with the sight of his smashed face, a reminder of a time everyone was doing their best to forget and an awful reproach to those who had got through it without too much hardship; a mute and unacceptable pang of conscience from which most fled like cowards.

'All right, Antoine?' Léon called. 'It's been an age since we saw you.'

'Three months. I had an accident. My knee in plaster. This is my first long trip.'

'Well, that's good anyway. You're not like the others.'

They dined together on the balcony, wreathed by clouds of moths that whirled around the hurricane lamp and singed their wings. Léon was a man of truth. Unlike Charles Ventadour, the war he kept going back to was a squalid conflict, but it was his conflict, his alone, revolving around that attack when his head had been blown apart. He needed to talk about it, to go over it ceaselessly as though it were still possible, six years later, to take that one sideways step that would have saved him when the German 77 burst. And so great was his desire for that step that he seemed, at odd moments, almost able to erase the tragedy and recover his face as it had been, and his morale and cheerfulness, only to fall back again, harder than before, into the depths of a despair so bitter it had the taste of death about it. More than anything, he could not forgive the involuntary aversion of those who saw him for the first time. A curse had fallen upon him, and his uncomplicated and still sound spirit could not overcome the vast injustice that separated him from the rest of the living.

'You don't know what goes on,' he said to Antoine. 'My daughter and her mother do their best not to look at me. I don't make love any more. It would be unsightly, and everything around me is so beautiful. Roquebrune is the prettiest place on Earth. The people who come to the Côte are happy, they're beautiful, I turn away so that I don't make them sad. Sometimes I say to myself: Léon, you're not a man, you're not a man any more, you're like a dog, you're a pest, you've got to hide away.'

'You're a very unhappy man,' Antoine said.

'Maybe that's it. You're the only friend I have. We talk to each other. We drink grappa and the hours go by. Then you leave, and I wait for months for you to come by again. It's not your fault. I know you have a family and friends and, judging by your car, plenty of loose change. Maybe you're unhappy too. But you get around. I'm stuck here. That's my life. It's all I've got.'

Antoine stayed the night. Léon put up a camp bed for him in a bare room behind the kitchen. Mosquitoes descended on him and he stayed awake till first light, his head heavy with grappa fumes and his senses sharpened by the thought of Marie-Dévote lying in Théo's arms.

Léon came in, bringing a cup of coffee.

'It'll wake you up for your visit to your daughter,' he said.

'Yes, it will.'

But Geneviève was no longer at the clinic and Antoine, a prisoner of his family's habit of secrecy, did not dare admit it. Two years earlier, she had left Menton to spend the winter at Marrakesh. From there she had gone to Brazil, and recently they had received a postcard from her, sent from Japan. Who she was travelling with, who she was spending time with or, to be more accurate, was keeping her in such luxury – since she seemed to lead a sumptuous existence whatever latitude she found herself in – nobody knew. At La Sauveté nobody spoke of her. A fiction had taken root: Geneviève needed to get away from unhealthy climates. She would never return to Normandy. She needed air, sunshine, and the sea or snow-covered mountains outside her windows. Questioned, not without mischief, by her friends, Marie-Thérèse du Courseau invariably answered, 'Our children are nothing like we were. Geneviève is in love with freedom. It's the gift the war gave to her generation. I think we're modern parents. In 1923 you don't bring up children the way they were brought up fifty years ago.'

So Antoine pretended to spend a couple of hours at Menton, greeted Léon Cece with a blast on his horn on the way back, stopped to kiss Marie-Dévote, and slept at Aix after a second evening with Charles. On the road from Aix to La Sauveté he did his best to knock a few more minutes off his previous record. As he drove through the gates that evening in October 1923, he glimpsed Adèle Louverture, with Michel under her arm gesticulating and trying to kick her. He had just broken Jean's tricycle by taking a hammer to it, and Antoinette was kissing Jean to try to make it better.

Jean was pretending to read. The lines were dancing in front of his eyes. If he rested his forehead on his hand, he could lower his eyelids, make the unreadable page disappear, and go back in the minutest detail to the circumstances in which he had seen and then very gently kissed Antoinette's bottom. It had happened that afternoon at the foot of the cliff, behind a heap of fallen rocks. Of the scene, which had hardly lasted more than a minute, he retained an anxious feverishness, as though they both had deliberately committed a sin that defied the whole world. He felt proud of himself, and at the same time wondered to what extent his feverishness, which periodically felt just like dizziness, wasn't the punishment he risked, the sign that would betray him to the abbé Le Couec, his father, his mother, and Monsieur and Madame du Courseau. But between four o'clock and six that evening most of them had had plenty of time to read his thoughts, to question him, to notice how he blushed when they talked to him, and now he felt that their blindness was a serious blow to an infallibility that they had, in their different ways, fashioned into a dogma. Hadn't Antoinette said, 'If you don't tell, no one – do you understand? No one on Earth – will ever know.'

'Well, my dear Jean, you're not getting very far with your reading. Aren't you interested?'

At the sound of the priest's voice, Jean jumped as if he had been caught red-handed. The abbé was behind him, ensconced in the only armchair in the kitchen, his legs flung out straight and wide apart, stretching the coarse threadbare cotton of his cassock.

'That boy's ruining his eyes with reading. Always got his nose in a book,' Jeanne said, quick to take her adopted son's side.

'I wasn't blaming him!' the abbé answered. 'I'm just used to seeing him more engrossed in what he's reading.'

Albert, who was playing *trictrac* with Monsieur Cliquet, raised his head and said with finality, 'Anyway, there's nothing to be learnt from books. Newspapers and life will show you everything you need. I've never read a book in my life, and I'm no idiot, am I?'

He had allowed Madame du Courseau to pay for Jean's education with great reluctance. To his way of thinking, it would simply mean that the boy would later become a dropout instead of a good gardener who knew and loved his work, because if progress was one of Albert's key words he also entertained, within that vast idea, an illusion that society, advancing with even step towards human well-being and the mastery of life, would do so with its beneficial inequalities and necessary hierarchies intact. By not continuing the tradition of gardeners in the family, Jean was sowing disorder. But he also conceded that a mystery hung over his birth, and that such a child could thus not be tied down to the Arnauds' profession from father to son. He had to be given a chance to decide his own destiny, and his seriousness and application consoled Albert.

Captain Duclou, who, with his elbows on the waxed tablecloth, was completing the delicate manoeuvre of inserting a ship into the narrow neck of a bottle, whose three masts he would subsequently raise with a complicated arrangement of threads that he would tie off and snip with the help of long tongs, showed that for all his absorption he was not missing a word of the conversation.

'At sea there's no use for books. Everything you need for navigation, you learn from your elders and betters.'

'Come along,' the abbé said, 'let's not exaggerate. Moderation in everything. We don't come to God on our own. We need the Gospels.'

'Your turn, Albert!' Monsieur Cliquet said, holding out the dice cup to his cousin to remind those present that he took no part in such conversations and considered them pointless.

Jean resumed his daydream where it had been interrupted, and behind his lowered eyelids recreated his picture of Antoinette's bottom, a white, soft, well-rounded bottom that went into dimples where it met her back. Antoinette's face was not especially pretty – her nose was a little too long, her cheeks too plump, her small eyes, which sparkled with suppressed amusement, rather close together – but her body was firm, with well-shaped muscles beneath its roundness. She swam, cycled, rode and played tennis with unflagging vigour. She radiated an attractive vitality, and in her company you felt the same strong desire to exert yourself and to imitate and follow her. She had very recently started to develop into a young girl, and her bust joggled nicely when she ran across court playing tennis or stood on her pedals to climb hard up the road from Dieppe to Grangeville. Jean, under a spell of admiration, was almost always with her, breathless, furious, happy, enchanted by this creature four years older than he, who protected him from the endless stream of traps Michel laid for him.

She had asked him without warning, 'Do you want to see my bottom?'

To be honest, her bottom did not interest him very much. He would have preferred her breasts, but they would be for later, another time, and anyway Antoinette only ever did the things she wanted to do. The two of them had found a place concealed by a rock, where it was hard for them to be seen even from the top of the cliff above them. Antoinette had lifted up her skirt and pushed down her white cotton knickers, uncovering two lovely, smooth fresh globes that exuded a sense that being naked like that filled them with joy, making them want to burst with health and pleasure. The cleft disappeared into a shadowy fold between her thighs. Beyond, other mysteries began that Jean would have liked to find out about and whose importance he sensed without knowing why.

'So?' she said.

'It's very pretty.'

'You can kiss it!'

He had put his lips on the soft skin, so soft it had a sweet taste, and had managed to hold back from biting, a maddening impulse that suddenly started up like hunger somewhere between his teeth. He had not been upset when in an abrupt movement she covered up her two marvels, for their contemplation was making him dizzy. Mademoiselle du Courseau straightened her skirt, and they dashed back up the gully together, hand in hand, to fetch their bikes and pedal frantically all the way to La Sauveté …

'Yes, Father,' Jeanne said, 'you're right. In books we learn how we must behave in life. But there are also books that are dangerous for people's good sense.'

'What are you reading, Jean?'

'Treasure Island, Father. It was a present from Uncle Fernand.'

'Always stories about sailors!'

Fernand Duclou looked up. 'Well then, father, perhaps you'll tell us what you've got against the navy, you, a Breton?'

'Nothing, my dear man. It's perfectly true that stories about sailors are generally a good healthy read.'

'Because there are no women on board sailing ships' Monsieur Cliquet said mischievously, taking the dice cup from Albert. 'Whereas,' he added, 'there are women on trains and even Madonnas in sleeping cars.'

He was referring to a novel that had sold a fabulous number of copies, whose title was known even to those who were illiterate. Jeanne coughed, covering her embarrassment, and pulled her chair closer to spread her knitting over the kitchen table, above which hung an electric bulb and its china shade. The light was yellow and it flickered, but it was a novelty they were becoming accustomed to, not without the anxiety that it would be more expensive than their oil lamps. Jeanne stretched out the sleeve of the jumper she was knitting

71

and compared it with the one she had just finished. Captain Duclou poured warm blue wax into the bottle, and the three-master bobbed on a sea stirred up by a swell.

Albert had won. He sat back and lit a pipe, reached for his newspaper and after reading a headline, said bitterly, 'They'll have his hide, and then we'll have another war.'

'The war is over, for all of us,' the abbé said.

'Oh, they'll wait until Jean's old enough to be called up.'

'Well, that gives us a bit of time, and as for your Aristide, no one will miss him.'

'Briand equals peace!' Albert said forcefully.

'Peace equals a good navy,' the captain said. 'We no longer have one.'

'And a decent transport system,' Monsieur Cliquet said firmly. 'How can we mobilise today's wonderful modern armies with a network as out of date as ours? If the government thought that there would be another war, it would take the railways in hand. It's not doing that, and I therefore deduce that there is not going to be a war in the near future.'

'Now, now!' Jeanne said. 'There's no need to go having an argument when everyone agrees.'

The abbé protested. He did not agree, and he did not care for Briand, calling him an 'orator' and beginning to imitate rather grotesquely his famous 'Pull back the machine guns, pull back the cannons' speech. He then raised the embarrassing matter of his criminal record. In his eyes Briand embodied the worst aspects of the centralising republic that got itself mixed up in the affairs of the world willy-nilly, while denying its provinces their rightful cultural freedoms.

'Just listen to the Chouan!'[2] said Monsieur Cliquet, who had voted radical socialist since his youth.

The priest roared with laughter and leant over to borrow Albert's tobacco pouch to roll himself a cigarette between his fat peasant's fingers.

Jean was no longer following their talk, his mind having gone back to the delicious picture of Antoinette's bottom. He now badly wanted to see it again, and stroke its cool skin.

'It's time you went to bed,' his mother said. 'You have to be up at six tomorrow.'

Jean closed his book. In bed he would be alone in the dark, with no one to interrupt his reverie. He kissed everyone goodnight and went upstairs. Each year at Christmas Marie-Thérèse du Courseau gave him something for his bedroom, bookshelves, an armchair or some leather-bound books, and the simple room, whose only window looked out onto the park, was set apart by its taste from the rest of the house, where waxed tablecloths, the chimes of Big Ben and kitchen chairs reigned. Albert naturally disapproved of such luxury, which seemed to him devoid of sense.

'One day that boy will be ashamed of us,' he said.

Jeanne shrugged her shoulders. She did not believe it, and little by little had begun to indulge herself in dreams of a great future for the child who had fallen into her lap. Besides, how could she refuse? Despite being repeatedly rebuffed, Marie-Thérèse du Courseau interfered relentlessly in Jean's upbringing. Hadn't she recently been talking about him having tennis lessons, as Michel and Antoinette did, and wasn't she always picking him up whenever a Norman accent crept into his speech? But for the moment Albert's fears were unjustified: Jean admired him and adored Jeanne, and even if he showed enthusiastic gratitude to Madame du Courseau for her many kindnesses, he didn't really understand her attitude and its apparently arbitrary mixture of reprimands and generosity. He remained scared of her and never entered La Sauveté without apprehension, equally on his guard against Michel, who continued to nurse a deep, though veiled, hostility towards him that was more dangerous than kitchen knives or rat poison.

*

73

A few days later the Briand cabinet fell. Its end affected Albert deeply. War was around the corner, now that the one man who could prevent it had been removed. His successor, André Tardieu, nicknamed 'Fabulous'[3] in political circles for his cigarette-holder and personal elegance as much as his grand bourgeois manner, inspired confidence only among the bankers. They doubtless needed it, being in the middle of a recession, but the magic formulas that were apparently overflowing from Tardieu's pockets were already too late. The country's industrial base, including its armaments industry, was crumbling. Antoine du Courseau himself, having for a long time done no more than glance indifferently at his notary's warnings, found himself having to contemplate the sale of half the La Sauveté estate. The ink was barely dry on the contract when he left for the Midi, as though unable to bear Albert's reproach-laden look or his wife's indulgent smiles, laden with commiseration. Marie-Thérèse was admirable in her stoical dignity. She might of course, without straining herself an inch, have used her own fortune to save the park, but such an idea never occurred to her, and, it has to be said, nor did it cross Antoine's mind to ask her to do so. A wall went up, which Albert covered with ampelopsis. The view out to sea vanished and was forgotten, its only reminder the herring gulls that swooped over the beeches and continued to land on the lawn in front of the bluffs of rhododendrons. They alone betrayed the continued presence of the great disappeared space, the infinity of the sea that had been rendered so finite.

Jean was hardly aware of these changes. He quickly forgot the lost park. Antoinette filled his thoughts. Not all of them, to tell the truth, as though he had already guessed that a man lives better with two passions than one. Certainly Antoinette dominated, because she was there every day, but Chantal de Malemort reigned by virtue of an almost fairy-like absence and her pure, transparent graces. It was, therefore, the little girl he caught sight of once a month if he was lucky, in the course of a formal visit, who captured his heart's

74

most passionate impulses. If she had decided to reveal to him the same secrets as Antoinette he would have detested her, just as he would have detested Antoinette if she had decided to stop exciting his imagination with her carefully arranged exposures. In fact he did end up detesting her several times when, as much out of caprice as to gauge the extent of her power over him, she refused to show him that part of her body that had so fascinated him one afternoon at the foot of the cliff. She was also prudent: without her foresight and coolness they would definitely have been caught. Jean went slightly mad. He demanded his due everywhere, in the garage, in the woodshed, even in Antoinette's bedroom when he managed to slip in there. Their difficulties increased when Michel's attention was aroused and he began to follow them, but Antoinette knew how to shake him off with a mischievousness worthy of her age, and Michel would get lost in the back ways to the sea while the two accomplices sprinted down the gully and hid themselves under the cliff. Jean's pleasure was spiced with remorse: what would Monsieur du Courseau think if he found out? Their secret understanding, born six years earlier after the incident of the punctured hosepipe, had continued and strengthened, without any need for great declarations. A wink from time to time, a word here and there, had been enough to reassure Jean. Actions and opportunities would come later – but what a disaster it would be if, before that happened, a shadow were to fall between them! Jean did not even dare imagine it. On the other hand, at Christmas there would be a problem: to receive communion he would have to go to confession, and there was no question of confessing to any other priest than the abbé Le Couec. But how would he react to what Jean would have to tell him? By early December Jean was feeling increasingly anxious, and he decided to ask Antoinette about his problem. She burst out laughing.

'You stupid boy! Why should you confess it? It's not a sin. Don't be such an idiot, or I shan't show you anything any more.'

'I'm sure it is a sin. It's called lust.'

'Oh my gosh, just listen to him! Who do you think you are? A man? For heaven's sake, there are no children left.'

Impressed, Jean did not say any more, and on Christmas Eve went to confession with the village children. The abbé Le Couec officiated in his icy church, chilled by a west wind that whistled through the porch and made the altar-cloth ripple magically. The dancing candle flames twisted the shadows of the Sulpician statues of Saint Anthony, Saint Thérèse of Lisieux and Joan of Arc in their niches. Huddled in his rickety confessional, the abbé Le Couec listened to the piping litany of childish sins. When it was his turn Jean knelt, trembling, and with his voice shaking with emotion recited an Our Father as if he were clinging to a lifebelt, then fell silent.

'I'm listening, my child,' said the priest, who had recognised his voice.

Jean confessed to some venial sins that he wasn't even sure were sins. The abbé's silence worried him. Was he there, listening behind his screen? What trap was waiting, right next to Jean, in the darkness of the confessional? What if there were no priest on the other side at all, but a huge ear sitting on the wooden bench, an ear of God with hearing so acute it could listen in to the most secret thoughts.

'Is that all? Well, that's not too bad. Those are not really sins, more weaknesses that a boy like you ought to be able to put right with no trouble. Two Hail Marys and two Our Fathers. You can go.'

Jean left the confessional, hands clasped together and head bent, and walked to the altar where he knelt and prayed, his heart heavy with his remorse at having deceived a man as good and generous as the abbé Le Couec.

At La Sauveté Antoinette was waiting in Jeanne's kitchen, where Jeanne was ironing in front of the range on which she was keeping the iron hot. As soon as he walked in, his gaze met Antoinette's, and he knew that she was waiting to make sure he hadn't weakened. He held her look and grinned.

'So did you make a good confession, little one?'

'Very good, Maman. The abbé Le Couec told me my sins aren't really sins.'

Antoinette's eyes shone with pleasure. She kissed Jeanne on the cheek, shoved Jean playfully, and skipped back to La Sauveté. A few days later, when they were out for a walk together, she showed him her breasts, which had already grown into two charming, nicely firm little domes. Jean was filled with happiness, and his remorse at having deceived the good abbé steadily faded. He was beginning to lose his trust in the absoluteness of a religion that was unable to penetrate the secrets of people's souls. You could escape from God's omnipresence, and trick his ministers, without the earth opening up beneath your feet. The idea was not yet clear in his mind, but a glimmer flickered on the horizon: if a person watched where they were going, they ought to reach a world less full of threats and menace. Wasn't Albert an unbeliever? And Jean could not imagine that a better person than his father existed.

However strong Antoinette's hold on him was, she could not remove Chantal de Malemort from his thoughts, where she continued to reign discreetly as a figure of pale and dark beauty, pink-lipped, slender and modest. On New Year's Day, Madame du Courseau drove the children to a party at the Malemorts'. That afternoon, during a game of hide and seek, Jean found himself alone with Chantal in the trophy room on the château's ground floor. Dozens of stuffed birds crowded the shelves, and the whole of one wall was covered in the antlers of stags hunted in the forest of Arques by three generations of Malemorts. The room was icily cold and smelt of dust, a dead, faded smell that caught in Jean's throat. Chantal pulled back a brocaded curtain that hid a recessed door.

'Hide in there!'

'What about you?' he blurted out, so close to the object of his admiration that he was unable to stay calm.

'I'm coming with you, of course!'

The heavy curtain fell back over them and they stood still for a moment, side by side, not touching, their backs against the door. Shouts rang out in the corridor. Michel was looking for them. He entered the room and called out, 'Come out, I saw you!'

Chantal made a slight movement, and Jean put his hand on her arm. They held their breath, shoulder to shoulder. Michel marched around the room, looking under the table, opening cupboards.

'I'll give you three seconds to come out!' he shouted.

Jean held Chantal's arm more tightly and she didn't move. They heard the door close again, and the sound of a stampede in the corridor.

'He's gone!' she said.

'It's a trick. He's going to come back as quietly as he can.'

Two minutes later the door creaked, and Michel burst into the room.

'Hey! I saw you.'

Terrified, Chantal hid her face in the hollow of Jean's shoulder. He felt pure happiness. For years afterwards he remembered that impulse she had had to claim his protection, and the firmness with which he had kept her close to him, wrapping his arm around her, with his nose in her fresh-smelling hair. Chantal de Malemort never belonged to him more than she did at that moment, as a child-woman.

When Michel finally gave up his search and left the room, Chantal detached herself from Jean, pushed back the curtain, and pulled him by the hand. They ran to the hall, where the Marquis de Malemort was pulling off his mud-plastered boots and drenched oilskin. He had just been out to take oats and straw to his horse and gave off a strong smell of stables. Jean admired this handsome and solid man, who owned a château and was favoured with a title that belonged in the kind of fairy tales in which kings and princes have daughters more beautiful than the dawn's meeting with the night. That this character was real did not intimidate him, quite the contrary. He liked his strong, earthy presence, and the way he swore with the same manners as Madame de Malemort and the same gentleness as Chantal. A bond united this family – the château, the name – a bond whose subterranean ramifications Jean had only just begun to perceive, through snatches of conversations whose meaning he did not always understand, but which seemed to exclude him. In short, Chantal belonged to a caste that put her beyond his dreams, in a virtually magical firmament in which she glided on the tips of her feet without touching the earth at all. Left to himself, Jean might eventually have doubted the superior existence of Chantal de Malemort, but he had Marie-Thérèse du Courseau, née Mangepain, to influence his thoughts, a woman sugary to the point of crystallisation in her decorum, hungry to add ever more titles to her conversation and gather like nectar, from one country house to the next, the crumbs of a decaying society of which she would have adored to be a part, even if it meant being swallowed up along with it. Her admiration – stripping her character of every natural quality – helped to sustain the existence of a tradition that had been more overwhelmed by several years of recession than it had been in a hundred and fifty years of revolutions.

However kind the Malemorts were to him, Jean never saw them without a feeling of guilt, as though his place was not among them. He was the son of Albert and Jeanne, caretakers of La Sauveté. If he ever forgot it for an instant, Michel made it his business to remind him with a wounding word. Michel's unpleasantness hurt him because, even though he did not love Michel – how could he? – he genuinely admired him for his talents. He would have given anything to sing like him at mass, or create the crib figures he made with his own hands, or paint the colourful landscapes that had already been shown in a gallery at Dieppe, and then at Rouen. What did he, Jean Arnaud, possess that he could shine with, in the eyes of the Malemorts? Nothing, apart from his strength, his physical agility, and some secrets passed on to him by Monsieur Cliquet and Captain Duclou, incommunicable secrets that Chantal would never need to use: the history of locomotives through the ages, and how to predict the weather.

I sense that the reader is eager, as I am, to reach the point where Jean Arnaud becomes a man. But patience! None of us turns into an adult overnight, and nothing would be properly clear (or properly fictional) if I failed to illustrate the stages of our hero's childhood in some carefully chosen anecdotes. This is, after all, the period when Jean is to learn what life is, or, more specifically, when he is to experience a range of feelings, aversions and passions which will imprint themselves deeply on him and to which he will only discover the key very much later, around the age of thirty, when he begins to see things more clearly. At the time that I am talking about, he is still a small boy, and beyond the walls of La Sauveté the wide world that awaits him, with all its cheating and its pleasures, is a long way off. So far away that you might as well say it doesn't exist. Jean had an idea of it, however, thanks to an encounter that I want to record and to which I implore the reader to pay attention. It happened under the premiership of Camille Chautemps, which is entirely irrelevant, I hasten to add, and which lasted for nine days, a record equalled in the Third Republic only by Alexandre Ribot and beaten by Édouard Herriot. Returning from an errand in Dieppe, Jean was pedalling back up the hill to Grangeville in a fine drizzle that was working its way through the cape he had spread across his handlebars. Despite his sou'wester, rain was also dripping down his neck, and his soaked feet were squelching on the pedals in shoes that were too big for him. Coming round a bend, he saw a car that had stopped on the verge. It was a car that impressed as much by its size – it looked as large as a truck – as by its yellow coachwork, black mudguards and white wheels. A chauffeur in a light blue tunic and peaked cap was crouching next to the offside rear wheel, whose tyre was flat, and trying to remove the wheel. He must have been lacking an essential tool, because, seeing Jean, he hailed him. Jean slowed and stopped and stood open-mouthed: the chauffeur was black. His face, wet with rain, shone under his cap, and when he opened his mouth Jean was struck by the size and yellowish colour of his teeth.

'Is there a mechanic near here?' the chauffeur asked.

'Yes, at the bottom of the hill.'

'Is it far?'

'Maybe a kilometre.'

'You wouldn't like to go and get him for me, would you?'

'It's hard to ride back up the hill. I've already done it once.'

'Will you lend me your bicycle?'

'It's too small for you.'

'I'll manage.'

The chauffeur took off his cap and tapped on the rear window, which opened with a squeaking sound. A face appeared, pale and with grey semi-circles under the eyes. The neck disappeared into a tightly tied blue silk scarf. It was impossible to say whether it was a young man ravaged by a hidden illness that gave his cheeks and forehead a parchment-like translucency, or a much older man whom death would soon blow apart, splitting an envelope stretched to breaking point over a fragile skeleton.

'Monseigneur,' the chauffeur said, 'this boy is lending me his bicycle to go and fetch a mechanic. There's one at the bottom of the hill, he says.'

'Hurry then! We have to pick Madame up again at five o'clock.'

The man's voice matched his physique, thin and fragile. Jean was dazzled: he had heard the chauffeur call his passenger with the blue scarf 'Monseigneur'. This passenger now turned and looked at him sympathetically and added, 'You're not going to stand out there in the rain. Come and sit by me.'

The chauffeur opened the door and Jean shook out his rubber cape and climbed into the passenger compartment, where the man pointed to a folding seat.

'What is your name?' he asked immediately.

'Jean Arnaud.'

'And do you live near here?'

'At Grangeville.'

'It looks as if it rains rather a lot here.'

'Oh, it depends! There are fine days too.'

Jean's eyes began to get used to the half-darkness inside the car, whose luxury seemed fabulous to him. The seats were of glossy black leather, the carpet of animal fur, and another pelt covered the knees of the traveller, who was bundled up in a black overcoat with an otter-skin collar. A tortoiseshell telephone connected him to the chauffeur, who was separated from his passenger by a glass panel. Beside the folding seat there was a drawer of some rich hardwood, filled with crystal decanters and silver goblets.

'What are you looking at?'

'Everything … everything, Monseigneur.'

'I see that you're well brought up. This is a great strength in life. What do your parents do?'

'My parents are the caretakers at La Sauveté. My father's a gardener. He lost a leg in the war. He doesn't want me to be a soldier.'

'He's right.'

'What kind of car is this?'

'Hispano-Suiza. Have you ever seen one like it?'

'Never. It's beautiful. It must cost a lot of money.'

'I don't know. They bought it for me. I'm a very lazy man. I don't buy anything myself.'

'Then people must steal from you.'

'Perhaps, but never mind. That's the price of my peace of mind.'

The man coughed into his closed fist. He peeled off one of his tan kid gloves to take a phial out of a small box next to him, from which he dripped a few drops onto a handkerchief. A strong medicinal smell filled the car.

'Are you ill, Monseigneur?'

He nodded his head, put the handkerchief over his nose and breathed in deeply before answering.

'I have asthma.'

'Can't the doctor cure you?'

'No.'

'That's very sad!'

'You are a very kind boy.'

Jean looked at him intensely, and the man smiled back.

'Can I ask you a question?' Jean said.

'Yes, but I cannot promise I'll answer it.'

'How do you become a monseigneur?'

'It's a very old story. I didn't become a "monseigneur". My father was a prince. And my grandfather, and my great-grandfather. You would have to go a long way back into history to find the first of my ancestors who became a prince, in the year 318 of the Hijra, which is to say in AD 940, which you will understand better, I dare say, being a little Christian. At that time there reigned at Bab al Saud an extremely powerful king, named Salah el Mahdi. He was good, but arrogant, and had a serious fault, which was never to know when people were lying to him. When I say "serious fault", it was almost an illness with him, he made so many mistakes about other men. Haroun, his vizir, who looked after the affairs of the kingdom in the company of a dozen or so emirs who had sworn loyalty to him, used his position to accumulate an immense fortune by extorting money from country people and merchants alike and by using the royal fleet for pirate raids across the Mediterranean, as far as the coast of France. The king suspected nothing. He believed that his kingdom's finances were prospering, because the vizir very skilfully denied him no luxury. When the vizir offered him a sumptuous present he did not suspect that it was the hundredth fraction of the pirates' booty, of which the wretched band in power kept the other ninety-nine hundredths. His harem was populated with beautiful, pale, almost diaphanous creatures captured from Christian ships, whom Haroun assured him were gifts from foreign kings dazzled by his reputation, when they were really poor Greek girls snatched from their families or passionate light-skinned Sicilians kidnapped by the crews of pirate feluccas. Haroun and his henchmen were so greedy that after several years had passed they began to believe that what they were giving the king was still too much, that the hundredth of the spoils that they were forgoing to keep him happy would do just as well in their own chests. So they arrested Salah el Mahdi and would certainly have cut his head off if a prophecy known to everyone had not promised that decapitated kings would turn into vampires when it got dark and return to suck their executioners' blood. Instead they shut him up in a fortress where he was to be guarded by a company of warriors, the fiercest in the kingdom, incorruptible mountain fighters commanded by an officer who knew only his duty. The poor king understood nothing of what had happened to him. Shut up in a narrow cell where he hardly had room to lie down, he was only allowed to walk for two hours each night, chained to his gaolers. A hole in the wall allowed him to glimpse a tiny square of sky and a mountain peak, which he saw covered in snow three times before the vizir, deciding that it was another unnecessary expense to keep under such heavy guard a deposed king who was too lazy to escape, dismissed the warriors and ordered their commanding officer to escort him to his tribe. That officer, Abderrahman al Saadi, which means the Avenger of the Just, was my ancestor. He knew only his orders and that, as he had been told, the king was responsible for the country's great misery. He treated him like a slave and made him clean his weapons, forcing him to carry out tasks that normally were only done by women. The king humbly accepted his lot. The years of captivity had matured his spirit and he recognised his error – a capital error for a sovereign

84

– in having surrounded himself with double-dealers, toadies and grasping officials. He never complained, suffering his ill-treatment with resignation. Then one day it happened that Abderrahman al Saadi discovered that his prisoner, even though he was famished himself, was sharing his miserable rations with a hunting dog that had been wounded during a chase and could not compete with the other dogs for its supper. He was astonished that such a vile being, whose cruelty and rapacity had been so vividly described to him, could have any such impulse. He had him brought to his tent, and the two men talked all night. Abderrahman al Saadi understood the injustice of which he had been made the instrument. He prostrated himself before Allah and swore to deserve his name of Avenger of the Just, and then went to the king to beg his pardon for having so insulted him. Within a few weeks Abderrahman had raised an army of fighters, every man among them as fierce and as courageous as could be. This small army represented less than a tenth of the vizir's army, but on its side it had faith and the desire to avenge a king too easily abused. Instead of confronting the regular army head on, Abderrahman decided to act by stealth. He invited Haroun to a great celebration at the gates of the capital. His best horsemen were to compete against each other at a game of skill that would later be called polo. Flattered and pleased to be entertained without it costing him a penny, the vizir accepted, and a great camp was set up in a field. Abderrahman insisted that Haroun come with his personal guards, who would be massed around the main stand. These were all black warriors of two metres in height, chosen for their colossal strength and skill with a spear. On the appointed day Haroun arrived at the celebration and watched the game and then the races until nightfall, when Abderrahman announced an archery competition. Mounted on galloping horses and led by a masked rider, the competitors were to fire their hundred arrows at a target in the middle of the hippodrome, held by an impassive warrior. Filled with enthusiasm for their skill, the vizir asked for the crack bowmen to be introduced to him. Led by the masked rider, the archers formed up in a line in front of the vizir's stand.

'"Who are you?" Haroun asked.

'"Do you truly want to know?"

'"It's an order. Who are you?"

'"Your king!" cried the rider, tearing off his mask and firing an arrow straight at the heart of Haroun, who collapsed dying as the hundred horsemen took aim at the vizir's guard and planted a hundred arrows in their bronze breastplates. Night was falling, and the crowd's cries of terror turned to panic as they saw that the city was burning. Abderrahman's spies, making the most of the dignitaries' absence, had set fire to the palace and the barracks. The zeal of the incendiaries was doubtless somewhat excessive because, in the space of a day and a night, the whole capital burnt down. Salah el Mahdi, having regained his throne but without a palace, decided to live in the mountains with the warriors who had given him back his kingdom. He built himself a fortress and entrusted the country's administration to my ancestor, whom he made a prince so that the word "vizir" would never again be heard in the country. There you are, Jean Arnaud. That's how you become a prince.'

'Goodness, it's not easy!'

'No, you're right about that, and one must also admit that there are fewer opportunities today than there once were to become a prince.'

'Yes, that's sad!' Jean said, thinking of Chantal de Malemort, who would not hesitate to marry him if he suddenly became a prince.

There was a tap at the glass, misted by the rain, and Jean made out the blurred face of the chauffeur, who was laughing. His passenger wound down the window, and the black man took off his cap.

'Monseigneur, the mechanic is here. He is completing the job. We'll be able to get on our way.'

The window rose again.

'This is thanks to you, Jean. I'm very grateful to you.'

He unbuttoned his overcoat and took out a wallet, from which he withdrew two thousand-franc notes.

'I hope that you have a money box.'

'Yes.'

'Then put these two notes in it, and write your name and address in my notebook. I'll send you a souvenir when I remember.'

'I can't accept them. What will my father say?'

'He won't say anything.'

'He'll never believe I met a prince at the side of the road. Things like that don't happen.'

'Sometimes the most unlikely things are the most easily believed.'

He slid the notes into Jean's cape pocket.

'There you are, it's done. Let's say no more about it. Goodbye, Jean.'

He seemed very tired, ready to close his eyes and go to sleep. The mechanic was tightening the bolts of the spare wheel with a few last turns while the chauffeur watched him with a superior expression. Jean picked up his bicycle and climbed the rest of the way up the hill as fast as he could, though not fast enough to stay ahead of the Hispano-Suiza, which caught up and then overtook him. To his great surprise, he found it stopped again outside the gates of La Sauveté. The chauffeur waited by the passenger door, umbrella in hand. A young woman in a fur coat dashed out of the house and through the rain and threw herself into the car, which drove away immediately.

'You took your time!' Jeanne said when he came in, having shaken out his cape in the hall. 'It's too bad that you missed Mademoiselle Geneviève. I told her about you, and she very much wanted to meet you.'

'Was it her who was leaving as I arrived?'

'Yes.'

'Well, I talked to her husband.'

'Her husband?' Jeanne said.

'Yes, the monseigneur.'

'What are you talking about? She hasn't married a bishop.'

'No, another monseigneur. A real one. A prince. He gave me this!'

He took one of the thousand-franc notes out of his pocket, a reflex that he only understood later holding him back from producing both.

'A thousand francs!' Jeanne cried. 'But he's completely mad!'

'I lent him my bike.'

'You lent your bicycle to a prince?'

'No. To his chauffeur, a black man in a blue tunic.'

'I don't understand a word you're saying.'

He had to explain from the beginning, and then explain a second time to Albert, who to Jean's astonishment decided that the thousand-franc note was proper treasure trove and pushed it into Jean's money box. Yes, Geneviève had been there that afternoon. She had come directly to the lodge to kiss Jeanne, before going across to La Sauveté to see her parents and her brother and sister.

'She hasn't changed, our little one,' said Jeanne, trying as she invariably did to link the fearful present to a reassuring past where everything had been kindly and good.

'What are you talking about? She's twelve years older and looks it!' Albert said, turned as ever towards the future.

'I mean that her heart's still in the right place. She gave me a stole and a bag which will be just right for mass on Sunday.'

After dinner Madame du Courseau appeared, and Jean was sent to bed. Grumbling, he went upstairs, leaving his bedroom door slightly open. He could not hear everything, but he realised that Marie-Thérèse had come to find out whether Geneviève had unburdened herself to Jeanne any more than to herself. Jeanne was stony in her replies, answering in monosyllables until the conversation was interrupted by the familiar rumble of the Bugatti being driven out of its garage. This one was a Type 47, the largest cubic capacity ever produced by Ettore Bugatti, a 5.35-litre engine that effortlessly accelerated to 150 kilometres an hour.

'It really is far too late to be going out for a drive,' Madame du Courseau said in an offended voice.

Antoine had been left feeling confined and stifled by the emotions that Geneviève's visit had aroused. For several days he had wanted to try out the new car, delivered three months earlier from the Molsheim workshops, over a proper distance, but as it was late he switched his itinerary and took the road for Paris, where, arriving shortly after midnight, he stopped for a *demi* and a ham sandwich at a café at the Porte Maillot. Not having been to Paris since 1917, he found the city changed. He remembered black streets and empty boulevards, in which glimmers of blue light escaped from behind blinds placed over windows: a city of often beautiful women, of whom he had been instinctively suspicious. Now he wandered in search of memories and found none, and as in such circumstances we generally find what we would like not to, on Place de l'Étoile he overtook a yellow Hispano-Suiza driven by a black chauffeur. He let it pass him and followed it to a side road off the Avenue du Bois, where it stopped outside an *hôtel particulier*. The chauffeur opened the door. Geneviève stepped out first, waiting for the prince, tall and slightly stooped, to follow and take her arm. Antoine accelerated past them so that he would not be recognised.

It was two o'clock by now, and the only life to be found was at Place Pigalle, Montmartre, where he abandoned the car and walked. Because the girls who began to accost him bored and repelled him, he pretended to be part of a group that had just alighted from a bus and were hastening towards a nightclub whose entrance was in the shape of an enormous red devil's mouth. English was being spoken around him, then German, as a trilingual guide steered the group, sat it down at small tables and clapped his hands to call the waiters, who arrived with demi-sec sparkling wine in champagne flutes. Antoine found himself sitting between an American woman and a German, facing a nondescript individual who laughed for no reason and who, for as long as the show (pretty bare-breasted girls playing with snakes) lasted, kept his hand in his trouser pocket and did rather unspeakable things, apparently without conclusive result. Scarcely had the show finished than the guide collected up his herd and stuffed them back into their bus. Antoine followed. At this late hour no one was counting the tourists in search of the legendary Paris by night, and in any case it was highly likely that some had been mislaid en route, either too drunk to go on or spirited away by some hungry seductress. The bus drove on to Bastille, from where the passengers had a brisk walk to a dance hall on Rue de Lappe. At the tourists' arrival the band struck up. Bad boys in shiny black shirts and striped trousers danced a rakish waltz with molls in plunging necklines. Antoine found himself with a Swedish couple, who were beside themselves with pleasure. They asked him where he was from, and when they discovered they were talking to a Frenchman their joy was boundless. The woman was not bad-looking, with attractive breasts that stretched the fabric of her low-cut dress; when Antoine distractedly stroked her thigh under the table, she bit her lip. They drank warm white wine and nibbled slices of soft sausage that were supposed to get them in the mood. Antoine was looking forward to enjoying himself when the bad boys and their molls had left the dance floor, but no one was brave enough to follow them and the guide gathered his tourists together to go. The tour was over. The bus discharged its dazed and exhausted night owls at Place de l'Opéra, which was deserted except for the street-sweeping machines sluicing it clean with great jets of water. The Swedish woman looked around for Antoine, but he was already gone, walking quickly up towards Trinité and then via Rue Blanche back to Pigalle, suddenly anxious for his car, which he had left with the hood down in the fine drizzle that had started to fall over the city, varnishing its empty, dirty streets strewn with dustbins. Girls leaving nightclubs as they closed ran, pushing up their coat collars. The blue Bugatti was where he had left it, its handsome leather upholstery soaked and its steering wheel dripping. Antoine dried both with an old raincoat and set off slowly in search of the Porte d'Italie, to which a policeman on a bicycle eventually directed him. Day was breaking. He shivered in his still-wet cockpit, but the engine's organ-pipe sound was on song with such evident pleasure that Antoine kept going to Fontainebleau, cutting deep into the frosty forest that sparkled in the morning light. On the main square he found a brasserie and ordered a bowl of coffee, as he waited for a barber and a shirt-maker to open their doors. He felt pleasantly light-headed at the change he had wrought in an itinerary that for ten years had been immutable. He had a pang of regret about the Swedish woman – the warm skin between her stocking and knickers had seemed very welcoming. But one cannot have everything, and at the other end of the Nationale Sept[4] there was Marie-Dévote and little Toinette and at Roquebrune Mireille Cece, the daughter of poor Léon. It was already plenty. Antoine was no longer twenty years old. He even admitted to being fifty-six, and though he had lost weight at Marie-Dévote's express request – despite her shamelessly filling out herself – he could no longer lay claim to a young man's adventures. Shaved and roused by coffee, he set out again and made Lyon without stopping, where he slept for twelve hours and opened his eyes on a deep, swirling fog. A pea-souper, thick and dirty and clinging, had come in through the window and was raking his throat. He could not see as far as the end of his bed. The foggy moods of the Saône and Rhône were joining forces. Antoine remembered the nickname given to Lyon by Henri Béraud: Mirelingue-la-brumeuse.[5] The Lyonnais, accustomed to this miasma blanketing their city, seemed not even to notice it. Antoine eventually found the Vienne road, and immediately the fog lifted, revealing the Rhône valley, green and grey and lovely under the winter sun.

At Aix he halted outside Charles's garage, under the sign saying

Chez Antoine. Charles no longer got his hands dirty, and instead oversaw his mechanics from a small glass office which he filled with caporal tobacco smoke while reading books about the war. Hearing the Bugatti's engine, he came straight out.

'All right, Captain? Well, well, the new one, eh?'

He spread his arms wide, as if the Bugatti was going to jump up and hug him. The engine was idling, and he put his ear to the bonnet to hear the tick-over.

'Terrific!' he said. 'Really terrific.'

'Twenty-four valves, single overhead cam. Like a watch: I averaged 112 between Lyon and Aix. In October I'll have the 50: double overhead cam and supercharger.'

'Ye gods! ... This one must do at least 200 an hour.'

'Only 175,' Antoine said modestly.

They drank a pastis together, standing by the car, while a mechanic changed the plugs and the engine oil. Charles insisted that the captain dine with him.

'We have business to discuss,' he said.

Antoine shuddered inwardly. The most recent warnings of his notary at Dieppe were fresh in his mind, and as people only ever discussed business with him with one purpose in mind, he was on his guard. The garage was big enough as it was; and he would say the same to Marie-Dévote, who was planning a new wing to her hotel, and to Mireille, who wanted to add a long terrace to her restaurant that would face Cap Martin and the sea.

Charles, not imagining for a second that anyone might want to run from his company, asked anxiously, 'How's the little one? Nothing serious, I hope?'

'Nothing at all. She's as right as rain.'

Antoine's heart beat faster. He thought of Toinette, the little girl he had had with Marie-Dévote, so slight and skinny, who had just recovered from typhoid fever. Charles, who for some time had known everything that went on in his captain's life, added, 'What about Mireille?'

'She doesn't often write. She prefers me to visit.'

'It's understandable.'

Night was falling.

'I've still got a good way to go,' Antoine said.

'What a shame! Jeannette would have made us tomato soup.'

'Tomato soup?' Antoine repeated, seized by weakness.

'I can send a lad over to let her know.'

'No!' Antoine said, agitated at the thought of all these banquets costing him so dearly. 'Next time!'

'As you like, Captain.'

The Bugatti was ready. A mechanic started the engine, with one eye on the dipstick. Antoine shook Charles's hand and sat at the wheel.

'Till the next time!'

Charles turned to the mechanic, who still held Antoine's tip in the palm of his hand.

'A little beauty!' he said with a wink.

'A real beauty,' the mechanic said thoughtfully. 'It would take me two years of working without eating or drinking to afford one of those.'

The Bugatti was already gone, leaving behind it a bluish trail of oil. Antoine reached Saint-Tropez two hours later in a cold, cloudless night. The hotel was extensive now, with twenty or so rooms, a lounge, a large dining room and an enormous kitchen. There was no off-season any more, and during the summer Parisians who did not fear the sun, and were sometimes even incautious about going out in it, occupied the rooms vacated by the painters, who preferred the months of winter, bathed in its limpid light.

The hotel's door opened, and Marie-Dévote appeared with her back to the light. Her southern beauty made the most of a certain plumpness, a bigger waist and more splendid bust, and Antoine felt happier the moment he set eyes on her and she ran towards him, kissing him tenderly on both cheeks while he still sat in the Bugatti's cockpit, the engine ticking as it cooled.

'I was longing for you to come! Come inside quickly, it's cold out here.'

He followed her into the kitchen, where, since her mother had died, one of Théo's aunts had taken over, an immense and rather strong-smelling woman, a genius at making fish soup, tomatoes *à la provençale* and *pissaladière*. He was cold through from the drive, having come all the way with the hood down, and they served him a hot supper there and then on the kitchen table.

'When I've warmed up, I'll go up and kiss Toinette. How is she?'

'Wonderful. And first in school too. This evening she came home with two more good marks.'

'Is Théo in bed?'

'He's in Marseille. He's coming home tomorrow or the day after. He's buying himself a new boat to take the Parisians on trips next summer.'

Antoine was content. Tonight there would be no complications, none of the innuendos that irritated him so much. His cares instantly slipped away, he thanked aunt Marie with a gentle slap on her bottom, and took the stairs that led to Toinette's bedroom two at a time. She was asleep in a four-poster bed draped in pink silk, and was every inch his daughter: pale skin, blond hair with a tinge of chestnut, and long, blue-veined hands. In any case the doctors had confirmed to Théo that he could not have children. Antoine pressed his lips gently on her fragile temple, and Toinette turned over in her bed with a little moan. He was so happy that he put his hand up Marie-Dévote's skirt as she came to stand behind him.

'Antoine! Not here,' she chided him. 'You don't have any morals at all!'

He would so much have liked to. But how do you explain these things? As the years went by, she was becoming more and more bourgeois. In a sense it was reassuring, because with all the artists

94

who came to lodge with her for the winter, she could easily have been making love every night. But she joined him later in his bedroom and left him the next morning, shaking him vigorously as she went.

'Antoine! Your daughter ... '

'What about my daughter?'

'She's going to be late for school ... '

There were rituals, then. Every time he visited he drove their daughter to the Saint-Tropez primary school. With a ribbon in her hair, dressed in pastel colours that went with her Nordic complexion, Antoinette made an arrival that the children chattered about for weeks.

'Uncle Antoine, the other girls, they really want to be me.'

'Do you think so?'

'Their uncles don't have Bugattis.'

'Well, I've always had one, so it doesn't seem very unusual to me.'

'Will you come and fetch me at lunchtime?'

'Yes, if you like.'

He returned to have breakfast at the hotel. Three painters were there. He didn't recognise them and so, reserved as usual, he pretended to ignore them. The dining room was full of pictures, some of which commemorated unpaid bills, others Antoine's purchases. It was beginning to acquire a reputation, and people often came a long way to admire the Derains, Dufys, Dunoyers de Segonzacs and Valmincks hanging on its walls. Théo was starting to worry.

'Soon there won't be any more room ... What are we going to do with all these daubs?'

Marie-Dévote, whose instincts were more sensitive and who overheard what passing visitors said, was beginning to see the daubs as a good investment.

'You don't know anything. One day they'll all be famous, and then you'll be following them around, begging them to do you a drawing on the paper tablecloth.'

'You'll always know how to make me laugh.'

*

When he was at Saint-Tropez Antoine dressed in old trousers and a turtleneck sweater and went for long walks along the beach, during which he contemplated his life. He would have liked to rectify two of its big events, his marriage and the war, but in its present specifics it pleased him. He had to acknowledge, for instance, that Théo's equivocal indulgence added fire to the few nights he spent with Marie-Dévote. If Théo had not balked at letting him enjoy her more freely, she would have had more power over him, and perhaps his appetite for her would have been sated. He loved her without her being close to him, and in truth no one was really close to him, not even his children, Michel, Geneviève and the two Antoinettes. He was essentially a shy man and, like most shy people, had impulses of tenderness that were not always returned. He was realistic; he harboured no illusions about Charles's friendship, or the love of Marie-Dévote or Mireille Cece. Money stimulated warm feelings, and that was what one used it for, to create those momentary illusions. Without money, he would have known nothing, and if he happened not to have any one day, his existence would be a desert and no part of it would be worth living.

He left the beach and came back through the woods. He loved the fragrance of the pine groves and the silvery-pale sheen of the olive trees. At Saint-Tropez, as he waited for school to finish, he paused at La Ponche beach and sat on the terrace of a fisherman's bar. The weathered boats pulled up on the shingle were unloading red mullet, bass and rock lobster. He drank a second pastis, and his lost rapture returned. No one talked about the war here. Had it ever happened? He could almost have believed that the past twelve years had wiped it from memories and hearts, if he himself hadn't continued to be troubled by terrible dreams. And then there had been the death of Léon Cece, from the live grenade he had clutched to his stomach so that he exploded like a pig's bladder. Others like him were still

96

suffering, but now they hid themselves away. Their morbid trains of thought disturbed the pleasures of peacetime and put the younger generation off their food. Léon had killed himself so that he would stop being a blot on the world's happiness. At La Ponche Antoine gradually found himself talking to everyone. When he bought a round the fishermen exaggerated their southern accents, and he was not fooled: that too was part of the act that everyone was putting on and that seemed, year by year, to become more real than reality.

As soon as Antoinette appeared at the school gate, she ran towards the Bugatti and climbed in next to him.

'Uncle Antoine, will you take me for a drive?'

He drove her as far as Grasse to buy *fougasse* flatbreads still warm from the oven, which they ate with bars of chocolate as they rolled slowly back to Saint-Tropez. They had bought perfume for Marie-Dévote, who loved to soak herself in lavender water.

'How are you my uncle?' Toinette asked. 'You're not my papa's brother, or Maman's, yet everybody says I look just like you.'

'I'm the uncle of your heart. When you love a little girl very much from the day she's born, she gradually starts to look like you.'

'Is that really true?'

'Truer than anything! I swear it.'

Antoine left then, before his heart got any softer. At Roquebrune he parked outside Léon's restaurant, which had been renamed Chez Antoine after it was extended. Mireille greeted him with a well-rehearsed tantrum and then, when her sulking and reproaches were over, this strange little vine shoot wrapped herself around him, locked the kitchen door and gave herself to him among the pots and pans. A waitress drummed on the door and went away laughing. Antoine usually stayed for a day or two, never longer, attracted by a basic and violent desire, but was eventually driven away by Léon's ghost, which wandered through the house with its terrible smashed face, impossible to contemplate. The restaurant was doing well, and Mireille had discovered that she had ambitions after she had been written up in the food columns of several newspapers. When Antoine arrived her mother faded into the background. Sitting on a chair at the roadside, her hands lying in her lap on a grey apron that partly covered her black dress and cotton stockings, she fixed things and people alike with a look of complete vacancy, like an Indian fakir trying to escape from his earthly self. Her relations with Antoine were limited to a nod when he arrived and left. Mireille was not, strictly speaking, beautiful in the way that Marie-Dévote was, but her ascetic skinniness, the fire in her eyes, her blue-black hair curled tightly about her small face, emphasising her sharp features, the nerviness of her body with its taste of saffron, and the impression she gave of being ready to flare up at the slightest spark, attracted Antoine irresistibly. Yet each time he left her without regret. She was too fiery for his temperament, and he was afraid of getting burnt. On the road back he stopped again briefly at Saint-Tropez, kissed Marie-Dévote and Toinette, listened distractedly to another of Théo's new plans, and drove north to Aix where he stopped at Charles's garage but, less vulnerable to its owner's charm, listened noncommittally, not to his war stories this time – that era had been exhausted – but to his fabulous speculations for Provence's future.

Ah, the wonderful way back! The Bugatti sang. Antoine worked the engine hard up the Rhône valley, and as though it preferred the roads that led to cooler climates where it could carburate more happily, it gobbled up the kilometres, glued to the road and without a squeal through the bends, flew up the hills and strained at the descents. At garages where he stopped, mechanics flattered the engine with their caresses, scarcely daring to touch it, so perfect did it seem, like the creation of some heavenly watchmaker or a wizard of the road.

When he arrived home from his trip of February 1930, Antoine was surprised to see that work had already started in the part of the park he had sold at the end of the previous year. In flagrant disregard of the agreement signed at the time of the sale, the new owner, a Parisian, Monsieur Longuet, the proprietor of two fashionable bordellos at Montparnasse, although he preferred to claim that he had made his fortune in hardware, had begun building what looked like a two-storey villa for himself, his wife and son. From the first floor they would be able to see everything that went on at La Sauveté. Marie-Thérèse was only waiting for Antoine to come back so that war could be declared. He had not got out of the car before she came running to him.

'Have you seen? A week! A whole week just to put up that scaffolding. We'll be just in time to get the building stopped.'

'Let's plant trees instead.'

'They'll take fifty years to grow.'

'Not if you plant pines or eucalyptuses.'

'They're not trees from around here.'

'Then let's put up with it.'

Marie-Thérèse shrugged angrily, turned on her heel and went back inside to scold the new Martiniquan, a Mademoiselle Artémis Pompon, who worked in the laundry, the children having grown too big to have a nurse. Artémis aroused no feelings in Antoine: she was a skinny nag, always barefoot in the house, with a disappointing bosom and a dropping lower lip. She was nevertheless a dutiful girl, who had been told that her employer would sleep with her for the same price as her predecessor, and had appeared on her first morning, giggling, at Antoine's library door, where he, in his dressing gown and smoking the first cigar of the day, had received her with astonishment.

'Artémis, you are mistaken. I want peace and quiet in my house. Go to bed. You need to rest. I know Madame treats you badly, but there's nothing to be done, it's the way she is.'

Satisfied – sometimes even beyond his capacity – he now preferred to devote his early mornings to reading, so much so that in a bold step, uncharacteristic of his conservative nature, he had bought in a sale at a Dieppe bookseller's a complete edition of Alexandre Dumas, whose pleasure he had not yet managed to exhaust.

About fifty people had crowded onto the pavement facing the offices of *La Vigie*: pensioners with their caps on straight, young workers with theirs jauntily over their ears, children. No women. But many bicycles stood next to their owners, one in particular, that of Jean Arnaud, red and with derailleur gears and racing handlebars taped up with gutta-percha. Whenever an employee emerged through the glass door and placed his ladder against the wall beneath the blackboard above the exhibition area, there was an 'ahh' of satisfaction from the waiting crowd. Calmly, in a round, well-turned hand, the man wrote in chalk 'Stage: Nice–Gap. 1st André Leducq, 2nd Bonduel, 3rd Benoît Faure'. In the overall placings, of course, Leducq had retained the yellow jersey. The crowd dispersed, disappointed, almost without comment. Reawakened in 1930 by the return to a system of national teams, French chauvinism was bored by a victory that lacked drama. That André Leducq, a great sprinter but lamentable climber, should have won a mountain stage proved that, unless the dice were loaded, it was all over. The 1932 Tour, in stark contrast to the previous year, when there had been victory for the great Antonin Magne combined with a heroic sacrifice by his young team-mate René Vietto on the Col du Lautaret, would finish in tedium. Jean got on his bike and set off for Grangeville, this time climbing the hill without standing up on his pedals. He had been feeling on top form since the beginning of the Tour, and his bike, a Peugeot, was worthy of a champion. He had bought it at Easter with his savings, supplemented by two postal orders from the mysterious prince. Nearly thirteen years old, he looked sixteen or seventeen; he was five foot seven, with long legs and a well-developed upper body. Jeanne now bought his clothes at the men's department in the Nouvelles Galeries. The term before, he had liberated himself from Madame du Courseau's yoke by starting to ride to school at Dieppe, refusing a lift with Michel in her new Ford V8, still rather high-bodied and old-fashioned, but powerful and silent. He preferred his bike, however steep the hill back up to Grangeville. His height earned him the frequent (cautious) mockery of his schoolfriends, who themselves wisely remained below average in that respect. Jean stood up to their meanness without pleasure. He recognised Michel's sly handiwork in these skirmishes: in the year above Jean, he was the one anonymously orchestrating the taunts and rallying cries. Less innocent now, Jean began to keep a tally. One day he would put an end to Michel's campaign. His fists itched, but for now Michel continued to enjoy the aura of his family. He was the brother of the delicious Antoinette, with whom Jean's excitements were becoming more and more specific. He was also the son of Antoine du Courseau, with whom he, Jean, had made a secret pact that was still in force, despite Antoine's frequent absences. And he would have wounded his parents deeply by attacking one of the du Courseaus who, despite their accumulating difficulties, retained a certain magnificence for Jeanne and Albert.

Arriving at La Sauveté, Jean found his mother sitting, very straight, on a chair in the kitchen. Tears were rolling down her cheeks. She was a picture of suffering too deep to be expressed, but she managed nevertheless to stutter, 'Your father's waiting for you with Madame.'

He had just stepped into the hall when Antoinette, half-opening the door of the small anteroom, grabbed his arm and hissed imperiously, 'Say it was you!'

She shut the door again immediately, and Jean walked into the drawing room, where his father, Marie-Thérèse and Antoine du Courseau were waiting for him. He understood that he was facing a tribunal and that this tribunal, presided over by a woman flanked by two further judges, did not expect to show clemency. Albert's face expressed a vivid wrath, while Antoine's was indifferent, almost absent. As for Marie-Thérèse, after several rehearsals in front of her mirror she seemed ready to play her role with the necessary dignity. It was she who found the first words, the most idiotic, obviously, that revealed very clearly her understanding of her relations with those around her.

'Jean, we must speak to you very seriously, as we would to a man, since you insist on behaving like a man, despite being only thirteen years old. Do you recognise that up until today we have treated you as we would one of our own children?'

'Of course, Madame.'

She sighed, and pretended to hide her face in her hands for a moment before continuing.

'To Michel you're like a brother—'

'Do you really think so?'

She dismissed his doubt with a wave of her hand.

'Oh, I know … little rivalries between boys. When you both grow up they'll be quite forgotten. I should add – which is of capital importance – that to Antoinette you're also a brother—'

'Of course I am!' Jean exclaimed. His legs were shaking.

'You little beast!' Albert shouted, raising his hand as if to slap him, in a gesture that was entirely out of place.

'Calm down, Albert,' Antoine said.

'Captain, he is a little bastard.'

'What have I done?' Jean asked in a strangled voice.

Marie-Thérèse intended to lead the investigation in a proper judicial manner.

'Where were you this afternoon?'

'In Dieppe. I was waiting for the Tour results. Leducq won the stage.'

Marie-Thérèse's smile indicated that she had expected just such an alibi.

'With whom, may I ask?'

'With his team, of course.'

'I'm not talking about your grotesque Tour de France, whose vulgarity exasperates me beyond measure, I'm talking about you. Who were you with at Dieppe?'

'I was on my own.'

Her smile widened.

'Naturally! And you didn't speak to anyone!'

Jean hesitated for a moment, thinking who he could have seen that afternoon.

'No. No one.'

Antoine looked at him intensely. Jean met his eyes fixed upon him and found new courage.

'What are you accusing me of?'

'You know very well. This afternoon you were not at Dieppe. You were at the bottom of the cliffs, at the far end of the gully, well concealed behind some fallen rocks.'

Jean paled. He did not notice that she had said 'this afternoon' and thought he had been found out. Tears welled up in his eyes.

'Good!' Marie-Thérèse said triumphantly. 'We have no need to spell it out to you. I hope you recognise the seriousness of what you have done. Is today the first time you have done such a thing, you and Antoinette?'

Jean realised his error and straightened up.

'I was in Dieppe today.'

'Don't lie!' Albert exclaimed. 'Or I'll disown you.'

'I'm not lying.'

He was not lying. He never lied. He might have sinned by omission at confession with the abbé Le Couec, when he 'forgot' his and Antoinette's games. Then his heart sank as he remembered what Antoinette had hissed in his ear: 'Say it was you!' He would not say it, but he felt a chasm open up at his feet: who had she been with this afternoon at the bottom of the cliff? He wanted to die. Antoine's gaze gave him the courage to withstand his despair. Wanting to save Antoinette, he bowed his head and said nothing.

'What you did is disgusting!' Marie-Thérèse said. 'You are not the only guilty party. She is too. But I shall no longer look on you as one of my children.'

'You ungrateful wretch!' Albert said.

'Now, now,' Antoine said. 'Let us just strike it from the record, and never mention it again.'

'I'm confiscating his bike for the rest of the summer.'

Jean looked at his father meekly, despite his anguish.

'That will hardly undo the harm he has done!' Marie-Thérèse said acidly.

Antoine broke in. 'All right! It's done, it's over. And may it never happen again.'

He stood up, to put an end to Jean's ordeal, which he shared. Albert led his son away, grasping his arm as if he was going to try to escape. He himself was too agitated to speak. Jean walked past his mother, who pretended to be scouring a saucepan in order not to see him, and went to his room. Through the open window he caught sight of the Longuets' villa, which a trellis covered in ivy failed to conceal. Jean shook his fist at the house, an enemy twice over, closed his shutters, and threw himself on his bed and sobbed. Over, it was all over. He would never speak to Antoinette again. A tart, an utter tart, the worst bitch of all the bitches. And how would he ever see Chantal de Malemort again? He wept until midnight, eventually falling asleep, and woke up early the next morning, his only thought that it must all have been a bad dream. But as daylight filtered through the slats of his shutters, he again felt the sinking feeling that had finished him the day before. It was completely true: Antoinette's betrayal, Michel's victory, his bike confiscated, and, even worse, perhaps worse than all the rest: he would never be taken to Malemort again, he would never see Chantal again. His life spread out ahead of him like a desert. He cried again briefly, then got up and, his eyes still blurred with tears, pushed back the shutters. Albert was watering marigolds along the boundary wall. Behind that wall lurked his rival, the big pimply lecher, Gontran Longuet, whom he had seen shamelessly hanging around Antoinette since the beginning of the summer. What was he doing with a name like Gontran? None of it would have happened if René Mangepain, Madame du Courseau's brother, had not re-established relations between the two warring families. Albert, militant as ever in politics, had been outraged. It had almost been enough to make him subscribe to *Action française*,[6] which every morning directed its spotlight on the depravities of the majority-party politicians. After keeping a low profile as a deputy in the Chambre Bleu Horizon,[7] René Mangepain had switched to full-blooded radicalism. He spoke of 'my party', tensing his already enormous neck. Politics for him was little more than the crumbs of his daily bread, but they were crumbs he clung to with a fierce appetite. No deputy could ever remember him mounting the gallery to address the Chamber, and his rare contributions recorded in the official register provoked hilarity, even among party colleagues. What rottenness connected him to the ghastly Longuet, the sources of whose enrichment Jean was perfectly well aware of? And how adroit they were, these traffickers in human flesh! Hadn't even the abbé Le Couec taken to repeating 'To every sin its pardon!' since Madame Longuet had paid for the repairs to the church roof? Life was truly vile. He would go and punch that Gontran-my-arse in the face. The thought gave him the courage to brave the disapproval of the adults who had condemned him blindly the day before, in the absence of any evidence. And then there was Antoinette: he could already feel the satisfaction of the slap he was going to give her. Jean took one of those decisions one feels one will definitely stick to for ever, and which evaporated at the first application of her charm. Although for a few days he strenuously avoided her, it was impossible for the situation to go on without an explanation, and one morning when

Jeanne sent Jean to the grocer's at Grangeville to buy some butter, he walked straight into Antoinette, stopped on the bend in the path, wearing a tennis skirt, her legs bare, pushing her bicycle. The slap that Jean had promised himself did not happen. Antoinette may have been disappointed. She was expecting a torrent of reproaches, and did not suspect that her sudden appearance, her hair pulled back in an Alice band and her pretty breasts unconstrained under her white sweater, would confuse Jean to the point that he would forget everything he had sworn to himself to say to her. Thus did he become acquainted at the very early age of thirteen with that immense power that women have to disarm us by their innocence even when they are guilty.

'Hello. Are you still cross with me?'

He said 'yes' at the exact moment when he realised that he no longer was, that Antoinette, there in front of him, in all the freshness of her seventeen years, a little plump but so sleek too, and as fragrant as a young peach, still had an inexpressible power that he was far too inexperienced to detach himself from in a single encounter. It was to her that he owed the discovery of wonderful sensations. But how could she give them to someone else, to others? Tears filled Jean's eyes, and he clenched his fists to keep his emotions in check. Seeing him, Antoinette guessed the reason for his furious silence and tried hard not to show her delight too quickly.

'Will you come for a walk with me?' she said.

'We're not allowed to see each other.'

'I know a barn——'

'Who else have you been there with?'

'Nobody.'

'Liar!'

Antoinette's face hardened, and Jean was overcome by panic. What if he lost her? He wouldn't be able to bear it, any more than he could bear being with her and her huge dishonesty.

'I didn't lie to you,' she said. 'I don't lie to you.'

'But you said it was me that you did your horrible things with at the bottom of the cliff.'

'I didn't say that.'

'Who said it then?'

'Do you really want to know?'

'Yes.'

'You won't try to get your own back?'

'Tell me ... you can say anything you like, can't you?'

'Michel.'

'Oh the ... I hate him! One day I'll kill him.'

Antoinette smiled. Jean's noble vow enchanted her.

'Just this once, you would be wrong. He really thought it was you. Ever since he started trying to catch us out. He confused you with Gontran.'

'Have you been doing it with him for a long time?'

'It was the first time.'

He did not believe her but felt too upset to be angry and make her realise how shameless she was. Besides, he could no longer think about anything except slipping his hand inside Antoinette's sweater, stroking her sweet girlish breasts, feeling their points stiffen under his hand. A mist passed across his vision, and he bowed his head.

'Come quick,' she said. 'I promised to be home by six.'

Jean cut across the fields while she cycled on. They met up again on a path next to a hedge that ran around an abandoned house. The barn was invisible from outside the hedge. Antoinette hid her bicycle and they climbed over the wooden barrier. Inside they caressed each other in the straw, but Jean sensed that he could not go as far as Gontran. He cursed his inexperience. Antoinette promised that it would be for another time.

'You're only thirteen!' she said. 'It could be bad for you, and you could make me have a baby.'

Defeated, he accepted his pleasure from Antoinette's hand as his reward, and afterwards they spent a good fifteen minutes laughing as they pulled off all the stalks of straw that had stuck to their hair and sweaters. Antoinette cycled cheerfully home, reassured and joyful. Jean dashed to the grocer's and bought the butter.

'You've been away a long time, my boy!' Jeanne said, busy ironing in the kitchen.

'I met Antoinette!' he said impulsively.

'Oh!'

Jeanne held the iron close to her cheek and put it back on the range.

'It would be better for everybody if you kept your meetings to yourself.'

'You know, Maman … it wasn't me with her, down at the cliffs.'

'I believe you … but why didn't you stand up for yourself?'

'Because of her!'

Jean's heart was beating madly. The warmth in his mother's face filled him with remorse. He knew that he was just playing with words, and that what he had been doing an hour ago was the same, apart from one detail, as what Gontran had done with Antoinette. At least I'm not the idiot who gets caught in the act, he thought.

'Your father's been very upset. He says he no longer dares to look Monsieur Antoine's family in the face. We thought about giving up our place here, but then we'd be penniless: when you're fifty-five and you've got one leg less than everyone else, there's no work to be had.'

Jean was appalled that he had not, for a single moment, considered the extent of what had happened.

'I'll talk to him,' he said.

'Try, my child … but there's none so deaf as those who don't want to hear.'

'And I'll talk to Monsieur du Courseau.'

'Madame would be better.'

'No, not her.'

Jeanne smiled indulgently.

'You owe her a lot.'

'To you, to Papa, I owe a lot. Not to her.'

'One day you'll understand.'

Jeanne kept so much goodness hidden inside her that it was enough to tell her there was no such thing as evil for her to believe it and for her pious, honest soul to rejoice that she lived in an unblemished world. Albert might have been the same, if the horrors of war and the sacrifice of his leg had not produced an authoritarian outlook that mistook itself for intelligence. He had ideas: firm, clear-cut, and to a certain extent immovable. Jean had little hope of convincing him by a confrontation. On the other hand, something told him that Antoine du Courseau might show himself to be understanding. He had to be brave enough to talk to him, but Antoine was a man who discouraged conversations that he had not initiated. At the first sign of difficulty he climbed into his Bugatti and vanished for several days, returning when those who had stayed behind had dealt with the problem for him. Jean would have continued to hesitate if he had not been so angry about being deprived of his bike for the rest of the summer. Not daring to go to the house, he resorted to a letter, which he rewrote ten times over before he was sure that it was short enough for Antoine to deign to read it and not throw it straight into the wastepaper basket.

Monsieur,

May I permit myself, in the name of our very old pact, agreed when I was a small boy, to ask you for an interview. I will explain to you that I am not guilty and why I have allowed people to think that I am. I will say it to you because you are the only person whose opinion matters to me. Your
  Jean Arnaud

He posted the letter at Grangeville, and the next morning the

Bugatti, nosing out of the park, took the drive that led past the lodge. Jean had been looking out for it, and ran down and jumped in beside the driver. Antoine put his foot down, and they sped to the Dieppe road; reaching the docks, they halted at a café where hot shrimps, washed down with an honest sparkling cider, were served around the clock.

'Thank you, Monsieur!' said Jean, after Antoine urged him to start.

'I suspected you weren't guilty. But to tell you the truth, and I'll say it only to you, I wouldn't care if you were. Antoinette is seventeen ... Some girls are like that. She has my temperament ... '

Jean did not know exactly what he meant by temperament, but guessed it had something to do with a predisposition to forbidden pleasures, and he smiled so understandingly that Antoine smiled back, then said, 'What do you want to do when you grow up?'

'Uncle Duclou wants me to take the merchant navy examinations, but I'm not very good at maths ... and Uncle Cliquet is pushing me to work on the railways—'

'And you think it's boring!'

'Really boring.'

'And you don't have any idea of your own?'

'No. All I know is that I'm not going to be a gardener, and I am going to travel.'

'Ah!' Antoine said casually, buttering a slice of brown bread.

Jean, on the brink of other confidences, stopped short at Antoine's rapid loss of interest.

'I suppose,' Monsieur du Courseau went on, 'that you took the blame to spare my daughter from getting into more trouble.'

'I like her a lot. Sometimes I even think she's my sister.'

'What about Michel?'

Jean looked down and did not dare to answer.

'I see,' Antoine said. 'You know, I feel exactly the same about him. What a strange idea to have gone and told everyone what he

110

saw. He turned the house upside down. You and I are obliged to hide to talk to each other, and my wife is not about to forgive you in a hurry.'

'I'm even more cross that my father won't forgive me. He's so upright and so good. I feel ashamed.'

'I'll do my best to fix that. Man to man, you can say what you want.'

'You won't punish Antoinette?'

'Punish Antoinette? I've never done such a thing. And in any case, my little Jean, I'm not blameless myself. I have another life … Far away … '

He broke off to watch an English couple who had walked into the café, a tall, slim blonde woman and a man in a tweed jacket and grey trousers. All his attention was taken up by the young woman. She sat down and attempted to decipher the menu that she had been given by a good-humoured waiter. Her husband took the menu from her and ordered mussels and white wine without consulting her.

'They're aliens!' Antoine said.

'Yes, they're English.'

'No, no, I mean they weren't born on the same planet as us. Like the Chinese, the American Indians, the Arabs or the Africans. Our planet is here, Normandy. They'll leave it behind on the midday packet, and tonight at six o'clock they'll be at Newhaven, where they'll drink tea and eat ham squashed between two pieces of rubbery bread with the crusts cut off.'

'I'd still really like to go to England.'

'There's an idea! Would you like to go and explore? Geneviève is living in London at the moment. I can write and tell her you're coming.'

'Papa will never let me go!'

'Leave that to me.'

Antoine drank the last of his glass of cider and called the waiter to ask for the bill. When he had paid, he walked out, climbed into the car and drove away, forgetting Jean, who had gone back to fetch his cap, which he had left hanging on a peg inside. Without a centime to his name, he could not even catch a bus, and so he walked back to Grangeville that warm August day, seething every time a cyclist passed him. He was arriving at La Sauveté when he met the abbé Le Couec, huge and red-faced, striding along.

'Jean! Heaven has sent you to me!'

'Father, you were looking for me?'

'Yes, I need you.'

The priest's iron hand clamped the boy's biceps, and for a second he thought he had been taken prisoner.

'My parents will be thinking that I've run away … '

'That is indeed what's happening! Let us go to the rectory. I need to talk to you and to introduce you to a hero.'

'They'll punish me.'

'I'll square that, don't worry.'

'I've already lost my bike for the whole summer.'

'You'll get your bicycle back. Come along … time presses.'

We shall call the man hidden at the rectory Yann, for the sake of convenience. Jean saw a tall Celt, with yellow, wavy hair, eyes of a clear blue and hollow cheeks, who shook his hand and immediately addressed him as a man.

'Jean Arnaud, the abbé has told me about you. Just by looking at you, I know that I can count on your discretion and your loyalty.'

'Yes, Monsieur.'

'The police are looking for me. Don't ask me why, but a false move, a word in the wrong place, will put me in prison for many years. We have to be certain of your discretion and your complicity.'

'Yes, Monsieur.'

The abbé took out of his cupboard a bottle with the sort of label children use on their school exercise books: 'Monsieur Le Couec's calvados'. He filled two glasses, and was about to fill a third when Jean stopped him.

'Father, I mustn't ... being fit ... you know ... I'm trying to stay fit even though I don't have my bike.'

'You'll have your bicycle back tonight, a priest's word on it.'

'Papa won't give in that easily.'

'I know how to persuade him. But before dinner you need to go to Tôtes and meet someone at a café.'

'In that case, it's Maman who won't let me go so easily. She doesn't like me going out on my bike at night.'

'I'll take care of it.'

'The man you'll meet at the café – it's Les Amis de Tôtes,' Yann said, 'will be wearing a white carnation. He'll be drinking cider, and you'll go up to him to shake hands and say, "Good evening, Monsieur Carnac," and he'll reply – pay attention, it's important – "All right, son?" After you've exchanged a few words, you're to leave together and bring him here. He will have a car, a motorbike or a bicycle. He's short, clean shaven, and his hair's going grey. You won't know his real name, any more than you know mine.'

The abbé emptied his glass of calvados. Red blotches appeared at his neck and throat.

'Now I'm going to see your father,' he said.

Albert, who had just had to deal with a lecture from Antoine du Courseau about the absolute necessity of returning Jean's bicycle to him, felt like the victim of a plot when the priest then came to him demanding the same thing. It irritated him to be, as he saw it, pushed around, and Jean was briefly in real danger of having his bicycle confiscated until he was twenty-one. Monsieur Le Couec guessed what had happened, and quickly changed his insistent tone to one of gentle flattery, with the result that Jean found himself reunited with his cherished bicycle. He immediately set about oiling its chain and hubs and pumping up its tyres.

'I'll take him with me,' the priest said. 'We have things to talk about. He can sleep at the rectory tonight. I'll send him back to you for his breakfast, because I have nothing to give him.'

'Behave yourself!' Jeanne implored, no longer knowing whether her child was a monster or a man already worthy of a priest's company.

On the road to the rectory, the priest offered Jean a monologue all to himself.

'God is all goodness. He will forgive me, after my penitence, for having lied to your parents. Lives are at stake. One day all of this will be much clearer to you than it is today. This evening I only ask you to trust me, as your spiritual guide and your friend ... In fact, as I am your confessor, how is it possible that I don't know why you have been so severely punished by your father?'

Jean began to think his legs would fail him. The confessional lent itself to the lie of omission, but here on the road, face to face with the priest, who had stopped and was staring at him in his rough and tender way, it was infinitely harder to wriggle out of the truth. He made a vague gesture to signify everything and nothing, intending to play down the matter.

'Oh, it was nothing, just some stories about girls!'

'Is that all it was?' the abbé said. 'Hardly enough to hang a Catholic, I'd have said. If you knew what I heard at confession. But you're a bit on the young side, all the same ... It's true that you look a good deal older that thirteen ... Girls could easily think you were older. Anyway, you're not having your head turned, are you?'

'No, Father.'

'That's the essential thing. We'll talk about it again. At this moment, what needs our attention is Monsieur Carnac. I knew him at the seminary, but he gave up ... didn't have the vocation ... Some are like that ... I'm not talking about myself. When I look at my life, I don't think I could have been anything but a priest. Well, I am a priest and there's never been a day when I haven't been happy to be one, when I haven't thanked God for having taken me into his service, for having given me the health that my ministry demands, and the strength – or innocence if you prefer – not to have been undermined by any doubt.'

They arrived outside the rectory. Monsieur Le Couec took a large key from his pocket and opened the glazed door. Yann was sitting next to the stove, positioned so that he could not be seen from either the window or the door. He put down a book and Jean read its title: it was an anthology of poets. How could a man who was being hunted by all the police in France be interested in poetry? Yann intercepted his look.

'Do you sometimes read poems when you're alone?'

'No, Monsieur. Only in class, when the teacher recites them to us.'

'And what does he recite to you?'

'Jean de La Fontaine, Victor Hugo, Albert Samain.'

'La Fontaine I understand ... some nice lines in Victor Hugo too ...

Yesterday from my skylight was a view
That I blinked at with stares like an owl's,
Of a girl waist-deep in the Marne who
Was washing brilliant white towels

or this, which isn't bad:

The dreamy angel of the dusk who floats upon its breezes
Mingles, as it bears them off in the flutter of a wingbeat,
The dead's prayers and the living's kisses.

115

But Samain is for idiots.'

Yann had uttered the few lines of poetry in a tone that made Jean shiver, and he stared intently at the handsome giant, who had been suddenly altered as he recited Hugo in his steady, calm voice with a lack of restraint that was almost embarrassing.

'A fine time for reciting verses,' the abbé broke in. 'Time's getting on. How long will it take you to get to Tôtes, Jean?'

'Thirty kilometres ... at my usual speed I should be there in an hour and a half.'

'Perfect! Before nightfall. And then you can do the return trip with Monsieur Carnac in the dark.'

Yann began to walk up and down, stroking his chin and looking so distracted that both Jean and the priest watched him for a moment without daring to interrupt.

'He needs to go!' Monsieur Le Couec said finally.

'I know ... I've just thought of something. There's still a danger. What if there's a gendarme there instead of Carnac?'

The abbé sat down hard on a rocking chair that nearly overturned under his weight.

'Jesus, Mary and Joseph!' he exclaimed. 'That would be the end of everything. My dear Jean, I can't let you run that risk.'

'Father, don't worry, I won't talk ... They won't get a word out out of me.'

'No,' Yann said firmly. 'On the contrary. I'm not going to send you there unless you undertake to give us away if you find that a policeman has taken Carnac's place. It's an order I'm giving you. We'll exonerate you immediately ... Swear it!'

'I can't swear something like that.'

Monsieur Le Couec jumped up, his expression threatening.

'Swear it!'

Jean, who had begun to acquire a certain talent for equivocation, crossed his fingers behind his back and murmured, 'I swear.'

'Louder.'

'I swear.'

'All right, you can go!' Yann said.

The priest kissed Jean and then, to conceal his emotion, opened the cupboard and took out the bottle of calvados again to pour himself another glass.

Jean was so happy to have his bicycle back that he set out for Tôtes without a second thought for the importance of his mission. From the moment the abbé had lent his support, he did not even wonder what it was all about. There would be plenty of time for the mystery to be cleared up later. His bike was riding divinely, without a sound, even though he had perhaps very slightly over-tightened the chain. It was a question of adjustment, just as it was for the tyres, hardened by their immobility over the recent weeks. Jean concentrated on regulating his breathing to the speed of his pedals, pacing himself progressively. A decent average demanded good tactics and knowing how to use the road conditions, Georges Speicher had told a reporter from *L'Auto*. You pedal with your legs but also with your head. It's pointless to over-stress your heart by racing every time you're challenged on the flat, otherwise the slightest gradient becomes an ordeal. Jean, his attention fixed on the road ahead, did not allow himself to be distracted by anything, except for the drive leading to the Malemorts' château, where he slowed down to glance through the open gateway: the marquis, in riding boots, was unsaddling his bay mare, which Chantal was holding it by its bridle. After Malemort he gave himself up to the enjoyment of a series of wild ups and downs in the road, diving with the fields into pretty hollows with brooks at the bottom and then climbing back up to apple orchards and an old church or a farm of red bricks with meadows around it. Just before

Tôtes his rhythm was disrupted by potholes, and he had to zigzag his way around the areas where the road was being repaired and occasionally take to the verge, among the loose gravel. The setting sun was softening the landscape's colours: greens turning to grey, copses darkening as if, suddenly, life was about to stop, to freeze for the night and only awake with the new dawn and the breath of the dew, with colours freshly alive, an opal sky and sheep on their knees nibbling the brilliant grass in their pasture.

As Jean approached the village he caught sight of a Renault Primaquatre belonging to the *gendarmerie*, which had stopped a car. A sergeant was asking for the driver's and passengers' papers. Jean slowed down and cycled past them, sitting up, hands on the flat of his handlebars.

The café called Les Amis de Tôtes sat with its terrace at a crossroads. Jean parked his bike, and ignoring the pinochle players and two pensioners sitting idly outside counting the cars coming from Dieppe and Rouen, went inside. He saw Monsieur Carnac's carnation instantly, a white fleck on the lapel of a man tucked away reading *L'Ouest-Éclair* in a corner of the room. He walked over to the table, gave the password, and received the expected answer.

'Would you like a drink?' Monsieur Carnac asked.

'A shandy, please.'

The waitress poured beer and lemonade together and put the glass down in front of Jean, who sipped politely, even though he was very thirsty.

'How are your parents?' Monsieur Carnac said.

Jean immediately lost his composure.

'Do you know them?'

Monsieur Carnac glowered as if the whole world was listening, despite the room being empty. There was only the waitress, wiping a table near the door with a tired and dirty cloth that left spiral-shaped smears on the slate.

'How are your parents?' Monsieur Carnac repeated more firmly.

'Very well, thank you. They're expecting you tonight.'

'Drink your beer and we'll be off.'

'There are policemen stopping cars on the road out of Tôtes.'

'I haven't got a car. I borrowed a bicycle in Rouen.'

'I've got a bike too.'

'How far is it?'

'Thirty kilometres.'

Monsieur Carnac frowned.

'You can take my wheel.'

'Take your wheel?'

Monsieur Carnac clearly knew nothing about cycling terminology. Jean's explanation received an incredulous reaction. How could staying glued to the wheel in front help you if you were the unlucky rider pedalling behind?

'All right,' Monsieur Carnac said, 'let's see how it goes. If I need to rest, we'll have to stop.'

Jean decided not to explain that to stop, far from helping, was extremely bad for your hamstrings. He was surprised to see Monsieur Carnac pick up a milk can and a small loaf of bread from the chair next to him and remove the carnation from his buttonhole. Jean finished his shandy standing up and followed him outside, where several bicycles including his own were parked.

'That's a nuisance. I can't remember what the bike I borrowed looks like.'

'Didn't your friend tell you what make it was?'

'I didn't borrow it from a friend, to tell you the truth, but from someone I don't know who is probably, at this moment, combing the streets of Rouen and pouring his heart out to a policeman.'

'Did you steal it?' Jean said, horrified at the idea of a theft that affected him personally. The bank robberies and corruption of government ministers that Albert enumerated every evening left him cold. But a bicycle thief was a man without soul or scruples, who deserved the severest punishment.

Monsieur Carnac read Jean's indignation on his face and hastened to reassure him.

'I left a car in exchange, whose registration number the police know only too well.'

'Oh I see!'

He didn't see anything, but it didn't matter. So long as the abbé Le Couec was involved, everything was all right. To locate the right bicycle all he had to do was decipher the compulsory registration plates above the excise stamp. Monsieur Carnac knew nothing about traffic regulations, so Jean pretended to tie his shoelace in order to crouch down and inspect the plates, among which he found one from Rouen. Monsieur Carnac hung his can of milk on the handlebars and fixed his loaf of bread on the front carrier before getting on clumsily. Night was falling as they left Tôtes, and a moment later found themselves halted by the beam of a flashlight.

'Where are you going?'

'Home, where else?' Monsieur Carnac said in an accent that was more Norman than the Normans.

The sergeant came closer and shone his flashlight on the can of milk and bread, which seemed to reassure him.

'Fine,' he said. 'On your way.'

The cool evening air reinvigorated Jean, but he felt as though he was dragging a heavy weight on an invisible thread behind him. Monsieur Carnac wheezed and spluttered and spat and loosed torrents of swear words, threatening continuously to get off and continue on foot, reduced to fury by the slightest gradient. The return journey took them more than two hours, and when they arrived outside the rectory they glimpsed through the lighted window the figure of the abbé Le Couec pacing up and down, his hands clasped behind his back. He opened the door in such a state of emotion that he could hardly speak as he enfolded Jean tightly in his arms.

'Jean, my dear Jean, I was afraid ... I should never have forgiven myself.'

Monsieur Carnac came in, carrying his bread and milk can. Yann appeared and shook his friend's hand, before taking Jean by the shoulders and looking him squarely in the face.

'My boy,' he said, 'we owe you a great debt, and one day it will be repaid! I won't ever forget it.'

'We might make a start by hiding the bike,' Monsieur Carnac interrupted. 'I stole it in Rouen.'

'Stole?' the abbé said.

Jean looked at Monsieur Carnac anxiously. He was a short man with thick hair that was already going grey, though he was certainly no more than forty. He looked like someone with a short fuse, hot-tempered and violent, but his face, weathered by the sun and creased with very mobile wrinkles, expressed a ruthless determination.

'Yes, stole! One pinched bike is worth a man's skin, I'd say.'

The abbé crossed himself and murmured a few almost unintelligible words.

'Come on, my dear abbé,' Yann said, 'let's not panic … the cause justifies the means.'

'I would like to be as certain of that as you always are.'

'If not, we would never have got our young friend of the poets mixed up in this business.'

'Young friend of the poets?' Monsieur Carnac said, arching his left eyebrow, as if he was about to screw in a monocle.

Jean felt transfixed by his hard stare.

'And may one know which poets you honour with your friendship, dear boy?'

'La Fontaine and Victor Hugo,' Jean answered, swiftly forgetting Samain, whom Yann had thought fit for idiots.

'Exactly right,' Yann said, 'just earlier on I was reciting those lovely lines from "Crépuscule":

The dreamy angel of the dusk who floats upon its breezes

Mingles, as it bears them off in the flutter of a wing beat,
The dead's prayers and the living's kisses.

Monsieur Carnac burst into sarcastic laughter.

'Oh, that's a good one, that is! You're forgetting – intentionally, I imagine – the first line that rhymes with "wing beat":

Love each other! 'tis the month when the strawberries are sweet.'

'Every poet has their weakness!' Yann said, annoyed.

'Unforgivable! Unforgivable!'

The abbé Le Couec was in a state of some irritation. The question that was bothering him was not Victor Hugo's weaknesses, but the stolen bicycle. What were they going to do with it? Monsieur Carnac suggested throwing it in the sea. Jean shivered. The abbé wanted to compensate its owner or return his property to him.

'Returning it is out of the question,' Yann said. 'It would be putting the police on our trail immediately. Let's write down the owner's name, and I'll send him a postal order from somewhere in the north, when we get there.'

The abbé offered to go himself, under cover of darkness, and fling the bicycle into the sea.

'Details, details, we can deal with all that later!' Monsieur Carnac said. 'At this very moment I am dying of hunger.'

Jean's hopes rose. After the excursion hunger was gnawing at him too. The hot shrimps he had eaten that morning were a distant memory. The abbé opened his wire-mesh pantry door and threw up his hands.

'A hunk of bread, a pot of cream, butter … but it's true, I do have some buckwheat flour and a drop of sparkling cider left over from last autumn, two or three bottles.'

'What are we waiting for? Let's get the pancakes on,' Monsieur Carnac said, dropping his jacket on a chair, turning on the stove and starting to prepare the mixture.

'I can go home to my house,' Jean suggested.

'No, you can't, young man,' the abbé said. 'Tomorrow at six you can serve mass.'

'I haven't confessed.'

'I give you absolution. Two Paters and three Hail Marys before you go to sleep. Three because it's the Holy Virgin who is particularly responsible for protecting us in this undertaking.'

They ate the pancakes off chipped plates with their fingers, standing up next to the range. The cider was undrinkable. The abbé offered calvados, which was refused, so he was obliged to replace the bottle on the shelf without touching its contents, after which he sent Jean to sleep in his bed, the only bed in the rectory.

'My friends and I have matters to discuss.'

Even though he would have liked to hear what they said, Jean obeyed, and slipped between the abbé's coarse bedclothes. A strong smell of leather pervaded the room, and when he peered under the bed he discovered an enormous pair of patched work boots, the priest's pumps, and his seven-league boots that helped him take the word of the Lord into parishes that lacked a priest and to square up to the bishop of Rouen. Spent with fatigue, Jean fell asleep without even trying to overhear what the three men gathered in the neighbouring room were saying.

Monsieur Le Couec woke him up shortly before six, as the sun rose. He himself had slept briefly in an armchair after Yann and Monsieur Carnac had departed.

'They won't hear mass?' Jean asked, disappointed not to see again the two strange characters who stole bicycles and tossed lines from Hugo at each other.

'No question of mass for them for the moment. They're in hiding. They're good Christians. Brave too. Come on. We shall go and pray, you and me, so that they won't be arrested.'

'You mean they're not real thieves?'

'No. They're heroes. But you must never talk about them, even if the police start asking questions.'

'I won't, ever. I promise.'

'To anybody?'

'Not to anybody, Father.'

'That's good, it means you're a man.'

Jean thought that if Monsieur Le Couec were to say these words in front of Antoinette she would no longer think him a child and would let him take the same liberties with her that she had allowed that swine Gontran. But such a thought stained his soul before communion, and he chased it away. He did his best to serve mass well, and afterwards followed the priest into the sacristy, where he helped him take off his chasuble. One of the ladies who lived next to the church brought them bowls of milky coffee and thick slices of bread and butter that they devoured at the sacristy table.

'Now it's time for you to go home, my son. Lips sealed.'

He planted a kiss on both of Jean's cheeks, kisses that smelt of milk and coffee.

As Jean reached the doorway, the priest called to him.

'Tell me, these stories about girls that got you such a wigging? There wasn't anything in them, was there?'

'Oh no, nothing, father … nothing at all.'

Pedalling home in the glorious morning, Jean told himself that in fact his stories with girls were nothing at all, that real life was the life that men like Yann and Monsieur Carnac led, heroes who moved in the shadows. Everything else was childishness, kids' games with little hussies. Gontran could indulge himself with Antoinette all he wanted. He wouldn't be challenging him for her.

At La Sauveté he found Jeanne and Albert at the kitchen table, their bowls of coffee in front of them.

'At last!' his mother said.

'I served mass at six o'clock.'

'Oh, that is a fine way to start the day!'

Albert grumbled that no priest should be disturbing the good Lord's rest at such an hour. It was in poor taste.

'Don't listen to your father!' Jeanne said. 'He served mass more often than his turn and now he's just talking big.'

'It's not about talking big. I'm for freedom of conscience!' Albert said, with a mouthful of bread and kidney beans.

Perhaps for the first time, Jean realised his father was talking nonsense, and it pained him, in the way it pains us when someone we admire suffers a humiliating defeat. Antoine du Courseau had disappointed him in a similar way: how could you be so removed from life, so distracted? It felt like a sort of resignation, when men like Yann and Monsieur Carnac were living life's great adventure. One day he, Jean Arnaud, would defy the forces of the law for a noble cause which was yet to reveal itself, but which the grave events announced by Albert would doubtless make sure they brought about.

Jean never discovered the reason why Yann and Monsieur Carnac had been forced into hiding. The secret has stayed well kept. We may nevertheless advance a hypothesis by consulting the newspapers of the period. During the night of 6–7 August, in other words two days before the arrival of Monsieur Carnac at Tôtes, a person or persons unknown had blown up the monument erected at Rennes for the quatercenary of the union of Brittany and France. This act of vandalism could have been justified on aesthetic grounds: the work of one of those sculptors much cherished by the Third Republic of Doumer and Lebrun, the monument symbolised the triumph of overblown pomposity. It showed Brittany on her knees before the king of France. The clandestine nationalist movement Gwenn ha Du had been determined to demonstrate with maximum impact against the visit of Édouard Herriot,[8] who in turn had responded with more modest impact by refusing to attend the mass said at Vannes by Monseigneur Duparc, bishop of Quimper and Léon. Were Yann and Monsieur Carnac numbered among the perpetrators of that act? It is possible, even probable, but nobody knows any more today than they did then, and we leave the reader entirely at liberty to imagine other hypotheses that justify the attitude – singular for a priest – of the abbé Le Couec. What is certain is that, overnight, Jean Arnaud matured by several years, learning that a priest may also be a plotter, and that without being thieves or murderers men might have to hide from the police because they were defending a noble cause. The world was not built of flawless blocks, of good and bad, of pure and impure. More subtle divisions undermined the picture he had so far been given of morality and duty. For another boy than Jean, this discovery would have been dangerous. It was only useful to him because his innocence kept him out of temptation's way better than all the lessons he had been taught. He therefore decided, in the days that followed, not to punch Gontran Longuet in the face the next time he saw him, and to forgive Michel du Courseau his spiteful nastiness towards him. What had Gontran really done, apart from make the most of what he was offered and would have been a hero of Spartan self-denial to refuse? And if Michel loathed him, it must be because Michel had guessed a long time ago, with remarkable intuition, that one day Chantal de Malemort would elope with his rival. And if Antoinette found it hard to keep her knickers on, it was a quality she had inherited from her father, about whom there was enough gossip among the locals for Jean to be fairly fully informed. In short, the world was not just full of guilty parties, and if you looked hard enough, you could find an excuse for everything. This philosophy has no technical name. For young Monsieur Arnaud it is called the Arnaud philosophy, for Jean Dupont it is called the Dupont philosophy. Each practitioner shapes it in the way that works for him or her, with personal variations. It was in this state of mind that Jean, with a return ticket from Dieppe to Newhaven in one pocket and a thousand-franc note in another, both given to him by Antoine du Courseau, wheeled his bicycle on board the ferry at the end of August 1932, en route for London. His fingers also frequently felt for the visiting card that Antoine had given him, to make sure it was still there. It was for Geneviève, Antoine's daughter, and had these few words written on it: 'Here is Jean Arnaud, whom I spoke about in my letter. A few days in London will complete his education. Be kind and look after him, and send him back to us at the end of the week. With love from your affectionate father, Antoine.'

When Marie-Thérèse du Courseau heard the news of Jean's departure, she displayed all the symptoms of an attack of nerves, but she was also one of those intrepid, dauntless souls who, in the face of catastrophe, find the means to triumph over circumstances yet again with their composure and coolness.

No, no, I have not forgotten Mireille Cece, Marie-Dévote, or Toinette, Théo or Charles along the way. Before I recount Jean Arnaud's London expedition, it may indeed be a good thing – so as not to displease readers who might be interested in what happens to them – to pass on news of them, even if only in a few sentences. They are still there, although removed from the theatre of our action – Jean's adolescence – as that becomes clearer; for they belong to Antoine du Courseau's secret existence, which is a secret we can only draw out by following Antoine south to the Midi. Jean may have left for London, but Antoine will not leave La Sauveté at the end of August 1932. The heat, the crowds on the beach, the packed roads are not to his taste. He no longer recognises the pretty, quiet port where he discovered a little café at the edge of a sandy beach. Hotels have sprung up, the fishermen no longer fish, and everyone hams up their southern accent to charm the tourists, to the point where one might imagine one was listening to some northerners acting in a play by Pagnol. At Marie-Dévote's hotel, big changes are afoot. She no longer serves in bare feet, nor is she even to be seen at the reception desk, where she has taken on a Swiss clerk to attend to the details. She has instead an office, on the door of which is written 'Manager'. There are eighty beds in the hotel, a car park, and the beach is more or less for guests' use only. A lifeguard is on duty, a handsome fellow who rolls his shoulders and whose wandering hands make the more mature ladies coo. The hotel does not interest Théo, who has bought his 'yacht', a former submarine hunter with two powerful diesel engines, and from early June to early September he is available for charter. His secret pleasure is his collection of naval caps: caps from every country, with gold insignia he has no right to wear, but he does not care, he is happy. Toinette is eight years old, and we shall have more to say especially about her in 1939. One more thing to add: on the walls of her office Marie-Dévote, now well and truly overtaken by middle-aged spread, has a Picasso and a Matisse. Chez Antoine is featured in the guidebooks for its collection of paintings. Antoine's early purchases have been added to with work by the Surrealists: Dalí, Tanguy, Magritte, De Chirico, Max Ernst. Antoine still knows nothing about art, but he is a lucky buyer, and has a gallery in Paris to advise him so that he scarcely puts a foot wrong. All of it is in Marie-Dévote's name.

At Roquebrune things are no longer quite as they were, and Antoine has given up stopping there since the day when he arrived unannounced and found Mireille in bed with a customs officer. Throwing herself at him, she cried, 'Why didn't you come sooner? He seduced me. He hits me. Defend me.'

The customs officer (his trousers meticulously folded on a chair and his képi hung on a coat hook) opened his eyes wide. He could have sworn that it was the other way around, and thus did he become rudely acquainted with Mireille's impressive impudence. Antoine sighed: it is always unpleasant to be on the receiving end of infidelity, but with Théo he had got used to it and it no longer wounded him so much. As the naked Mireille, still clinging to his neck, continued to sob, and the customs officer retrieved his long underpants from the floor, a ruthless calculation surfaced in Antoine's mind. To break it off would have several advantages, chief among them that he would save a good deal of money, and then there were also Mireille's amorous demands, which were beginning to exhaust him. At fifty-eight, well, he was no longer a young man. He thus assumed a dignified and offended air, held up his hand to the customs officer, who was pulling on his braces, and begged him to stay as he was. Mireille flew into a terrible fit of temper, but Antoine was immovable and, having forcibly detached her, he walked out, slamming the door behind him, through the restaurant full of diners finishing their lunch. A Parisian designer had transformed the bistro into a country restaurant that was more Provençal than Provence. Poor Léon would have found it unrecognisable. He had done the right thing by dying.

As for Charles, he is the agent for an important car manufacturer, running his own garage, and has launched a political career: for the moment he is merely a radical-socialist departmental councillor, but the future is bright, or at least he believes it is.

Such was the situation as Jean boarded the ferry at the end of August 1932, his pockets full with his thousand-franc note, return ticket, Mademoiselle Geneviève's address and another that Monsieur Cliquet had given him of a friend of his, a retired employee of one of the British railway companies. Captain Duclou had likewise showered him with introductions for the crossing, which, though it lasted barely six hours, would without the shadow of a doubt awaken Jean's vocation as a sailor. The ferry captain was a former officer of Uncle Duclou, and when Jean had stowed his bicycle in steerage, a sailor led him to the bridge, where the captain, having looked him up and down with a great pretence at severity, pointed to a place next to the helmsman that he was not to leave at any price. It was from there, with a beating heart, that Jean followed the difficult manoeuvre of the ferry as it left the quayside and turned into the channel leading to the harbour mouth. The boat hardly seemed to move, although he could feel the vibrations of its engines, whose speed the captain held back by spluttering into a sort of large tube fixed to the deck of the bridge. They had scarcely inched past the harbour mouth when he ordered the engines full speed ahead. Jean had the impression that the ferry was sitting down in the swell, then hurling itself forward at the long green waves. I am sorry, for the sake of the story, to have to report that the crossing was perhaps the most uneventful of the year. After departing at ten in the morning, the ferry was at the quayside at Newhaven at six that evening. Not once did anyone shout, 'Man overboard!', and there was no mustering of passengers on deck to sing 'Nearer, my God, to Thee' as the ship sank. Jean had lunch at the captain's table. The fat, rotund man with pink cheeks disappointed him a little. There was nothing of the master mariner about him, and it was difficult to imagine him as a young lieutenant rounding Cape Horn in a gale aboard a mixed cargo of the Messageries Maritimes, as Uncle Duclou had related. Did he even remember those days? Jean told himself that the monotonous Dieppe–Newhaven crossings through the Channel shipping lanes, jammed with traffic, had gradually erased all spirit of adventure in this man, who kept two canaries in his cabin and talked about the flowers in his garden. At Newhaven the captain entrusted Jean to one of the ferry's officers, who led him to a bungalow with a sign outside saying 'Bed and Breakfast'. An old lady with curly grey hair opened the door, letting out a smell of Brussels sprouts. Yes, she had a room, and tomorrow morning she would serve him a nice big breakfast before setting him on his way to London. Jean thanked the officer and stepped into the smell of Brussels sprouts. The few words of English he had remembered from the lycée were enough for him to be able to ask questions the answers to which he did not understand. In any case the lady had a slight pronunciation defect as a result of her loose dentures clicking as she spoke. Whenever she moved, she gave off a smell of cheap face powder that quickly became nauseating. Jean's small but pretty bedroom at La Sauveté made this one look hideous. Everything in it smelt of cold sprouts. The sash window looked out onto a yard full of rotting horse-carts. As the sun set, lights began to go on in the houses that backed on to his bungalow, and Jean caught sight of mothers and children gathered around tables laid with teapots and plates of sandwiches. A radio, louder than the others, broadcast a stream of unintelligible words into the yard. It was a funny country, this England, with its low houses built of brick and its sky blackened by the smoke of ships entering and leaving port. It didn't look anything like what he had read about it in class. He consoled himself: he had not seen anything yet. The old lady knocked and walked straight in without waiting for him to answer, and started gibbering. He understood that she was saying 'tea' and followed her. In a living room decorated in flowery cretonne, she had laid a low table with a light meal of sandwiches, tea and chocolates. She smiled, delighted to have this young guest to banish her solitude temporarily. Lipstick had run into the wrinkles around her thin lips. Jean still understood nothing, fascinated by the movement of her dentures in her mouth and the fantastic feet in front of his own, wearing patent leather shoes with buckles. She showed him a photograph in an oval frame of a soldier with tapering whiskers, wearing a beret with ribbons. Was it her husband, her father, her son? Thinking what would be best, he said, 'Husband?'

She nodded her head and tears rolled down her cheeks, creating two channels in her make-up. When he had finished eating, she disappeared for a moment into the kitchen, to return wearing an irresistible three-cornered hat and carrying a small handbag in green needlepoint. She smiled and pointed at the door. Jean was alarmed. Was she going to leave him alone amidst the flowery cretonne, watched over by a soldier who had met death on the battlefield?

'I come!' he said.

The handbag twirled with pleasure on the old lady's arm. She knew exactly where she was going, and forged ahead between indifferent passers-by along pavements lined with identical houses of red brick. The weather was exceptionally mild, and men in shirtsleeves were trimming their box hedges in their minuscule gardens and mowing their meagre lawns. Jean was finding it hard to keep up, and wondered where she was leading him with such lightness of mood and a mysterious smile at the lipstick-smudged corners of her mouth. No one at home having apprised him of the bizarre customs of this exotic people, he felt no anxiety and concluded that his landlady's athletic strides must be her preferred form of exercise before going to bed. Night was falling and everything looked darker. A succession of enormous protuberant eyes peered out at the edge of the street, the bow windows whose yellowish glow was reflected on the road surface, and he felt as if he was walking between the tentacles of an enormous slumbering octopus in a town that was being crushed in the darkness. After more than ten minutes of this brisk walk, the old lady turned into a street that was better lit, with illuminated signs and shop windows. Jean just managed to dash in behind her as she entered a smoke-filled pub, in which all he could initially make out was the men squeezed together around the bar, each holding out a hand full of change. Behind the counter a barman in a striped waistcoat, bald but with a face embellished by a fine waxed moustache, lowered and raised steel levers, handed out large glasses of beer, and took the money immediately, without a smile or a word. The old lady did not seem in the least frightened by the bustle and unselfconsciously elbowed her way through to the holy of holies, from which she returned with a glass of cider for Jean and a whisky for herself. They drank standing up, resting against a pillar and exchanging smiles. When he refused the third glass of cider she seemed to think he needed a 'just so you know', because she led him towards a swing door marked 'Gents'. A constant flow of men was emerging, buttoning their flies as they did so. Out of politeness Jean followed suit. The old lady meanwhile had moved on to drinking beer and brandy alternately, a swig of one followed by a swig of the other. Everyone seemed to know her. They greeted her good-humouredly, without the slightest mockery. Jean learned her name: 'Eliza' or sometimes 'Mrs Pickett'. At the rate she was going, it was evident that she would soon be completely drunk, but she bore up very well, if a little red-faced beneath her make-up, which was beginning to crack in the heat of the room. An unintentional elbow nudged her hat. Thinking she was putting it straight, she replaced it completely askew without losing any of her dignity. At about eleven o'clock the barman stopped serving drinks, and Mrs Pickett gestured to Jean that it was time they went back. She had spoken to him several times without his being able to say anything in response apart from 'yes', which was about the only word in English he felt more or less sure of. He told himself that in any case she wasn't listening. When she left the support of the pillar, which had held her up since the beginning of the evening after each of her sorties to the bar, the pub spun in front of her and she had to grip onto Jean's arm. They set out down the street, but she could hardly place one foot in front of the other. Repeatedly tripping over herself, she finally stopped, pulled off her buckled pumps, handed them to her companion and walked a little more steadily in her cotton stockings. Jean saw her swaying more and more and offered her his arm. For the last five hundred metres he had to half-carry her. She weighed nothing, a little package of mummified skin and bones. Thanks to Jean the key was turned in the lock. Mrs Pickett tossed her three-cornered hat onto a coat hook, did a little dance, and sat down heavily on the ground, where she began to laugh madly. Jean picked her up, without force, and laid her, still cackling, on the living-room sofa and piled some cushions on top of her. Eliza Pickett shut her eyes immediately, but as he was about to turn out the light and go to his room, she sat up and said in French, 'Would you give me a glass of water, my dear?'

Jean fetched a glass of water from the kitchen and brought it to Eliza's lips. She grimaced with disgust.

'Oh no, not like that! This water stinks!'

With her thumb and index finger she took out her dentures, dropped them in the water and closed her eyes again.

'Put it on the floor!' she said. 'And now goodnight.'

She was already asleep. Jean left on tiptoe and went to his room. He had landed in a strange world, where old ladies got shamelessly drunk. What would Chantal de Malemort think about it? Late as it was, in the darkness the image of Chantal, so fragile and lovely, would not leave him. How he would have loved her to admire him, all in one day crossing the Channel, setting foot on British soil, and spending his evening in a pub! He felt capable of astonishing her with even greater feats than this, of crossing vaster seas, of discovering unknown lands, and being as much at ease among the Kanaks as the old ladies of Newhaven. He had made up his mind. He would travel far away to win Chantal and her parents' respect, and come back to her loaded with knowledge, or perhaps he would even take her away with him, a long way from her château and from her family who stifled her, from the covetousness of Marie-Thérèse du Courseau. You are not truly a man until you have, there in front of you, a woman's happiness to complete, an immense task with which to fill your heart with joys and anxieties. Jean swore to himself to be worthy, to yield no longer to any weaknesses, to disregard Antoinette and her cheap ways. Love demanded purity. Antoinette confused his vision of love with her delicious whiff of sin, her plump thighs and her pretty pink breasts. Yes, they were very pretty, Antoinette's breasts, soft when his fingers squeezed them, her skin of a tenderness that inspired respect. He must not think about them any more; but at night when sleep was slow to come, her 'girlish' games unsettled the sternest of resolutions. What if Antoinette was actually the devil? After several false starts Jean finally fell into a sleep that mingled Chantal's pale blue eyes, sweet almond smell and white skin with the softness and perfume of Antoinette du Courseau's silky down.

He was woken by the noise of wirelesses. He was alone in bed, in an unknown bedroom, an unknown town, on the brink of discovering London, the home of Scrooge and Jack the Ripper. Grey daylight filled the window. He got up and went into the corridor with the firm intention of fleeing Mrs Pickett, who would surely be ashamed to see him, but the sizzle of frying greeted him, and as he came into the hall Eliza Pickett appeared in her dressing gown, made up like a china doll, bright-eyed and every inch the happy hostess. Breakfast was waiting in the kitchen. He thanked her in French and she looked at him, astonished.

'I don't understand French!'

He attempted to explain to her that the previous evening she had expressed herself perfectly in that language, and in a charmingly superior manner she responded that he must have been dreaming. Jean's vocabulary was too limited for him to argue. Breakfast was there, he was hungry, and before he set off he needed to build up his strength. Without too much disgust he ate a fried kipper, Brussels sprouts, toast and marmalade in the time it took Mrs Pickett to polish off two cans of beer.

Half an hour later he rode out of Newhaven on the London road, making sure that he kept to the left. I shall not linger on his long ride through the countryside and small towns of Sussex and Surrey, during which he did his best to keep up a solid average so that he would arrive in the capital before it got dark. The English roads were easy, well surfaced and used by streams of high-bodied cars that swayed through the bends like Madame du Courseau's old Model T Ford. On the other hand, he met few cyclists, except around the villages he passed, and when he did they were usually girls perched on antediluvian machines. Their sit-up-and-beg riding position forced them to show their legs, which they did with a charming immodesty and, it seemed, inconsequence. Towards the end of the afternoon he arrived at the outer suburbs of London and, believing that it was the city itself, was horribly disappointed. Everything was ugly, and appallingly monotonous. He asked the way to Kings Road, and was directed to a narrow street where children were playing among the rubbish. Mademoiselle Geneviève could not live there, she who had departed from La Sauveté in a prince's Hispano-Suiza. He retraced his steps and looked for a policeman whom he eventually found, very preoccupied, at a crossroads. The policeman studied the address Antoine du Courseau had written down and mumbled something incomprehensible. However, his gestures indicated that Jean should follow the cables of a trolleybus. Jean obeyed and pedalled on over oily and slippery roads until he saw signposts pointing towards Chelsea, Westminster and the City. It was already dark when he cycled over the Thames at Battersea Bridge and finally discovered the Kings Road and, off it, a lovely street lined with pretty houses painted in a motley of reds, whites and greens. Geneviève lived in Chelsea's artists' quarter.

And here I would be glad to be allowed a small digression about Geneviève, a character who remains minor and intermittent so far, but whom we will see more of later. If, despite the temptation I have felt on several occasions, I have forced myself only to talk about her when she actually appeared, Geneviève is none the less one of the keys to this story. In 1932 she is about thirty years old and at the peak of her beauty, a beauty of the kind that nowadays makes us smile affectionately: shingled hair, dripping with real and paste jewellery, eyes made up from the moment they open in the morning, short skirt, and oversize sweater on a bust that might belong to a boy. She speaks English and Italian and occasionally swears in Arabic. In London she could easily live in Eaton Square or the nicer parts of Kensington if she chose, but she knows that it would not be appreciated, because she is a kept woman. Judicious, intelligent, perfectly in tune with her times, she surrounds herself with actors, painters, musicians, writers. In the more chic districts she would be snubbed for her pretension. In Chelsea people beat a path to her door precisely because, absurdly, they want to slum it, to meet some real artists who dare to despise the gentry and their boring dinners. Her house in Chelsea is a witness to the Thirties. In it you could see, hanging on exposed wires from the picture rails, the same painters as those at Chez Antoine at Saint-Tropez, a drawing room strewn with black and white furs and no other furnishings, apart from a red Steinway and Negro masks under glass globes placed directly on the rugs. Guests sat Indian-style on the floor, and Salah, the black Egyptian in a black and white boubou, passed around coffee, cigarettes, sweetmeats and a hookah.

One can imagine Jean Arnaud's disorientation when, with his knapsack on his back, he knocked at the door and it was opened by a servant in frock coat and white gloves. The Ali Baba's cave that he was entering bore no resemblance to anything he had known. He had landed on another planet from the one inhabited by Jeanne and Albert, or even the du Courseaus and the Malemorts in their antiquated luxury. Here everything was new and scary, including this valet who immediately turned out to be French. Yes, he had been waiting for Monsieur Arnaud, but Madame was not in London. She had telephoned to ask that her young guest be looked after. After his first astonishment, , Jean grew anxious about his bicycle. He could not leave it outside the front door. The valet picked it up with infinite delicacy and parked it between two statues of Negro boys in polychrome wood, bearing gilded candelabra.

'Madame's guests will like that very much,' he said. 'If Monsieur would care to give me his luggage and follow me.'

'Oh no, that's all right. I'll carry it myself.'

'In that case, if Monsieur would be very careful on the stairs where there are many pictures!'

Jean carried his haversack in his hand and was shown to a small bedroom which had green-lacquered Cubist furniture and walls overloaded with naïve paintings. The window looked out onto a charming garden, in which the greenish beam of a spotlight illuminated a spherical head that was eyeless and had an only just discernible nose.

'Would Monsieur like me to run him a bath?'

Jean thanked him with a certain embarrassment. He found the haste of this servant in wanting to wash him rather suspect, but when he looked closely at himself in the bathroom mirror he realised that after more than a hundred kilometres of riding through the dust, heat, and lorry exhausts, a bath was a far from indecent suggestion. Unfortunately, all he had to change into afterwards was a pair of trousers that had been crushed in his haversack, a short-sleeved shirt Jeanne had bought for him in a sale at the Nouvelles Galeries at

Dieppe, and a sweater she had knitted. After he had amused himself with the bath salts, shampoo, moisturising cream, perfume for men, and other beauty products that were lined up on a glass shelf, he washed himself conscientiously. A ringing telephone summoned him from his bath, and he ran to pick up a strangely baroque instrument apparently made of shells.

'Monsieur's dinner is served.'

Jean promised that he would come down immediately. His heart beat faster. Perhaps Madame Geneviève had come back from the country. But he was disappointed: the valet was waiting for him in the hall where his bike was still parked amidst the Venetian sculptures and amorphous metallic objects. He ate alone in a candle-lit dining room, a low-ceilinged room with no other decorations apart from the table silver. Because he was hungry he couldn't feel intimidated. He gobbled his dinner and let himself be served as if he had had a footman standing behind him since he was a baby. He nevertheless felt his thoughts wander to Chantal de Malemort: why was she not there, at the other end of the table, her sweet face lit by the candelabra's unsteady glow? She was made for luxury like this, and one day he would offer it to her, in a brilliant existence among foreign lands. They would only – when there was no valet with them – have to reach out their hands to touch each other's fingertips and reassure and repeat to each other that they were quite alone in the world. Jean's heart sank from anxiety. Where was she at this moment? Madame du Courseau was closing her net. Michel could see Chantal any day he wanted to …

Jean did not refuse the *crème au chocolat*. The valet disappeared and came back with a telephone.

'Madame wishes to speak to Monsieur.'

Jean picked up the receiver. A young and dulcet voice, slightly breathless at the start, said, 'Dear Jean, I'm so desolate not to be with you. I hope they're looking after you.'

'Oh yes, they are, Madame.'

'I'll be back in town tomorrow. Make yourself comfortable, and treat the house as if it were your own. In the morning the chauffeur will drive you to the Tower of London and Westminster Abbey, if you'd like that. Or you can jump on a riverboat and go to Hampton Court. It's delightful and awfully relaxing. How is my father?'

'Very well, Madame. He's at La Sauveté.'

'And my dear Jeanne, your maman?'

'She gave me some jams to give to you.'

'That's so thoughtful. Till tomorrow, dear Jean. Lots of love.'

She hung up. Jean tried to go on listening, but the crackle on the line separated him from the lovely dulcet voice. The valet took back the telephone and it disappeared as if by magic. Everything seemed enchanted in this house: thick carpets muffled the sound of footsteps so that you could never be sure you were alone, you could shine a bright light on an object and turn it into a transparent ball; walls slid back and forth to reveal or conceal rooms that were either bare or packed with paintings. So far Jean had only seen the valet. Was he alone, assisted by robots, or was there, behind these magic partitions, a magic people making sure that the house worked magically?

'Monsieur,' Jean began.

The servant interrupted him in a superior tone. 'My name is Baptiste, Monsieur.'

'Baptiste? Gosh, that's not a name I've heard very often.'

'And nor is it my name, Monsieur. Baptiste is the name Madame gives to all her butlers. I accepted the post and the name. I shall have my own name back when Madame no longer has need of me.'

Jean went back to his room. Someone had turned down his bed and laid out his striped cotton pyjamas next to the pillow. In the garden the spotlight still lit up the golden head. Jean opened empty drawers and a wardrobe in which there hung a silk dressing gown. He read the spines of some cloth-bound books on a bookshelf: Daniel Defoe, Dickens, Ruskin, Joyce, Pound, and a signed copy of Paul Morand's *Londres*: 'To Geneviève, in London when the £ was at 28 francs, her friend Paul.' He began reading, and only stopped hours later, far into the night, his eyes blinking. So that was what this great city that encircled him was really like, the city that he would see tomorrow, before he had even been to Paris? He experienced a vague fear at the extent of his discovery, his solitude, and his ignorance; but helped by the tiredness he felt from his long ride, despite the excitement of so much novelty he fell asleep the second his head hit the pillow and opened his eyes again to see a white and blue silhouette and a pink face with a forehead topped by a starched cap.

'Madame!' he said, thinking this was Geneviève.

'I am Mary!' the young woman said, opening the curtains and letting in the light of a radiant September sun before pushing a trolley to his bedside.

Mary smiled at him and lifted the silver dome from a plate to reveal fried eggs and bacon and a grilled tomato. She was far prettier than Eliza Pickett, and as she bent over to pick up Jean's shirt and lay it carefully on the armchair she also revealed the pretty backs of her knees and the beginnings of soft thighs. He hoped she didn't drink beer in the morning, like the only English woman he had met so far and who – no, really, it was impossible – could not be the paragon of all other Englishwomen.

'What luxury!' he said out loud when she had gone.

The day was just beginning. Going downstairs, Jean was thrilled to catch sight of his bicycle, carefully restored to a brilliant shine. His heart leapt, and he stroked its saddle, its handlebars and its shining red frame. He and it would visit London together. Refusing Baptiste's help, he tucked it under his arm and walked down the front steps to come face to face with the black chauffeur whom he recognised and who immediately also recognised him. In the rain, on the hill up to Grangeville, this same chauffeur had borrowed his bicycle to fetch a mechanic. The yellow Hispano-Suiza with black mudguards and white wheels was waiting, parked by the pavement. In the narrow street it seemed even bigger, excessive, with its long bonnet whose radiator cap was in the shape of a silver arrow, perhaps the very silver arrow that had struck Haroun, the king's enemy, in the heart. Things were becoming clearer: the prince and Geneviève enjoyed a close relationship, probably a very close one.

'Hello!' Jean said. 'We've met already.'

The chauffeur laughed and raised his cap.

'My name is Salah, and I have been ordered to show you around London.'

'What about my bicycle?'

'Let's leave it here.'

'I really wanted to ride around London a bit. Apparently it's very flat.'

Salah scratched his head.

'We can put it in the boot, and when you want to ride it you can take it out and I'll follow you.'

Reluctantly Jean accepted. The bicycle did not completely fit in the boot and they had to resign themselves to leaving a wheel sticking out. Despite Salah's formal protests, Jean sat next to him in the front.

As night had fallen the previous evening, he had only seen an indistinct grey, rather dirty mass. In the morning light he discovered another city altogether, joyfully coloured, white, pink, red and olive green, full of beautiful balconies in wrought iron; a very gay city, which caught the slightest light, held it in its streets, and shone with pleasure. Obviously I shall not recount Jean's sightseeing, his surprises, and his sudden and intense friendship for the chauffeur. Salah was Egyptian. He spoke French and English. He had travelled all over Europe and the Middle East with the prince and often Madame too. He seemed very attached to both of them, but was more attached still to the Hispano-Suiza. It was his thing, his baby, an enormous machine whose size simply crushed the little English cars, the sparkling yellow of its coachwork creating a respectful gap around it. Silent, but responsive too when it was called upon, it drank fabulous quantities of petrol. Jean was careful not to say that deep down, and by a long way, he preferred Monsieur du Courseau's Bugatti, which was a real plaything, noisy and highly strung, that would fly down any road you pointed it at.

After the Tower of London, Jean insisted that they go to Hyde Park. They bought spongy sandwiches and bottles of lemonade that they ate and drank on a bench facing the Serpentine, which ran gently between two banks of lawns. At lunchtime the young secretaries left their offices and came to stretch out on the grass and eat a packet of biscuits, pecked by pigeons. At least a hundred Eliza Picketts walked past them, in three-cornered hats and buckled shoes. Salah explained that the English loved two things more than anything: lawns and animals. Apart from that, nothing, or almost nothing. He also mentioned that the prince had been very tired for a number of months and now rarely left his country house in Oxfordshire, and that Madame could not stay in one place. She drove in her Bentley coupé from one grand house to another, came back to dine at Chelsea, left again the next morning at dawn, always full of vigour and happy to be alive. Yet people said that she had been ill like the prince and that they had met in a nursing home.

Two three-cornered hats stopped in front of them, stared at them in astonishment, and said something before continuing on their way.

'What are they talking about?' Jean asked.

'The first one,' Salah explained, 'said, "There's a Negro", talking about me, obviously, and the second one said, "I didn't know they were allowed to sit next to children in Hyde Park." Do you think I should have said something to them?'

'Yes, but what?'

'Something like, I'm really just rather suntanned, and in a generation half of London will be black-skinned. But they would not have believed me.'

'It would have been funny.'

'Yes, but you have to keep your mouth shut and know your place. I've learnt that. As I have learnt the scorn of the scorned.'

143

'You speak really cleverly for a chauffeur, Salah.'

'My father is a proper Egyptian, a minor provincial aristocrat, if you like, pale-skinned, and I'm the son of a Sudanese mother, a sort of slave girl. They sent me to a school run by the Lasallians, the Brothers of the Christian Schools, but I only ever had one thought: to escape from Egypt and see the world. The prince took me with him. I respect him because he speaks to me like a human being. You'll see him: he is an immensely good man, a very rare thing among Arabs, especially Muslims. I say that as a Muslim myself, who never eats pork or drinks alcohol and respects Ramadan.'

'You're a very good friend to me,' Jean said.

Salah smiled, half-opening his wide, scored lips and showing his yellow teeth. A Semitic nose inherited from his father clashed with his black skin and frizzy hair. His long, fine hands lay on his knees. Jean was impressed by their grace and by the care with which he looked after his nails. He was more familiar with Albert's rugged hands or with the abbé Le Couec's big paddles or Monsieur du Courseau's paws. Somehow Salah's hands reminded him of Chantal and her long, fine fingers and fresh, pink rounded nails, as if these two beings, so different in their skin, habits, sky and God, had some mysterious common origin.

Opposite where they were sitting, on the other bank of the Serpentine, a girl sat down on the grass, crossed her legs and started to read a book that she had placed on her lap. Her tow-coloured hair framed a plump, rather round face. She was chewing a bar of chocolate, oblivious – in reality or just pretending, it was impossible to say – of the sight she was offering the man and boy facing her: a panoramic view beneath her dress of sturdy thighs of a sugary whiteness and a pair of screamingly loud pink knickers. Salah and Jean both fell silent, fascinated by her immodesty. They had finished their sandwiches and lemonade. The day was wearing on, and they would have stayed talking to one another a while longer if this obscene

144

apparition had not come to disturb the friendship that had suddenly grown up between them on a calm English afternoon animated by swans, old ladies in three-cornered hats and daydreaming couples lounging on the grass. Salah was the first to rouse himself. Getting to his feet, he put his chauffeur's cap back on, pulled on his gloves, and bowed.

'Where would sir like to go?' he asked with exaggerated deference.

'Wherever you like, Salah.'

The Egyptian looked at his watch.

'I have a suggestion: we shall keep Westminster Abbey for tomorrow, and if it doesn't bore you too much, we'll go to the British Museum instead, where I'll leave you for a moment to go and have a French lesson with my teacher who lives very close by, in Soho.'

'But you don't need any lessons, you speak very good French.'

'Yes, I speak, but unfortunately I write very badly. Mostly phonetically. If the dear Brothers read my writing, they would blush to their roots. I've found an excellent teacher, a grammarian. Her lessons don't last longer than half an hour, and in the evening I do the homework she gives me.'

'The British Museum it is, then.'

At Piccadilly Jean asked who the statue was, balanced on its pedestal.

'Eros!' Salah said, grinning. 'This is his spiritual home, everywhere around here.'

The god of love! Jean's thoughts went straight back to Chantal. Their first journey would be to London and their first visit to this statue. The Hispano-Suiza turned into Shaftesbury Avenue, which bore no resemblance at all to the clean and fashionable London of Chelsea or Kensington. All along the grimy pavements were cinemas with garish posters, theatres with jangling bells, Italian cafés whose proprietors took your money as you went in, cigars clamped between their teeth. A pervasive smell of vanilla, dust, chip fat and petrol hung in the air, as if everything had been gathered up together, stirred and cooked in desperation, and finally exhausted.

The British Museum belonged to another, more reassuring district. Jean had never seen anything quite so impressive when Salah set him down at the main entrance.

'I'll pick you up in an hour,' he said. 'In any case, I'm not going far. Odeon Street is just around the corner.'

Jean was not passionate about museums. Painting quickly bored him, especially the official kind of painting that glorified British victories in Portugal, in Spain, at Trafalgar and Waterloo. These British devils had always won everything. William the Conqueror was the only one who had taught them a lesson, and as a Norman himself Jean was proud about that. He turned his back on these disagreeable reminders and headed for the sculpture rooms. Greek history and Roman history were still fresh in his mind. There, at least, in those vast halls you could still dream, even if it was permissible to doubt Lord Elgin's right to take down half the surviving friezes of the Parthenon and enrich his country with their incomparable sculptures.

As he was contemplating one of the friezes, a bald man in his fifties, with red lips and dressed in the black suit and white collar of a clergyman, approached him.

'Are you French?'

'Yes,' Jean said, surprised to be so easily identified.

'I thought as much from the way you look.'

'The way I look?'

'Something which is unmistakable and common to every French person. I've lived in your country. Are you interested in Greek sculpture?'

'Er ... yes, sir.

'Do you like Greek history?'

'It's very interesting.'

'It's much better than that!' the minister said, raising his finger. 'It's the only history that matters.'

146

He spoke so close to Jean's face that Jean felt gusts of cold tobacco buffet him. The minister looked into his eyes with chilling insistence.

'Greek beauty!' he said again. 'Impossible to imitate. It has disappeared for ever, corrupted by foreigners. Look at that young athlete, his slender neck and his torso, in which you can follow the play of muscles beneath the skin and even the ripple of the veins in their exertion … '

The man's hand grasped Jean's arm and squeezed it with unexpected force, as if to prevent him from running away.

'And yet … and yet!' he went on. 'Yet one does find sometimes, like a gift from heaven, yes, I really mean a gift from heaven, without blaspheming, the trace of Greek beauty in isolated individuals. Its seed has mysteriously come down the centuries, and beauty is reborn, unaccountably, in almost all its purity … You don't have any Greek ancestors, do you?'

'No,' Jean said, trying to disengage himself and distance his face from the other's with its blue, staring gaze that was making him nervous.

'I thought so. Well now, come and have a look at this extraordinary coincidence: a young athlete who is twenty-five centuries old and looks like your brother.'

The minister dragged him to the end of the room. A twisting staircase led to a dark room where spotlights illuminated a series of metopes in a line, the metopes of the temple of Bassae.

'Look! Look!'

Jean saw nothing but some high reliefs of definite grace, but whose faces all looked the same and who, he felt, bore no resemblance to him whatsoever. On the other hand, he definitely felt the minister's arm slip around his waist and pull him close; and when the tobacco-breath mouth tried to press itself against his own he gagged, wrenched himself away and stood ready to defend himself.

'You horrible pig! Dirty old man!'

'Be quiet! Be quiet!' the minister hissed, his cheeks puce.

A couple appeared in the doorway, and Jean dashed away, hurtled down the stairs and ran as far as the museum's exit, his cheeks burning. He must be as red in the face as the minister. Nothing like that had ever happened to him before. He did not actually know what it meant, only having heard about such things in crude conversations between those of his classmates who were always thirsty for smut, but just from the gagging sensation he had had, he was certain he had escaped from something horrible. He should have ... oh yes, what shouldn't he have done! Smashed his fist into the nose of the dirty old swine, called an attendant, got the old lecher arrested. He became ashamed that he had run away. Wasn't it the churchman who should have run away? If only Salah had been there! But Salah was having his French lesson and would not be back for half an hour. Visitors were coming and going, staring at the tall boy with red cheeks and dishevelled hair. Jean thought that people must be able to read on his face, as clear as day, what had just happened. He had seen the direction the Hispano-Suiza had taken after it left him, and he started walking that way. Odeon Street was difficult to find in the labyrinth of narrow streets lined with pubs, nightclubs and restaurants. By a stroke of luck, and what he considered to be an unheard-of thing, a youngish woman, albeit rather heavily made up, smiled at him. He stopped and asked, 'Odeon Street, please.'

Expecting not to understand a word of her reply, he was startled to hear her say, with a pretty Toulouse accent, 'Young man, are you sure you're old enough to be hanging around here?'

'You're French! Oh what luck. I'm thirteen.'

'Well, at the age of thirteen you don't hang around in Odeon Street. Do me a favour and go home to maman.'

'I'm looking for the chauffeur.'

'What chauffeur?'

'You haven't seen a big yellow Hispano-Suiza, have you?'

'Salah's Hispano?'

'Do you know it?'

'Do I know it … a bit.'

'It's time for his French lesson.'

The painted lady raised her black-pencilled eyebrows.

'Oh … ah, I see, Monsieur. Well, take the second street on the left and you'll see his Hispano. Good luck, young man … '

'Thank you, Madame!'

He quickened his step and almost immediately he came upon the car parked outside a fairly run-down house. On the half-open door he saw three printed cards:

Miss Selma Undset
Swedish massages
Massages suédois
Massagii suedese
1st floor, 1er étage, 1° piano.

Beneath in gothic letters:

Fräulein Loretta Heindrich
Elocution lessons. Oral only.
2nd floor.

The third card must be the one:

Madame Germaine
French teacher
very strict
3rd floor, 3e étage.

The building was wretched. A spiral staircase climbed upwards between walls corroded by saltpetre, but instead of the habitual smell of sprouts that oozes from this sort of building there was a stomach-turning mixture of face powder and disinfectant. On the third floor he stopped outside Madame Germaine's door. A cord of multi-coloured hemp cloth hung above the notice that announced the same words as on the ground floor, this time underlined: '*very strict*'. Poor Salah! Who was this person he trusted to teach him perfect French? Jean listened for the sound of raised voices. All he could hear was murmurs of encouragement, and he pulled on the cord. There were whispers, the sound of steps, then a small panel he had not noticed slid open beneath the printed card and a woman's voice with a southern accent said, 'It's not time yet, love.'

'Yes I know, but I need to speak to Salah.'

'Who are you?'

'Jean. Jean Arnaud.'

From the other side of the door he heard Salah's voice.

'Open it, let him in, it's a friend.'

A chain rattled and the key turned twice. Why did they need to lock themselves in for a French lesson? It was true that the district seemed pretty shady, and there were all sorts and races in the streets and a lot of over-made-up ladies. Eventually the door inched ajar and a woman appeared in the half-open doorway, her black hair loose, her face coated in cream, her lips mauve. She seemed to be wearing a dressing gown or long dress of gold polka dots. Jean couldn't see all of her, and Salah had already moved her aside to step onto the landing.

'What's going on? It was agreed that I would come and pick you up at the British Museum.'

Jean recounted his ordeal at the metopes of Bassae. Salah looked dismayed.

'I shouldn't have left you on your own, even for such a short time. It's my fault.'

'No it isn't, it really isn't. How could you have known?'

'I should know everything. Would you like me to find him and smash his face in?'

'Oh no, not a scene, that's the last thing I want! I want to go back. I'll ride my bike and you can go in front to show me the way. Have you finished your French lesson?'

150

'That's not at all important. Let's go.'

The door was still half open. Jean glanced behind Salah. Madame Germaine was brushing her hair in front of a mirror, and all around the mirror hung whips and chains. Their eyes met, the woman's reflected in the mirror, sultry and velvety and at the same time loaded with menace, to such an extent that Jean felt a shiver in his spine, for no more than a second, because Salah immediately shut the door behind him after calling 'till the next time' to Madame Germaine. As they went past the second floor, they passed a man who pulled his hat over his eyes and covered his mouth with a handkerchief. He was on his way to an elocution lesson with Fräulein Loretta. Despite its mysterious ways, its grimy appearance and its smell, the house was a serious place of work. The masseuse on the first floor was the only element that was out of place in this artistic and intellectual atmosphere. On the way down they heard a guttural voice, chanting in time with the sound of slapping: one, two, three … one, two, three … without pity for the raucous, panting breath of its patient. Salah led Jean quickly outside.

'It's the rush hour,' he said, 'we shall get stuck in the traffic. I think we had better postpone your ride until tomorrow, particularly as I should be at home soon in case the prince calls me to go and fetch him.'

Jean was disappointed, even though it was only a postponement. He would have liked to ride in London, where he had so far seen no other bicycles, squeezing between the hearse-like taxis and the red buses boasting the virtues of chicken stock and toothpaste. Salah appeared preoccupied.

'I'm sorry I interrupted your lesson with Madame Germaine,' Jean said. 'But she doesn't really look like a teacher. Is it true that she's very strict?'

'Oh … yes, in a way, but not with me. She knows how to be very tolerant too. With her English customers she uses the strong method. She has a lot of customers … I mean students.'

Jean remembered the whip and chains. How did she deal with the bad students exactly? What a strange country. He remembered having read in a book somewhere that there was still corporal punishment in English schools. Madame Germaine must have adapted her teaching methods to the English style … Salah was driving his Hispano-Suiza with an absolute dignity and certainty that he would dominate the evening crowds. He cut off a black Rolls-Royce as if it were a donkey-cart. They crossed Hyde Park as the shadows were lengthening and drove down Sloane Street to the Kings Road. It was pleasant to come back to a district lightened by the colours of spring, to women who did not make themselves up outrageously, to a complete absence of clergymen with red lips and staring eyes.

Baptiste opened the door, and Salah took the bicycle out of the boot and replaced it in the hall.

'Did Monsieur have a good ride?' the butler asked.

'Unfortunately not. There were too many cars. I think I'll go tomorrow, early in the morning, and do a circuit of Hyde Park, otherwise I'll start losing my fitness.'

'Madame telephoned. She deeply regrets that she is unable to come this evening, but she will do her best to be here to meet Monsieur before he leaves.'

It might have struck the reader that Baptiste was exaggerating in his unctuous use of the third person. Jean himself wondered whether the florid-cheeked, grey-whiskered butler, who seemed to be chewing his tongue all the time, was not having a joke at his expense, as the son of a gardener and housekeeper. The feeling that this sententious dogsbody was almost certainly looking down his nose at him made Jean uncomfortable. He would have liked to make Baptiste understand that he was not quite as pitiful as he looked, despite his haversack and short-sleeved shirts with their threadbare collars, and a sweater with its elbows darned by Jeanne. Had he not been to tea at châteaux where this snobbish flunkey would only have been invited to pass the petits fours? But it would be humiliating to tell him so.

Jean learnt that day to hide his ill humour by going along with other people's view of him as something he was not. Or perhaps was, for after all a son of Jeanne and Albert was no better than a Baptiste. He was not yet aware of the infallible intuition among servants that makes them able to detect instantly a person displaced into a milieu which is not their own. Let us remember that Jean was not so well-read at thirteen, and that the revelation would dawn on him later, when he came to read Swift's *Directions to Servants* and learn by heart his advice to those employees: 'Be not proud in prosperity. You have heard that fortune turns on a wheel; if you have a good place, you are at the top of the wheel. Remember how often you have been stripped and kicked out of doors; your wages are taken up beforehand and spent in translated red-heeled shoes, second-hand toupées, and repaired lace ruffles, besides a swingeing debt to the alewife and the brandy-shop.'

So Jean had dinner alone, as he had the previous evening, served by Baptiste, whose affected respect came to feel increasingly insulting. Geneviève did not telephone, and he said to himself that she must be an odd person, too indulged by life or, more specifically, by the prince. He promised himself that he would question Salah about the latter. Behind a mask of kindness and generosity, the prince concealed his true self with all the majesty of his person. You could only guess at what he was really like through the devotion he inspired in Salah and the luxury he provided for Geneviève. Jean would have liked to thank him in person for the postal orders that had helped him to buy his red bicycle, but would the prince even remember sending them?

The next morning a new maid pushed the trolley containing his breakfast into his bedroom,

'You're not Mary!' he said, disappointed.

'No. I am María.'

She spoke French with what Jean supposed to be a strong Spanish accent. Where Mary was blonde and fresh as a strawberry, María was black-haired with a dark complexion and sultry expression. In an entirely different way she was also very nice to look at. Knowing that she would have to draw the curtain, as Mary had, he eyed her legs, which were a bit too wiry and muscled although certainly pretty, even though on that point he might not yet have very well-formed ideas or a reliable definition of female beauty. María was more familiar than Mary, and sat down on the end of his bed.

'So, are you enjoyin' yourself in London?' she asked, revealing a set of fine teeth.

'Very much, Mademoiselle.'

She burst out laughing.

'You mus' no' say Mademoiselle, you mus' say: María. I am the maid.'

It should perhaps be pointed out that the low-paid slovens lately taken on at La Sauveté by Marie-Thérèse du Courseau had none of the tantalising quality possessed by Mary and María, with their lipstick and varnished nails. (Marie-Thérèse had put a stop to the Caribbean girls of the past; Jean barely remembered the last pair, who had been nowhere near as pretty as Joséphine Roudou and Victoire Sanpeur.)

'What are you thinkin' about?'

'That you're very pretty for a maid.'

'Well, bless me!'

She stood up, did a complete turn on tiptoes and looked at Jean with knitted eyebrows.

'You are startin' pretty young!'

As soon as he had finished breakfast, Jean went down to the hall. His cherished bicycle had not moved, but Salah appeared, his cap in his hand.

'First we're going to Westminster Abbey, and then we'll see.'

'What about my bike?'

'Let's leave it here. Baptiste will look after it. Where we're going is not very good for bicycles.'

Regretfully Jean agreed to leave his bicycle behind. The Hispano-Suiza was waiting at the kerb, so familiar now that it no longer impressed him. At Westminster he felt cold. He preferred the church at Grangeville, with its smells of candles and incense and the sound of the abbé's big feet plodding between the pews. The visit did not last long.

'Now what would you like to see?' Salah asked.

'I don't know. Where do those boats go to?'

Large boats were taking on lines of passengers at Westminster Bridge.

'To Hampton Court. It's a long way. You get there in time for lunch, and you come back in the late afternoon.'

'Actually I'd really like to go for a boat ride on the Thames.'

Salah was very reluctant, and Jean had to persuade him that it was safe to go on his own. It was not every day that one encountered lecherous clergymen.

'If anything happened to you, Madame would never forgive me.'

'On the telephone she told me herself that I should go to Hampton Court. Nothing will happen to me. Go and have a French lesson.'

Salah smiled and allowed himself to be convinced. On the boat at first Jean saw only old ladies in frilly dresses, clutching cups of milky tea. He counted three three-cornered hats and a number of shoes with buckles. The first part of the trip, past docks and wharfs, was gloomy, but the old ladies expressed themselves delighted. They found it 'charming'. The truth was that they were short-sighted and not actually looking at anything, but entirely taken up with refilling their teacups from the urn that was provided. Fortunately Jean found an unusual couple to distract him at the boat's stern: a short, stocky, bald man who had a jaw like Mussolini's and a Borsalino jammed on his head was literally licking the face of a mulatto woman with bleached and not very well straightened hair. Everyone seemed to be ignoring the woman's antics as she tittered and squirmed, crossing and uncrossing pretty legs sheathed in fishnet stockings, and those of the man, who was getting increasingly impatient. Their Anglo-Italian pidgin seemed to be delighting both of them. Jean watched them, fascinated, until the man caught him looking and glared furiously. The boat slid on up the black, slack river between banks occupied by factories and empty spaces. Just before Hampton Court the countryside finally appeared, soft and green and rolling, dotted with pretty houses with slate roofs and surrounded by gardens in bloom. He imagined them inhabited by army officers with ruddy cheeks, children in velvet breeches, and pretty tennis players. The old ladies on board, stimulated by their innumerable cups of tea, waved enthusiastically at everyone they saw. Having found the docks charming, they had no words left to admire the English countryside. The man with the Borsalino went on licking his mulatto, who was squirming like a dog on heat; her pointed tongue looked as if it had been dipped in raspberry jam.

At the landing stage the old ladies rushed away like clumsy sparrows towards the palace and the park, where Jean stretched his legs for a moment before going back to the bank of the Thames. Young men were launching sharp, arrow-shaped skiffs with varnished hulls. Pale-skinned, with red or blond hair, they rowed with an application and seriousness that Jean admired. The blades of their oars dipped without a splash into the dark water and their boats, as if seized by sudden inspiration, flew over the still surface of the river. The cox's sharp instructions paced the exertions of the rowers, upright and tense like machines, and Jean promised himself that one day he would try rowing, a noble sport that had sculpted fine athletes and imparted to generations a sense of teamwork. It was not a popular sport in France, probably because, as Albert liked to say in his best flights of philosophical fancy, the French were a bunch of dirty individualists who only thought about getting ahead. Besides, rowing's joys were best experienced on expanses of calm water that reflected nature arranged by man, parks of beech and cedar that sloped down to drink at river and lake, country houses whose images wobbled, vanished and reformed in the passing of motor cruisers and barges.

The boat left again at two o'clock. Jean was first on board, followed by the old ladies, who fell on the tea urn to refill their cups with pungent, scalding tea, and the crew was about to cast off when the flamboyant mulatto rushed up, dragging by the hand her companion in the Borsalino, who was breathless, his clothes half undone. They settled themselves back on the bench at the stern, giggling like children, and then the woman put her hand in her coat pocket and pulled out a pair of bluish lace knickers that she put back on without ceremony. Which bush had they been playing behind? The scene left Jean mystified, and led his thoughts back to the games of Antoinette, to the sweet ecstasies of their incomplete pleasures and the happy silence that followed. There must, then, be two sorts of love, one horrid, rude and immodest, and the other secret, sparking off dreams and gentle pleasures.

Salah was waiting at the landing stage. Jean stepped ashore behind the lustful pair and was astonished to hear Salah say a curt 'Good evening' to the mulatto, who immediately stopped laughing and dragged her companion away. The old ladies collected their bags of needlepoint and baskets of food and trotted to a waiting bus.

'Did you enjoy yourself?' Salah asked.

'Enjoy? No, not really. Well, I suppose I saw some things. Do you know that lady?'

'Slightly. Jamaican, I believe.'

Jean told him the story of the knickers discovered in her coat pocket and replaced without fuss. Salah's stern expression cracked and he laughed.

'A strange girl,' he said. 'Not to be recommended. You definitely are going to leave with a curious idea of London ... I regret now that I let you go off for the whole day. Madame came to lunch. She was hoping to see you.'

'I'll see her tonight.'

'I'm afraid she has just driven away in her Bentley again. She's spending the weekend with some friends in Kent. I also have to tell you something that may annoy you ... She arrived with three friends, a poet, a painter, and the sculptor John Dudley. Mr Dudley is very bizarre. He makes extravagant sculptures from all sorts of things: he will weld an old coffee-maker to an iron, a saucepan on top of a clock, whatever. Apparently it sells. Art lovers can't get enough of his work. Anyway, when he saw your bicycle in the hall he decided that it was a sublime object and that he would construct a masterpiece from it by crushing it in his hydraulic press. Madame allowed him to take it away ... '

'What?' Jean exclaimed, his eyes full of tears.

'Madame asked me to buy you another one tomorrow morning.'

'Oh Salah, it's impossible. My bike ... you don't know how much I love it. Let's go and get it back from this man straight away ... '

'I'm afraid the damage will already be done.'

Tears rolled down Jean's cheeks. He could have faced almost anything, but not some mad sculptor crushing the bicycle that he cherished above everything else, his finest possession, a perfect bicycle, such as he had never known before and would never know again.

'Don't cry, for goodness' sake! You're a man, and tomorrow I'm going to take you to buy another one.'

'An English bike, Salah! You must be joking! The English have never made a proper racing bike. They ride around on bikes that date back to Louis XIV.'

'Well, look, I've got the money, I'll give it to you and you can buy yourself another one in France.'

'It won't ever be the same. That bike was my bike. My bike, do you understand? And how am I going to get back to Newhaven?'

'I shall drive you there in the Hispano.'

As soon as they got back to Geneviève's house, Jean dashed up the steps two at a time and rang the bell, hoping that it would turn out to be a bad dream, but Baptiste opened the door with a prim expression.

'Monsieur has heard?' he said. 'His bicycle has become a work of art: yes, of ART!'

Jean spent a profoundly unhappy evening, despite a letter that Geneviève had left for him.

> *My dear Jean, your bicycle so excited Mr Dudley that I allowed him to take it away. I do hope this won't upset you. Salah will drive you to a bicycle shop tomorrow and you will have a replacement. I was so sorry not to see you today, but now I must go to see some friends and shan't be back till Monday. Enjoy your last three days here. Salah is an excellent guide. He knows everything. He is not just a chauffeur, he is also a friend. Please kiss my parents for me, and Antoinette and Michel too, and especially your maman, dearest Jeanne, who was so good to me when I was a little girl.*
>
> *Your*
> *Geneviève du Courseau*

But next morning Jean rejected every bicycle he was offered. They were all fitted with English rod brakes, that work well enough but make the machine much heavier. As for racing handlebars, not one dealer knew what he meant. In the end Salah handed Geneviève's money to Jean, who almost gave it straight back: it was roughly enough for at least three bicycles fitted with the latest derailleur used by Leducq in the 1932 Tour. Instead he started to dream. Salah dropped him off at museums and parks and picked him up at the exit. Geneviève was right: the chauffeur was also a friend, thoughtful, intelligent and discreet. Mysterious too from time to time, skilfully avoiding answering embarrassing questions, such as the one Jean asked on his last day. Each morning he had been woken by a different

159

maid, and every one was called Mary, or María, or even Marie, who was French and whom he was amazed to identify without a shadow of a doubt as the over-made-up girl from Toulouse who had given him directions in Soho to Odeon Street where the Hispano-Suiza was parked. The Chelsea house was not so grand that it required a very large staff, especially since the prince almost never used it, and Geneviève was touring the English countryside every weekend. Even if she invited a dozen of her friends to lunch or dinner, there was still no need for so many staff. And why were these interchangeable maids all called Mary? Why were they, if not beauties, all at least good-looking girls? Jean had also made a disturbing discovery when he had gone downstairs one evening, around midnight, to fetch a glass of water from the kitchen. He was still on the stairs when the front door opened. Baptiste was returning from an evening stroll, and was followed by a woman Jean immediately recognised as the mulatto from the boat. Baptiste behaved a good deal less civilly with her than with Geneviève's guests. Jean was surprised too by what she was wearing: a short, very tight-waisted green suit, a loud scarf decorated with a pearl, and a blue cap tilted over one ear. She was smoking. Baptiste told her she had better go and throw her cigarette outside if she didn't want a good slap, and the previously exuberant creature obeyed without a word before following Baptiste into the kitchen. Jean went back upstairs on tiptoe and stayed awake for a good part of the night, attempting to work out what it could all mean. The next day Salah made no answer when he asked him about it.

On the Saturday the Hispano-Suiza took Jean back to Newhaven. Because the packet was an hour late, he decided to visit Mrs Pickett, and found her little house and sign – 'B and B' – with ease. The old lady opened the door with her hat and coat on. She was just going out for a short walk. Oh, not far! Just around the corner. Jean gestured to Salah, who opened the door of the car, and Mrs Pickett climbed in without being asked. It doubtless seemed perfectly natural to her that Jean, having arrived on a red bicycle, should come back to visit her in a yellow chauffeur-driven Hispano-Suiza. They stopped outside Mrs Pickett's favourite pub, where her arrival caused a small sensation which she did not deign to acknowledge. Salah refused alcohol, which surprised her a little, and when he explained to her that he was a Muslim she gave him a charming smile and said, 'That's awfully bad luck, you ought to convert.' They left her, supported by her pillar and already happy, after Jean had tried again and failed to speak to her in French. No, she knew nothing of that barbaric language. The mystery remained.

The packet was edging alongside as they drove onto the dock. Salah contemplated the boat with a melancholy look.

'There are days when I would like to get back to Egypt,' he said, 'to my Nubia where I was born, Djebel Chams, next to the Nile. My father is getting older and there is a chance I may not see him again. It's not because he showed me very great kindness. He thought I was too dark-skinned. I have two very pale half-brothers, almost like the English, and he has always been prouder of them than of me, even though they are both useless fools who sponge off our father and are completely idle. Of course he doesn't know that I am a chauffeur. I pretend that I have a job in a bank, and as I regularly send him money he thinks I'm rich and regrets a little that he did not have confidence in me.'

'I'd really like to go to Egypt with you,' Jean said.

'In that case, I'll take you there. I promise. We shall go up the Nile by boat and arrive loaded down with presents for my father … '

'And your mother.'

'No, she's dead,' Salah said. 'I hardly knew her at all. She was just a slave in the house, and I was brought up by my stepmother.'

Jean caught sight of the captain on the gangplank. His familiar face dispelled a little of the sadness that choked him as he got ready to leave England and Salah. When would he see Salah – his first proper friend – again? They shook hands. With his haversack on his back, Jean walked up the gangplank. On deck he went straight to the rail to catch a last glimpse of the chauffeur and his beautiful Hispano-Suiza, gleaming in the late afternoon sunlight, but the car had already driven away and disappeared behind the docks, leaving no trace on the streets or seafront of this red-bricked, soot-blackened town. His gateway to England was closing on many unanswered questions. Some things would become clear in time Not all. And Jean would draw from it the conviction that it was better not to know exactly why Mrs Pickett spoke French at night when she was drunk, nor why, in an elegant house in Chelsea, the maids were all called some version of Mary and were different every morning. After all, what did it matter? His view of the world had broadened. In future he would no longer live inside La Sauveté's walls the way he had lived until now.

On that hot afternoon at summer's end, graceful clouds scudded across the sky: gazelles, lambs, melting snowmen. Dust rose from the avenues at La Sauveté as vans and carts passed over them, loaded with furniture. The official auctioneer, Maître Prioré, arrived from Rouen in his black suit and tie, mopped his brow with a cambric handkerchief and drank large glasses of water flavoured with a drop of grenadine. He was no longer enjoying himself. His zest was dwindling with the indecision and and timidity of the final bidders. The coat stand was snapped up for thirty francs, the umbrella-stand only found a taker at ten. Yet people were not leaving. Initially respectful, they had begun wandering through the empty house, where paintings had left behind large, lighter oval and rectangular patches on the worn wallpaper. Others strolled through the park, and from his window Albert had seen some of them picking flowers or sitting on the hallowed lawn. He had not moved when one stranger had stolen his watering hose and a woman had taken a pot full of climbing geraniums. Having been weeping since the morning, Jeanne now seemed dazed, and sat on a kitchen chair, her large hands, bleached by endless laundry washing, motionless on her knees. Albert lit a pipe, and the smell of tobacco drifted through the kitchen. He caught sight of Monsieur Le Couec, who, with an air of feigned indifference, walked among the crowd, exchanging a word with those he knew and staring in surprise at those who were carrying something away: a pitcher, a bowl, a box, a copper planter. Occasionally he allowed himself some reproach that went uncomprehended by his interlocutor. The auctioneer bent down to one of his assistants, who shook his head. There was nothing more to sell. La Sauveté had been emptied in an afternoon by an

163

invasion of ants who had left the house with only its old lace curtains and rugs so worn that they tempted no one. A silence settled, then the murmuring started up again. The bookkeeper was enjoying himself with various sums in his large black oilcloth ledger. With a drink or two, the whole sale might have been turned into a festive occasion, but elements conspired against it: the heat, the absence of the du Courseaus, the shyness of the bidders and the embarrassment, at least for the people who lived nearby, of plundering this house whose modest grandeur had for a long time contributed to the fortunes of the neighbouring village. People gossiped to each other that the new owners, still known only to the notary, were Monsieur and Madame Longuet. The gossip had quickly spread: they were going to knock down the dividing wall and demolish La Sauveté, or convert it into one of those welcoming establishments that had been the basis of their fortune. Monsieur Le Couec would be its chaplain. Did he not have something of a weakness for Madame Longuet who, being from Alsace, kept him well supplied with alcool blanc, raspberry or plum according to the season? No one had seen the Longuets during the general sell-off, but an antique dealer from Rouen was thought to be their straw man. This person had bought the family portraits, which could only have been for clients who wanted to invent a lineage for themselves. One further absence, which had met with favourable comment, was that of the Malemorts. They stayed away from any public event that risked descending into a free-for-all; the only exception was when they went hunting in the forest of Arques. Marie-Thérèse du Courseau, with Michel and Antoinette, was living with them while she waited for the villa she was having built on the cliff on the road out of Grangeville to be finished. Some praised her dignity in the face of ruin, others declared that the ruin was not hers but that of her husband, from which she could have saved him with a single gesture. As for Antoine, no one had seen him that day. For good reason: he had spent the afternoon at the Café des Tribunaux in Dieppe, playing draughts with Jean Arnaud. Jean was leading by five games to four when the auctioneer arrived, having swapped his black suit for a sports jacket and grey slacks. At the wheel of a red Alfa Romeo roadster, he was a different man.

'We can be fairly satisfied,' he said. 'The day has gone better than I expected.'

'What will you have?' Antoine asked.

'Scotch for me!'

'Scotch? I don't know if they have any here.'

Antoine's slur on the Café des Tribunaux was unfounded. There was indeed Scotch for the locals, as the British never ordered it, addicted as they were to white wine from the moment they disembarked.

'Will you do me the pleasure of dining with us?' Maître Prioré asked, intrigued by Antoine's Olympian indifference. 'I mean, with my bookkeeper and myself. And Monsieur as well, of course.'

Jean was not often addressed as 'Monsieur', and he looked up at the person who had just disturbed his game.

'I'll take you back after dinner,' Antoine said.

Jean accepted. The auctioneer asked to see a menu and the head waiter. He wanted sole. He had come to Dieppe to eat sole. But before deciding whether he would have them *au gratin* or *meunière*, he needed to see them. A lavish choice was presented to him, because they were all very different sizes.

'Do you have a preference?' the auctioneer asked for form's sake, believing that Antoine did not give a damn, as he did not about everything else.

'Yes. Small. Two hundred and fifty grams at the most, because I like them *meunière*.'

'Well all right, *meunière* you shall have if you like, but have this big fat one instead. It's truly only here that they have such enormous ones.'

'No, they're like that at Oléron too,' Antoine said, 'but so fat that they only taste good *au gratin*, with the skin on. Small ones you skin, they have a more delicate taste. Medium size, you stuff them, which I'm not wild about. I don't like shallots or peeled shrimps. The stuffing kills the flavour of the fish. Naturally I exclude anything prepared with tomatoes or mushrooms, which is for people who are tired of life, and that's not the way I feel at all, nor you, I sincerely hope.'

'No, obviously not. Well then, let's follow your advice.'

The bookkeeper protested mildly. He wanted a salad with some ham. No one listened to him. On the choice of wine Antoine was equally categorical: there would be no wine. The patron kept a few bottles of a personal reserve of sparkling cider, which survived the summer thanks to a cool and remarkably well-insulated cellar.

'I'm completely in your hands!' Maître Prioré said. 'You're a true epicure.'

'Sometimes, though more and more rarely. When I travel, I'm happy with saucisson and red wine.'

'You travel a good deal for your business, I imagine.'

'I get around. It's not exactly business, which I understand nothing about and wish to understand nothing about. Besides, you wouldn't be here this evening if I had known how to look after myself.'

'You haven't even asked me how much the sale this afternoon amounted to.'

'No, I haven't, and yet the cheque you'll hand over represents all that I have left … '

Abandoning his sole, which he had been clumsily picking at, the bookkeeper made a grab for his black ledger, on the bench beside him.

'We have plenty of time,' Antoine said.

The auctioneer gestured irritably at his bookkeeper. Antoine du Courseau surprised him, and he was extremely curious to know who this man really was, so untroubled at his separation from his fortune. He tried politics.

'The Front Populaire has ruined France in the space of three months.'

'Do you think so?' Antoine asked, pouring himself some cider. 'I don't. Money's being redistributed, that's all, and I generally think that's a good thing.'

'People tell me that the strikes in the armaments industry have driven any number of small companies to the wall.'

'We're anachronisms. Others will come and take our place.'

'Even so, you won't deny that if things continue as they are, we'll soon start losing the will to work, even for our children's sake. Thanks to my father's hard work I've been able to acquire my position, and if I'm not mistaken your own company was founded by your father.'

'I didn't manage to hang on to what he left me. He took a lot of trouble for nothing.'

'A great shame for your own son! Isn't that right, young man?'

'I'm not Monsieur du Courseau's son,' Jean said.

Maître Prioré began to feel uncomfortable. Plain speaking and platitudes generally worked much better than this. He had aimed too low, thinking he was dealing with an unsophisticated Norman ruined by his own stupidity, and discovered that beneath his provincial appearance Antoine concealed a profound well of contempt. The auctioneer was annoyed, and could not see how to backtrack easily and show that he was the kind of man he felt himself to be (and in reality was, with a slight self-over-estimation that was normal in his smooth-tongued profession): a connoisseur of dependable taste, possibly the best expert he knew in English furniture, and a great collector of enamels. It is always difficult to switch from one tone to another when one has made a mistake. Flight is usually the only way out. There is nothing like it for leaving your mistakes behind. They decay, forgotten and alone.

'Shall we meet tomorrow?' he asked.

'Is that really necessary? I'd intended to make an early start. I'd like to be at Saint-Tropez in time for dinner.'

'In which case you've no time to lose: it's 1100 kilometres.'

'Oh, I can do that in ten hours.'

'In an Alfa Romeo, I'm guessing?'

'Absolutely not. A 57S.'

'A Bugatti?'

'Who ever told you a 57S was anything other than a Bugatti?'

'Yes, you're right of course, forgive me. Which model?'

'The Atalante.'

The intelligent, cultured auctioneer, at ease with everyone and in every situation, crumbled. He could be criticised for his taste, his collections or his reading matter, but not for his car. He would rather have been cheated on, arrested for a breach of trust, or molested by a meharist in the middle of the desert than bested in his choice of wheels.

'You're still loyal to Bugatti!' he said, with a twisted grin. 'He's been finished for four or five years.'

'Is that so? I wasn't aware of that. Let's see, we're 1936 now: that would mean that Bugatti hasn't won anything since 1932.'

'Very minor races, Monsieur.'

'Achille Varzi made Tazio Nuvolari look pretty foolish in the 1933 Monaco Grand Prix.'

'An unfortunate mechanical problem!'

'Oh yes … at the gasometer bend he took the lead from under his nose like no other driver could have done with any other car.'

'Then Nuvolari overtook him on the hill up to the Casino—'

'And over-revved his car and sent it up in flames. He had to finish the last lap pushing it. And name me another constructor who has won the Targa Florio five times in a row. Last year the first continental car to win the Brooklands 500 was Earl Howe's Bugatti. Apart from that, and this year's ACF Grand Prix, Bugatti is definitely washed-up as a constructor.'

'That isn't at all what I was trying to say, my dear Monsieur, but Alfa Romeo, Maserati, Mercedes and Auto-Union are winning everything else.'

'All of Italy, all of Germany are behind those makes. Bugatti races alone. He's nothing short of a genius, and in France geniuses are condemned to isolation. But tomorrow I'll be happy to take you on. Dieppe to Saint-Tropez. Eight o'clock start. The first to arrive wins the bet, as much as you like.'

'Sadly tomorrow's impossible. What about Sunday?'

'I'm not going to sit languishing here from now till Sunday. A thousand regrets! But speak to me no more of Alfa Romeos. It annoys me. Good evening to you, Maître.'

There was nothing superior in his tone, he was just weary. The auctioneer became bad-tempered.

'You think you know everything!'

'I don't know anything,' Antoine said. 'Nobody knows anything. I'm simply saying that you don't compare a Rolls-Royce to a bicycle.'

He stood up and gestured to Jean. The draughtboard was waiting for them at a neighbouring table.

'Shall I sign your cheque?'

'If you'll be so kind.'

He pocketed it without a glance and moved a draught forward.

'Goodnight to you,' Maître Prioré said.

'Goodnight.'

Jean won the game. They were at 6–4, and decided to stop rather than desperately chase a draw. Antoine had a cognac, Jean a lemonade. A few couples lingered, an elderly English pair and a girl of twenty with a man in his fifties with whom she appeared to be in love. Antoine thought about Marie-Dévote. Another twenty-four hours and he would be with her. He would stroke her still glorious though over-ample breasts. Lying next to her, he would know the meaning of peace. The shells would stop bursting and Marie-Thérèse would stop shouting.

'I'll drive you home,' he said to Jean.

'But where will you sleep, Monsieur?'

'At La Sauveté.'

'There's nothing left there.'

'I don't need anything.'

There was no light, except in the lodge. Antoine drove through the park and stopped in front of his door. It was not locked. What was there left to be stolen? They went in and walked through empty rooms that still smelt strongly of the removers. Through the windows, their shutters open, the full moon spilt long yellow splashes on the carpets and rugs. Antoine reached his bedroom where, after pulling a flat silver flask from his hip pocket, he sat on the floor with his back to the window and took a long swallow.

'You still don't drink?'

'No. I think I'll like to drink one day, but later. I'm rowing on Sunday.'

'Just look how pretty my Atalante is in the moonlight.'

The Bugatti cast its long bluish shadow across the gravel. The chrome of its radiator grille glittered in the moon's unworldly silver light. It sat there silently, placidly, sure of its strength. Jean thought it was as beautiful as a scull.

'Do you remember this room?' Antoine asked. 'You were a small boy.'

'The burst hosepipe. I've never forgotten it.'

'I liked you very much that day. It seems to me that we've got on well since then ... apart from one small mishap ...'

'Yes, the Antoinette thing ... I swear it wasn't me.'

'We don't swear to each other. We only tell the truth. Who was it?'

'Gontran Longuet.'

'That littlesquirt! Poor darling Antoinette, how lonely she must have felt to descend all the way down to his level. I shall have to talk to her, tell her how very much her papa loves her ... But why did Michel say it was you?'

'He must have thought it was me.'

'He hates you.'

'Hate's a strong word.'

'No, I think he must do.'

Antoine drank from his hip flask again.

'We're really all right here, aren't we? Without furniture, a house becomes itself again. I was born here. Geneviève, Antoinette and Michel were born here. And you were born next door.'

'I don't believe it any more,' Jean said.

'Hey now, come on, what's going on in that head of yours?'

'Michel came out with it last year, he taunted me and told me I was a foundling.'

Antoine stood up and paced to and fro several times, moving out of the shadows into the rectangles of light where his own shadow suddenly lengthened, deforming into an imposing and grotesque shape.

'We decided we would never lie to each other.'

'Yes, Monsieur.'

'In that case I'll tell you the truth. It's correct to say that you're a foundling. You were left in a basket on Albert and Jeanne's doorstep. They adopted you. They are therefore your parents.'

'I love them and respect them and I couldn't hope for better parents, but I feel … different from them. Papa doesn't understand me. He's always getting on his high horse when I try to talk to him.'

'He's a first-class man. Everything that isn't absolutely first-class irritates him.'

'At the moment he's really irritated.'

'He always has been. You didn't notice it so much when you were a child. My father was always irritated too. I was afraid of him. The outcome was not perfect, as you can see for yourself. Everything he left me has gone up in smoke. It's nothing to be proud of. I've loved this house, you know … '

Jean heard a catch in his voice, which fell to a murmur. Antoine opened the door onto the landing. There was no Marie-Thérèse there listening, her ear glued to the keyhole.

'Follow me,' he said. 'When there are two of us, the shadows are afraid.'

They walked on through the silent, wasted house. Parquet creaked, hinges squeaked. Everywhere the light of the moon lit up the shape of windows on the darkened walls. Antoine opened and closed the curtains and tried a tap, only to turn it off immediately. In the kitchen, at the back of a cupboard, they found some bottles without labels.

'They must have got forgotten. Let's have a look … oh yes, it's calva. I'll take them. They belong to me. Farewell, Normandy. I'm going to live in the sun. Do you know what the women of the Midi are like?'

'No,' Jean said. 'Apart from the trip to London you treated me to four years ago, I haven't budged from here.'

'Why budge, if you already understand everything?'

'I'd give anything to really know a big city, or to see the Mediterranean or the Pacific, the Sunda islands, or Tierra del Fuego.'

'How boring! On this planet of ours, only women are a big enough mystery to be interesting.'

'In Grangeville they aren't going to come running to me, are they? I have to go to them.'

Antoine swigged from the bottle and walked into the butler's pantry, where two stools had escaped being auctioned. He handed one to Jean and picked up the other one.

'Let's break them!'

The stools crashed against the wall. The leg of one flew at the window and the glass shattered. A dark head appeared, framed in the hole, and the abbé's voice boomed into the kitchen.

'What on earth has got into you?'

'We're breaking what even the rats had no use for.'

'And have the rats drunk everything?'

'No,' Antoine said. 'Come in, Father. We can't let such an occasion go uncelebrated.'

The head withdrew. Another shattering was heard. Monsieur Le Couec, parish priest of Grangeville, was using his back to push out the last of the glass, after which he clambered into the kitchen.

'You're not hurt, Father?'

'No, Jean. I too am perfectly transparent.'

He straightened up for a moment on the tiled floor, a shadow so enormous it woke up the whole house.

'I wondered where you were.'

'We were talking. We were bidding it all adieu.'

'Adieu is a word I like, when it is pronounced correctly, *à Dieu*.'

'Come now, Father, come now, no proselytising in an empty house. We're all men here. I've no glasses. Drink from the bottle.'

Monsieur Le Couec took a swig.

'Revolting! I suppose it was kept in the kitchen to flambé the game.'

'Never mind the bottle –'

'Oh ho! I'll stop you there, if you don't mind, Antoine du Courseau. Calvados was not invented for idiots … '

Jean giggled.

'No, Father, it was invented for you.'

'My dear boy, belt up. Sport is a very fine thing, but don't go round trying to convert everybody.'

'Jean doesn't drink,' Antoine said. 'He's getting ready for the future, for that uncertain planet on which I have no desire whatsoever to land. I've never led you into temptation, have I, Jean?'

'Yes, you have, Monsieur, but without knowing you were.'

'From today, you're to call me Antoine. It will annoy my wife intensely. I ought to have thought of it earlier.'

'Thank you, Antoine.'

'Can I point out,' the abbé said, 'that we've nothing left to sit on? My feet are aching. This whole place looks like a rout.'

They sat on the floor, on tiles strewn with sawdust by the removers. The abbé was on form.

'Well, this is a moment to take stock. A unique occasion. Not a terribly solemn location. Thanks to the moon we can see a little of

173

each other. Not too much. Besides, we all know each other's faces: my ugly mug, Antoine's, which has collected a certain ruddiness of its own, with age and training, Jean's handsome countenance. Let me take this opportunity, dear boy, to point out to you that in this life a handsome face is a handicap to be overcome. You are going to arouse some serious resentment. By way of compensation, girls will fall into your arms like manna upon the poor and needy. Mind how you go. That is what an elderly priest advises. Now, where were we? Who has bought this house?'

'The Longuets,' Antoine said.

The abbé tipped up the bottle and swallowed another mouthful. He did not like embarrassing situations. This one deeply offended his sense of tradition, and he hesitated over the standpoint he should take. Madame Longuet was perhaps not such a saintly woman as he liked to tell himself, but, at least towards him, she behaved with uncommon generosity. He even believed that deep down she was sincere in her faith, trying to leave her past behind and working with all her being towards redemption, of her soul and others'. Of course Monsieur Longuet did not inspire much confidence, and as for young Gontran, he had the makings of an out-and-out miscreant, despite his mother's good example.

'Well, Father, what do you think?' Jean asked, delighted to see the priest on the defensive.

'Nothing, my child. I think absolutely nothing. People do what they wish with their money. The Longuets have money. It is no more a crime to have money than not have any. I believe they will respect La Sauveté.'

'What about my parents?'

'Your father has had words with both Monsieur Longuet and the son. He should have shown more patience—'

'I wonder if they've emptied the cellar,' said Antoine, who could not care less about the Longuets. 'Actually there wasn't much left. A cellar is the work of a lifetime. I drank my father's and I'm not leaving one for my son. I was right about that, at least. He only drinks water.'

'Antoinette would definitely have appreciated it!' Jean ventured to say.

'Antoinette? Do you think so?'

'Let's go and see,' said the abbé, rather interested in the idea.

When dawn broke they were to be found outside, on a bench, with two empty bottles at their feet. Jean slept. Grangeville's parish priest was a little pale, but his speech was clear. Antoine felt tiredness overwhelming him and calculated that caution dictated a departure later in the day. A silhouette roused them from their lethargy. Albert was watering the flowerbeds. Antoine called to him.

'Who are you watering for?'

'For the honour of it, Captain.'

'There's no honour left.'

'You'll never make me believe that. And Jean would be better off in his bed. I hope he hasn't been drinking.'

'Don't worry. He's a man now, and a responsible one.'

Jean opened his eyes onto a new world. La Sauveté, emptied of its furniture, no longer symbolised anything for him, and despite his persistence he had been unable to extract any information about his birth from either the abbé or Monsieur du Courseau. He felt weary and stiff, the opposite of how he wanted to feel for Sunday's challenges.

'Well, dear boy, we slept!' the abbé said, retying his bootlaces before he set out for the rectory.

'Nowhere near enough. I don't feel at all well.'

'You sporty types! What weeds you are! Now at your age—'

'At my age, Father, you definitely weren't rowing.'

'Not rowing! What's punting, then?'

'We're not talking about the same thing.'

Jean was feeling increasingly resentful towards the abbé. He was an excellent man, but he knew ... Was he still supposed to feel bound by the seal of the confessional in a case like this?

'Go to bed!' Albert said in a tone that he intended to sound peremptory.

A day of the purest pink was breaking behind the trees. Antoine kissed Jean.

'We shall meet again. I shan't forget you.'

'How will I know where you are?'

'You and I don't need an address. You'll find me.'

The abbé, standing, stretched out his arms. He looked like a scarecrow. A strong smell came from his threadbare cassock.

'I have a mass at seven o'clock.'

'See you later, Father,' Jean said.

'See you later, my boy.'

Jean walked past Albert, who pretended not to see him. Antoine stroked the Bugatti's bonnet, damp with dew.

'We shall see the priest home, and then set out for the south!' he whispered to his car.

'I shall walk, if you don't mind,' the abbé said. 'Some gentle *jogging*, that's the way to stay healthy.'

'I didn't know you spoke English.'

'Neither did I!'

'Farewell, Albert. Don't hold all this against me.'

'I don't hold it against you, Captain. Jeanne was the one who cried all night.'

'My family didn't cry at all.'

'It's not the same thing.'

Antoine decided not to pursue the subject. He opened the driver's door and climbed into his coupé. The Atalante's starter turned once and was replaced by the engine's soft rumble. He smiled. He waved joyfully to the gardener and the priest who were watching him, their heads bare, and he did not even glance at the house he was leaving behind him. It meant nothing any longer. He was already thinking about Marie-Dévote's breasts and Toinette's cool little arms around his neck. As he drove out of the gates he told himself that he would never see this house again nor, very probably, his children. Life had gone by very quickly, and all that stood out from its colourlessness were the sparkling pictures of the bay of Saint-Tropez as it appeared on the way down the scent-drenched slopes from Grimaud, and of Marie-Dévote as a girl, her skirt hitched up above her long olive-skinned legs, washing the gutted fish in the wavelets that lapped and spread on the flat sand. He was tempted to try to make it to the Midi without stopping, but after making a small misjudgement on a bend he realised how tired he was and decided to sleep just outside Rouen. After dinner, fed and rested, he set out for Lyon as night fell. The 3.3 litres of the 57S accelerated effortlessly to 150 kilometres an hour, and on the straights the speedometer needle ran out at 200.

Let us leave Antoine du Courseau for now. Relieved of all that weighed upon him only the day before, he is driving away to the only life he loves, carrying a cheque in his pocket that represents his last assets. But despite what he says, he is not a man to fear the future. When he is near Marie-Dévote, the future does not exist. Nothing counts apart from her. We are, as you will have guessed, in 1936. Léon Blum has been prime minister since June. Sylvère Maes, a Belgian, has won the Tour de France, and at the Olympic Games Germany, with forty-nine gold medals, has become the leading nation of the sporting world. We French have had to make do with Despeaux and Michelot's golds in boxing, Charpentier's in cycling, Fourcade and Tapié's bronzes in the coxed pair, and Chauvigné, Cosmat and the Vandernotte brothers' in the coxed four. But cycling has lost its fascination for Jean. Even Antonin Magne's victory at the World Championship has failed to keep his interest alive. He has abandoned racing handlebars and competition rims for a touring bike with low-pressure tyres. Rowing has taken over as his passion, from the day he saw young Englishmen rowing on the Thames at Hampton Court. With Geneviève's money and another postal order from the prince, he has bought himself a scull and trains regularly, every Saturday and Sunday. He has taken part in several competitions, so far without success, but he has been noticed and at Dieppe Rowing Club the coaches are keen to team him with another rower in a coxless pair. He is not sure, he prefers to row solo, find his own ideal rhythm, because he has a slow start but always finishes faster than his opponents, despite so far failing to make up all of the lost time. Rowing entirely satisfies his idea of what sport should be. It demands total energy, consummate skill and a permanently alert tactical intelligence. It's also the most complete sort of athleticism, developing shoulders, biceps, stomach muscles and legs. At seventeen, Jean is a superb young man of almost six foot, broad-shouldered and with long, strong legs; he is not particularly talkative, as if he is afraid of wasting his strength or disapproves of the futile verbal excitement of the world he lives in. When a competition finishes he is not to be seen mixing with other club members, but in the changing room, where he showers at length as part of his rigorous routine of hygiene in both physical and dietary spheres. Lastly, in June he took his baccalauréat in philosophy and passed with distinction. Jeanne was all the prouder because she has no idea what philosophy is, and feels, with her habitual modesty, that it is too late for her to ask Monsieur the abbé to explain it to her. Albert, apparently better informed, grumbled something along the lines of 'philosophy doesn't put food on a man's table'. Albert is ageing, and recent events have given his pacifism a battering. He votes socialist more out of loyalty than credulity, and no longer believes in the slogan 'Socialism for peace'. Germany is back, united and terrifying. Not yet armed, as a nation it nevertheless represents an enormous physical mass at which no one wants to take the first shot. Its youth and enthusiasm are humiliating in a lamentably weak and divided Europe. Albert no longer knows what to think. There are times when he would prefer to die, so as not to have to see what is going to happen. To be proud of Jean he would have to forget that this handsome, healthy, intelligent boy isn't his son. He cannot. Jean is so utterly different. And as the months go by, the gulf between them widens, though the boy has never expressed the slightest suspicion or made the least wounding remark about his adoptive parents. Does he know? Albert wonders. Too many people around the family do. Somehow the truth must have come out.

On the evening of his baccalauréat result, after a long series of skirmishes, Antoinette at last allowed Jean to go the whole way. It happened at La Sauveté. Marie-Thérèse du Courseau was away, driving Michel to Switzerland. Antoinette organised things well, and the ceremony took place according to certain rituals that she had imagined for a long time. First they drank a bottle of champagne in the kitchen, and then she said, 'My bra is awfully tight.'

'Well, take it off then.'

He could not work out exactly how she managed to undo it without unbuttoning her blouse, but within a minute the bra was on the table and he was touching it, a simple, modest item of girl's underwear, its only concession to decoration a tiny satin rose stitched between the two cups. He held it to his face and breathed Antoinette's smell. She smiled and looked down. Her blouse was transparent, and Jean marvelled at the softness and poise of her breasts. He stopped listening to her almost as soon as she began to tell some inconsequential story, no doubt to hide her own confusion, equal to his, now that he knew the moment had come. All the pain of waiting, of being forestalled, was swept away. She was there, facing him, barely protected by the width of the pine table, in which the cook's knife had scored dark lines that danced before his eyes like cabbalistic signs. The moment was approaching and, having desired it for so long, it was delicious to postpone it a little longer with bold teasing and feigned modesty. A few minutes later, as she walked upstairs, she unhooked her pleated skirt, revealing her soft, prettily rounded bottom encased in girlish white cotton knickers. On the landing she took off her blouse. They kissed each other for a long time, standing up, leaning against the banister rail and stroking each other affectionately until Antoinette pulled Jean into her mother's bedroom and onto a four-poster bed overlooked by a heavy crucifix. There she undressed him with disarming tenderness and countless kisses. Antoinette was no more beautiful than before, with a fairly ugly nose (her father's) and dull blond hair (her mother's), but her creamy skin and well-rounded figure, her deliciously soft thighs, her marvellous breasts, so free and mobile under his fingers, and the scent of her neck filled him with hunger. She was one of those creatures that you want to eat more than penetrate, as if their skin, when you bite it, will satisfy some deep, unacknowledged greed. What a mistake it would be just to enter her! He felt he would like the opposite to happen, for her to melt and disappear inside him, inside his chest, his stomach, his legs and arms, so that they would then be just one and the same being, taking its pleasure from itself. Of course he was clumsy the first time. He wanted her so much, and had so often dreamt of this precise moment, when she would squeeze him between her thighs, that he was unable to wait. Antoinette consoled him, stroking the back of his neck, before leading him into her father's bedroom, where there was no crucifix, only some prints of the Battle of Hastings. There he managed to be less clumsy, and by the time they began again in Michel's bedroom he had learnt how to watch for the beginnings of Antoinette's climax by the way her pink mouth began to tremble. Finally she drew him into her own bed, where they stayed until dawn, repeating their caresses without drawing breath, and then one last time, on the floor in the hall, where she came to see him out and shut the door behind him.

'That's it, it's done,' he said to himself, heading back to the lodge, where Albert would soon be getting up, strapping on his wooden leg and making his coffee before starting his first round of morning's watering. Jean's body was on fire; he was bruised all over and exhausted. In a few days he would be seventeen. It was not too early or too late. He spared a thought for Bergson and creative evolution, which had inspired such a brilliant philosophy essay that Antoinette had finally granted him the reward he craved. Thank you, thank you, Bergson! As that summer began, life was starting to open up for Jean. In future all women would be like her, except that perhaps they would not often have the same fresh and creamy taste, and going to bed with them would not be such a glorious act of bravado. That night, the two of them had exorcised La Sauveté, they had got their own back on Marie-Thérèse and Michel, and even though Jean slightly regretted having used Antoine's bed, he would never forget their last lovemaking on the hard, threadbare rug in the hall.

Jean slept, recovered his strength and, waking, wanted Antoinette all over again, but she remained invisible. He thought himself liberated from desire the following day, taken prisoner again the day after, freed once more when he saw her with Gontran Longuet in his car, a Georges Irat two-seater convertible, an inept copy of the famous English Morgan. How dare the daughter of a Bugatti-lover agree to park her bottom on the seat of such a phoney sports car? He felt sorry for her inability to appreciate the gulf that separated the two machines.

At Dieppe Rowing Club he asked his coach what he thought about women. The coach answered, 'Jean, physical love is physical exercise like any other. Certainly it tires you, and I wouldn't recommend it the day before a competition, but I'm not as rigorous as many coaches I know: there are muscular exertions a man can't do without. Love, on the other hand, is a catastrophe: I mean being in love. I've seen first-class sportsmen reduced to crybabies because some salesgirl stood them up. Everything that happens below the belt is healthy. Everything that attacks an athlete's competitive concentration is unhealthy. I hope you understand what I'm saying.'

'Yes, Monsieur.'

So how, from this point onwards, should he think of Chantal de Malemort? Jean reflected that she had never tormented him nor beguiled him with false hopes, that when they met in secret in the forest of Arques they talked to each other as friends would, with genuine sincerity, though when she left him he always felt slightly light-headed. The meetings had become increasingly important during the summer of 1936. Early in the morning Jean would get on his bicycle and ride to the forest, where he would put on his spikes and set off on his training run, heading for an intersection of two paths marked by a handsome clump of beeches. It was unusual for her not to arrive at the same time as he did, on her bay mare. They would push on together, further into the underbrush, he running, she at a trot, for half an hour before returning to the cross-way, where they would finally sit down together on a stump, catch their breath and talk. Chantal had not disappointed expectations. She remained the same pretty, frail-looking creature, although I say *frail-looking* because you only had to see her on a horse to judge her energy and her strength. Her hair had darkened and the healthy life she led at Malemort, on horseback and on her father's tractors, had put some pink into her complexion. Her voice was no longer small and shy, which at her age – the same as Jean – would have sounded vapid and sentimental.

What did they talk about? We might be surprised to learn that two such young people, feeling a more than negligible attraction, never confided to each other what they fretted about when they were apart. The subject remained taboo. An invisible barrier separated them, of which they were not even aware. Yet the more they believed they were talking about nothing in particular, the more they were confiding to each other.

'Have you noticed,' Chantal said, 'how sad a season summer is? The days are shortening, and we're getting ready to go into the dark. The weather is lovely, but it's an illusion. I prefer winter, when the trees have no leaves, the woods are full of skeletons, and the days are lengthening again. You feel as if you're coming out of a tunnel.'

'I don't know any more, I can't decide. I think I'd like to live in the tropics: six months' wet season, six months' dry. You know exactly where you are. Spring and autumn are both silly seasons, neither one thing nor the other.'

Or:

'What are you going to do after your exams?' she asked. 'My father says studying is no use, you need to get to grips with life very early. Apparently the world is full of specialists and you can't find anybody who knows how to do everything: harvest the wheat, drive a tractor, buy a horse, cook, sail a yacht, help a woman give birth on a desert island, or fix a tap.'

'I completely agree with your father, but mine is self-taught, so knowledge fills him with suspicion and secret desire in equal amounts. He hoped he'd make a gardener out of me, but flowers bore me, and now he has decided that I should be, as he says, a "scholar". You can see what he's doing: it's his dream, to make up for what he never had.'

'What sort of scholar? You're not very good at maths, are you?'

'Do you suppose my father really makes a distinction between maths and literature?'

'Well … '

'I don't think so!'

Having plucked up courage, he burst out, 'I'm not Albert and Jeanne Arnaud's son. I'm a foundling they adopted.'

'I know.'

'Does everybody know?'

'Everybody? No. Some people.'

'So I was the last to find out.'

'Does it upset you?'

'No, I'm just asking myself questions all the time. And I'd like to know everything about where and how I came into the world. Who's going to tell me?'

'You shouldn't think about it.'

'I can't help it.'

Sometimes they liked to talk about their favourite sport.

'Don't you want to ride sometimes?'

'No. I like having my feet on the ground. Or wheels. Or maybe a scull. In a scull I fly over the water. Speed isn't everything, because there are ways of going a lot faster, but in a scull I feel weightless. The oars skim the surface. You can't imagine the delicacy of what you're doing. The drive, the catch, the recovery are all calculated to the centimetre. I'm the machine. I'm proud of that.'

'But there's one thing missing. The pleasure of control. I control my horse, and from the horse I control the places I go to, as if I was a giant.'

'I'd be scared to marry a giant.'

Chantal was silent. He had contravened their unspoken agreement. Not by much, but enough to make her feel uncomfortable.

'Some giants can bend their knees,' she said finally.

'That's reassuring.'

One day he mentioned Michel.

'You shouldn't say anything against him,' she retorted. 'He not only doesn't say anything against you, he actually admires you.'

'Michel admires me? Now you're making fun of me. He's hated me since we were children.'

'Perhaps he envies you.'

'He has everything. I have nothing. He draws really well. Maybe he'll become a great painter. His name is Michel du Courseau, and his mother will give him anything he asks for.'

'Then why do you think he's always drawing portraits of you?'

'I didn't know that. His main models are the neighbours' son, who's very handsome, or Élias, the Longuets' young gardener.'

'His mother has shown us lots of drawings of you. Apparently his bedroom walls are covered in them.'

Jean tried to remember the night he had made love to Antoinette on Michel's bed. He hadn't looked at anything surrounding him, hadn't looked at anything at all apart from Antoinette's white body.

'The idea gives me the creeps,' he said. 'Anyway, why is his mother always pushing him in your direction?'

'I know, it's a bit comical. In the beginning I thought he was shy, then I thought he must have some sort of aversion to me. Now I don't really think about him at all. I think we could be friends. But he's so strange … '

She mounted her mare and rode off at a slow trot down the empty path, which the sun riddled with shafts of light between the leaves. Jean waited for her to disappear before sprinting back to his bicycle at the edge of the wood.

In the first two months of 1936 Jean had found a part-time job in a bookshop at Dieppe. The bookseller was a young man, Joseph Outen, who had started the business recently and was full of enthusiasm. Jean had met him at the Rowing Club, where they trained together on Sundays. In the changing room Joseph expressed surprise at Jean's absence the last three Sundays.

'You're wrong not to train regularly. Regularity counts more than anything else.'

'I was taking my philosophy bac.'

'Did you pass?'

'Yes.'

'What did you you get?'

'Distinction.'

Joseph looked at Jean in a different light. Questioning him, he perceived that he was intelligent but incredibly ignorant. He explained to Jean that sport for sport's sake was a folly as great as literature for literature's sake … The young bookseller was an agile, muscular athlete who had a nicely dark, clipped beard and smoked a pipe. He loved literature and sport with an equal passion, and treated all writers with suspicion until he discovered their view on the subject. For a single excellent page about boxing, he had read everything Maeterlinck had written. He thought highly of Giraudoux, a former university 400 metres champion, Morand who drove racing Bugattis and hunted foxes, Montherlant because he had written *The Eleven Before the Golden Door*, Hemingway for his short story 'Fifty Grand', Byron for having swum the bay of La Spezia from Portovenere, Maupassant because he loved sailing. One can hardly disagree that, though not the only way to get interested in books and writers, as biases go it was far from stupid, and there were and are plenty of others a good deal less reliable. Jean's ignorance, however, was not because of sport but because he lived in a house without books. Yes, we have seen him reading one evening, in the kitchen, during one of those family gatherings from which he preferred to keep his distance. He could borrow books from the lycée's library, but had to wait his turn. Albert and Jeanne had never read a book in their life. Albert would say it wore out your eyes to no purpose, and Jeanne that, once read, a book was no more than a dust trap. Marie-Thérèse du Courseau, having given Jean several volumes of the Hetzel edition of Jules Verne for Christmas, had stopped giving him presents after the alleged incident with Antoinette. Captain Duclou had given him an atlas and Monsieur Cliquet a book about railways. The school curriculum betrayed a considerable mistrust of literature, using it simply as a pool of texts selected for their value as grammatical examples, of which Lamartine's 'The Lake' was the apogee. Joseph Outen, with his passion for books, broke through this torpor. He had wanted to write, but had rapidly resigned himself to not being the equal of his great models and to introducing them instead to a public intimidated by such literary audacity and diversity. His job, as he saw it, was to guide those timid souls who came into a bookshop on the pretext of buying an envelope, and as they did so stole secret glances at its forbidden fruits, in the shape of the new books on display. Practised as an apostolic mission, bookselling is a philanthropic task. Joseph Outen began the conversion of his Rowing Club teammate-cum-sales assistant, and immediately found such fertile ground that they decided to shut the shop at five o'clock to give themselves up completely to reading. Jean was overwhelmed. He had imagined writers merely as glorious statues, yet here was a man as famous as Stendhal confessing his youth in all the naïve unsophistication of its first impulses and presenting his account to his readers with perfect ingenuousness. There was, then, no shame in being young, not the way adults wanted to make you believe, saying every time you advanced the slightest opinion, 'Wait till you've grown up a little. We fought at Verdun. When you've done what we did, then you can speak.' According to Stendhal, it was no crime to make mistakes, to give in to your enthusiasms, to be happy or unhappy because a girl made you suffer. Writers whose memories were preserved by literature revealed their youth, unvarnished.

At the beginning of September 1936, Joseph Outen was obliged to admit to Jean that business was not going well. In the face of the last three months' economic and social tumult in France, everyone was reacting the same way. They did not go without a litre of wine or a can of petrol, but they went without books. Publishing's doldrums had reached the bookshops.

'I'm sacking you,' Joseph said. 'Without notice, with nothing. Since you're not a union member, don't even think of taking me to court …'

'I'll stay. For nothing. Not a centime.'

'That would be capitalist exploitation. No. Let's go our separate ways. I've infected you with a vice. It's your bad luck. Deal with it the best way you can. Here's your month's money. Take your bike and go wherever you want.'

'Wherever doesn't exist. I want to know where.'

'I don't know … go and look for Stendhal in Italy.'

'Where exactly?'

'On his tomb it says, "Arrigo Beyle, Milanese". Go to Milan. Look. You'll find it.'

'To Parma?'

'That's the one place he isn't. You need to go further.'

'Then I'll go to Civitavecchia too.'

'As you like. It's nothing to do with me. Send me some postcards. Goodbye.'

Joseph Outen knew how to be offhand when he had to. He would continue, alone, the tireless task of bringing lost and lonely customers to the pleasures of literature. Jean would have liked to kiss him, as he would have a brother, but between two athletes it was not done.

'I shan't forget!' he said.

'We'll see about that.'

We will come across Joseph Outen again, following a new destiny. He still has to go bankrupt, to start and abandon a thousand things, to join up in 1939, serve in the infantry on the Maginot Line, and answer the call in a prisoner of war camp. But let us not get ahead of the story.

The same day Jean began the task of winning his father over to the idea of his journey. Albert was so flabbergasted that he did not know what to say. He had consented to the London journey four years earlier because Antoine du Courseau had been the instigator of that escapade. But Italy! In that nation of Fascists, who knew what might happen? They assassinated socialist leaders like Matteotti, and force-fed their opponents with castor oil after throwing them into the fountains in Rome. At the Vatican there lived the world's obscurantist-in-chief. Here Jeanne protested in the name of the Holy Father. If her son could receive the Sunday blessing from the window of Saint Peter's, she would be as happy as if she herself had made the pilgrimage there. Jean saw a chink of light. Where Fascism was concerned, he was entirely in the dark. He wanted to see palaces, monuments, sculptures. He did not mention Stendhal, whose name would have meant nothing to his parents. Albert declared that there were more than enough monuments and châteaux in France for Jean not to need to bother to see what there was in Italy. The discussion might have gone on for ever without the intervention of the abbé, who took Jean's side. He had been to Rome when he was young and had retained a dazzling memory of it, even though in his hotel for ecclesiastical visitors he had been robbed of two pairs of underpants and a missal. Albert gave in, with an obscure premonition that he was losing his son for good. But could he say 'his son'? Each time he had the thought he found his paternal authority paralysed. Besides, Jean had earned the money for his journey. He could not, in all fairness, be refused the opportunity to use it as he wished.

Ten days after the sale of La Sauveté, Jean boarded the train for Paris. He had never visited the capital, but he did not stop there. A taxi took him and his bicycle to the Gare de Lyon. The bicycle was loaded into the baggage car, and the train for Milan pulled out. But that is another chapter.

Certain to leave one another tomorrow, we hasten,
my colonel and I, to say to each other in a few words
all the most interesting things we have to say.

Stendhal

Was this truly the town that Henri Beyle had so loved? You might not have thought so. Trams clashed in the narrow streets, shaking windows that remained permanently shut, cars chased pedestrians onto pavements, people advanced with urgent steps, head down and cheeks unshaven, a low cottony sky crushed Milan beneath its factories' smoke, owners of palaces barricaded themselves behind studded doors guarded by bulky doormen in white gloves, and La Scala was shut. Of course in the Galleria, where it emerged onto the Piazza del Duomo, it was still possible to find some of that easy -going atmosphere Stendhal had liked so much: the *disoccupati* in sandals rolling cigarettes of dark tobacco, the girls in pairs, arm in arm, pausing in front of shop windows to examine their pursuers, the ice-cream sellers bawling their monotonous cries of '*gelati*' that ricocheted off the glasswork, a man in discussion with another suddenly making an obscene gesture with hand and elbow, a blind man offering lottery tickets beneath the suspicious gaze of a couple of carabinieri whose white leatherware and wide red stripes down their trouser seams were incongruous in the daily grind of a crowd surviving on espresso coffee and watermelon seeds.

Jean rapidly discovered his inability to see behind the mask of this foreign city, where the only people who addressed him were those who had something to sell and the only people who smiled were tarts painted as though they were on their way to mass. He wrote a postcard to Joseph Outen: 'Arrigo wasn't at the meeting place. I'm pushing on further.' Further was Parma, 150 kilometres away, covered in two days at the meandering speed of a tourist, sleeping in a barn and washing himself in a fountain where an old woman, cackling, drenched him with a large bucket of water. The weather was ideal for a fine ride along a well-maintained road between plump fields bordered by young poplars. If not for the cars that nearly grazed him as they raced past at terrifying speed, he would have felt complete pleasure at letting himself roll southwards on his comfortable bicycle. What was it with Italians and cars? They drove around in patched-up Fiats and Lancias with open exhausts and thought they were Tazio Nuvolari, the wraith-like champion in the yellow shirt who walked off with every prize for Alfa Romeo, or the burly Campari in his checked cap, or the battler Ascari. Jean noted that they rarely rode bicycles. Cycling had been in decline since Bottecchia's 1925 Tour de France victory. The country needed a new champion. People were starting to talk about a pious, athletic young man named Gino Bartali, but the lack of international prizes in the last decade had kept bicycles out of fashion, while the successes of Alfa Romeo and Maserati, battling wheel for wheel with Bugatti, Mercedes-Benz and Auto-Union, had raised Italians' mechanical passion to fever pitch. The country was in the grip of a hysteria of popping exhausts and speed. Jean was thus delighted when, after his wash at the fountain, he saw a boy of his own age approaching on a black bicycle with sit-up-and-beg handlebars. He had straw-coloured hair, a blushing complexion, and wore leather shorts with shoulder straps. He was also shirtless. Luggage elastics kept a sleeping bag and large satchel strapped to his carrier. He spoke French very well, with a strong German accent, and introduced himself straight away by his first name: Ernst.

Ernst is called on to play a role in this chapter, for which I crave your forgiveness. The proper thing to do would have been to talk about him in the opening pages, as also another character, Constantin Palfy, who is about to make an appearance. But I am not writing a novel. All we are talking about is the life of Jean Arnaud, and it is inevitable that in the course of the story this boy found in a basket will see a good many people enter his life: some will stay with us, others will detach themselves, like the lowest branches of a tree. So let me say here and now that, even though we are still four years away from 1940, we will see Yann and Monsieur Carnac again, and, soon, the prince and Salah. Geneviève, the invisible Geneviève, will appear at a moment of her choosing. We will be bringing back, briefly, Antoine du Courseau. As for Marie-Thérèse, Antoinette and Michel, they are not the sort of characters to let themselves be tossed aside. Mireille Cece is not far away. Marie-Dévote, Théo and Toinette will keep us waiting, but their return will not lack for unforeseen elements. Sadly we must lament the passing of a few faces. Captain Duclou is getting old. He will die the day the Germans excavate his garden on the cliff top to build one of the bunkers for their Atlantic defences, take down his weathercock rigged on the highest ridge of his roof, and remove his aneroid barometer, which they judge to be dangerous. He will have himself buried with weathercock and barometer in his coffin. Monsieur Cliquet will fare no better: obsessed by the go-slow strikes of 1936, he spends his time calculating impossible itineraries to Nice, Lille and Istanbul, though he has not moved from Grangeville for more than fifteen years. The delays he encounters, however fictitious, demoralise him to such an extent that people begin to wonder if he is not becoming a little strange in the head. His absurd end is something I shall recount later. Saddest of all is undoubtedly the fate of Albert and Jeanne. We shall come back to them in good time. But let no one accuse Jean of ingratitude. He loves his adoptive parents dearly and will be loyal to them till the end, yet he is from a different stock, and now that he has broken out from their very restricted universe by travelling to London, sleeping with Antoinette, reading the books lent to him by Joseph Outen, and, at this moment, riding far and wide with Ernst over Italian roads, he will never go back.

Our young German is, therefore, an occasional character. It would certainly be enjoyable to imagine that during the great upheaval that will, by its end, have whittled Europe away to almost nothing, he will again meet, at some bend in the road or the bottom of some shell-hole, his French friend from the summer of 1936. What a marvellous scene one could write, recounting their reunion in enemy uniforms! I can already see them shaking hands instead of murdering each other as the rules of war demand, recalling to each other their happy hours on the Lombardy plain, their climb up to the Passo della Futa between Bologna and Florence, their arrival in Rome browned by the sun. Unfortunately the war, so potentially fertile in coincidences, will not supply that opportunity, and each of them will pursue his destiny without influencing the other. I can even tell you at once Ernst's fate in the great cataclysm to come: enlisted in a tank regiment in September 1939 for the invasion of Poland, sergeant during the French campaign, in which he and his unit will reach Bordeaux, lieutenant by spring 1941, as Panzer divisions flatten the Soviet wheatfields. Attached to the Legion of French Volunteers as an interpreter, he will glimpse, along with his French mercenaries posted to the vanguard by Hitler in memory of Napoleon, a signpost indicating 'Moscow 12 kilometres', before retreating with his comrades and being promoted to captain outside Stalingrad. In 1943 we shall find him in Italy again, a tank officer without a tank, first fighting an infantry battle against General Juin's Moroccans at Monte Cassino, then against partisans in the Abruzzi. In 1945, at twenty-five, he will be a major, Iron Cross first class, wounded three times, never seriously, and will return home, boots full of holes and uniform in tatters, to discover that his home in Cologne no longer exists, that his father, mother and sister were all killed in a bombing raid. He will commit suicide by biting a cyanide capsule as two members of the British Military Police arrive to arrest him in the cellar, where he has taken up residence with the rats.

This devastating future of fire, blood, glory and desolation did not yet weigh on the young man who leant his bike next to Jean's and thrust his blond head into the fountain. When he straightened up with his eyelashes glued together and hair, suddenly less blond, plastered to his head, he burst out laughing.

'You're French?' he asked.

'Yes. How do you know?'

Ernst burst out laughing a second time, pointing at the maker's name on Jean's bicycle.

'I know everything!' he said. 'Except whether you're heading north or south.'

'South.'

'Like me. Shall we ride together?'

'With pleasure. I'd like to stop at Parma this afternoon.'

'There's nothing to see at Parma,' Ernst said.

'Yes, there is. Some Correggios, especially a fresco of a Madonna blessed by Jesus in the library, which moved Stendhal to tears.'

'Stendhal? That sounds like a German name.'

'No, he was from the Dauphiné. His real name was Henri Beyle.'

'Is he your god?'

'I don't have a god yet. To be honest, I'm utterly ignorant, as I discover every day. Three months ago I didn't even know Stendhal's name.'

'I didn't know it two minutes ago.'

'You've got an excuse. What's your name?'

'Ernst. In French it's Ernst. What's yours?'

'Jean. How do you say it in German?'

'Hans. If you like I'll call you Hans and you can call me Ernst.'

'Okay. Shall we make a start?'

Riding with Ernst was a pleasure. He kept up a steady pace without the slightest exertion and produced an unbroken stream of conversation. Very soon Jean knew that his father was a philosophy professor at Cologne, and that as he was on the point of leaving, his father had played a rotten trick on him.

'As it happens, I'd packed a copy of *Mein Kampf* in my satchel—'

'What's *Mein Kampf*?'

'What? Don't you know? I can see you really are an ignoramus. Have you ever heard of Adolf Hitler?'

'A bit. My father says he's a warmonger, and Léon Blum says at the next elections the socialists will cut him down to size.'

Ernst again burst into laughter. His cheerfulness appeared to be indestructible.

'Is your father a socialist?' he asked.

'Yes. A pacifist socialist. He fought in the last war and lost a leg.'

'That's uncanny! My father fought in the last war too, he's a social democrat and he lost his left arm in the forest of Argonne. Maybe they both shot each other? Who knows.'

'Yes, who knows. What about your *Mein Kampf*?'

'In a book that he wrote in prison, Hitler spelt out his whole programme step by step: how he'll annex Austria, take back Dantzig, remake Poland's borders, and gather into one great Reich the German minorities who have been oppressed since the Treaty of Versailles. And he will do it, I guarantee it. Your Léon Blum can't have read *Mein Kampf*.'

'And I urge you to notice that your Hitler hasn't yet accomplished his programme.'

'Yes, he has. The first point. And only this year – France has a short memory – he remilitarised the Rhineland.'

'That's true, I'd forgotten. Well, let's see what happens next. It's nothing to gloat about, nobody tried to stop him. So what about this *Mein Kampf*?'

'Well, I was sure I'd packed it in my satchel. But my father took it out and replaced it with a copy of Goethe's *Italian Journey*. I was beside myself with fury. I almost rode back to Cologne, but on the endpaper Papa had written, "To my dear boy, for him to dream now and then." So I said to myself, All right, this is my holiday. When I get back from Italy I'll have plenty of time to study *Mein Kampf* in the evenings at my Hitler Youth meetings.'

'You're a Nazi?'

'Of course, like every boy my age. What about you?'

'Me? I'm not anything. I don't care and I don't understand their blasted politics. I sit my exams and when I have a few hours free I row at Dieppe Rowing Club.'

'Rowing? I'd like that. But you French weren't all that brilliant this year at the Olympics, were you? What's wrong with you?'

'I don't know what you want. In cycling the medals all went our way: road race, team road race, team pursuit, 1000 metres time trial, sprint and tandem sprint.'

'All right, all right. Don't get cross, Hans. Cycling's a great sport. What about rowing?'

'Only two bronzes.'

In the middle of the day they stopped at a small trattoria in a village that dozed at the side of the main road. Three steps led down to a low, vaulted room invaded by flies. Workers, their chins stuck out pugnaciously, sucked large forkfuls of spaghetti in tomato sauce, wiping their mouths with pieces of bread they then chewed slowly, with dreamy expressions on their faces.

'Watch how they do it!' Ernst whispered. 'It's a special technique. When we've worked it out, we can order some. It's not expensive and it's nourishing. Before we do, we can try some polenta. It fills you up, and I'm famished.'

They devoured two portions of polenta each. Jean thought he might choke and asked for some wine. He was served with a red Bardolino that was as thick as shoe cream. When they had finished eating, they staggered outside and wobbled several kilometres down the road before stopping next to a field.

'I suggest we have a lie-down,' Ernst said.

'I think that may be preferable. My legs feel like cotton wool.'

They fell asleep in the shade of a hedge and were woken up by an elderly farm labourer with his dog, cursing them. Ernst could only laugh. The man had a stick, which he raised. Jean grabbed it from him and threw it over the hedge. The old man picked up a stone. The dog barked furiously. Ernst pulled out a flick knife.

'No!' Jean said. 'We should go.'

'I'm going to teach the old fool how to behave.'

'No! Get on your bike.'

They rode away, pursued by the old man's curses and youths armed with sticks who came running from a neighbouring field.

'It's the first time I've seen that in Italy,' Ernst said. 'They're usually so welcoming.'

'It was bad luck.'

'Never mind! In an hour we'll be in Parma.'

They arrived at Parma at the end of the afternoon. Unluckily the library was closed, and there were no Correggio frescoes to be seen.

'Are you sure your friend Stendhal saw them?'

'I think he exaggerated a good deal, but does it matter?'

On the outskirts of Parma they saw a fine, shady grove of trees with a stream running through it.

'Let's stop!' Ernst said. 'We can sleep here.'

'But I haven't got a tent or even a sleeping bag.'

'We don't need them. It's a warm evening.'

He lit a fire, and they toasted bread and sardines splashed with olive oil. Jean pulled apples and sugar from his haversack and baked them in the embers.

'Delicious,' Ernst said. 'Only the French really know how to eat.'

'Who says any different?'

'My father. He and my mother only ever argue about that one subject. She's from Alsace, it has to be said, so she's a bit French around the edges.'

'What do you mean, "a bit French"! She's completely French, even if she was born before 1914.'

'Of course she was born before 1914, on German territory, in Strasbourg.'

'Ernst, you're pulling my leg.'

'Pulling your leg? I don't understand.'

'You're getting on my nerves! Now do you get it?'

Ernst was laughing.

'I get it. It's something I do. Now, listen carefully—'

'No. We've settled the Alsace question. French territory.'

'In *Mein Kampf*—'

'Oh, stuff *Mein Kampf*. Hitler's a crybaby. You only have to stamp your foot and he'll back down.'

'Stamp your foot. Go on.'

Jean pretended to stamp.

'There you are, all over. No more Hitler.'

'Well done!' Ernst exclaimed. 'Peace is declared.'

'And there wasn't even a war. Do you want another baked apple?'

'Not for me. Let's get some sleep. We can wash in the stream.'

Ernst was fixated with washing himself whenever he encountered fresh water. He soaped his pink and white body and rinsed himself in cold water, whistling the *Horst Wessel Lied*. Jean followed suit. Night was falling. A hundred metres away, cars roared along the road to Modena. They kept the fire going, to keep the mosquitoes away, and lay down side by side on the bare earth, sharing Ernst's sleeping bag as a pillow. Between the trees they glimpsed patches of black sky, glittering with stars.

'I'm happy,' Ernst said. 'We're living through a great time. The world is ours. We must defend what we have, but let's do it with a song on our lips, and if we have to die, we'll die so that our children can enjoy a golden age.'

'I'd be obliged if you would note that neither of us has children, so far, and no one is attacking us.'

'Ach, you filthy French sceptic! You're well fed, you don't belong to an oppressed minority, and you have no idea what it's like to hear your downtrodden brothers call to you for help when you've been disarmed and your hands are empty.'

'Listen, Ernst, let's talk about all that tomorrow. Tonight I'm ready to drop, and you're aggravating me with your oppressed brothers. Go to sleep!'

At midday the next day they arrived in the centre of Bologna. For both of them it was their first great Italian city for art. Ernst stopped in a square to read his Goethe. 'Venerable and learned old city … ' He wanted to climb a belfry to see the tiled roofs lauded by the poet. 'Neither damp nor moss attacks them.'

'What funny ideas he has, your Goethe! I wonder if anyone's still interested in details like that.'

'Goethe is a universal man. Nothing was alien to him. What does Stendhal say?'

Jean opened his little Beylian guide. 'A few lines, no more. He went to two concerts here. He was introduced to some scholars. "What fools!" he writes. "In Italy you get either raw geniuses, who astonish by their depth and lack of culture, or pedants who haven't the slightest idea."'

'Is that all?'

'Absolutely all.'

Ernst appeared deeply disappointed. The levity of the French was incorrigible. He set about demonstrating as much to Jean, but Jean was not listening, half dreaming instead of the plump young man who dashed to hear eighteen-year-old singers and discuss music endlessly with other music-lovers, while Goethe, driven by sudden inspiration, shut himself away to rewrite *Iphigenia auf Tauris*.

That evening they wandered under the arcades, mingling with much less excitable crowds than those in Milan. The girls they encountered were in groups of four and five. Their teeth gleamed as they laughed. They smelt sweetly of soap, and their young, sumptuous bodies seemed happy to be alive in the rediscovered coolness of the night.

'They're pretty,' Jean said.

'But not very fit!' Ernst remarked. 'I can't see any of them running the hundred metres.'

'Who's asking them to?'

'Me! You have a completely retrograde conception of women, Hans, as if they exist for enjoyment, for the pleasures of the pleasure-seeker. In Germany women are our equal. Their womb is the nation's future.'

'Ernst, you are a sad sack. I don't suppose your Goethe wrote anything about Italian women either.'

Ernst was silent. Goethe did not talk about women. He took no risks, unlike Stendhal. He was not a man to die from a badly treated dose of the clap. Ideas, poetry above all! And health! ! Ice-cream and cake vendors were calling out their wares on street corners, and the Bolognese were outside to sample one of the last fine summer evenings, deserting their stuffy houses with shutters closed on narrow streets that shook disagreeably at the passage of a tram. Behind bourgeois parents skinny little maids from Emilia-Romagna, bare-headed and dressed in black with white aprons around their waists, attempted to restrain children who shouted and squabbled. There were no beggars to be seen; they were forbidden. From this spectacle Jean drew a number of conclusions: that Italians liked to live in the street, where they could use loud voices and expansive gestures; they all knew each other and loved to lavish magnificent Signors, Signoras and Commendatores on each other. They were satisfied. Business was doing well. An order reigned of which they were proud. In Ethiopia their legions had reconquered an empire. Many of them loved to recite Gabriele d'Annunzio's poem, Mare nostrum. In Lombardy they were cold and prim, but the closer one got towards more human latitudes, the warmer they were and the more hospitable and curious about strangers. Ernst, on the other hand, felt uneasy at this loquacity, this good-humoured self-indulgence, this nation that sang so well individually and so poorly as a choir. The Hitler Youth had tried to forge closer ideological and military relations with the Fascist Balillas.[9] Without success: Balilla leaders considered the Nazis johnny-come-latelies at the party, absolute beginners as Fascists.

Around midnight Ernst and Jean reclaimed their bicycles from the garage that was looking after them and pressed on towards Tuscany. They found the road hard going, stopped at a village, found a barn to sleep in, and set off again early. Alone, either of them would have taken three days to make it over the mountains, but together, riding in relay to lessen the airstream, they reached the Tuscan border in a day. Late afternoon had plunged the clean, ordered, garden-like landscape into silence, and it lay resting there in its dense, handsomely dark ochre soil on which trees wrapped in white ruffs stood out. As they came closer they identified the trees as olives, being harvested by women with poles. In sheets stretched out below, children gathered up the olives that were then taken away by men with heavy basket-weave hoppers on their back. Workers called to them to offer them bread moistened with oil, tomatoes and onions, and a light, graceful, flower-scented white wine.

'If people get kinder and kinder the further south you go,' Ernst said, 'what must they be like at the equator? There must be a limit.'

'Why don't you go and find out! I'll wait here.'

'Don't be an idiot. Every country has its south.'

'Even Germany?'

'Even Germany. The Bavarians are our Italians.'

Jean still thought of himself as a Celt. He was wary of the south, believing it would soften him. Yet these Italians were bursting with pride. They seemed cheerful and welcoming, laughed easily, offered everything they had to impoverished passing strangers. What if Albert was wrong? What if the country luxuriated in Fascism the way Poppaea Sabina luxuriated in her bath of ass's milk? Ernst was a Nazi. Didn't he laugh all the time? Jean needed some explanations.

They asked if they could sleep in a barn. After supper they were shown to a double bed into which they fell, snoring like pigs, to be awoken the next morning by a fine male voice singing a popular song.

'Why don't we help them?' Ernst suggested.

They picked olives all day, with their backs aching and their legs weak from the pitcher of white wine being urged on them too often.

'I bet you,' Jean said during a brief pause, 'that your Goethe never picked an olive in his life.'

'What about Stendhal?'

'Nor him, as far as I know. But maybe at the end of the eighteenth and beginning of the nineteenth centuries it wasn't thought good taste to speak of the fruits of the earth. Having said that, I grant you that just this once Goethe and Stendhal stand shoulder to shoulder.'

At the end of the day they said goodbye to the farmer and his wife and son. It was time to get on to Florence. But they must have drunk too much white wine, and had to stop to sleep at the roadside. Finally, at midday the following day, they arrived at Florence and made straight for the Arno and Ponte Vecchio, greeting them with shouts of admiration. Muddy water of a handsome cream colour flowed either side of its enormous pillars. Ernst reached for his Goethe, then looked up, crestfallen.

'What's the matter?' Jean asked.

'I cannot tell a lie. These are the four lines he devotes to Florence: "I hastened through the city, saw the cathedral and its baptistery. Here again there opened to me a quite new world in which I did not wish to linger. The Boboli gardens are delightfully situated. I left as precipitately as I arrived." What about your Stendhal?'

It was Jean's turn to burst into laughter.

'He's no better. Listen: "Florence, situated in a narrow valley in the middle of bare mountains, has an unjustified reputation."'

'Ah, you reassure me. Might they both be mistaken?'

'Definitely.'

They spent two days in Florence, staying in a noisy and dirty small hotel. The Uffizi and the Duomo aroused their admiration, but no one addressed a word to them. They agreed that Florence was much too secret a city for the time they had to devote to it. In truth, Goethe and Stendhal had had the same impression, the first dreaming only of the Rome of the Caesars, the second only of opera.

'We'll come back,' Ernst said. 'Another time, when we have the key to Florence. I'm afraid that for now we're wasting our time.'

'You could be right.'

Eight years later Ernst was to pass through Florence again, after the battle of Monte Cassino. Standing in a truck, all he saw was Italians with their backs turned, the fires that had broken out in the wake of the shelling of the city, and the bombed Ponte Santa Trinità. He would never know Florence. He thought about Jean then, wondering what the great cataclysm had done with his companion from his first visit to Italy. In the pitiless mess of war, those who were forsaken looked vainly for their former brothers and encountered only the face of the enemy.

After Florence Goethe and Stendhal's routes had diverged. One had gone on via Perugia and Terni, the other had headed for Rome via Viterbo. Jean observed that Stendhal had overtaken the German. Ernst declared that it was not worth coming to Italy just to do everything as fast as you could. Besides, Goethe had talked to everybody, soldiers, carriers, smugglers and gendarmes, while Stendhal had only sought out the devotees of bel canto. The two young men halted at the roadside to discuss again at length the merits of their respective guides. In fact neither was being entirely sincere. Ernst found Goethe heavy and pontificating, and Jean was uncomfortable at Stendhal's pursuit of pleasure, which seemed too similar to his own. Had he been more sure of himself, he would have recognised in the little consul of Civitavecchia, so mischievously caricatured by Alfred de Musset's pencil, an equal in sensitivity and a fellow enthusiast.

Their one point of agreement was that, as they continued south, their haste gradually left them both. They pedalled with hands loosely gripping their handlebars, casual, relaxed, eyeing up girls who refused point-blank to notice them. How could they attract the attention of these fabulous Italians who paraded slowly across the shimmering road in front of them, their legs bare, in black skirts and white blouses?

'Have you ever made love?' Ernst asked.

'Yes, once. Or rather, lots of times, but the same night, with the same girl.'

'And you didn't try with someone else straight afterwards?'

'Who else? It's not that easy.'

'Next year I'll invite you to one of our summer camps. They're mixed. We never have that problem, on condition that we restrict ourselves to girls from our race.'

'What race?'

'The Aryans, of course. Poor Hans, you really are an idiot. Didn't anyone ever tell you you were an Aryan?'

'I can tell you that I don't even know what it is.'

Ernst demanded that they stop, on the shore of the lovely pale green waters of Lake Bolsena, while he explained what Aryanism was to his ignorant Celtic friend. Jean also learnt that 'his' prime minister was Jewish. Later, when he was better informed, he regretted not having pointed out that Ernst's Hitler was also a little Jewish. Generally his friend's theory seemed flimsy and fairly absurd. At school, for rhetoric, he had had a teacher called Monsieur Pollack, a charming man who had shown unflagging kindness towards his class of little blighters, all of them grossly ignorant. Monsieur Pollack had also fought at Verdun, for which he had been awarded the Légion d'Honneur. In what way could he possibly fit the description Ernst gave, apart from the fact that he was bald and had a curved nose and large ears?

'Your theory doesn't stand up,' Jean said. 'I know a Jewish teacher —'

'Blah blah blah … Everyone has their good Jew.'

'There are others.'

'Well, your reaction doesn't surprise me. You French are rotten to the core. You don't even realise the difference between an Aryan and a non-Aryan. When the next war comes, we're just going to thrash you.'

'Will you shoot at me?'

'No. Not at you. At your friend, yes. You can be my good Frenchman.'

They swam in the lake. Jean swam faster and better than Ernst. He beat him over a short distance, and as the price of his victory held Ernst's head underwater for a good minute.

'You're not completely rotten!' Ernst spluttered as he surfaced, red in the face.

'I'm not rotten at all.'

'Let's be allies, the whole world will be ours.'

'We won't do anything with it.'

'Wretched dilettante.'

'I'm not a dilettante. At the next Olympics in 1940 I shall win gold for my country with my scull.'

'That I have to see!'

'No question about it.'

They quarrelled like this as far as Rome, happy to be alive, to confirm themselves in opposition to each other. Jean could not resist the pleasure of reading to Ernst the pages Stendhal had devoted to Goethe. '"The Germans possess only one man, Schiller, and two volumes worth reading out of Goethe's twenty … We shall read the latter's biography, for his excessive absurdity is worth reading about: a man who believes himself sufficiently important to tell us in four octavo volumes the manner in which he had his hair dressed at the age of twenty, and that he had a great-aunt called Anichen. But this proves that in Germany they do not possess the *sense of absurdity* … In literature the Germans have only pretensions."'

Ernst appeared sincerely devastated, and Jean regretted having gone as far as he had. He consoled his companion.

'I should never have read you those pages. They're a bit too French.'

'Why not? It's not me you disappoint, it's my father. He swears by Goethe, and I can promise you he means it. He would have done better to leave my *Mein Kampf* in my satchel. I'm going to burn Goethe. Stendhal's right.'

They rode through Civitavecchia, which seemed to them to correspond entirely to the boredom Stendhal had felt there when he served as consul. Joseph Outen received another postcard. 'This city can only have known one moment of glory in its long history, when our dear friend livened up a bourgeois society that was dying of depression. Tomorrow, I enter Rome. Greetings and brotherhood!'

As they arrived, Rome appeared so majestic to them that they both instantly dug into their luggage to find a clean shirt and long trousers. Since they had met on the road to Parma, they had been riding in shorts, shirtless. Ernst, having narrowly avoided turning the colour of a lobster, had developed a warm tan colour that ennobled his handsome blond barbarian's head. Jean had turned a bolder brown. Neither of them passed unnoticed, but their youth preserved them from self-consciousness and vanity. Their eyes were so wide open, all they could see were the ruins of the Forum and the Colosseum. Nothing distracted them from their rigorous sightseeing. Ernst was better informed than his companion. Since childhood he had heard talk of Rome from his father, a gentle man who had brought him up to respect Roman virtues and intellectual recreation. Ernst could, without fuss, quote Seneca, Livy and Tacitus. At home they had practically spoken only of them, at mealtimes or when they were out walking. Jean realised the full extent of his ignorance. At La Sauveté such names were unknown. He knew them only through extracts set at school, and the stale tedium that hung over his Latin compositions, but Ernst treated these authors as living writers who had vanished too soon, young men full of ardour, burning for pleasure like Virgil, or adults whose stern maturity was masked by irony, like Seneca. Ernst no longer opened his Goethe. Jean read, in secret, a few lines of Stendhal on the character of the Romans. He would have liked to meet them, but the girls he encountered were reticent and well-behaved, and at the youth hostel where they slept the old woman who polished the stair-rail said nothing when he spoke to her. Other young men of their age, from Finland, England and America, stayed the night and moved on, more intoxicated by the sun and beaches than ruins. On Sunday Jean went alone to Saint Peter's Square to receive the blessing of Pope Pius XI. All he could make out was a little man in a white skullcap, whose arm rose to make the sign of the cross over a crowd of inquisitive and not very contemplative faithful. But Jean would be able to tell Jeanne that he had attended, and Monsieur Le Couec would draw a deep satisfaction from his pilgrimage. Ernst had refused to accompany him.

'To mingle with the congregation? No thanks. I don't care for that sort of crowd. Masses fed on homilies aren't going anywhere. I'll invite you to Nuremberg for next year's First of May. You'll see the difference.'

When they were not visiting museums, churches and palaces they would stop at a Roman piazza, and for the price of a drink on a café terrace observe for hours on end the procession of tourists photographing fountains and girls in pairs talking with a delightful vivacity and hand gestures that seemed to harmonise with their musical accent, that Roman sound that was so lovely, serious and light at the same time. Despite their best efforts, the two friends had not managed to meet a single one. As soon as they ventured a word, the girls turned away, giggling, and quickened their step. The only women who would have listened to them were the tarts they saw in their greatest numbers one evening when they deserted their favourite haunts – Piazza Navona and around the Pantheon – for Via Veneto. Dazzled for a moment, Jean and Ernst were rapidly disgusted. This was not their Rome, among these tourists, among the pretentious spoilt youth and girls with aggressive smiles, whose breasts made their satin blouses gape. They felt themselves more strangers there than in the city's poorer districts, where a constant flow of shabby Romans tried to sell them all sorts of things, unable to distinguish them from the thousands of other visiting punters. Their lean look of nondescript youngsters gorged on sunshine but ill-nourished held no interest for the society of the Via Veneto. Both were so disappointed by this aspect of Rome that they fled to the Trinità dei Monti. From there and the Pincio, at least, the city welcomed everyone who came: red and ochre at sunset and dawn, veiled in bluish smoke that wafted between domes and steeples, enlivened by a continual murmur, as though a single confused being, the people of the streets, adjusted its quarrels and shouts to the time of day.

As they walked past the Adler Hotel, Jean suddenly caught sight of a Hispano-Suiza whose yellow coachwork and chrome gleamed mockingly at them in the light from the streetlamps. A black chauffeur in a white uniform was reading a book balanced on his steering wheel.

'I can't believe it! It's Salah!' Jean said.

'Who?'

'A friend.'

'Do you mean to say that that Negro is your friend?'

'He is a great person. He knows everything and understands everything.'

Ernst gaped. He looked from Jean to the chauffeur, absorbed in his reading, and back again, and failed to discern why there should be a friendship between the two.

'Listen, dear Hans,' he said, 'that man is a Negro, a servant. I'd also like to point out that, according to the car's Arabic registration plates, he is an Arab's chauffeur, that is to say a Semite. You must explain to me how you could make such a mistake about this individual. Up till now I liked you. Of course you've mocked Goethe, but it was because of your Stendhal: it's a French quirk, as my father says. I forgive you much because I myself don't terribly like Goethe and because you've opened my eyes, in a sense. However, I must warn you that if you come over all chummy with that Negro, you will no longer be my friend.'

'Ernst, you're a perfect fool! That man is as good as we are, a hundred times over. In London he was my mentor.'

'Ach, obviously in London … London is a very special sort of decadent place, a cesspit that Europe sensibly wants nothing to do with. The white race has given everything to the world. The world owes it everything. But it can only take on that mission if it defends itself against racial pollution. I am warning you: I'll agree to laugh with you at my enthusiasms, but I refuse to go along with your weaknesses.'

Jean was not listening. With Salah's presence on the other side of the road, memories he had nursed fondly since his last journey came crowding back: the London light, the mystery of Soho, Hampton Court and the revelation of the glories of rowing, his beautiful bike sacrificed on the altar of modern art by an unknown sculptor.

'Wait here for me!' he said.

'No. If you speak to that Negro I shall leave.'

Jean crossed the road and approached the chauffeur.

'Salah!'

Salah did not recognise him immediately.

'You don't remember me? In London, my red bicycle, Madame Germaine, the Maries of Chelsea?'

'Jean Arnaud! A man now. You've grown into a fine, healthy-looking lad. Well, well … I was not expecting to see you here.'

He put down his book and got out of the car to take Jean by the arm.

'It was written … we were meant to see each other again. But why in Rome? Only God knows the answer. Ah, my dear Jean, I didn't forget you. At least you won't find any lecherous vicars here. But I know two people who will be happy to see you … '

'The prince?'

'Yes. And Madame Geneviève. They're here. I'm waiting to take them to dinner in Parioli, they should be here any moment now. Are you on your own in Rome?'

'No, I'm here with a friend, Ernst, he's German.'

Jean turned around to look for Ernst, but he was no longer standing on the far pavement.

'Isn't he with you?'

'He was, but it looks as if he's run away. He's shy.'

'Unless he doesn't like people with black skin,' Salah said, lighting a cigarette.

'I don't think that's the reason. He's really just very unsociable.'

Jean admired himself for lying so well, but Ernst's disappearance disconcerted him.

'He must be waiting for me at the bottom of the steps. A strange boy: he can stand there for hours watching a fountain. Oh, Salah, I'm so glad to see you again.'

'Me too, me too. How many years has it been?'

'Four.'

'No time at all. Are you still on your bicycle?'

'Yes, but no more training, no more races. I've got an old man's bike. I'm rowing now, at Dieppe Rowing Club.'

'Ah, now I understand why you look so fit.'

'How's your father?'

210

'He died. In my absence my half-brothers and sisters took everything he possessed. One less thing for me to worry about … Ah, here comes the prince.'

The doorman from the Adler, cap in hand, walked ahead of a tall, thin man in a coat with a velvet collar who, despite the warmth of the evening, seemed about to faint from cold.

'Monseigneur,' Salah said in French, 'this is Jean Arnaud.'

'Little Jean from Grangeville?'

'Yes, Monseigneur, it's me.'

'I don't recognise you, but I'm sure it is you. What are you doing in Rome?'

'I'm visiting with a German friend. I must thank you. It's thanks to you—'

'I hate people saying thank you. If you want to thank me one day, you must warn me in advance.'

The doorman was holding the door of the limousine open. Jean did not know what to say. Salah, witnessing his embarrassment, came to his aid.

'Are we waiting for Madame, Monseigneur?'

'Madame is tired, she won't be coming.'

As if he had realised the terseness of his last remark, he added in a softer and more controlled voice, 'Come with me, Jean. Salah will bring you back here when he has delivered me.'

Inside the Hispano-Suiza it was almost pitch dark. The car could have been driving through the London suburbs, and its passengers would have been none the wiser. It was apparent that the prince was doing his best not to show his ill humour. Was Geneviève really tired, or had they quarrelled?

'It's a very good thing to travel,' the prince said after a silence. 'Boys like you must see the world. There are so many things to learn. I hope you have everything you need.'

'Everything, Monseigneur.'

'Have you taken your baccalauréat yet?'

211

'Yes, with distinction.'

'Your parents must be very pleased.'

'I think they are. They haven't told me so.'

'La Sauveté has been sold, apparently.'

'Yes.'

'To whom?'

'Some neighbours. The Longuets.'

'Longuet? That name rings a bell.'

'To you, Monseigneur?'

Jean saw him smile in the dark.

'Perhaps it's a namesake. I vaguely remember meeting a Longuet once. His wife was from Alsace.'

'That's them!' Jean said, surprised.

'Extremely vulgar people. The sort of vulgarity that reaches the heights of comedy.'

'That's definitely them.'

'So I see.'

They both fell quiet. Through the coupé's glass panel Jean gazed at the back and white cap of Salah, who was driving like a silent automaton.

'What are you going to study now?' the prince asked.

'My father would like me to go to a technical school: radio, or mechanics.'

'And you?'

'I'd like to work. To earn my living. Be independent.'

'And what will you do with your independence?'

'Row. I row for Dieppe Rowing Club. I've got four years to be selected for the 1940 Olympic Games.'

'I admire your confidence in the future. Nineteen forty? What could happen between now and then? Never mind … I am a pessimist. I shall see if I can find something for you. My secretary will write to you at La Sauveté.'

The Hispano-Suiza slowed and stopped outside a ravishing, brilliantly lit palace. Two valets in white gloves and high-cut frock coats stood at the gate.

'Goodbye, Jean,' the prince said. 'Salah, take our friend back to his hotel. I shall see you here at eleven.'

'Yes, Monseigneur.'

Jean watched the frail figure climb the steps of the little Renaissance palace.

'Let's go and have a drink,' Salah said, taking off his cap and white jacket.

Jean got in the front, and the car silently descended the slopes of Parioli into the centre of Rome. Salah stopped near Piazza del Popolo and led Jean into a brasserie that had nothing Roman about it. Everyone was drinking draught beer, and men were smoking strong cigars whose pungent aroma filled the room.

'Why here?' Jean asked.

'Someone is meeting me here. What will you drink?'

'The same as everyone else, I suppose.'

Salah ordered beer and a lemonade for himself.

'You still don't drink!'

'No,' Salah said. 'It's a rule of dietary hygiene. So tell me. What has happened in the last four years?'

Jean told him in a few words the story of La Sauveté, its sale, Antoine's departure for an unknown destination somewhere in the south of France, and Madame du Courseau building a house for Antoinette and Michel on the cliffs. A page had been turned. Did Geneviève know?

'Ah. It's hard to know what she knows.'

'I had an impression that the prince was cross with her this evening.'

Salah laughed, his dark face lightened by his fine teeth.

'She can be capricious, I must admit, but everyone loves her that way. If she were to change, no one would pay any attention to her any more.'

'I would really like to meet her.'

'Tomorrow, maybe. She is somebody … how can I put it … she's volatile. Her charm is extraordinary, and she exploits it.'

'It's amazing how well you speak French, Salah. Do you still have lessons with Madame Germaine?'

'Madame Germaine? … Oh yes. Poor thing.'

'Why poor thing?'

'She died … murdered, I think. Perhaps by a student she treated too harshly. No, I don't have lessons any more, but I read a lot. A chauffeur's life is marvellously lazy. You wait. That's all. I make the most of it by devouring books. At the moment I'm reading my way through the whole French nineteenth century. When you found me, I was deep in *Sentimental Education*. Have you read Flaubert?'

'A bit,' Jean said cautiously.

In fact he had read only a single extract from *Salammbô* at school, and remembered a dictation in which an old servant appeared with her hands bleached from doing the laundry. He decided to steer the conversation to Stendhal.

'Yes, he is more exciting,' Salah said, 'but so terribly French that I can't always understand him. Compared to him, Flaubert is perfect. You think you're hearing—'

He broke off. The glass street door had just opened, and a woman in a bright red dress and hat entered. She saw Salah and came to their table.

'Hello,' she said in English, 'am I late?'

'No, sit down … Maria, Jean.'

Jean felt that he knew her face, and her dark and slightly too powdered complexion. She took off her hat, freeing a mass of frizzy blond hair that was obviously dyed. On Via Veneto she might have been glimpsed walking with her bust thrust out aggressively, but she wasn't on Via Veneto, she was Salah's girlfriend, speaking English more easily than French or Italian.

'It's nice to meet some pals.'

Jean's memory was working at high speed to try to put a name to the traces this strange creature had left there. She held out her hand with its red claws to take the glass of beer the waiter had brought her.

'Cigarette?' she said.

'I don't smoke, as you know very well.'

'What about this young man?'

'No thanks.'

'A handsome boy like you!'

'I do a lot of sport,' Jean said, looking away from her.

He was sure now that he even knew the woman's voice.

'What sport?'

'Rowing.'

She heaved a sigh.

'I thought only the English rowed. I used to love watching them training on the Thames ... before I buried myself in this bloody holy city with that sad sack Gino ... '

The veil fell, and Jean experienced an indefinable relief. He recognised her, with her mulatto's complexion and her dyed hair. On the boat from Westminster Bridge to Hampton Court an Italian wearing a seedy Borsalino hat had licked her face, and after some escapade in the bushes she had pulled out her knickers and put them back on in full view of the other passengers. On his last evening in London he had caught sight of Baptiste, the butler, threatening to slap her in the hall of the Chelsea house. Her life had apparently improved since then, if her jewellery was to be believed. She had even filled out a bit. Her double chin wobbled. Did she still have such good legs? He would have had to look under the table. While she was talking in English to Salah, he wondered to himself whether he would really enjoy going to bed with her. He decided that he might,

215

as a disinterested experiment. But it took two to make it happen. She had doubtless married her Italian with the Mussolini jaw, the Gino she had described as a sad sack. Perhaps Salah could help. Unless he himself was the girl's lover, as Baptiste had been. How could he find out? He finished his beer and stood up.

'Salah, I have to go and find my friend. Can I see you tomorrow?'

'You're leaving ... Tomorrow? Yes. Around the same time, outside the Adler. I'll warn Monseigneur and Madame, who will certainly want to meet you.'

'I'll be there. Good evening, Madame.'

The woman stared intensely at him, opening wide her big black eyes with their thick false eyelashes. The moment Jean was back out in the street, he forgot her. Ernst was the only one on his mind. Jean was afraid that his friend would not forgive him for having stayed with Salah. Could a person really be so stubborn? If several million young Germans, enlisted in the Hitler Youth, all reacted like that to the sight of a black person or a Jew, they were doomed to stay within their country's borders. Stendhal had been right to say that the Germans 'need never reproach themselves for anything so personal as an opinion'. When he reached his hotel he was told that Ernst had just returned and gone up to the room they shared, a broom cupboard overlooking a courtyard where women shrieked and children whinged from early morning till night. They were too young not to crash onto their mattresses and sleep like logs when they were tired, and Jean was unsurprised to see Ernst, naked, stretched out on his narrow iron bed with his face buried in a pillow. Fine. Explanations could wait until tomorrow.

The explanations did not take place, Ernst suggesting, as soon as they opened their eyes together – awoken by a more intolerable screech than usual – that they leave the city for Ostia.

'I've had enough of old stones, seminarians in crocodiles, icy churches and baking piazzas. Let's go and swim.'

'Fine by me,' Jean said, eager to repair the wrong he had done, even if it was imaginary. 'But tonight I need to come back to Rome, I have an appointment.'

Ernst did not ask with whom. They retrieved their bicycles from the garage.

'What do you say we use the occasion to leave this horrible hotel?' Ernst said.

'Where will we sleep?'

'I don't know … on the stones in the Forum, on the Appian Way. We'll find somewhere … Don't worry.'

They loaded their belongings onto their luggage racks and pedalled out in the early light of morning all the way to Ostia, where they found themselves a beach of soft sand to rest on. The sea beat lazily against the shore with a knowing sluggishness. Fat women in black, their sleeves rolled up to reveal arms even whiter by wrists and hands weathered by the sun, vegetated beneath parasols, regularly called their straying children back from the water where they were paddling up to their ankles, like clucking hens. Fortunately there were some prettier creatures too, beautiful Italian girls of fifteen or sixteen with olive skin and velvet eyes and here and there foreigners, mature-looking English girls, Americans in flower-covered swimming hats, Scandinavians with tanned skin and pale hair. After Rome's segregation and over-solemn atmosphere, that made it impossible to get to know the city quickly, they rediscovered others of their own age who had also cast off their clothes, setting their bodies free beside a sea that gave itself to them, warm, blue and calm, without a past. Jean and Ernst dived into the water like children, came up for air, and got into a game with two Swedish girls, no goddesses but in their scanty swimsuits terribly naked and desirable. Conversation in English, their common language, turned out to be too hard, and they gave up and sat at a mobile stall that served salted veal in paper cornets.

'It was a good idea of yours,' Jean said. 'We were starting to feel that we were the new Goethe and Stendhal. Did either of them ever talk about going for a swim in the sea?'

'I don't think so … Perhaps it's time we summoned them to answer for their errors.'

'We're not a court.'

'But that's where you hold someone accountable.'

'Accountable? How, dear Ernst? No one has ever been perfect.'

'Dilettantes! That's what they were, the pair of them. And there's no place for dilettantes in the new Europe. You go and talk to the workers, the peasants, you'll see what they think of dilettantes. National Socialism will sweep away such parasites. Listen carefully …'

'No, Ernst, you're seriously getting on my nerves now. Here we are at Ostia, sitting on a beautiful beach, and there are girls playing catch right in front of us. Do you really think this is the time and place to be solemn? Save your propaganda for another day.'

With their mouths full of bread and salted veal, they continued to argue, half-serious, half-laughing.

'No one will believe we could have been such stupendous failures on this trip,' Jean said.

'Failures?'

'Clumsy, pathetic.'

'Why?'

'We haven't managed to pull a single girl.'

'Does that interest you so much?'

'Yes. I'd like to. I'd have the feeling of being a man, at last.'

Ernst could not hide his disappointment.

'Poor Hans, that's not how you become a man. If every Frenchman is like you, within two or three years your country will be a German colony…'

'… which will colonise Germany. It's true that I don't know a lot, only the curriculum for the bac, but according to the history books, those who are devoured will devour their devourers, in other words the best forces that Germany can muster will be undermined by the example of our carelessness and frivolity ... Remember how the decadent Greeks corrupted their Roman conquerors.'

'Ah, you believe that ... but you're talking about Latins and Greeks. They're not Aryans. Aryan men are not so vulnerable in their victories, and Aryan women—'

He did not finish his sentence, but sprang up from his stool. Two boys, jumping on their bicycles, which they had left on the seafront, clearly in view, were about to ride away. In a single movement Ernst was on the first one. He grabbed him by the throat and rolled on the ground with him, followed by Jean who caught the second and had him full-length on the cobbles when he abruptly noticed that Ernst's thief had the upper hand. He rushed to his aid, seizing the thief, who was pummelling the German's already bleeding face, and holding him in an armlock. There was a brief struggle, amplified by the shouts of passers-by and the panic of the girls on the beach, and the thief was knocked out. The two friends stood up, to discover that in the course of the fight Jean's bicycle had vanished. Someone pointed out the direction it had taken and they dashed that way. The bicycle appeared at the end of a narrow street and disappeared again. Ernst's nose was bleeding, and his chest was splashed with blood.

'Are you hurt?' Jean asked, out of breath.

'No, not at all. But what are you going to do without your bicycle?'

'Had it. Gone for good. All my things too. My swimming costume's all I've got left.'

'We'll share everything.'

'That's very decent of you, Ernst, but I've got to look after myself.'

At the beach a circle of passers-by and bathers had surrounded the thief, who sat on the ground spitting out his teeth. A policeman was bending over him, questioning him. An elderly gentleman in a boater and alpaca suit shouted at Jean in French, 'You ought to be ashamed of your brutality! The boy only wanted to play a joke on you. Where do you think you are? In a land of savages? Well, I can tell you you're not, you despicable brute, you're in a civilised country, a thousand times more than your own ... '

Dismayed, Jean scanned the curious faces around him, and the policeman who was regarding him with an inquisitive look. The boater and alpaca suit inspired respect. If it was his word against Jean's, people might believe him.

'What about the other one?' Jean said. 'He went a bit far with his joke, going off with my bike.'

'If you hadn't attacked his friend in such a cowardly manner, he would have given it back to you straight away, and if it wasn't a joke the police would have arrested him. We do have a police force, Monsieur, and it knows what to do.'

Turning to the policeman, who was listening uncomprehendingly, he repeated his last sentences in Italian. The policeman, less convinced of his force's effectiveness, nodded his head with a dubious expression and began a long explanation that the bystanders followed with interest, while the thief attempted to slip between their legs. Ernst stopped him with a kick in the ribs. The man in the boater flew into a rage and raised his stick at the German. He seemed to have convinced several onlookers. Ernst, unable to reply in his language, interrupted the policeman's speech and indicated that it was time to go to the police station. They could explain themselves there, as could the thief, who was now lying in the road moaning, his face swollen.

'What a nerve!' the elderly gentleman said, furious.

'Monsieur—' Jean tried to reply.

'Commendatore!' the other corrected him.

'Commendatore, would you like to explain to this policeman that my bicycle has been stolen by this thief's accomplice?'

The man sniggered. 'Ah, ah, ah! But what proves you had a bicycle in the first place? Show us your papers.'

Jean was astonished by his ill will, which far exceeded anything he had experienced up till then. A police car arrived, cutting the discussion short. Ernst and Jean were bundled in, along with the thief. The commendatore handed his card to the policeman. He would act as a witness whenever he was required. At the station they found a young inspector who spoke French. The affair seemed to him as clear as day. He was also familiar with the so-called commendatore, and his false visiting card. He was a skilful fraud who managed a young band of thieves and pickpockets. The inspector called the policeman a naïve fool. If he had had his wits about him, he would have arrested the man in the boater. The two men embarked on a violent discussion, ignoring Jean completely.

'But what am I going to do?' he finally said. 'I can't go back to France in my swimming costume, without money or documents.'

'You'll have to ask your embassy to help you.'

'Where?'

'In Rome, of course.'

'How can I get to Rome in a swimming costume?'

The inspector made an evasive gesture. The question did not interest him.

'I can give you a shirt and shorts,' Ernst said. 'But I've got almost no money left, only just enough to get back to Germany. How will you manage?'

Jean felt overwhelmed. He thought he might have cried if Ernst had not been there. The worst part was the casual way in which the inspector announced that, as the superintendent would not be coming that afternoon, they would only be released the following morning. They were offered benches to sleep on. They slept badly, tormented by insects, and when the superintendent arrived next morning at ten o'clock, all he did was offer his terse apologies: they should never have been detained. They were free to go as soon as they had signed their statement. They were served with coffee and a slice of bread, then found themselves on the road back to Rome, Ernst pushing his bicycle, Jean barefoot and wearing a pair of German shorts that were too short and a shirt that was so tight he couldn't do up the buttons.

However, Jean refused to view the situation too tragically. At the Adler, Salah would let the prince and Geneviève know what had happened, and he would arrange everything. He reassured Ernst.

'Don't worry. They'll help me. And I haven't lost anything precious, apart from my Stendhal that Joseph Outen gave me. None of the rest amounted to much.'

'You're not telling me that you're going to accept help from that Negro or his Semite employer?'

'Why not?'

'They won't give you anything for nothing.'

'They are the most generous people I know.'

'Don't believe it … They will own you one day, and you'll be one of their creatures.'

'Ernst, you are truly obsessed. I've had enough of your theories. You could be the best friend a person could have, if you weren't always reading from a script.'

'I'm saying it for your own good. One day you'll understand.'

'Never. And while we're waiting, we're not walking all the way to Rome. You go on ahead, I'll try to hitchhike.'

Ernst refused to leave him. He waited until a van stopped for Jean. The driver dropped Jean off on the outskirts of Rome. From there he walked barefoot along burning pavements until, an hour later, he saw the Pincio. He was dying of thirst, and hungry. The Adler's doorman was walking up and down in front of the hotel. He looked superb in a tightly tailored linen uniform with gilt buttons, and a cap with a brim as wide as a Soviet general's. He might be a flunkey, but he could not be hoodwinked. The rich gave tips, the poor got kicks up their backside. Jean's build saved him from such treatment, but he had to threaten the man to make himself heard. The doorman in turn threatened to call the police. Jean told him he would punch him in the face, and, because he was pale with fury, the doorman finally understood that some strange relationship could link a half-naked and

222

shoeless young man wandering the streets of Rome at lunchtime with a prince who travelled in a Hispano-Suiza with a black chauffeur and a blonde mistress. Thus Jean learned that his one remaining possibility of assistance had left early that morning for Venice.

Ernst appeared on his bicycle, pink and dripping with sweat, having pedalled like fury to catch up with his friend.

'Now I am in a mess,' Jean admitted, sitting down at the top of the Spanish Steps.

'No. Never. We stick together.'

'My poor Ernst, you're a very decent friend, but you can't do anything. I'm going to hitchhike back home.'

'Without papers or money?'

'I'll work my way back. As for papers, when I reach the border I'll explain what happened.'

'You're really breaking my heart. At least take some money. Half of what I've got left. I'll work my way back too.'

'You're awfully decent, but you make me feel ashamed.'

'Think nothing of it. I owe you for stopping my bike getting stolen. If you hadn't come to my rescue, that fellow would have run off with it. Logically I should give you half of it.'

'That would get us a long way.'

At the bottom of the steps a florist was making up a bouquet of red carnations for a fat woman in her Sunday best whose sandals tortured her swollen feet. As she climbed the stairs, her arm extended to protect the flowers, her gleaming handbag bumping against her short thigh, she passed close to the two friends, murmuring, with a look of disgusted pity, '*Che miseria!*' although it was impossible to tell whether she was sorry for them or just found their youth intolerable.

'It's a shame you can't beg in this country any more,' Jean said.

'It's not that you can't,' Ernst corrected him. 'It's that there's no need to any more. In Fascist Italy there's work for everybody. You'll see the same thing when you come and visit me in Cologne.'

'Right at this moment, Fascist Italy has not seen fit to serve us lunch and I'm ravenous.'

They bought bread, ham and two apples, which they ate sitting on the edge of the fountain of Neptune in Piazza Navona. Rome was gently dozing. The street vendors, sitting in the shade, daydreamed behind their stalls of watermelons, filled rolls and ice cream. Two girls, so alike that they must be sisters, came and sat on the lip of the fountain, laughing and dangling their dusty feet in the cold water. They were not particularly pretty, and had that yellowish complexion that was common among the city's workers, but they were happy and when they laughed they showed teeth as fine and healthy as their free, young figures under their loose cotton smocks. The friends gave them their apples, which they accepted straight away and bit into, still laughing. After a superficial exchange, the girls jumped down with a cheerful '*Arrivederci*' that ruled out any idea of following them. In any case Jean was no longer able to walk, for his feet had been burnt by the asphalt of the streets and the pavements' flagstones. He needed to find a pair of sandals at all costs. When sandals had been bought, the friends counted the money they had left: enough to feed themselves with bread and salami for a week and sleep under the stars.

'You ought to ask your consulate for help,' Ernst said. 'And some papers to get yourself out of Italy.'

At the consulate Jean was only able to speak to a thin-lipped young official who looked him up and down with an expression of profound contempt. How dare he present himself in such a holy place with bare legs and his shirt undone to the waist?

'Papers? Who says your name is really Jean Arnaud? Do you have any witnesses?'

'I only have my friend Ernst, a German.'

'A German! Are you making fun of me?'

'What can I do then?'

'I shall write to Paris and ask them to make enquiries at your town hall at … '

'Grangeville, Seine-Maritime.'

'As soon as I have an answer, I'll draw up a provisional paper for you.'

'Tomorrow?'

'Now you really are joking. A week's time, at the very least. Allow ten days to avoid disappointment.'

'In ten days I'll have died of hunger.'

The young man raised his arms to the heavens. Consulates were not charitable institutions. Jean studied him without rancour, with iron in his soul. His last hope had faded. This testy, disdainful consular official symbolised the first of his encounters with the world of administration. He looked more closely at him: flabby around the neck, a shiny nose on which sat horn-rimmed spectacles, a suit of beige tussore set off by a loud tie, a podgy hand wearing a signet ring with two intertwined initials. The initials restored some of Jean's composure. He remembered a sarcastic remark of Monsieur de Malemort's once about a bourgeois who, lacking a coat of arms, had sported similar initials on his signet ring.

'You heard what I said,' the young man said. 'Come back in ten days' time.'

'Has no one ever told you that it's bad taste to wear a signet ring engraved with initials?' Jean asked, in such a faraway tone of voice that he was surprised himself, as though the remark came from someone else.

'What? What are you talking about?'

'You heard very well what I said. Goodbye, Monsieur.'

'Get out of here, you cheeky wretch!'

'No one can tell me to get out of a place where I have a perfect right to be.'

'You don't have the right to insult me.'

He had stood up, scarlet with fury, strangled by his starched collar. Another mistake, Jean thought, noticing that he was barely

225

more than five foot tall. Behind a desk he could maintain the illusion; upright, he was to be pitied.

'I ask you kindly to get out!' he yelled.

A secretary opened the door, alerted by the raised voices.

'What's happening, Monsieur?'

'Nothing. In ten days' time this man will return to see if we have received an answer about his papers. Now leave me, I need to work.'

The secretary kept the door open for Jean, who walked from the room, smiling at the woman. She looked at him with anxiety. Her hair was grey but fine and soft, and she had gentle eyes.

'You've had your money and your papers stolen, haven't you?' she said, in a pretty singsong accent.

'Yes, Madame.'

'Poor boy! How could someone do that to you? People truly are too bad. In Rome?'

'No, at Ostia.'

'It makes me feel ashamed. I'm Italian, married to a Frenchman. Will you let me help you?'

She picked up her bag from the table and took out a fifty-lire note. Tears had welled in her eyes.

'I can't say anything, I'm his secretary … but I'd feel I was helping to right a wrong if you would accept. I have a son like you. He travels too, and I would be awfully sad if something like this happened to him … '

'I'll send you the money as soon as I get back to France, if you'll give me your name and address.'

She gave them to him, and he went out into the street to find Ernst, who was waiting with his bicycle.

'No papers,' Jean said. 'Just fifty lire that the secretary lent me because she took pity on me. I was treated like a dog.'

He recounted the consular official's welcome.

'You see,' Ernst said, 'if something like that happened to me at a German consulate I would immediately denounce the man to the party.'

'Denounce? No, that's too disgusting. You don't do that!'

'Why not? He's a saboteur. You would be doing your country and your party a service.'

'There isn't one party in France, there are thirty-six ... Listen, Ernst, we don't think the same things, and even so we're great, and true, friends. Right now I only have one thing I want to do: to get to the border. After that I'll manage on my own ... '

'Then you need to find a car or a truck to take you to Ventimiglia. Let's get out of Rome.'

They walked to the edge of the city, and at the Florence road stopped next to a petrol pump. They waited two hours before a truck stopped. The driver poked a superb head, shaved like a Roman gladiator's, out of the window.

'*Dove vai?*' he asked.

'*Francia.*'

'*Anche io. Francese?*'

'*Sì, sì, Francese.*'

'*Allora, monta!*'

Jean only had time to say his goodbyes to Ernst and promise to write to him.

'I thought of a present for you to remember me by,' Ernst said. 'You've got nothing left, so take my *Italienische Reise*. One day perhaps Goethe will be your companion, as he is my father's. You're more like my father than you are like me, and Goethe could have been a French writer if he hadn't chosen, when he was twenty, to write in German.'

'Thank you, Ernst. I'll take it, and when I get home I'll send you a Stendhal.'

'Goodbye, old Hans.'

'Goodbye, old Ernst.'

They shook hands vigorously, and Jean climbed up to sit next to the driver, who spoke a little French.

'Anda de baggages?'

'No baggage. Everything was stolen.'

'*Porca Madonna!* All righta, tomorrow nighta you will be in your country. Ligha me a cigaretta. My name eez Stefano. Yours?'

'Jean.'

'Jean, *Gino! Bravo. Andiamo.*'

Stefano let the clutch in and Jean watched his friend's sorrowful face. But at seventeen there are no adieus. Life's road is long, and you believe it will be paved with reunions.

Between Rome and the border he lit a good thirty cigarettes for Stefano, who drove his heavy truck like the devil, stopping every six hours to sleep for a few minutes, his hairy arms folded across the steering wheel. He spoke little, sang a lot, switching often from Italian to Tino Rossi's French ballads. At the border he hid Jean behind a crate. It was seven in the evening as they drove through Menton. Jean asked to be dropped there.

'No, my young friend. You are 'ungry. You 'ava no money. Come to my girlfriend's.'

They took the high corniche road, and a while later Stefano pulled up outside a restaurant with a striking sign: Chez Antoine. Mireille Cece had recognised the sound of his engine. She was standing on the doorstep.

The author wishes to express a purely personal feeling: that it is sad to have abandoned young Ernst in the previous chapter, to leave him to go on towards his dreadful destiny. Yes, it is undeniable that from the autumn of 1939 onwards this young man will sow death all around him, but he will be repeating a lesson he has been taught, and without that lesson that subjugated so many souls in the young Germany, victorious at the recent Olympiad, victorious in the diplomatic sphere, and soon victorious militarily throughout Europe, without that lesson he would doubtless have been a romantic young man with a heart after his own father's. He was being readied to perform the role of a robot, and the robot would only break when it faced the revelation of the extent of the disaster it had helped to create. Adieu then, Ernst, of whom we will perhaps speak once or twice more without glimpsing again that face of a young Germanic god, with his straw-coloured hair, blue eyes and prominent cheekbones. To console us, though, here is Mireille Cece, of all unexpected people, standing in the doorway of her restaurant in a red dress with white polka dots. She throws her arms around Stefano's neck. In the balance she would not weigh heavily beside Ernst. The moral balance, I mean. But much as the young man's dogmatic idealism still possesses a certain charm – a naïve charm – so her carnivorous realism is impressive. Her unfortunate experience with the customs officer has not cured her. At the same time as keeping up enthusiastic and disinterested relations with Stefano, whose hairy chest and powerful thighs trigger an almost ecstatic frenzy in her, she has found a successor to Antoine, indeed gone one better than a mildly libidinous sugar daddy: an amorous prefect, who ensures that his gendarmes turn a blind eye to her small-scale smuggling. She is thirty-three and her vine-shoot look is at its peak. Sinewy, swarthy, almost flat-chested, restlessly in motion, she is not one of those voluptuous creatures between whose bottom and breasts some men love to lose themselves. On the other hand, there is not one eligible bachelor who, passing within range, fails to guess what flame keeps her warm. I feel that we are edging towards the trivial, that we would do better not to elaborate, and merely limit ourselves to six words: in bed Mireille is a bomb. She has lost her girlish softnesses, to the benefit of her feminine confidence. Her black hair, tied back, severely frames her taut, lively face and large, constantly sparkling black eyes. All the more sparkling now that Stefano has hardly taken her in his arms and she can already feel through her light dress how badly he needs her. And then there is Jean, in an open shirt and a pair of shorts too short for him, standing on the roadside, wondering if he still exists. Fortunately Stefano is a true friend, one who knows how to master his emotions.

'Mireille,' he said, 'Gino eeza French friend. He eez 'ungry and I wanta you to find 'im a bed for de nighta.'

Mireille opened her eyes and caught sight of Jean, looking gauche and embarrassed. Her immediate thought was that he was handsome, and then that something could be done for him.

'Come with me,' she said.

Jean's tiredness was so great that, having wolfed down some dinner, he collapsed onto a camp bed that had been put up in the pantry and only awoke the next day when Mireille appeared in a dressing gown with a steaming bowl of coffee.

'Stefano has gone,' she said. 'He told me what happened to you. You can write to your parents from here. Where do they live?'

'Near Dieppe.'

'Do they have a telephone?'

'No, it would be difficult, but perhaps they can send me a postal order. While I'm waiting I'm going to look for work.'

'Work? There's plenty here. You can help in the kitchen.'

And so there is Jean, washing dishes in a restaurant. It is surprising that Mireille, a simple soul, did not ask the question, 'Near Dieppe? Do you know an Antoine du Courseau?' but she had never left the Alpes-Maritimes, and the name Dieppe meant little to her. We should add that Antoine had never revealed his real surname either. She had taken him to be a commercial traveller, a good father and husband, generous, although protective of his anonymity. In any case it was ancient history, and since the unmasking of the customs officer plenty of vigorous lovers had shared her bed, erasing the memory of her first benefactor.

The restaurant was full every evening. They came from Menton, from La Turbie and Monaco, to sample a selection of Provençal and Italian recipes. Mireille no longer cooked herself. She had taken on a chef from Marseille who, after two nights in her bed, had shown himself to be the most obedient of slaves. This man, a former infantry marksman, had the fortunate ability to drown his jealousy in streams of pastis. He stood over the stoves, his eyes bloodshot, glass in hand, utterly indifferent to everything that was happening around him. The waitresses called him Tomate, a witty distortion of his real name, Thomas, because he cooked nothing without tomato sauce. Jean appeared one day through a haze of pastis, and he took no more notice of him than of a new cat in the kitchen. Jean himself was given the very humble task of scouring the pans. The day after his arrival, he wrote to his mother.

Dear Maman, I'm writing to you from Roquebrune, a pretty little village in the Alpes-Maritimes near the Italian border, where I have just arrived after my excellent journey to Italy. I've found a job which will allow me to get back home before very long. Actually, at Ostia near Rome I had a bit of bad luck: my bike was stolen, along with my papers and all the money I had left for the return journey. Thanks to a German friend, and then an Italian truck driver, I managed to get as far as the border. So do not worry if I'm away a bit longer than you expected, I'm only making enough money to get home. Reassure Papa too. With warmest love from your

Jean

PS. I received the papal blessing at Saint Peter's and thought of you very much at that moment.

He posted the letter that evening before dinner and took up his position at the sink, bare-chested, having washed his only shirt. Mireille inspected the kitchen and said a few words to him. He found her curt and bossy, now that Stefano had left for Italy again. But a few days later, writing to Joseph Outen and having told him the Ostia story, he added:

… I'm not unhappy to have a job washing dishes. All the great businessmen started by selling newspapers or shining shoes. I scour pans under the glassy stare of a certain Tomate. It's not very instructive, but in my situation I don't have the right to ask for too much. With my first week's pay I bought a shirt, a pair of trousers, a comb and a toothbrush. It was my return to the human condition. Unfortunately I have nothing to read apart from Goethe's Italian Journey *and, since I don't understand a word of German, it would be the torture of Tantalus if dear Ernst hadn't already put me off by reading some extracts to me. Be kind and let me cadge a book or two from you. I promise to pay you back when I get richer.*

The patronne is a very strange woman. A real volcano. Not my type at all. I like them slender and distinguished for affairs of the heart, or nice and plump for a fling.

I read in L'Auto *that our eight got thrashed at Mâcon: fourth out of five. What ignominy! As soon as I go away it's a catastrophe. Wait for me to get back, if you want to avoid*

making yourselves a laughing stock. Every morning when I
wake up I treat myself to 200 press-ups. What could be better?
    Your friend,
    Jean

The second letter to Joseph Outen, ten days later, shows the
subsequent course of events.

Dear Joseph, thank you for the books. Such a sarcastic parcel is
just what I'd expect from you. The Physiology of Taste *and*
the recipes of Alexandre Dumas! But I've had it up to here with
kitchens and their smells. My hair and skin are slowly becoming
impregnated with garlic and tomatoes. When I get out of here
I'm going to need a lavender bath to get rid of them. The worst
of it is that I haven't even been allowed to pick up a spoon and
stir a sauce. I scour pans, and that's it. About that I know a lot.
In any container used for braising, for example, you end up
with a crust that's unbelievably hard to get off. Wire-wool pads
won't touch it. You have to use your nails. When mine are worn
out, they'll just get rid of me. Unless ... too bad, you'll have
to hear everything: the patronne sees me. Until now I was only
ever on the sharp end of remarks about my work. Yesterday
our eyes met. She looked away. But then Stefano came for
two days, and she disappeared with him. The bedroom where
they frolic is underneath the pantry. At night I don't miss a
moment of what goes on there. It makes me a bit melancholy. I
dream about someone else. Look, it's fairly excusable, I'm only
seventeen, after all. Anyway, to summarise in a word: yes, the
patronne sees me. It's making me shiver already ...

Jeanne did not answer her son's letter. As she said, 'I'm not very
good at writing.' Albert only wrote to newspapers to insult their
leader writers. The abbé Le Couec answered for them. He envied

Jean his papal blessing and was not at all surprised to hear his bicycle had been stolen. Hadn't something very similar happened to him with the theft of two pairs of underpants and a missal? Jean's parents were well, but they were preparing to leave La Sauveté. The Longuets had entrusted the park to another gardener, a supercilious Parisian who was living with them and waiting for the Arnauds to leave so that he could move into the lodge with his wife, a lady of severe aspect who dressed in black and wore costume ruby earrings. There was no call for Jean to hurry back. His parents expected to find shelter temporarily at Madame du Courseau's. Jean should work and amass the money for his return journey. Then, at the beginning of November, he could enrol at the law faculty in Rouen or at a technical school. They would discuss it. The abbé Le Couec sent Jean his warmest wishes and advised him not to drink, a vice that could be picked up very easily in a kitchen, where you were always hot.

A week later, Jean wrote to Joseph again.

> *Dear old thing, I'm afraid from now on you're going to have to speak to me like royalty, in the third person. I am sleeping with the patronne. To tell you the truth, it's more the other way around. She is sleeping with me. And to be even more precise, she ravished me. I didn't fancy her at all in the beginning ... No, it's too bad, you'll have to hear the whole story. A couple of days ago, having scrubbed my last pan of the evening and steered the chef to his bedroom where, as usual, he flopped onto his bed without getting undressed (or even taking off his toque), I went out to the terrace to get some fresh air. The view was magnificent: the lights of Menton and Monaco, the dark mass of Cap Martin. Moonlight to boot. Leaning on the balustrade, I was musing on the idea of one day bringing here someone I like very much, a creature so perfect I just want to go on keeping the secret I've been keeping for the last seventeen years. Anyhow,*

*there I am dreaming, when suddenly the patronne comes up. I
thought she was going to tick me off for some pan or the state of
the sink, but it was nothing like that! Wrapped in a black wool
shawl, she leant her elbows on the rail next to me and said in a
voice that I didn't recognise at all:*

'Beautiful, isn't it?'

*What would you have said if you'd been me? 'Yes, Madame.'
Obviously. Well, it didn't put her off a bit. She heaved a sigh
that didn't exactly pierce my soul, but it did put me on my
guard. She was wearing perfume and didn't smell too badly of
garlic. Anyhow, I mean: she didn't even smell of garlic at all,
although there must have been a strong whiff of it coming off
me.*

'You're not feeling too lonely?' she added.

*'Lonely? Oh no. I'm thinking about other things besides
work. I'm dreaming.'*

*She must have seen in me some sort of high-flown creature, a
poet lost among the pans, one of those social injustices the Front
Populaire has forgotten to put right. She ruffled my hair with
her hand and she said, as enthusiastically as if she'd stroked
my flies: 'There's a lot going on in there!'*

*Enough! I'll keep it brief. She talked about herself: her hard
life, her depressed father, horribly disfigured by his injuries,
the restaurant going downhill, her useless mother, how she'd
brought it back from the brink by sheer hard work, alone,
admirable, one of those orphans you see crowned with a garland
of roses for her virtue. Stefano? A friend. Just a friend. He
looks after her, her, the weak woman. Nothing like what mean
and vulgar gossips might make it out to be (or hear from the
bedroom above). Was I likely to be able to do better? I asked
myself that question.*

'How hot it is!' she said.

And she opened her black shawl a little to fan herself. She was naked underneath. Dear old thing, there's no scene of that sort in Stendhal, nothing in Byron, nothing in Maeterlinck. Where is its equivalent in literature? To cut a long story short … We go to her bedroom. The bed was ready. She makes me have a shower. Did I shine afterwards? She'll tell you better than I can if you happen to be passing this way. In a word: I didn't close my eyes all night. At eight in the morning she sent me to the kitchen. All day she cold-shouldered me, ignoring me. In the evening it starts all over again. Fitness comes with training. Sadly, with one dreadful consequence: when I woke up, I couldn't manage more than 150 press-ups. Yet I can swear to our dear coach, hand on heart: there's no emotion lurking down there …

That's about where I am. Your absence weighs on me. I'm badly in need of help. In a fortnight I'll have earned the money I need to go home. But will I go home?

The same evening Stefano's truck stopped outside the restaurant door. The Italian jumped down, grinning, unshaven, exhausted. He had come from Venice non-stop with a load for Marseille. He swept his Mireille off her feet; she must have weighed as much as a wisp of straw in his arms. He asked for news of Jean and came to find him in the kitchen.

'Hey, my frienda, you are still scrubbin' de pans. Leave it! Eeza time to enjoy ou'selves!'

Mireille frowned.

'There's work to do!' she said.

'No' for friends! *Andiamo, Gino!*'

Jean sat at their table, on Mireille's left. They had dinner in the main restaurant, which was already full. Jean admired Stefano's poise, so superior to his own, an adult and an Italian poise that did not feel out of place anywhere. This warm, powerful man longed to share his happiness. He drove like a bull for whole days and nights to

236

be able to allow himself his stops at Roquebrune, where he opened his arms and his heart to friendship, to love. What beast would he have been transformed into if anyone had revealed to him that Jean and Mireille ... But graces of state exist, if not states of grace. What was so obvious to the eyes of everyone, what made the waitresses almost unable to conceal their giggles, passed him by. He ate, drank and slid his hand under the tablecloth to stroke Mireille's skinny thigh; she shivered as nervously as if he had crept much higher. Jean was astonished to find that he was not jealous and could quite calmly face the noisy night in his narrow bed in the pantry while Mireille and Stefano made love on the floor below. It even occurred to him, not without pleasure, that he would get a night of rest and the opportunity to resume the rhythm of his 200 press-ups, without which he could not hope to be worthy of taking up his old place at Dieppe Rowing Club. Stefano was picking his teeth with wholly Italian assiduity, leaning back in his chair and flexing his powerful wrestler's torso. At this time of night he was friends with all the world. Mireille was still trembling. Something awaited her that she had sampled before with savage joy, but which had changed its taste over time and with Jean's appearance. She enjoyed fresh meat, and at the same time felt panic-stricken at abandoning Jean for more violent pleasures. She laughed, embarrassed, stood up to give instructions, telephoned to make sure that the prefect would not be passing this evening, ticked off a waitress and went down to her bedroom where, tearing off her dress, she threw herself naked onto the bed to wait for her man.

Stefano had had a carafe of grappa brought. He filled two glasses to the brim. The spirit unleashed friendly and protective feelings, and he set about demonstrating to Jean that Fascism was rejuvenating nations and would save an exhausted Europe from its decadence. Even so, it was important to make a distinction: only the Mediterranean revolutions would bear fruit. Everything being cooked up north of a line from the Brenner Pass to the Loire could be left to the Teutons. The Italians had shown the way with the march on Rome. The Portuguese had rallied to the banner of Salazar. The Greeks were marching behind Metaxás, the Turks behind Mustafa Kemal Ataturk. And at last the Spaniards were waking from a nightmare: last 18 July, their generals had crossed the Rubicon. What was holding France back from adding its voice to history?

Jean did not know how to answer this question. He nevertheless possessed enough common sense not to want to be shot down for parroting his father's solution. Having encountered authoritarian ideas in troubled times, he had also been impressed, without being able to see very clearly where the flaw in the argument lay. It was obvious that Ernst's Nazism and Stefano's Fascism had little in common, except that both appealed to an instinct for revenge among populations that had been bled white by the last war. People's thinking would evolve in time.

Stefano was getting carried away. He was now speaking only Italian, and Jean was surprised to understand him so well, trying to remember who Joseph had quoted when he said, 'The Italians are the French in a good mood.' Oh yes, Cocteau. He smiled to himself, and Stefano, seeing his expression, stopped talking and said, 'You makin' fun of me?'

'No, I was just thinking about something a French writer once said.'

'Oh? What was dat?'

'That the Italians are the French in a good mood.'

'Yes, dere eez a lot of truth in what Cocteau sez.'

Jean raised an enquiring eyebrow. It was clear that driving was not a profession of ignoramuses. First Salah, and now an Italian trucker quoting a French writer whom Jean himself scarcely knew.

'How do you know Cocteau?'

'Oh, you know.'

Trying to look modest Stefano poured himself a second large glass of grappa with a steady hand, grasping the the neck of the carafe with calm strength. Jean had discreetly emptied his glass into a flowerpot

238

in preparation for his morning training session. He felt ashamed not to be as fit as he had been. What you lost in a few days took weeks, even months, to catch up, if you weren't a force of nature as Stefano was. Sitting opposite, his shirt open on his hairy chest, his powerful forearms resting on the table, with his enormously thick neck, he was a man who had been brought into the world to stop charging bulls. Yet Jean was allowed a secret smile because Mireille was cheating on that man. In the strongest among us there is always some pitiful weakness, an Achilles heel. An interesting lesson, Jean said to himself as Stefano, finishing his panegyric to Mediterranean Fascism as the sole bulwark against Teutonic heaviness and Slavic lifelessness, stood up without showing a sign of drunkenness, even though he had drunk, on his own, a full half-bottle of grappa. Truckers were the lion-hearted knights of modern times. At the wheel of their trucks they thundered across nations, imposed their own laws of the road, aided the poor (Jean), mocked the rich in their sports cars, flouted customs inspections and, when they stopped, jumped into bed with creatures they whipped into such a state of passion that at dawn they left them panting on unmade beds in rooms that reeked of the heavy smells of diesel and axle grease. Signs indicated their secret trysts, little restaurants where waitresses tucked these weary giants up in their beds; and when they woke, day or night, they set off again across the highways of Europe, passing each other with deafening greetings. Occasionally one of them, imprisoned in his cab like a paladin in his armour, would send up a flare, lighting the nocturnal landscape with a glow that could be seen for many leagues around, summoning other wandering knights to him. What a magnificent life!

Jean admired Stefano even more when he could hear through the thin floor, from his camp bed in the pantry, the strange warbling sounds that the driver was drawing from Mireille. Nothing like the noises that he, Jean, elicited from the patronne. He had the impression that a wild, animal force was crushing and transfixing Mireille. Stefano handled his instrument like a virtuoso. When the performance ceased, a loud snoring ensued, and Jean imagined Mireille naked, exhausted, unable to sleep, staring wide-eyed into the darkness of her bedroom. What was she thinking about, as sleepless as he was? Jean called to mind the wonderful sequence of pleasures he had had in a single night with Antoinette, the shiver that ran through her all the way to her lips, her thighs suddenly as hard as wood, her eyes filled with tears, half-open to gaze at the inquiring face above her. Love took so many forms that one could not always recognise it. Why did Chantal de Malemort, when, alone in the night, he imagined her (because one day it would happen, he felt an absolute certainty), why did Chantal leave unanswered the same question asked of her?

Stefano left the next day, and the prefect telephoned. He sent a car to pick Mireille up and bring her to join him at a chalet near Peïra-Cava. Jean found himself alone and began a long letter to Joseph Outen.

> *First of all, one very important thing to say, dear Joseph: I'm not jealous. If I were, I'd really have something to think about. The patronne also sleeps with the whole world. It's given me a bit of rest for the last three nights and I've got back all my lost press-ups: 180, then 190, and then 200 this morning. I'm getting fit faster than I expected, and at the same time I'm thinking. I've bought myself a notebook where I've started making a few notes:*
>
> *a) Duplicity: absolutely necessary for a life without dramas. You have to harden your heart. I need to be capable, without blushing to my roots, of sleeping with a woman and then being a jolly decent chap to her lover or her husband. This is essential. Without it society would be impossible.*
>
> *b) Physical love is something you learn. I know nothing. Antoinette gave me one key, Mireille is offering me another.*

There's a world between them, even though both of them are nymphomaniacs. It's quite likely that every bit of totty's a different case. Absolutely imperative to vary my experiences. Sadly, for the moment there's no prospect of that! But I still have a lot to learn from Mireille.

c) I shan't go to university, or to a technical school. I want to earn my living straight away. My parents are old and apparently in difficult circumstances. It's time I helped them.

That's it for today. I'll keep you informed about my thoughts. Thanks for the books. This time you weren't pulling my leg. I've started Journey to the End of the Night. *It's marvellous. We're nothing compared to a man like Céline. I'm learning what misery is from a book. It will help me to recognise it and to put up with it when I encounter it in my life.*

Greetings and brotherhood,

Jean the baker's boy

Mireille returned from Peïra-Cava with passion oozing from every pore, and Jean was expected to rise to the challenge. After her short immersion in republican-masonic polite society she had become a little snobbish, and in order not to have to sleep with a scrubber of pans she promoted Jean to waiter. He learnt how to serve dishes, change plates, take customers' orders. The waitresses, three girls from Menton, giggled at him behind his back. He wrote in his notebook:

d) What a despicable lot domestic staff are. They really are the bottom of society's barrel. With one exception: Salah. But he's not a real servant. He has the manners and character of a lord. First prize for ignominiousness goes to that seedy Baptiste, the one in Chelsea who used to talk to me in the third person. In joint first place with the doorman at the Adler in Rome. The ancients were wise men: no free man was a servant. For all demeaning tasks they had slaves. When it abolished slavery, modern society started to dig its own grave.

Mireille, who had been born in a kitchen, knew everything there was to know about restaurant staff, whom she treated with a mixture of such severity, arrogance and pitilessness that she inspired respect. On two or three occasions she almost spoke to Jean the same way. He looked at her in such surprise that she realised her error. She was very fond of her 'boy', who filled her with delight and whose very inexperience was refreshing. He seemed tireless and took extreme pleasure in his lessons. He was learning quickly, and well. Yet Jean felt that the ardour he was showing was only lukewarm, because of the thought at the back of his mind: that his sweltering nights were followed by dismal mornings as his fitness routine plummeted. He was down to 120 press-ups now. A disaster. A letter from Joseph contained a warning. He was sliding down the slope of sexual obsession, a distraction that was fatal for a sportsman. At seventeen you couldn't only think of that, or if you did you'd find yourself with a wife and kid at twenty. Self-control involved more rigorous observance of the rules of procreation. Yet when Mireille was once again absent, Jean realised that, like an addict, he was suffering from withdrawal. He was unable to sleep, reliving in a sort of waking nightmare the crudest scenes of his nights with her and her suppressed fury that had to be quieted ten times before daybreak. She was devouring him. Very soon he would be a human wreck. Abruptly, one afternoon Tomate emerged from his permanent listlessness. The mask of his stare was torn aside, and Jean had the impression that the chef from Marseille was a man like other men.

'Jean, you're getting on my tits,' he said. 'A fine lad like you shouldn't fall into this trap. Go on, fuck off. Right now. No turning back. Another six months of this and you'll be a dishrag. Then she'll throw you onto the street. Fuck off, I tell you.'

Jean didn't need to think twice. Tomate's stare had glazed over again. The chef was returning to his dreams. He was right.

Mireille was due back that evening. Jean took what was owed him from the till, stuffed his things into a paper bag, and jumped on the bus to Nice, where he spent the night walking up and down the Promenade des Anglais, slumping only for a few moments on a bench from time to time, so afraid was he of the phantasms of insomnia. In the morning he drank several cups of coffee on Place Masséna, bought himself a knapsack and set out for Paris. The first truck dropped him off at Saint-Raphaël. The driver was going on to Saint-Tropez, a cul-de-sac from which Jean would have difficulty picking up a lift to Aix at the end of October.

I ask the reader's permission to pause here. You could be forgiven for thinking that we were going to follow, in reverse, the same path as Antoine du Courseau. Given the route of that particular truck, it would have been easy, but stories that pile up too many unhoped-for meetings lose all credibility, for life, as we know so well, is much meaner with its miraculous happenings. So no, Jean will not go to Saint-Tropez and come across another sign saying Chez Antoine, where he will find board and lodging, if not more sensual pleasures. Marie-Dévote is now a wise and moderate woman and Antoine has taken up fishing with a hand-line. Toinette is still too young. At this stage they do not interest us. Let us leave them there, a few kilometres from Saint-Raphaël. What is the good of disturbing their tranquillity? Théo is smoking 'the' cigar on the bridge of his 'yacht', reviling equally the recent elections that have wrought havoc with salary scales and the paid holidays that will bring penniless peasants flocking to the Côte, whose aspect and multitudes will send the select few tourists who already come here running for cover. Oh yes: this government doesn't give a damn for the luxury sector! Socialism would like to sacrifice thousands of respectable employees who like rubbing shoulders with high society to hordes of workers in caps and overalls. When he reflects on this, Théo shrugs his shoulders and makes a contemptuous, pitying face. Sometimes he sends a commiserating glance in the direction of Antoine, who in red linen trousers and vest is returning to port at the helm of the old boat whose motor leaves puffs of smoke in its wake. Oh yes, he's taking it easy. Sure, he has been as good as gold since he came to stay, but because fellows like him don't vote and don't care what happens in Paris, France is going under. 'She's going under, yes she is. Me, Théo, I'm telling you.'

Jean is a few kilometres from them, sitting on a milestone. He jumps up and sticks out his thumb in the direction of Aix every time a car or truck comes past. Let us leave him there for a moment and not forget Mireille completely, even though her part in the story is coming to an end; as you will have guessed, it is far from easy to get rid of someone so overwhelming. She hangs on like a leech, shouts, weeps, scratches, flies into terrible rages, then sinks into despondency before terrorising everyone around her.

When she came back that evening, she could not find Jean and thought he must be at Menton, although she had never known him go there, and then suddenly, in a flash of inspiration, she opened the drawer of the till in which her lover had left a receipt for the sum that she owed him. The scene erupted in the kitchen, where Tomate greeted her with admirable coolness.

'Gone? Well ... it's better that way. You were going to kick him out, weren't you?'

'Kick him out? Me?'

'I swear you were.'

'What do you mean, you swear? It's me who knows.'

'And what about me, then? Forget it, let's have a pastis together.'

The waitresses came in and out, looking poker-faced and sending the patronne into a fury. She was about to throw out several customers who had already arrived, but Tomate just managed to stop her.

'You'll regret it tomorrow. A fuck's only for the night, but the restaurant's your life.'

She drank two pastis in succession that were so strong she became instantly drunk and burst into tears. Once the explosion had occurred, Tomate clammed up and went back to his corner. Eyes drooping, slack-jawed, he watched his stoves, glass in hand. Alcohol had at least had the virtue of confining his interest in Mireille to two nights only, a fact on which he congratulated himself. Now he could treat her like a grumpy father. Mireille locked herself in her bedroom, came out a dozen times to make sure that Jean had not left a message with anybody, attempted to arouse Tomate's interest in her distress but did not succeed. The chef was back at his cooking, an ethereal realm where her problems had no purchase. Left to herself, she measured the extent of the disaster, which was not just emotional. Jean's young, pale, gilded body materialised in her dreams. She hugged him frenziedly to her without either of them coming to orgasm. In a decision worthy of antiquity she resolved to sacrifice the prefect to her vanished lover, hoping that by some magic this offering would bring young flesh back to her. Out of the futility of this sublime sacrifice she conceived a great bitterness and fastened more than ever onto Stefano, whose regular appearances helped make the excessively long nights bearable. She took a long time to recover, discovering in the process that excesses of sexual passion involve dangers that are sometimes fatal. Stefano saw nothing of this, or perhaps pretended to see nothing. He was a more mysterious character than one at first gave him credit for. Mireille should have expected it: he read books! Nearly four years after these events, at the end of June 1940, when Italian troops, thanks to the armistice, entered Menton, he turned up as an officer in the *bersaglieri*, with a captain's pips, and it rapidly became known that from his command post he controlled the intelligence service for the region. Since his affair with Mireille he had been covering the area with a close network of spies. Mireille and he renewed their relationship and, thanks to his influence, the restaurant at Roquebrune lacked for nothing during the four years of occupation, until suddenly the Italian soldiers – whose kindness and genuine distress at being involved in this absurd adventure against the French south, to which they felt so close, had not been sufficiently appreciated – were replaced by field-grey uniforms who began fortifying the hillsides against an enemy as yet invisible. Mireille hid Stefano for several weeks until he was able to join a group of partisans in the Abruzzi. At the liberation the French Forces of the Interior set up their command post inside the restaurant. Mireille was locked in the cellar, where at first, as she satisfied her new guests' urgent needs, she thought briefly that she might succeed in extracting herself at this lesser price, but the appearance of a rival group put paid to that hope. She was tried, and hanged from a tree. But not any tree, no! The oldest known olive tree in the world, planted nearly two thousand years before by the Romans. For two days her corpse swung there in the gentle summer breeze, until some sensitive souls found her a burial place in the cemetery next to her father and her mother.

That is it for Mireille. I am sorry: she will not reappear, a victim, like Ernst, of the Manicheanism of the times, the haphazard fortunes of good and bad. Stefano returned to Roquebrune and learnt of his girlfriend's fate. He had been responsible. Should he not have stayed to protect her? A great remorse grew in him; he thought of taking holy orders, hesitated and got married. On the day I write these words, he is a handsome old man who owns a thriving haulage business. From time to time, if there is a strike or a driver is off sick, he will still take the wheel and head onto the *autostrada*, without stopping, as if he were going to meet Mireille Cece again. In darkness pierced by the blinding beams of headlights, he sees again the irresistible body of the woman who waited for him on the bend at Roquebrune and whose fidelity he never had any reason to doubt. And when he does so he no longer feels alone, but drives on towards her and has the impression that nothing has changed, that the hair at his temples has not gone white and that pleasure awaits at the end of the road.

Let us return to Jean on his milestone in the Massif des Maures. He had been sitting there for two hours when a Renault Primaquatre driven by a commercial traveller stopped. The driver was bored and would happily have picked up a cow, so long as he could tell it about his problem, namely the sale of Isabelle chocolate below cost in the southern departments. Isabelle chocolate, in bars and in powder form, was not reaching its public. The company was skimping on advertising and counting on its sales representatives being everywhere. But in one of those irrational acts that demonstrate that managers inhabit another universe, far from the lives of those who actually have to work, Isabelle SA had just cut its sales force's expenses. Jean tried hard to follow the monologue of his travelling companion, a short, fat man with podgy fingers and clearly a lover of good eating, as he frequently broke off from his lament to give marks out of ten to restaurants in the villages they passed, accompanied by brief and very specific notes: an excellent saddle of hare there two years ago, a *coq au vin* as tough as old boots in that pretentious joint last month, or a lovely *vin de pays* at this bistro which doesn't look anything special, does it? These mindless ramblings about Isabelle chocolate and gastronomic preferences, which were enough to make an empty stomach turn over, nevertheless distracted Jean from what, or rather who, he was leaving behind him. For two hours, sitting on his milestone as he waited for a sympathetic driver to offer him a lift, he had thought of nothing but Mireille. He would have given anything to go back to her, but an invisible force pressed him into the seat of the noisy Renault, which had to change down to second at the slightest gradient. The soft shapes of the Maures near Saint-Maximin made him think of naked women, offering their round breasts up to the burning sun, and those clumps of black cypresses the tufts between their thighs or under their thrown-back arms. Tomate had been right, and he might even have been too late. Jean should have fled before he was overcome by Mireille's obsessive nocturnal habits. Would he ever escape from her? She was like a stain on his body and his thoughts ... The commercial traveller kept on with his grievances against Isabelle SA, a handful of ambitious, mean capitalists exploiting some grandmother's recipe, which was actually fortunate, in fact, because Isabelle chocolate, in bar and powder form, was the best France had to offer, perhaps even the best Europe had to offer. Jean nodded. You don't disagree if you don't know anything. And he knew nothing compared to such a man. A copy of *L'œuvre* was lying on the back seat, the daily paper Albert sometimes read in addition to *Populaire* for its articles by Michel Déat and the columns of Georges de La Fourchardière, whose caustic plain-speaking made him smile. Jean answered that he had heard this was true from his father, who read *L'œuvre*.

'Ahah, I see, a radical socialist like me! So what's he waiting for to enrol you in the Jeunesses Radicales?'[10]

'Do the Jeunesses Radicales really exist?'

The idea seemed completely laughable. The composite image of a radical socialist in people's minds generally consisted of Édouard Herriot's fat stomach, Ferdinand Buisson's goatee and the flapping trouser seat of the man Léon Daudet had nicknamed 'stuck-up Bonnevay'. When it came to life, the portrait had Édouard Daladier's gravelly voice, whose only intelligible words were 'my party'. Could young people really be tempted to rally to the banner of such men? The salesman appeared outraged by Jean's ignorance. He was a novice to be converted, to be trained so that France – a great democracy – would be, thanks to its young people's enthusiasm, the leading nation of Europe. Jean did not know how to answer this. To his immense relief they were coming into Aix, and the salesman pulled up at a garage to fill his tank and put some water in his radiator.

Jean was startled: the garage's name was Chez Antoine. For several minutes he was intensely miserable at the memory of Mireille's sign. Was she going to remind him of her existence like this all the way back? Let us note in passing that Charles Ventadour was not there. He rarely appeared at his garage since he had been elected to the departmental assembly and the board of a new company that was planning to build luxury villas on a plot of land on the Marseille road. It is true that Jean and he have no reason to be interested in each other. Their conversation would resemble that of the commercial traveller who, interested only in acquiescence, was so delighted by his travelling companion that in a surge of generosity he asked him to lunch.

'The patronne does all the cooking herself. A true woman of Aix, my young friend. Kind but firm at the same time. You'll have her chicken with Provençal herbs. She harvests her own herbs. It's turned on a spit over a fire of vine branches. We'll drink a Côtes du Rhône. There isn't much else around here. And if you want my advice, be careful with the rosés. They're only drinkable where they're grown, at the vigneron's. The minute they leave the vineyard, they get adulterated with all sorts of things.'

Jean accepted the invitation, although the man bored him to tears. When the dessert came, he excused himself, went outside, got his bag out of the Renault, and hid in the town until the angry salesman had left. Shortly afterwards, on the Montélimar road, an old Mathis driven by a priest in a beret stopped.

'Where are you going?'

'To Grangeville,' Jean answered absent-mindedly.

'Grangeville? Where's that?'

'Near Dieppe ... But I meant, anywhere that takes me closer to it will be welcome, Father, Montélimar, Valence.'

'Near Dieppe? Well, why not? I just wonder whether this car will last the journey. I lost a wheel this morning. Marvellous ... I saw it roll away in front of me but I was still moving, on three legs as it were. I came to a halt on the grass verge, and the hardest thing was finding the nuts again. In any case, the wheel's still holding with two. See … I can even let go of the steering wheel … '

The Mathis zigzagged dangerously across the road, to the priest's great enjoyment. He was a man in his thirties with a fairly prominent nose, yellowish skin, and black slanting eyes with the lashes of an Arabian dancing girl.

'You're not saying that you're going near Dieppe, Father?'

'No, I wasn't heading that way, but I have a taste for adventure. Having said that, I'm not certain that this Mathis will make it as far as Dieppe. She overheats as soon as I go faster than forty. You don't smoke?'

'No, thank you.'

'Ah, I see … keeping fit. I could have sworn you were a sportsman.'

He pulled a pipe out of his pocket, skilfully filled it with one hand, keeping his eye on the road, then held out a lighter to Jean.

'Get me going, will you?'

A delicious scent of tobacco filled the car that was nothing like the strong, sour smell of the caporal that Albert smoked.

'What is that?' Jean asked.

'My tobacco? Oh, a blend. I can give you the address: a little place in the City, behind the Stock Exchange. Ask for John Mulligan and tell him you're a friend of mine and you'd like my tobacco. It has a number, the 253.'

'You get your tobacco from London?'

'Why not?'

At the slightest gradient the Mathis panted and laboured. Jean wondered if they would reach Montélimar. The priest seemed entirely confident, laughing when he was overtaken.

'Mad! All quite mad! When we have our whole lives in front of us. How old are you?'

'Seventeen.'

'I'm thirty. My name's Constantin Palfy.'

'Jean Arnaud.'

The Mathis coughed, then sneezed. It sounded as if it really couldn't last much longer, but the priest took his foot off the accelerator, it cleared its carburettors with a series of misfires, and resumed its sedate progress.

'Admirable, don't you think?' Father Palfy said. 'The courage of the meek: do or die. She won't give up until she can't go any further. When she stops, it will be to lay down her bones for the last time. She will have earned her absolution.'

They thought she was about to earn it for certain when, a kilometre outside Pont-Saint-Esprit, she hiccuped and came to a halt at the roadside. The priest refused to be disheartened, however, and pulling a long, roughly calibrated stick from the boot, he lowered it into the petrol tank.

'Not a drop left! My father was right.'

'What do you mean?'

'The English say, "*Cherchez la femme*." My father said, "*Cherchez l'essence*." We shall push her to Pont-Saint-Esprit.'

Fortunately the Mathis was light, and in less than a quarter of an hour they were at a petrol pump.

'Fill her up, please, my friend, while I go and rapidly pray to Saint Christopher, because we still have a long road ahead of us.'

He disappeared into the church opposite, while the attendant filled the tank with an expression of disgust on his face. The abbé returned almost immediately, smiling broadly.

'Do you mind very much if I pay you in petty cash?'

'We always need change.'

They lined up the money on the counter in piles of centimes that had to be recounted several times.

'Is shrapnel all you've got?' the exasperated attendant said.

'My friend, it will be useful next time you go to mass.'

'The priest doesn't see me at mass a lot.'

'It'll come back, dear sir, it'll come back. The strongest of us turn to the Church's shelter when the time comes to shuffle off our mortal coil.'

'You're a barrel of laughs, Father, I must say.'

'Too true! There's no man more joyful than a priest. Goodbye, dear sir. If you ever feel in need of spiritual succour, don't hesitate to call on me.'

It was seven o'clock when they drove into Montélimar. As Jean was beginning to ask himself whether it was time to leave the ancient Mathis and its driver behind and wait for a truck, Father Palfy was rhapsodising over the distance they had covered.

'A hundred and thirty-five kilometres in five hours! Think how long it would have taken you to cover that distance on foot! Our civilisation's progress is meteoric. And one does work up an appetite on the road. Let's stop for dinner.'

'You must be my guest, Father.'

At dinner Father Palfy ate ravenously and drank without stopping talking. Jean wondered anxiously what the bill would amount to. A month's work had earned him enough to dress himself and buy a watch and a knapsack. What was left would not last him for several days' driving at an average of twenty-five kilometres an hour. Having said which, the priest took his mind off the gnawing memory of Mireille. He had thought less about her since leaving Aix, but now he was dreading the night to come, a second night without her. Wouldn't it be better to continue on foot, to exhaust himself physically, so that he could fall into a dreamless sleep?

'You're preoccupied, my boy,' the priest said, sensing that his audience was less attentive.

'A bit. It'll pass.'

'Was she good-looking?'

Father Palfy was on his fifth cognac, but his complexion was as yellowish as ever, unlike Monsieur Le Couec whose face reddened after a single calvados. The priest's extraordinary capacity could not be something he had acquired at the seminary. He was captivating and unsettling at the same time, without Jean being able to put his finger on exactly why. It was not just because his cassock went rather awkwardly with his relaxed and earthy way of expressing himself.

Jean did not answer his question, but merely looked down.

'I hope it's only about sex, my boy, not love!'

'Only sex, Father.'

'Oh, no more "Father", please. It's much too solemn. Call me Constantin. So you were stuck on this girl, and she left you?'

'I left her.'

'But that changes everything, my dear man. I was rather afraid that you were in love.'

'I am, but not with Mireille.'

'So she's called Mireille. Well, I know a Mireille who will be crying her eyes out tonight. It was good while it lasted, at least?'

'Yes.'

'Well then, don't worry! I shan't say it again. All right. No need to panic. One gets better. Have a little cognac.'

'I don't drink.'

'Impossible. Tell me … a wild guess … you're a sportsman, aren't you? You wouldn't have left this Mireille because she was ruining your fitness?'

Jean opened his eyes wide.

'How do you know?'

'Instinct! I know everything. What's your game?'

'Rowing. I belong to Dieppe Rowing Club.'

'I'll give your problem some thought. We'll talk about it again tomorrow. In the meantime let's find a couple of beds.'

He called the waitress, a large blonde woman who smelt of face powder and cooking oil.

'Tell me, pretty one. There wouldn't be a cheap little hotel in the vicinity that's as comfortable as a palace, would there?'

'The patron has rooms. Do you need two beds?'

'What do you think we are, a couple of queers?'

'Oh, Father, the thought never crossed my mind!'

She giggled and shook, hiding her laughter behind a hand with chipped red nails.

'Just because I wear a skirt,' Constantin Palfy assured her, 'doesn't mean that I'll let myself be insulted.'

'I wasn't thinking of that at all, Father!' the waitress said, getting frightened.

'In any case, the ecclesiastical estate is holy … Bring me another cognac. One for the road, or as our English friends have it, a nightcap. Go on, my girl. May God bless you … '

She walked away, wiggling her hips, and the priest murmured to Jean, 'You'll have noticed with what delicacy I omitted to add the ritual formula "… and make your hooter as big as my posterior".'

'I noticed,' Jean said.

They were shown to a room on the first floor that smelt of beeswax and lavender. Its amenities – a couple of pitchers of water and a bowl – were not worthy of a palace, but its two deep beds welcomed the weary men without a squeak. In the twinkling of an eye the abbé had stepped out of his cassock and revealed himself in vest and underpants. Almost as soon as he lay down he was asleep, and Jean struggled for no more than a few moments longer before he had also surrendered to a dreamless sleep.

It had been light for some time when he awoke to find that the bed next to him was empty and the curious priest had sneaked away. He got up and was splashing himself from the pitcher when the door opened on a beaming Palfy.

'Jean Arnaud, the road awaits. I have made my morning's devotions at the church next door. Breakfast is ready downstairs: sadly no China tea in this hovel, only an inferior variety from Ceylon. But I made the toast myself. Obviously there's no marmalade. We'll replace it with honey from the Cévennes. I hope you're not prejudiced.'

'Me prejudiced? No. I thought you'd gone.'

'I wonder what sort of a man you take me for.'

'To tell you the truth, I've no idea.'

Father Palfy held his sides. 'Please don't make me laugh on an empty stomach.'

The fat blonde woman served them breakfast in the restaurant, where the smells of the previous day's menu still lingered. Half asleep, in slippers and a flower-print robe, she brought the things one by one.

'She is a model of inefficiency,' Palfy said when she had left them.

But awfully natural … all the dereliction of the world is on a woman's face when she wakes: without enthusiasm, befogged and distracted, with an obscure resentment against what has dragged her from limbo.

Jean had paid for dinner, and the priest now paid for their room in small change and crumpled notes that he dug out of a huge pocket at the hip of his cassock.

'It won't inconvenience you if I give you my small change, will it, Mademoiselle?' he asked in an excessively polite voice.

'Change?'

'You don't mind if I pay with coins?'

'Coins?'

'Fifty centimes, a franc … '

'Er … no!' she said, after an immense effort of thought that furrowed her badly plucked eyebrows and put a bitter crease in her unmade-up lips.

They set out once more in the Mathis, which after a night's repose seemed rested and eager. It started immediately the priest cranked it and covered a good stretch of road before he thought he should check the level in the tank with his gauge. It was almost empty. They managed nevertheless to make it to the next pump, in a hamlet outside Valence. While the tank was being filled, Father Palfy disappeared in the direction of the church, from which he returned with a crestfallen expression.

'Can you lend me a little money?' he said to Jean. 'I've hardly got a sou on me.'

Jean paid without demur, and was then surprised in the afternoon to see that the abbé was once again in funds after two prayers in a church at Saint-Étienne. Of course we have realised before Jean has: Constantin Palfy was looting the collection boxes along the road, preferably those belonging to Saint Christopher, patron saint of travellers, an unlucky saint who thirty years later would not survive the great reform, so long awaited, of the Catholic Church. A priest looting collection boxes: I admit that it doesn't entirely make sense. We have a right to show surprise and indignation, especially as donations left at the saints' plaster feet are properly intended for the poor. Father Palfy was not poor, he was just short of money. He was not a priest either, since we are on the subject, which I know is not a mitigating circumstance. I hasten to make this clear for the sake of those souls who still respect the clergy and will, of necessity, have an interest in his case. Of necessity because Constantin Palfy makes a more than fleeting appearance in this narrative. He has entered it thanks to the fortunes of travel, and he has no intention of leaving it in the years to come. I should also like to add before I go any further that, contrary to what one might think, he is a character of many shades, and it would be hasty to judge him by appearances. Jean himself was surprised not to feel any disapproval when he discovered the truth on their second evening. Constantin Palfy had made himself a little additional pocket money from a church, and they were having dinner at an auberge near Saint-Pourçain when Jean asked him to recite the Benedicite.

'My dear boy,' Father Palfy said, 'you won't catch me out like that. I *know* the Benedicite, even though, as you have guessed, I'm not a priest. But I did spend three years with the good fathers. A conscientious pupil, it must be said, and gifted with a fine memory. Why, then, am I dressed like a priest? One has to dress like somebody. One can hardly walk the roads in one's underpants. The sacerdotal habit inspires trust, especially for those small exactions I'm reduced to making as a result of a very temporary lack of money. As to the moral aspects of the question, I owe you a confession: they leave me cold. I could invent good reasons – that the money of the poor is for the poor, or if you like, that I shall pay it back to the Church a hundredfold, or that this small change was offered to particular entities – saints – which have no earthly existence, so I'm not misappropriating a thing. I steal because I am in a situation where I have to steal to survive. Finally, and in short, thanks to a father superior who informed me of my expulsion from the college, I discovered the key to my character. "You cannot remain within our walls," he said to me, "despite the fact that you are not really bad, but you are incurable because you are *amoral*." The privative *a*, you see. I advise you therefore not to place any trust in me. Ever. Having said that, if my cassock offends you, tomorrow I shall appear in civilian dress, but we risk facing financial difficulties on the road ahead.'

'I've got a bit of money. We'll share it. And if we run out, we'll work.'

'Work is not my strong point, even though by happenstance I have been an interpreter, a chauffeur with a very aristocratic family, private tutor to a young prince and even a professional dance partner and I forget what else. But to be a proper worker you need to have known the worth of a good example. My father did nothing whatever. He spent his life gambling. As for my mother, she was too busy putting on her make-up to think about anything else. Not a good start, as you see.'

'So what about the future?'

'The future doesn't exist. Only the present exists. And by way of an example we shall now celebrate these confidences, with which

I'm usually very niggardly, by ordering a bottle of champagne if they have any in this joint, which so far has offered none of the usual hallmarks of a smart restaurant.'

They did. Jean accepted a single glass. Palfy's self-assurance fascinated him. He felt he was faced with a man who did not resemble the men he knew in any way, a monstrous, astonishing exception, who had opened up a gulf at his feet. At the bottom of that gulf a thousand charms sparkled, of an adventurous and carefree existence, while the rest of humanity buried itself in low and menial tasks. Jean met Palfy's dark velvet gaze; he was no longer smiling, but waiting for him to react. Jean extended his hand across the table. Palfy kept his arms crossed.

'A pact? I cannot have made myself sufficiently clear,' he said.

Jean continued to offer his hand.

'Let's try anyway.'

Palfy shrugged and shook the offered hand.

'If it makes you happy.'

At seven o'clock next morning, carrying their shoes, they went downstairs and left by a service door to make their way to the Mathis, waiting for them at the roadside. Ten kilometres further on, Palfy threw his cassock into a ditch and put on a tweed suit with a matching cap.

'You're very elegant,' Jean said. 'I look like a rag-picker in these cotton trousers and this sweater.'

'Elegant?' Palfy said, frowning.

'Yes, elegant.'

'Are you saying I look loud?'

'No, elegant.'

'Elegance is invisible. If I "look" elegant it means I must be ridiculous. And I *cannot* be ridiculous. My suit comes from Savile Row. In London I would not be elegant, I would be invisible.'

'All right. I didn't say a thing.'

'That's better. Now, the next thing we need to do is change our car. We can't go on in this dreadful rattletrap, which in any case threatens to give up the ghost every time it sees a hill.'

'Is it yours?'

'Mine? You must be mad. All I own is a suitcase that contains two suits and a few shirts. No! I borrowed it. And we are going to borrow another one. Are you scared?'

'Yes. To be honest, I am.'

'Well, you're lucky. I don't even feel scared any more. I've reached the point where it bores me. But sometimes you have to do boring things. Moulins is the place.'

And as he had said, at Moulins Palfy spotted a handsome little red Alfa Romeo parked outside a garage.

'Wait for me on the other side of town, on the Nevers road.'

An hour later Palfy came into view at the wheel of the Italian-registered Alfa.

'How did you do it?' Jean asked.

'That's my secret. Don't you think she's rather smart?'

'She won't be when I'm sitting next to you.'

'Come along, no false modesty. Jump in and let's go … '

We shall not follow their every kilometre on the last stretch of their journey, which was, as may be imagined, far more rapid than the first in the old and worn-out Mathis. The Alfa Romeo, with all due respect to Antoine du Courseau, was an agile, sparkling car that stayed glued to the road as if by instinct. Palfy nevertheless affected to consider it merely an amusing toy for the nouveaux riches. His taste was for English cars, and when in Rouen he saw, left for a moment by its owner, a majestic black and chrome Bentley with white-walled tyres, his hand flew to his heart.

'I'm lost, dear boy. Head over heels. I must have that Bentley. I know what you're going to say: it's not as good as the Rolls … '

'No, that isn't what I was going to say!'

'And actually it isn't as good as the Rolls, the most beautiful outward sign of wealth that can be imagined, but the Bentley is sensitive and responsive and not quite so noticeable. With a Rolls we wouldn't get far. With that Bentley we'll cross France all over again, and no one will notice.'

'I'd really like to get back to Dieppe.'

'Agreed, model son, but first a short detour via Deauville, which cost my father so dear that I rarely pass up an opportunity when in the vicinity to recoup a few of the notes he scattered on its green baize …'

Deauville was deserted in midweek, whipped by a wind laden with spray. Palfy explained the town's topography and pointed out the boardwalk that, as he assured Jean, he had walked up and down a hundred times, clutching his mother's skirts, around 1910. They pulled up in front of an exceptionally smart restaurant, where their appearance in a Bentley with English registration plates made a doorman snap to attention and greet them with a few words painfully learnt from a small book he kept at the bottom of his coat pocket. Jean had ceased to be surprised and did not even smile as Palfy began to speak with an English accent that was so affected it was hard not to laugh. But the Bentley, and his friend's blue blazer and flannel trousers, were more than enough to impress a maître d'hôtel.

'Understand,' Palfy said, 'that appearances are all on our side. The car, my clothes … and you …'

'What do you mean, me? I'm getting to look quite revolting.'

'That's what makes it real. I picked you up on the road, now I'm going to feed you, and for them there's no doubt about the outcome: tonight I shall take you to bed with me. We're two queers, do you understand? Few things inspire more trust.'

Jean thought to himself that they would have to pay when lunch was over, even so, this restaurant was not the kind of place where you could slip out through the toilets. Palfy seemed not to be worried in the slightest.

'Do you know how to eat?' he asked.

Jean was suddenly afraid that he did not know how to hold a fork or knife properly, despite the lessons he had been given over and over again by Marie-Thérèse du Courseau. Obviously he had not strolled the boardwalk at the age of four, clutching Jeanne's skirts, and faced with Palfy's poise – he seemed to have spent his whole childhood at spas and luxury seaside resorts – he felt paralysed. Eventually he understood that Palfy only wanted to make sure that the unimpressable maître d'hôtel was left a little surprised by his guests. First the chef was summoned, to take down a recipe for oyster soup.

'Careful with the onions,' Palfy reminded him. 'Diced very fine, above all. Then simmer. On no account let it boil, it will be a catastrophe if you do. Do you have a fresh mullet?'

'This morning, Monsieur.'

'Then serve it for us with a hollandaise sauce.'

'Monsieur means—'

'I mean a hollandaise sauce: egg yolks, flour, melted butter, a cup of stock. Careful, no boiling there either, or the sauce will turn.'

'Oh no, Monsieur, of course not.'

'The sommelier, please.'

Palfy crowned his performance by ordering a single wine, a blanc de blanc. Jean observed the reverse of a ritual he had watched at Mireille's, in a less refined version, from the pantry. Palfy was suddenly disclosing a whole new world to him. He could no longer be regarded in the same light, this Fregoli brimming with self-assurance.[11] His roguishness had greatness, it had something superb about it. If they were arrested by the gendarmes, he would make sure they knew it. But for how long would his luck hold? The first glass of blanc de blanc swiftly dispelled his anxiety about the final act, and when Palfy, casting a cursory look at the bottom of the bill, took out a cheque book and wrote a cheque drawn on an English bank, he hardly even experienced relief. Everything was turning out so well!

'Where did you find that cheque book?' he asked when they were outside.

'In the glove compartment. There usually is one in that sort of car. If there weren't, it wouldn't be much fun borrowing them … Now, I suppose you want very much to see your popa and your moma … '

'Yes … actually I don't really know.'

'Let's not go overboard. Everything must come to an end. Our little entertainment was a success. Not one snag. Let's head for Dieppe. Shall we keep the Bentley?'

'Why not?'

'I wonder if it isn't a little too pompous to turn up to your house in. A Traction Avant would be quite adequate.'

He replaced the cheque book in the glove compartment, and they drove slowly through the streets until Palfy spotted a Citroën that he liked the look of. By late afternoon they were at Grangeville. La Sauveté's gates were locked. They drove along the wall by the hawthorn hedge and stopped outside the door where seventeen years earlier unknown hands had left a basket containing the baby Jean. A woman in an austere black dress, her hair scraped into a bun on top of her head and thin lips made up with a single slash of lipstick, opened the door.

'What do you want?' she asked.

'My parents.'

'Your parents?'

'Albert and Jeanne Arnaud.'

'They don't live here any more.'

The door shut in Jean's face. The sun was going down. He could hear the magpies chattering in the park and the first gusts of the west wind that would blow all night, driving the Channel waves onto the high cliffs.

'I know that person,' Palfy said behind Jean, who had not moved.

'Who is she?'

'The former sub-mistress of Two Two Four.'

'I don't know what a sub-mistress is, and I don't know Two Two Four.'

'My dear innocent friend, a sub-mistress is the supervisor of a brothel, and Two Two Four is at 224 Rue Déroulède, the smartest whorehouse in Paris. Has she come to retire here, or to open a country annexe? It would be interesting to know. Meanwhile, we ought to find your parents. Who can put us on the right track?'

'Monsieur the abbé Le Couec.'

'A shame I chucked my cassock away.'

'Don't be an idiot. The abbé is the best man in the world.'

Monsieur the abbé, seated on a kitchen chair with his cassock hitched up to his knees, was soaking his feet in a bowl of cold water in which a fistful of rock salt was dissolving, after a hard day: mass at six o'clock, mass for the repose of the soul of Mathieu Follain at eight o'clock, baptism of Célestin Servant at ten o'clock, marriage of Clémentine Gentil to Juste Boillé at midday, a wedding feast that had finished at four o'clock, just in time for him to give extreme unction to Joseph Saindou. The wedding feast had been the most exhausting: seven courses, and so large a number of *trous normands*[12] that the groom had staggered out supported by two of the ushers and Clémentine, a girl who was usually rather reserved, had undone her bodice and let a white breast slip out, goose-pimpled like the skin of a plucked chicken. Monsieur Le Couec was musing about all these people who had been born, got married and died in a single day. He had accompanied them through their lives and to the brink of death, been present at their celebrations and their sorrows, known the fragments of secrets that they gave him during confession, and yet he knew nothing at all of whether they were happy or not. They did not listen to him very much, less and less in fact, and for several years he had been asking himself whether the religion of which he was a minister did not represent a formality for these people, in which God or the sufferings of Christ appeared to them as no more than magic potions. They remained loyal to it in order to guarantee themselves a little good fortune, out of superstition. Had he been right to follow his nature, to be familiar, bon vivant, understanding, sometimes even complicit? His attitude meant that people treated him as an equal, as a good fellow they respected, but knew that a full glass of calvados could make him all-forgiving. Where had they vanished to, those priestly wraths he had been armed with as he emerged from the seminary? Even from the pulpit he thundered no longer, stripped of the illusion that his sermons held the attention of his faithful. And so? He had only ever had a very relative propensity for asceticism, but in his idealistic moments he liked to imagine that his parish's destiny would have been quite different if he had shown the sublime, intransigent faith of Saint John Vianney – the *curé* of Ars – if his flock had believed that he was fighting every day against a devil trying desperately to overturn his potato soup or set his cassock on fire. It was true that the war had weighed heavily on him. You couldn't explain away that gigantic spectacle of filth, heroism and idiocy, and keep your faith intact. Jean-Baptiste-Marie Vianney had very prudently deserted before becoming a priest. The wise thing would have been to follow his example in 1914 …

The abbé was at this point in his sour reflections when Jean knocked and walked straight in, having glimpsed through the window Monsieur Le Couec with his feet in a bowl.

'My little Jean! The prodigal son returns! And I know two others, apart from me, who will be happy to see you. Come and let me kiss you.'

Jean kissed the abbé and introduced Palfy.

'This generous friend drove me here. We've just been to La Sauveté. The door was slammed in my face. Where are Papa and Maman?'

The priest's face darkened.

'Your mother isn't well, my boy. The sale, her eviction – I mean what I say, eviction – have deeply affected her. She's in hospital at Dieppe, where they're trying to coax her and treat her and bring her back to us. In a month she'll be bursting with health again, I'm sure. As for your father, he's living at Monsieur Cliquet's while he waits for Madame du Courseau to find him a position. He's bitter, I can tell you. To work all your life and find yourself on the street from one day to the next, without work, without a roof over your head and only the maximum invalid's pension to live on, it makes you think … Anyway, everything will work out now that you're here. And you, Monsieur, who are you?'

'A good-for-nothing, Father.'

Monsieur Le Couec looked disconcerted, more by the tone of the answer than by the evident accuracy of Palfy's self-judgment. Palfy smiled humbly and looked around him. In a glance he had gauged both the priest's state of penury and his character.

'There are no good-for-nothings,' said the abbé. 'First of all, you have brought my dear Jean back. Then again, you also exist and one day you will understand why.'

'I very much hope so. In the meantime there is no proof so far, and I sometimes get tired of waiting for it.'

'That is because it will take a form you don't yet know, that you cannot even envisage in the state in which you find yourself. In your place I should be very optimistic, even reassured.'

Jean was astonished to see the priest's words make an impression on Palfy. He would have thought his friend completely invulnerable to such reflections, much too ironical or cynical to listen to them without mockery. The priest dried his feet with an old towel and eased his socks and heavy boots back on.

'Let's go and see your father,' he said to Jean. 'He'll be having his supper with Uncle Cliquet.'

'What about Maman?'

'Visiting hours at the hospital are between midday and two o'clock. You can go tomorrow. If you would like me to, I'll telephone from the grocer's to ask them to let her know that you're back. Oh dear Jean, it is a great joy to have you back among us.'

*

We shall not describe in detail the reunions with Albert and Jeanne. Jean was shocked at how much they had aged in two months. He saw instantly that Jeanne remained shattered by events. She rambled sometimes, then realised what she was doing and sank into exhaustion. Albert was as proud as ever, but Jean guessed his distress. He talked about 'the release of death' before hostilities broke out again, which in his view was not far off. Monsieur Cliquet was still assuring him that what with the railways nationalised and the strikes and the sabotage, mobilisation was impossible. The government knew it and was playing for time. Captain Duclou was more optimistic: the French navy was ready as it had not been since the days of Louis XVI, its destroyer escorts and fast escorts would eliminate the German submarines within days, while British cruisers ensured the freedom of the seas. We are not going to rehearse in these pages the interminable conversations that took place after supper that evening in Monsieur Cliquet's modest kitchen. They would testify too well to the blindness of an era. Let us instead return to Jean and Palfy, who spent the night at the rectory. Jean would have liked his friend to stay on for a few days, but Palfy was loath to stay still. He explained very clearly why.

'You know, dear boy, being on the move is my only security. I have to stay mobile, especially when I sign bad cheques. It's not hard to understand. A crossed cheque paid in the same day is cashed the following day in the worst case, within two or three days in the best. Without putting my liberty at risk, I can stay in one place for twenty-four hours, forty-eight maximum, three days if I happen to sign a cheque on Friday afternoon. Thanks to the weekend, it will only be paid in on the Monday. That way, at the end of the week I get a well-earned rest before resuming my getaway.'

Palfy explained the mechanism of his swindles so clearly, in fact, and with such frankness that it was impossible even for a mind as fundamentally honest as Jean's to feel outraged. He found the looting of collection boxes in church more reprehensible than the bad cheques, promissory notes and worthless bonds. And even there Palfy had justified, in his way, his plundering of priests and the poor.

'I admire,' Jean said, 'your ability to live in such perpetual anxiety.'

'Anxiety? It is unknown to me. I live well, tell myself stories, dupe fools and enjoy myself without hurting anyone. For example, that cheque I signed at Deauville from the cheque book I found in the Bentley: I wrote the amount on the counterfoil. The owner, who is rolling in it, won't even notice. When there's a car involved, I always give it back it good condition with a full tank. As for the instability, it suits me completely. I can't stay in one place. During my childhood my parents never stayed more than a month in the same place. I acquired a taste for travel. I love travelling. So do you, actually. You've got the bug. Don't deny it.'

'It's true, and I don't know how I'm going to satisfy it. Not like you, anyway. One of these days you'll fall flat on your face.'

'One day? Yes, perhaps, and I accept it. It can end well too. Certainties are as dull as ditchwater. Let us live in delicious uncertainties.'

Jean could not wait to introduce Palfy to Joseph Outen. After his visit to Jeanne he met his friend at the Café des Tribunaux and took him to Dieppe Rowing Club, where the Sunday morning team training had just taken place. Joseph emerged from the shower, his hair and beard damp, his face taut from the morning's exercise.

'Holy moly,' he said, 'I thought rowing had lost you for good, buried alive beneath the pleasures of the flesh and the frying pan. When do you start again?'

'Tomorrow. Joseph, I'd like you to meet my friend Palfy, Constantin Palfy.'

With a rudeness too deliberate to be natural, Joseph examined the dandy before him from head to toe, in his grey flannel suit, blue shirt and English-style old school tie.

The disdainful scrutiny left Palfy unruffled, and he simply said, 'What are you training for? Coxed pairs?'

'Yes. Do you know about rowing?'

'Sadly I know nothing at all about coxed pairs. I rowed in an eight for Oxford, the last time in 1926.'

Joseph was visibly flustered, Jean embarrassed. It was probably untrue, but you had to know Palfy to guess that he was lying whenever he pretended modesty.

'And who won?'

'Cambridge. By a slim margin.'

'Where are you two having lunch? It's on me.'

'No, it's my shout,' Palfy said. 'You choose … '

They drove to an auberge in the Arques valley, where Palfy displayed one of his better qualities: he listened. Joseph began to shed his prejudices. Certainly he had a low opinion of such a well-dressed man; he could only be an imbecile. But Palfy had rowed for Oxford and although Oxford was, to his mind, a breeding ground for crashing snobs, that fabulous university town was also a place where incontrovertible sporting qualities were nurtured. To be more certain of what he was hearing, Joseph tossed out two or three writers' names, which were received with a blank stare. Palfy confessed his ignorance. Cars were his only interest. Jean was annoyed with Joseph for showing off and making no attempt to hide his amused condescension to his friend, not doubting for an instant that Palfy was of sufficient stature to be worth ten Joseph Outens. He began to wish Palfy would wake up and wrong-foot him. But Palfy continued to play the ingénu who was only too happy to attend to the pearls cast by a real intellectual.

'And you, Jean, what are you going to do?' Joseph asked.

'Look for work.'

'You'll be lucky. There's no work, except in the armaments factories.'

'Well, there's no armaments factory at Dieppe and I want to stay near my parents. They've aged so quickly.'

'I know. They've been appallingly tricked. That's what happens when you believe in the so-called goodwill of a paternalistic employer.'

'Don't say anything bad about Antoine du Courseau.'

'Why not? He's shoved off and left your parents in the soup. His bitch of a wife is worse, I agree.'

'I'll sort things out without anyone's help.'

'It's a shame you aren't able to come to England with me,' Palfy said. 'I would have found you something very easily in London. I have a lot of friends there.'

Jean did not react. It was the first time Palfy had mentioned leaving for England: a lie doubtless triggered by the Newhaven packet's appearance at Dieppe port two hours earlier. 'What on earth is that old tub?' he had asked. The answer had made him thoughtful. In the meantime the idea had taken root.

Palfy signed a cheque for more than the bill and pocketed the difference with a rueful smile. They drove back to Dieppe, where Joseph left them at Le Pollet.[13] He shook Palfy's hand and said to Jean, 'The film club is showing King Vidor's *Hallelujah!* at six. Do you want to come? It's a classic.'

'I thought you despised the cinema.'

'Not the classics.'

Joseph had begun his 'cinema' period in the wake of his 'sporting writers' period and was throwing himself into it with the same passion, trying to create a circle of young cinephiles in a town where Georges Milton and saucy innuendo were rather more popular with public taste than Charlie Chaplin and Greta Garbo. Jean agreed to meet him after Palfy had left. They parked the car on the Place du Marché.

'Is it true that you've decided to go to England? I thought you were saying it for effect, to impress Joseph.'

'I said it for effect, and now I've decided. What time does the ferry leave?'

'At five.'

'Plenty of time to buy a couple of tickets.'

'I can't come.'

'Jean, you disappoint me ... but I understand. If you change your mind, here's my address in London: the Governor Club, 22 Hamilton Street. I drop in there around lunchtime to pick up my post. My post and a glass of something. It's full of Oxford men.'

'So is it true you were at Oxford?'

'Absolutely.'

Palfy lifted his suitcase from the boot and left the keys on the dashboard.

'Tomorrow you might do something kind: an anonymous phone call to the police to report a stolen car on the Place du Marché. They'll let the owner know. He'll be getting anxious.'

'You are a credit to your profession.'

'Am I not? Have you got any money? I didn't make much at the restaurant, and at Newhaven I'll need to pay for my train ticket in cash.'

'I've got a hundred francs left.'

'Well, that'll have to do.'

At least Palfy was not the kind of conman who promises to pay you back. He borrowed without scruples or pretence, and doubtless lent the same way if he happened to be flush. They walked the length of the quayside and found the ticket office. Palfy bought a first-class ticket and asked what time dinner was served and when the first fast train to London was. Jean reflected a little gloomily that he was going to have to walk back to Grangeville on foot, since he no longer had even the two francs necessary for the evening bus.

'Jean, your film's at six. We've got time for a quick stroll before the boat leaves. This is not an adieu, it's an au revoir. You've been the most delightful companion, and right from the off I liked you, I can't think why. Possibly because I can be myself. Anyway, you've understood that caution demands one doesn't do the same with everybody. One day I'll tell you more, and we'll go for another wonderful spin together. Now I need to be serious: I've almost reached the bottom of the barrel, and if I don't want to end up in jail very soon I need to set up some pretty big ventures. Take note ... Only small-timers end up in prison. Never those of us with stature and ambition. For your immediate future I don't know what to suggest, except that it would be better for you not to hide yourself away at Grangeville. The countryside's all very pretty, but it doesn't lead anywhere.'

'My parents—'

'Yes, you're a good son. Wait a while, and things will soon become clearer. Reflect, observe, learn to judge your fellow human beings and see through them.'

'You were really cruel to my friend Joseph.'

'Cruel? You must be mad. He was delighted with his lunch, and thinking that he was shining at my expense. He's a charming boy, without a single original thought in his head: he borrows from everywhere and has no idea how to be selective. I have the impression that you know already how to be selective ... '

They walked along the pebble beach whipped by the wind. Above them gulls hovered, motionless, then plummeted like stones into the trough of the swell.

'I'd love to go to England again,' Jean said, 'come with you on the ferry, have a drink in the pub at Newhaven where Mrs Pickett gets drunk every night, then go to London and meet my friend Salah, see the prince and perhaps Mademoiselle Geneviève ... At the same time I'm happy to be back here in my shell, now that you're going ... There are reasons.'

'Have you left your love affair behind?'

'No, not really. But Grangeville's the only place where I'll get rid of it for good. You can't imagine how disgusted with myself I feel when I think of Mireille.'

'Then you're getting better ... Come on, come and see me off, and don't forget my address. I have a feeling we'll be seeing one another quite soon.'

From the dockside Jean made out Palfy's outline as he handed his suitcase to a steward and stood at the rail until the packet cast off. They exchanged a discreet wave. As the boat moved into the Channel they lost sight of each other, and Jean felt at once a gap in his life from Palfy's absence, though he had only known him for a few days. From now on things were going to feel very unexciting, and Joseph Outen would not be able to distract him from the bitter realities he found himself faced with.

Joseph was waiting outside the youth club, where he had hired a room at his own expense to show his repertoire of film classics. About a dozen young men were with him, members of the Rowing Club who had come purely to please him and were unimpressed by the supposed interest of old films that had gone out of fashion. Joseph hid his disappointment. Yet another. The bookshop was going downhill, and the film-club venture was going to eat up his last francs. The copy of *Hallelujah!* turned out to be as scratched and worn as it could possibly be, and the youth club's loudspeakers were so defective that the film's moving negro spirituals sounded more like a chorus of flayed cats. Joseph refused to admit the sad truth: with the resources he had available, he was simply vandalising the 'classics'. When the lights went up and he suggested a discussion about King Vidor's message, there was a shuffling of feet and every member of the audience had an urgent appointment. Jean stayed behind with his friend, who took him to a bar-tabac at the port for a beer.

'I'll get there!' Joseph declared. 'I'll shake them up, get them thinking. You'll help me.'

'How? I have to earn a living urgently. I haven't even got enough to get the bus back to Grangeville.'

'Good Lord, why didn't you tell me?'

'I'm telling you.'

'Here's ten francs. It's all I've got on me. Let's meet during the week. When are you going to start training?'

'As soon as I can.'

'You mustn't give it up, you have a talent. How many press-ups are you on now?'

'A hundred. Mireille wore me out in the last few days at Roquebrune.'

'You didn't pick it up again on the way back?'

'I'd like to have seen Palfy's expression, watching me do press-ups every morning.'

'I didn't like the man. I expect you noticed. His money doesn't impress me. He'd do better to spend some time improving his mind. Oh well, you can't always choose your travelling companions. Drop in at the bookshop during the week, I'll think about your problem, but these days life is hard, the crisis is hitting everybody.'

That evening, at the rectory, Jean opened his notebook and wrote:

e) It is wise not to mix one's friends. I should never have put Ernst and Salah or Palfy and Joseph in each other's presence. Ernst despised Salah a priori *because he's black and Salah despised Ernst's racism. Even though when you think about it it's hard to understand why: both are such generous and disinterested natures, they're made to get on with each other. The same difficulty when Joseph involuntarily made me think how dishonest Palfy is, dishonest in a way that I'd found entertaining up till then. Yes, I was a bit uncomfortable with it for a while, and felt guilty at benefiting from his swindles. So my moral sense was suddenly alerted because of Joseph. On the other hand, Palfy helped me, almost without a word, without comment, to see that despite his posturing Joseph is never going to rise very high. He's jinxed. Everything he touches turns to dust: today his bookshop, tomorrow his film club, even the Dieppe Rowing Club, where he's the most energetic and least talented member. Whereas everything works for Palfy: he steals cars without a second thought, finds a cheque book when he needs one. Everything amuses him because everything succeeds, and because success is his only criterion he believes himself justified in acting the way he does. The whole situation is a bit of a catastrophe: my friends don't get on, and their mutual discord shows both of them in an unpleasant light. It would have been the same if I'd switched them, Ernst face to face with Joseph, Palfy face to face with Salah. It's a good lesson to remember. Don't mix your friends. Put each of them in a drawer, and don't open one drawer without being certain that the others are tightly shut.*

At six in the morning the abbé woke Jean.

'I have no one to serve mass. Will you come, as you used to when you were a pious little boy?'

'Yes, Monsieur l'abbé.'

In a church numb with cold, lit by two mean yellow bulbs and a few candles, a moving, simple mass took place that was attended by three old women and a young man on his knees at a prie-dieu, his face hidden in his hands. After the 'Ite, missa est' the three women stayed behind, telling their rosary, and the young man crept towards the door as though he wanted to hide, but Jean was certain that the devout early-riser deep in prayer had been Michel du Courseau. Jean did not take communion, and when he was in the sacristy afterwards helping the priest to take off his chasuble and alb, Monsieur Le Coueé said to him sadly, 'That mass was intended for you, my dear Jean. You must have had your reasons for not taking communion, which I respect and shall not enquire further about. Let's go and have a bowl of coffee.'

The penury of the rectory was such that the abbé heated up his coffee over a spirit lamp, and for breakfast buttered two thick slices of a brown loaf he was given by one of the farmers every week.

'And now what will you do, my boy? We hoped you would go on with your studies. It's possible, there are scholarships—'

'I want to earn a living straight away. But what can I do here?'

'That is a very good question. Antoine du Courseau has gone, but we could speak to Madame du Courseau.'

'She doesn't like me.'

'You're wrong. Obviously there was that regrettable story—'

'I didn't do it.'

'Time has passed. She's a charitable woman.'

'When she's sure everyone around her will get to hear about it.'

The priest smiled and nodded his head.

'At your age it's a little sad to possess so few illusions. You're undoubtedly right. So let us make her think that everyone in Grangeville who matters will hear about her tireless generosity towards her gardener's son.'

They began to list a number of others who might be willing to help Jean.

'The Malemorts?' the abbé wondered. 'Hmm … alas, I fear that their own situation is not very splendid. The marquis has dismissed two farm workers, and I'm not sure I can see you working on a farm. There's the Longuets … '

Jean snorted, and the abbé reddened. He still had a soft spot for Madame Longuet and felt sincerely sorry for her having a crook for a husband and a future thug for a son. He felt that she was a victim. She had, apparently, pleaded the Arnauds' cause in vain to her intractable husband.

In the end it was Joseph Outen who found a job for Jean, at *La Vigie*. The newspaper also printed announcements, handbills, menus and cards. A dozen women made up the orders, and Jean stored them and delivered them in a van. It did not demand great genius, just physical strength and a character sufficiently cheerful to be able to withstand the crudity of the supervisor, a man named Grosjean who had fulfilled Jean's own role for nearly twenty years and whose promotion at his career's end, elevating him to the rank of supervisor, had dangerously intoxicated him. Jean left Grangeville on foot at six in the morning, started work at eight, and finished at six. In his lunch break he had a sandwich and went to Dieppe Rowing Club, where he rowed and trained with weights for an hour before going to see his mother in hospital.

Jeanne was not on the road to recovery. In truth she had quickly become used to the relative comfort of the ward on which she lived alongside several women older than she. Driven out of the place she had long considered her home, she found a ready-made community there, and unexpected company. Her neighbours' chatter delighted her and she realised that until that point in her life she had only ever talked to her family circle. The women's gossip, their fears and dreams, their nasty comments, opened up an unknown world to her. And for the first time in her life there were people serving

277

her and she enjoyed it. The sound of the trolley that brought her meals – the only interludes of those long days that began with the taking of her temperature and ended with her nightly infusion – filled her with pleasure. It made her quite forget the visitors sitting at her bedside, who suddenly discovered that their charitable gesture no longer interested the patient, who was overcome with joy instead at a very average hospital lunch. She rambled incoherently, especially with Jean and Albert, managed to mix up Madame du Courseau, Antoinette and the marquise de Malemort, and then the abbé Le Couec and Monsieur Cliquet, all of whom left each time with the impression that the doctors were keeping Jeanne captive, and that her stay in bed was making her weaker and weaker. Jean contemplated her with a sinking heart, remembering how often this half-disoriented woman, too unsteady on her feet to walk without help, had been good to him, how she had opened her heart to a baby abandoned in a Moses basket on her doorstep. He would have liked to question her – perhaps she knew the truth – but was afraid to upset her any more than she already seemed to be. Each time he saw her she asked him to tell her again the story of his papal blessing in Rome, and each time he patiently started again and watched her face take on a look of delight and serenity, her hands clasped together on the coarse brown bedspread.

Jean worked hard to erase his memories of recent weeks and was relieved to find that Mireille was easily forgotten, although her image nagged at him on certain nights so violently that it produced a real, physical pain. He did his utmost, walking, rowing and lifting weights, discovering that his youth required an almost demented expenditure of physical energy to resist the temptations of memory and imagination. He still had not seen Chantal de Malemort, and in a way he dreaded their eventual inevitable meeting, as if she would instantly be able to see on his face that he was no longer the same, that some inner torment had devoured him and left him changed, even after it subsided. Antoinette on the other hand used every ruse she knew to meet him, and he could not avoid her. On the pretext of visiting the house her mother was building at Grangeville, she walked over from Malemort every afternoon and waited for Jean at the top of the hill. He would see her at the last bend and slow his pace. As night fell they walked on side by side, Antoinette talking volubly, Jean saying little, answering with a yes or no. He could not understand why she now came looking for him after having behaved so casually towards him before, but Antoinette, who was more perceptive, had guessed without him saying so that something had happened, something that had spoilt the memory of her joyous reward for his bac. Now she wished she could forget him, for the bitterness of other flings whose short-lived pleasure had never come near the state of sweet tenderness she had felt with him had torn away the veil: it was Jean and no one else that she loved, fled from, and tempted back, and the certainty of being able to lure him back every time had concealed the one fact that makes love insistent and nearly unbearable: its fragility. Jean's absence, which was now no longer a physical absence but the absence of a response, profoundly distressed Antoinette without her being able to name the feeling that drove her to look for him every time she could slip away without attracting her mother's attention.

One evening she succeeded in persuading him to come with her to visit the new house. It smelled of fresh plaster, varnish and paint. The electricity had not yet been connected, so she lit a candle which they took with them as they pushed open squeaking doors and wandered through deserted rooms. The new floor creaked sharply under their feet. Antoinette led Jean by the hand through the labyrinth of bedrooms and bathrooms to a room that faced north for Michel to paint in and set up his printing press. Jean said nothing, and his silence put Antoinette into a state of panic. She could not understand, she did not understand anything any more, and looked desperately for the slightest sign that might bring back the closeness they had had before. Why didn't he speak, why didn't he hold her hand more tightly? In one of the rooms a bed had been set up for a cabinet-maker from Caen who had worked there for several days. Antoinette pulled Jean down onto the bare mattress. Despite the discomfort and the chill of the unheated house, she felt a pleasure so intense that afterwards she burst into tears. The candle's harsh glow lit her wet face with grimacing shadows and Jean was touched to see her suddenly ugly, stripped of her attractiveness.

'Why are you crying?'

'I can't tell you.'

He sat up, irritated. The guilt that had once weighed on him in his games with Antoinette had disappeared, and he felt only repulsion and sadness and even a sort of resentment towards her.

'Well, don't cry in front of me then. Let's get out of here. I hate this house.'

'Why?'

'It reminds me that my parents don't even have a roof over their head for their last years on this earth.'

'It's not my fault.'

'No, it's nobody's fault. Nothing is anyone's fault. I'm beginning to believe the whole world is under the spell of some sort of total irresponsibility. It's really comfortable, and I wonder why there are still a few idiots who worry about other people. Let's get out of here, I said, I hate this place.'

In a childish gesture, she dried her eyes with her cuff. She couldn't understand Jean's bitterness. What was he talking about? About a roof over someone's head, about ageing parents without a penny to their name, while inside her was a sorrow she didn't dare utter, and her distress felt to her like the greatest and the only distress in the world. Outside the rectory, Jean said goodnight to her. She picked up her bicycle, pedalled a few metres, turned round and came back.

'Don't you know what's happened to me?'

'No.'

'I'm pregnant.'

He did not move and watched her pedal away down the road, lit by the flickering yellow glow of her light. No. No, Jean repeated to himself. No. I'm not getting caught like that. He would not fall into her trap, and if she ever had the nerve to repeat those words to him he would just say, 'By whom? Anyone I know?'

Albert was waiting for him, chatting with the abbé, the bottle of calvados between them. He no longer foresaw any kind of future. His world was dying; he could not see what would follow this chaos. Jeanne's condition did not preoccupy him greatly. He had got used to it and refused to sink into a sentimentality that, as he claimed, was the undoing of men as well as governments. It was the spoilt peace, once more in jeopardy, that obsessed him. He could no longer bear Monsieur Cliquet's prognostications about the state of the railways or Captain Duclou's optimism about the navy. The abbé was the only man who understood him, and these two men who, ever since their return from the front, had not ceased to hurl brickbats at one another and cross verbal swords at every opportunity, had, in the current disastrous situation, rediscovered a comradeship that had something of the trenches about it. Albert had also watched with relief as his son got a job. He was now a worker, as he, Albert, had been, not a student, with all the distance that that would have created between them. Jean would forge his future on his own, if he had one, so long as they did not sacrifice him blindly to the Moloch of war.

'Well, my boy? You're late,' he said, seeing Jean come in.

'I met Antoinette, and she took me to see Madame du Courseau's house.'

'Was that her leaving on her bicycle?' the abbé asked.

'Yes.'

'Why doesn't she come to see me any more lately?'

'I don't know,' Jean said evasively.

Unless there was an explanation, and she really was pregnant. The abbé saw the shadow pass over Jean's features. It saddened him. The boy knew and would not say anything. All these children he had baptised, whose confessions he had heard, to whom he had given communion and nurtured in the principles of a solid religion, free from the sort of fine distinctions that risked misleading them, all of them were slipping away from him one by one. The only one who remained attached to him, Michel du Courseau, was also the only one he didn't truly care for. Which left Jean, but Jean dissembled.

'How's your work?' Albert said.

'You call it work, Papa? I don't. I carry parcels all over the place, and there's always a donkey braying at my heels, that Grosjean ... '

'What a blockhead! Fifteen years a lance-corporal. A record. To get him to leave the army they had to promise to promote him to corporal.'

'One day I'm going to punch him in the face.'

'Stay calm, Jean!' the abbé said.

'If he goes on behaving like a swine, I will, I promise.'

Albert filled his pipe to avoid replying. For some time he had been asking himself whether his son wasn't right. Why had he himself not rebelled earlier? His life would have been different if he had.

'You protest too much,' the abbé said, to change the subject. 'And you don't eat enough. How goes the rowing?'

'At lunchtime I'm all in. Knocked out ... At this rate I'll be good for nothing by next spring.'

'A society that has nothing but unskilled manual work to offer a boy like you is indefensible,' Albert concluded. 'Sweeping—'

With an expansive hand gesture he made as if to sweep around him, knocking the calvados bottle over, which the abbé, whose reflexes were always prompt, caught just in time.

'If they force another war on us,' Albert added in a loud voice, 'I hope we lose it.'

'You may not say such things!' the priest thundered, banging his fist on the table.

'I say them!' Albert declared placidly.

'Well, say them then … You don't believe a word of them.'

'I believe every word.'

The abbé raised his arms to heaven, opened his mouth to utter some imprecation that stayed in his throat and, suddenly calm, said, 'Mother Boudra brought me a dish of salt pork this afternoon. Jean, why don't you warm it up for us?'

Jean lifted the cast-iron pot onto the spirit stove. The aroma of the salt pork filled the room and the abbé fetched two bottles of the new season's sparkling cider from the cellar. They ate in silence, conscious that the slightest political allusion was likely to spoil the taste of the shoulder of pork and the lentils that went with it. In truth, sparkling cider was not the perfect complement to salt pork. They would all have preferred a solid red wine, and for an instant the abbé regretted being so poor, living from gifts and invitations. It was, none-the-less, a pleasant moment that justified the silent reflections of each of them on life and what was worth living for in this very lowly world.

After dinner Jean accompanied his father back to Monsieur Cliquet's. Albert had been walking with difficulty for some time. His orthopaedic leg hurt his groin, and to save money he refused to see a doctor, having decided that since he was no longer useful to anyone, he was not worth anyone's consideration.

'You're a good boy, and determined,' he said after a silence, as they were about to part at the gate of the cottage.

'I don't know if I can stand it much longer.'

'I wouldn't hold it against you. But what next?'

'Yes … exactly, what next.'

'I was careless, I didn't think I needed to make provision for a twist of fate like this, and now the Assistance Publique are paying your mother's hospital bills. We've become beggars.'

'It's not your fault, Papa.'

'Your mother and I'll come through it; I don't want you to worry about us. You keep pushing ahead. Make a life for yourself. Don't respect your elders too much, apart from our dear abbé. I was wrong to talk like that in front of him; I hurt him.'

'Not badly. He knows what you're like.'

'He's the only one you can rely on. It must be his religion. You see, I'll end my days believing there's something to be said for religion after all. What about you, do you feel religious?'

'No, Papa, I don't. But because of the abbé, who's been so good to me, I'll never say anything against it.'

'There's another thing I want to ask you. You know I've believed in peace ever since the armistice. I've voted socialist, because I thought socialism meant peace. Well, I was wrong. Socialism doesn't mean peace any more than the Right does. There's going to be a war, in two or three years at most. You have to promise me that you won't fight. How? I haven't a clue. But you'll see. When you were born, that was the vow I made: that this little lad would not be cannon fodder.'

Jean hesitated and murmured, 'When I was born?'

Albert seized his arm and gripped it violently.

'You know?'

'Yes.'

Despite the darkness, Jean knew that there were tears rolling down his father's lined cheeks and that, despite being so tough and reluctant ever to complain, he was silent now because he could not speak without his voice breaking. They parted after kissing each other goodnight. Albert disappeared into the shadows of the small garden and reappeared against the light of the glass-panelled front door, a limping silhouette whose left shoulder had started to drop some time ago, hunching his back. Jean returned to the rectory, where the abbé was already snoring. There was nothing to do but go to bed, worn out by the long day, and try to banish the image of Antoinette, her dress still rucked up above her bare stomach, sobbing into the mattress ticking.

At the end of the year Joseph Outen declared bankruptcy, closed his bookshop and started work at *La Vigie* in charge of the regional sports page. The film club swallowed half his salary, but a small core of cinephiles had formed, twenty or so young men and women who shared the costs. Their ambition was to collect enough money to invite a director to come and talk about his art. Joseph had written to René Clair, Jean Renoir and Marcel Carné, and all had responded favourably but regretted that they would be too busy in the months ahead. This had not discouraged him, and he still had a long list of interesting film-makers he intended to approach. Jean realised that the admirable thing about Joseph was his ability to rise above any disappointment; he was one of those men born to undertake all sorts of projects and never see a single one succeed. At the newspaper, Grosjean the supervisor looked furiously askance at the visits by one of the sacrosanct editorial staff, disturbing his drudge's labours. He disapproved of the mixing of 'classes'; it disturbed the rigid structure of a society founded on a hierarchy of workers and supervisors.

The winter was cold and gloomy and seemed to Jean like a long tunnel, and, because of his youth, he was scared that he could not see the light at the end of it. In an apathetic Europe France continued to show itself to be the least imaginative of nations. The one and only idea it could be commended for was the government's creation of a Ministry of Leisure, run by a charismatic socialist called Léo Lagrange. It was now on this man, far more than on Léon Blum, that the French rested their hopes. The number of strikes went down. Wages were no longer the unions' objective. They sought instead to purge the socialists from their own ranks of officials, while the communists reserved their fire for Blum, whom they nicknamed the 'social traitor', an insult that must have seemed mild to him in comparison to what Maurras called him, refusing to refer to him as anything other than 'that jackal-camel-dog'. But Jean could not get interested in politics, although people around him discussed it endlessly. He heard news from Ernst, who was going on with his history and philosophy course and researching a dissertation about Nietzsche. His solemn, enthusiastic letters were sprinkled with Nietzsche quotes, in which the democratic tendency was characterised as 'a decadent and enfeebled form of humanity, which it reduces to mediocrity at the same time as lessening its value'. Germany had found the 'new philosophers' Nietzsche had called for, he emphasised. Their names were Hitler and Rosenberg. German youth had found itself an incomparable leader in the shape of Baldur von Schirach. Jean showed the letters to Joseph Outen, who roared with laughter.

'Let them dream. They'll have a cruel awakening. The French army will retake the Rhineland in a week. In a fortnight it will be in Berlin. The Germans have no petrol or steel, and their army corps have no officers. A fortnight, I promise you, three weeks at the most. You can sleep soundly in your bed.'

That was all Jean wanted to know, even though he disliked the idea of a military excursion to Berlin. What would he do if he ever found himself face to face with Ernst? Shoot? Or throw open his arms? He gave up trying to decide the answer to that dilemma. Circumstances would tell. Meanwhile life felt pretty vile, so vile sometimes that he missed Mireille, her sunny restaurant balcony that looked out over the coast and the blue sea, and the life of relative ease there. He did not see Antoinette again until January. After her confession to him she had disappeared, and at Christmas Madame du Courseau moved into her house, which was finished at last. Albert had a job again: to create a garden where before there had only been a meadow and a few apple trees. Marie-Thérèse had nowhere for him to stay, however, and every morning he had to cover the two kilometres to the house on foot. The way back in the evening was, if anything, more painful.

At the slightest effort his orthopaedic leg hurt him badly, and he had developed varicose veins in the other leg. At least at La Sauveté he had had his own place, while at the new house, which was bourgeois and tasteless, he considered himself merely an employee. Not a word of complaint passed his lips.

At the end of January, coming home exhausted from his job at *La Vigie*, Jean learnt from the abbé that an ambulance had been called that morning to take Antoinette to hospital. The abbé knew nothing more.

'Go and see her at lunchtime tomorrow, when you see your mother. And let me know what's wrong. I feel everyone is spinning mysteries around me.'

Jean saw Antoinette the next day. She was in a room on her own, pale and swollen-faced. Lying without a pillow, she was not allowed to raise her head.

'I was waiting for you,' she said. 'I was waiting for you, no one else. Come here. Do you remember when you were a little boy and I adored you? I protected you … '

'I haven't forgotten.'

'I love you even more now.'

'You had a funny way of showing it.'

'Maybe. At least it taught me that I really love you.'

'I'd prefer you to tell me what's wrong with you.'

'Do you remember what I said to you that last evening we saw each other?'

'I didn't believe it.'

'It was true, and even if you find it boring I'm going to tell you what happened afterwards. I was pregnant—'

'You aren't any more?'

No. Gontran Longuet got me in trouble. He was like you, he

287

didn't believe me. I threatened him and yesterday morning he took me to Anna, you know, that woman who lives in your old house. She convinced me that it was nothing at all, and then she cut me up like a torturer, the witch, and when she couldn't stop me haemorrhaging she and her husband got scared. They put me in Gontran's car, and he drove me to the last bend before the house. It was a hundred metres from the door. I couldn't make it and I fell down. Michel came out and saw me. If I'm not dead, it's because of him.'

Jean took her limp hand, lying on the sheet. He studied her face, disfigured like the night she had wept in the deserted house. She was weak and defenceless, and above all she had reminded him of their childhood and the protective love she had wrapped him in then, before all the games that had led to their misunderstandings. Perhaps something else could grow between them now, a brotherly, watchful feeling. He squeezed her hand and kissed her fingers. A smile appeared on her bloodless lips.

'Promise?' she said. 'We'll tell each other everything—'

She did not finish. Her brother entered the room.

We have not seen Michel for a long time, apart from his recent furtive appearance at mass. Years have passed since his morbidly jealous childhood. He is tall and good-looking, if charmless, and the gaze he directs at others is one of haughty attention. Last December he gave a recital of songs from Fauré to Debussy at Paris, Bordeaux and Lyon, and was commissioned by an art-book publisher to produce twenty plate illustrations for a luxury edition of the Song of Songs. This recognition of his dual talent has contributed in no small measure to the making of the high idea he has of himself, and in a bedroom drawer he secretly keeps a scrapbook bound in red leather, in which his mother has religiously pasted the smallest newspaper cutting about him. His father's departure seems to have liberated the nervous boy he once was. The house was not big enough for two men, and the day Michel was asked about his ambitions and replied, 'I'm good at music and engraving,' Antoine had raised his eyebrows, looked at his son in astonishment, as if he were an impostor, and answered unexpectedly,

'You want to be an artist? It's entirely up to you, but artists bore me. They only ever talk about money.'

Michel had shrugged his shoulders, privately dismissing his father as a philistine. He would have been astonished to learn that in ten years Antoine had absent-mindedly purchased, piece by piece, almost never putting a foot wrong, a collection of modern works that was attracting more and more visitors to Marie-Dévote's hotel. Of course Antoine had seen several of his son's oil paintings, and noticed some of his engravings and lithographs, but Michel's talents as a painter were not evident to him and his engraving work, which was always dark, as if dominated by storms and haunted by the atrocities of martyrdom, and unsettlingly peopled by excessively beautiful young men, failed to appeal to a nature that now worshipped the light. He came within a hair's breadth of rejecting his son's work outright as old-fashioned, despite usually holding back from definitive judgements and relying purely on his emotions, although his own, more modest word for it was pleasure.

Michel kissed Antoinette and addressed Jean with a nod. Jean's presence visibly embarrassed him, and the demeanour he had adopted before entering the room no longer suited this meeting of all three of them, largely because Jean tried to catch his eye and in failing to do so discovered the older boy for the first time, so ill at ease with himself and yet so satisfied with his own inner tensions, which he had arrogantly elevated into a Christian quest for the soul. For a long period, until the story of what had happened at the cliff, they had been brought up as brothers. Then they had ignored each other. Now they stood face to face, both men and capable of clothing their feelings in a modicum of courtesy, but Jean identified something so all-enveloping and strange about Michel that he felt deeply uneasy, kissed Antoinette, and left without saying another word.

Jeanne was in a nearby ward. Jean crossed the sunny courtyard, where a few elderly patients were walking bundled up in their coarse blue Assistance cloaks. A ruptured aneurysm had recently affected Jeanne's faculties, and she had started to see Albert as her father and Jean as her husband, whom she attacked acrimoniously for leaving her a prisoner in the hospital.

'You wanted to get rid of me!' she shouted as he came to her bedside. 'I'll never let you. I'm going to stay alive, and even the spy you pay to inject me with poison every evening knows that I know. I'm not budging from here … At least they protect me … '

More than the senseless things his mother said, Jean suffered from the hostile, watchful silence of her bed companions. Around him toothless old ladies with flabby wattles and eyes clouded by leucomas or glaucomas gave him sly, hateful looks. They had ended up believing in Jeanne's demented speeches and took her part, pitying her when she broke off from her endless cogitation to dissolve into tears, repeating, 'Times are hard … times are hard … '

Jean stayed for five minutes, quickly disheartened, no longer recognising in this poor wandering old lady whose hair had gone white in the space of a few months the tirelessly kind woman who had brought him up so indulgently and generously. This was how people deteriorated with age and revealed their bewildered, animal soul. He would have given almost anything not to see her like this, for her to have had the chance to disappear before she deteriorated, leaving behind only noble and generous memories.

That evening as he came out of *La Vigie* he met Michel waiting for him on the pavement.

'I'm going to Grangeville. I thought I could give you a lift.'

For the last six months Michel had been driving a Peugeot 201, a present from his mother. When he used it, which was not often, he drove cautiously, with both gloved hands on the steering wheel, neck craning forward, hooting at every bend, and with none of his father's Bugatti-driving impulsiveness. Jean got in beside him, without thinking to thank him. He had had his fill of the day, whose habitual pointlessness had been increased by the sadness of seeing Antoinette ill and his mother half mad.

'I much appreciated your visit to my sister.' Michel said, 'Such occasions bring us closer. Yesterday I thought she was dying.'

'She'll be all right.'

'I prayed for her for a long time this afternoon.'

Jean refrained from making a comment that would have been repeated to the abbé Le Couec. In any case he found it hard to imagine that Michel seriously believed in the effectiveness of his prayers. Later he realised he was wrong: Michel really had cloistered himself inside a severe faith in which he fought against a forked demon with an angel's face. The secret of that struggle permitted him, he believed, to cast his implacable gaze over the rest of the world.

'My mother would like to see you,' he said.

'It's not hard.'

'There was a misunderstanding.'

'Who created it?'

'I did! I know. It took me a long time to find out the truth. I feel deeply remorseful about it.'

'Remorseful? You?'

'Why not me?'

'You always hated me.'

'Children can't control their feelings. When I became a man, I understood. Forgive me, Jean. Whenever I've thought about your generous and noble character, it has helped me be a better Christian. I want to thank you for the great lesson you've taught me. I shan't forget it.'

'Let's not speak about the past,' Jean said.

Michel disgusted him. He felt sick.

'There's someone else who would very much like to see you again,' Michel added.

'Who?'

'Chantal de Malemort. She's surprised you haven't been in touch since you came back from Italy.'

'Aren't you going to marry her?'

'No. An artist doesn't marry. My life will be solitary or it won't. I see Chantal often. She has a deep, beautiful soul. Pure and Christian. A transparent being.'

They had arrived at Grangeville, and the Peugeot stopped outside the rectory.

'It was good to see you again,' Michel said. 'We shouldn't lose sight of each other in future.'

'Does your faith have any room for charity?'

'Of course. Why?'

'My father's sixty. His orthopaedic leg hurts him badly and so does his good leg, every morning when he comes over to you. Go and fetch him in your car and take him home in the evening. It'll be your good deed for the day.'

'He's never said anything to us.'

'He puts up with pain in the name of peace. He's a proud man.'

'I'm perfectly happy to do that, although there are times when my work—'

'You decide. Good evening, Michel.'

Antoinette recovered, with the sad certainty that she would never have children. Widespread rumours accused the abortionist at the lodge, who would have gone to prison without the intervention of René Mangepain, Madame du Courseau's brother. The deputy paid frequent visits to the Longuets, who had moved into La Sauveté.

When people criticised him for his closeness, he defended himself on political grounds. Monsieur Longuet, despite having retired from business, represented real electoral power. 'Why,' René Mangepain asked, 'abandon men of such influence to a conservative and fossilised Right? Why should it always be the bishops who open their premises to pimps? Why, despite that industry's unfair contracts, shouldn't men of progress add their voices to those of the Left, bringing, I might add, a substantial clientele with them? We should have considered all this much earlier. I am now devoting myself to the task, despite my personal feelings of revulsion.'

In March, having saved enough from his pittance of a salary, Jean was able to buy himself a bicycle, and on Sundays he once again met Chantal de Malemort exercising her horse in the forest of Arques. They resumed their conversations, of which we have already offered an outline, full of veiled meanings, sometimes in both directions, and always ingenuous. At night, when the abbé's grumbling snoring kept him awake, Jean no longer thought of Mireille: it was Chantal's face he conjured up, her gloved hands on her reins, the smell of fresh grass or hay that she gave off, the seriousness with which she responded to everything. Yet she no longer appeared to be, as she had before, a disembodied creature to be shaken awake in the depths of the wood, but a woman, a desirable woman whose eyes he would have liked to kiss and whose stomach he would have liked to stroke. Where and how could that come about? Their intimacy, such as it was, remained buried, and whenever he glimpsed her unexpectedly in her father's company, even though the marquis was hardly any different on his tractor or in his stables from any of the other farmers on his estate, Jean was acutely aware of the distance that separated him, a porter at the *La Vigie* printing works, from a young woman wreathed in a fabulous past, one of her ancestors, Jehan de Malemort, having been the admiral commanding the squadron of Louis XIV that had routed the English in the North Sea. He was not in an entirely inferior position in relation to her, despite his being on foot or bicycle and a gardener's son and her on horseback and a marquis's daughter. For Chantal de Malemort had never left Normandy. She sometimes went to Dieppe to an aunt's house, or to Rouen to meet some cousins, but had not even been to Paris, whereas Jean could talk about Newhaven, London, Milan, Florence, Rome and the south of France. Their memory gnawed at his heart. What use was that first bagful of experience, if he had to spend the rest of his life portering parcels at *La Vigie* under the permanently furious scrutiny of that shit Grosjean? He was so acutely aware that his journeys constituted his one area of superiority that when he was with Chantal he began making up stories and pretending he was getting ready for another great departure on his eighteenth birthday.

'It's a secret,' she said. 'I understand. One you don't even want to tell me, who will not give it away. But I demand that you promise—'

'You don't need to demand.'

'You'll write to me.'

'At the château?'

'Why not? We're not doing anything wrong.'

He agreed that she was right, they weren't doing anything wrong, and he did not dare say how sorry he was that they weren't. Everything remained innocent and vague between them. Their growing friendship would perhaps never go further than that. Jean would have loved to perform some distinguished task for her, the kind of thing he had read in the novels of Alexandre Dumas: to chastise a ruffian, stop her runaway horse, save the marquis from a fire. He had only had one opportunity he could really boast about. Chantal had complained to him that Gontran Longuet was pursuing her in his absurd Georges Irat convertible. The brothel-keeper's son seemed to like overtaking her, calling out unfunny remarks and hooting madly, making her horse shy and bolt. One Sunday morning Jean was lucky enough to come across him on the track that ran past La Sauveté. Up till now I have hardly described Gontran, a character devoid of interest in any case, and yet impressive to some young provincial ladies merely by virtue of coming from Paris, driving a sports car, and spending money in bars. In 1937 he was a tall beanpole with slicked-back hair, on which there usually sat an English cap. He liked posing as a cad. Jean stopped him at the side of the track. Gontran demanded to know what he wanted with such contemptuous rudeness that Jean squeezed his fists in his pockets.

'Just to tell you to keep away from Chantal de Malemort.'

'We'll see about that.'

'I'm telling you to see about it, you prick.'

'No one's ever called me a prick.'

'Yes they have. Me. Just now.'

Jean was counting on his strength, but had not fought much in his life, just two or three times at the most at his lycée, and never with great conviction. He judged Gontran to be of about equal strength. He slapped him, knocking off his arrogant English cap. They exchanged a few almost cautious blows. Gontran was not jeering any more and his face was livid. Jean punched him in the eye and split his cheek. Blood ran. Unfortunately the brawls he had taken part in while working for his father had taught Gontran a vicious defence: twisting on his left leg, he smashed his right foot into his opponent's pelvis. Jean doubled up.

'And I suggest you don't start that again,' he said, retrieving his cap from the dirt.

Jean got off with a bruised lower stomach for the next fortnight. It might have been worse. But Gontran, with a split cheek and black eye, was the laughing stock of Grangeville. He no longer hung around Mademoiselle de Malemort. Joseph Outen, hearing what had happened, drew a moral from it.

'The truth is, you don't know how to fight. It's a gap in your education. I know a Japanese man here who gives judo lessons. Go and enrol—'

'No money.'

'He's a saint. He teaches for the greater love of Buddha.'

Jean attended the classes a dozen times and gave up. It was asking too much of his strength, when training was intensifying at Dieppe Rowing Club. In June he competed with Joseph in a coxed pair for the club heats and won. Two weeks later they faced the Rouen club. Fifty metres before the finish, they were leading and on the point of winning when Joseph drove his blade in too deeply. The scull nearly capsized and they came third. Joseph refused to accept the defeat and, blaming the equipment, gave up rowing. He was in any case at a period of great decisions in his life, and at the same time quit his job as sports editor at *La Vigie*, wound up the film club, sold his books and furniture, keeping only his Littré,[14] a bed, and a table and chair that he set up in a servant's room in an attic overlooking the port. He had wasted too much time. He was going to write a book, something completely new, in which he would make clear, by means of fiction, that humanity lives in a prison so long it refuses to divest itself of its need for love and money. He intended to finish by September, just in time for the NRF[15] to publish it before the prize season. A representative of that house had confirmed to him that they were urgently looking for new manuscripts. If the NRF could not promise him their full support for the Goncourt,[16] he would give his novel to Grasset.

'I'm taking holy orders,' he said to Jean. 'You understand what that means: blinkers on. Don't disturb me for anything. Find yourself another crew member at the Club. It wasn't the equipment that let me down at Rouen, it was me who let the equipment down. I wasn't where I should have been. I was already in my book ... '

A few days later, when he visited the hospital to see his mother, Jean was surprised to see a screen around her bed. She had died half an hour earlier. Marie-Thérèse du Courseau arrived from Grangeville with Albert who, numb and with trembling lips, repeated several times in a hoarse voice, 'It's happened to others besides me … it's happened to others besides me … '

The abbé Le Couec delivered a funeral oration so affecting and so simple that Albert suddenly understood the extent of his misfortune and the solitude to which he had been condemned. Jean had made confession the night before and this time took communion, kneeling at the altar next to Michel du Courseau, who stealthily squeezed his hand and murmured, 'I am your brother.'

At the cemetery, through tears that he kept in check with the greatest difficulty, Jean saw the Malemorts and their daughter crossing themselves as the coffin was lowered into the small vault. The marquis and marquise shook his hand, Chantal kissed him on both cheeks, and the intense happiness of her kissing him lightened the sad day. The next day he resumed work at *La Vigie*, where Grosjean behaved less odiously than usual. Pedalling back to the rectory that evening, he found Antoinette waiting at the top of the hill.

'I couldn't speak to you yesterday,' she said. 'There were too many people. You must be very sad.'

'Yes.'

'Are you going to go away?'

'How do you know?'

'Chantal told us. She knows more of your secrets than I do. What are you hoping for?'

'Nothing.'

'Don't leave me without saying goodbye.'

They walked together down a path that cut across the fields, where they kissed for a long time. Antoinette had lost weight after her terrible experience. She was no longer the deliciously ripe fragrant fruit he had stroked in the hay, but a nervous and desperate woman, who reminded him more of Mireille than anyone else.

'Before you leave,' Antoinette said, 'we'll go and spend the night in a hotel in Dieppe. I want to sleep in your arms and wake up next to you.'

How lonely she must be! Marie-Thérèse du Courseau's excessive love for her son had taken an aggressive form towards everything that upset him, even if it was no more than another presence. And how could she hope to marry Antoinette off after what had happened? Everyone knew. The only way out would have been to set her free, send her to Paris, but the idea of setting foot outside Normandy never occurred to Madame du Courseau. One married among one's own, in one's own milieu, never outside.

Jean promised. Weeks passed. He wrote to Palfy and by return received a long telegram.

> Marvellous! I'm expecting you. Come, and we shall invent the future. I'm putting the caviar on ice. Bring a baguette and a ripe Camembert. Business is going well. The world is our oyster. Constantin

Jean had his eighteenth birthday, and the only thoughtful present he received was an album bound in black leather of twenty drawings by Michel. They were all of him. He felt a sense of embarrassment and thanked Michel flatly, in a quiet moment, Michel having explained that his mother was to know nothing. Why such a mystery?

Albert took Jean's departure philosophically.

'I can't tell you to stay, though I can see nothing good in your journey. But I have no right to keep you in France. Everything here is rotten. Perhaps it's the same with the English, in which case you'll come back and be happy to see us again. If war breaks out between France and Germany, don't listen to the warmongers. Stay put, where it's safe …'

The abbé Le Couec added, 'I knew the demon of travel would not let you go. Be careful of life's many traps. Will you find work? The English are not pushovers. Anyway, you're a free man.'

And so everyone, apart from him, had known for a long time that he was leaving. Instead of the wealth of vague and innocent advice he received, he would have preferred a bit of money. His savings amounted to 2000 francs, enough to live on for a month once he had bought himself a suit. He left *La Vigie* on 31 July without bothering to tell his employers, resisting the violent impulse to punch Grosjean's face and shout at the women whose job it was to fold the print work that all in all they were the biggest bunch of idiots he had ever come across. He plucked up courage to telephone Chantal and invite her to a last meeting. She arrived on a bicycle. Her horse was lame. They left their bicycles behind a bush and walked in the lovely forest.

'I wanted to say goodbye to you. Can I still write to you?'

'Of course. What could be more natural?'

What else was there to to be said? One might have been tempted to add: alas! The two had known each other since they were children, and no shadow had ever fallen between them.

'I talked to my father about you. He thinks you're right. At your age it's suffocating here. You'll come back a man. You will come back, won't you?'

'Yes. I'll come back.'

The truth was that up to this point he had never thought about coming back, or leaving, for good. The commitment that she was asking of him was an important one whose significance seemed not even to occur to her.

'My father approves of you,' she said. 'He praises your spirit of adventure. He regrets … '

She stopped, embarrassed. Jean came to her aid.

'That I'm the son of a gardener?'

'Oh no. It's not that. We're only farmers ourselves now—'

'Living in a handsome château.'

'They're just appearances.'

'I can reassure you on one matter: I'm not a gardener's son, even if I wouldn't blush to be one.'

'I know.'

'You too!'

He could not understand how his origins had become an open secret.

'And do people know who my parents are?'

'No.'

For a moment his hopes had been raised. Was Chantal concealing something that he would perhaps find out one day, after everyone else? Seeing him looking so sad, she put up her hand and stroked his forehead, as if to chase away the clouds there. Jean grasped her hand and kissed it.

'I'm glad we're such good friends.' Chantal said, stepping away.

There would be nothing else between them, except for that ghostly gesture and its fleeting aftermath. Things needed to be that way in order to last. They carried on walking through the forest for a long time, both with heavy hearts, neither of them knowing whether the other suffered as they did. When they came back to their bicycles they kissed each other politely on the cheeks.

'Come back soon!' Chantal whispered.

He watched her pedal away down the path, her skirt revealing her pretty, pale legs, and only moved when she had disappeared around the corner of the gamekeeper's lodge, where the dogs barked as she passed.

The same evening, after his goodbyes to Monsieur Cliquet, Captain Duclou, his father and the abbé, he walked down to Dieppe with his single small case, asked for a room at the Hôtel de l'Océan and waited for Antoinette, who arrived just after he had finished dinner. They spent the night together. Their lovemaking was not the same any more. She wept, and he hugged her tightly until dawn began to lighten the sky and the gulls announced the coming day with their plaintive cries. Antoinette was still sleeping when he left, case in hand, and went down to the port to have a coffee by the landing-stage. Joseph joined him in espadrilles, cotton trousers and a turtleneck sweater. Two months of confinement had changed him almost beyond recognition. Eating and drinking only bread and butter and coffee, leaving his room only when he had to, he seemed unsteady on his long legs, and in his gaunt pale face, framed by a black beard, his eyes shone, feverish. Did he realise he looked like Dostoyevsky, like *The House of the Dead* revisited? Without the Russian's talent, alas, although the famous novel had made considerable progress, driven on by its author's whip.

'You're leaving, then,' he said. 'You've decided to run for it.'

'To run to the future.'

'When you come back, I'll either have won the Goncourt or I'll be the last of the losers. Don't write to me. I shan't have time to write back.'

The packet left at nine o'clock. Jean was abandoning his country to a new prime minister, Camille Chautemps, whose name the right-wing press invariably wrote by preceding it with a ∴.

'Have a look round it,' Palfy said. 'It's a monument. No two are the same. It was ordered specially in 1930 by Lord Albigate to drive around his estate in Suffolk, a distance of eighteen miles. A short expedition that he undertook once a year. Add it up: that makes 126 miles in seven years, not much more than 200 kilometres. It's new, in other words. Obviously its body doesn't have the same lines as a modern car. High wings, and the same radiator grille they've had since 1912, but that's the beauty of a Rolls-Royce. They've never thought of themselves as peanut sellers. A loyal clientele. Try to buy one if your name's Levy. They'll look at their order book and tell you there is nothing available until 1947. Albigate asked to see my certificate of baptism before he'd let me have it, forgetting for a second that he married a Rosenstein. But honour was satisfied.'

Jean walked around the silver Rolls parked at the bottom of the gangplank, gleaming in the afternoon sun as if it had just left the factory. The green hide cushions, the walnut burl dashboard, the internal intercom, everything was of a fully achieved and lordly distinction. It really was an extremely incongruous sight among the dusty production-line cars that were coming off the ferry and lining up to present themselves for customs inspection. Palfy had made himself worthy of driving it, in his golfing plus fours and his calves sheathed in green tasselled hose. He had not changed, though his face looked more yellow than before.

'I'm not sure,' he said, 'that you'll ever see a more beautiful example. To tell you the truth, I'm thinking very seriously, the day I no longer have the use of it, of burning it rather than see it fall into unworthy hands. Put your case on the back seat and let's go.'

After a rather rough crossing Jean could have done with a sandwich to settle his stomach, but it was quite clear that one did not eat sandwiches in a Rolls-Royce. One only drank, thanks to a silver drinks cabinet prettily built in to the rear compartment. At Palfy's suggestion Jean poured them each a neat whisky as they drove out of Newhaven.

'My outfit isn't nearly elegant enough for your car,' Jean said. 'I should stay outside, on the running board.'

'Outfit! Oh, the clumsiness! Certain people will judge you by your use of such words. We say suit. And yes, you're right, your suit reeks of off-the-pegness. We'll deal with all that. First I shall drive you to my tailor … '

'I have enough to live on for a month if I'm not extravagant.'

'You fool, who said anything about paying the tailor? Only the nouveaux riches have such egregious taste, and you'll see how fast it loses them respect in Savile Row. Trust me.'

'I haven't noticed you bringing much good fortune to those who trust you.'

'Are you becoming sarcastic in your old age? Be quiet, you're still a child.'

'All right. I'll be quiet.'

The Rolls-Royce sped noiselessly along a country road that Jean had travelled five years earlier, first on his bicycle and then in the prince's Hispano-Suiza, with Salah driving him. He saw it as a definite sign of his advancement, since one could hardly imagine anything more superior than a Rolls, unless it was the monarch's state coach. Had Palfy stolen this car, as it was his habit? It would all end badly one day, but the anxiety that Jean felt at sharing his friend's adventures again was also tinged with pleasure. It banished the last crushing year of mediocrity that he had spent in France, waiting for something, anything new to happen. It was a year that had passed desperately slowly, and now here he was, rolling at sixty miles an hour along a lovely road through little red-brick towns with bright red and apple-green shopfronts. It was impossible for this not to be the dawning of a new era, the beginning of a man's life of multiple twists and turns. Palfy had not changed. Precise, relaxed, he drove with a light hand, displaying an almost exaggerated courtesy towards cars he overtook or to which he gave way. It occurred to Jean that he did not even know which country his friend was from.

'That's rather complicated,' Palfy said. 'My mother was English, my father Serbian, and I was born in France, at Nice. So I'm French by accident, merely because my father was there trying out an infallible system at the Casino on the Jetée-Promenade. That said – since you're interested – I'll make a confession. I'm not just French by civil status, as they say, but in my heart too. It's true. It's my ridiculous side.'

'Why ridiculous?'

'Who still believes in the French? But who does things better than they do? Talking of which, I hope you haven't forgotten the Camembert and baguette.'

'No. They're there in my case.'

'We'll have them tonight. I have a couple of friends for dinner. The Ascots. Charming, both of them.'

'I don't speak English.'

'We're going to sort that out too. A good teacher—'

'Not too strict.'

Palfy roared with laughter.

'You really astonish me! How is it that you already know about such a typically English vice?'

'What vice?'

'The one with whips, chains, spanking.'

'I don't know anything about it, except that a few years ago I met a French lady in Soho who gave lessons and claimed to be very strict.'

'Goodness me!' Palfy said with a smile.

'A friend told me later she'd been murdered. She was called Madame Germaine.'

'I remember reading something about that. She was one of those many French prostitutes who offer their London clients the latest refinements on Masoch's pleasures. There are about a hundred of them in Soho, generally well thought of, so they quickly become rich. After working here for three or four years they go back to France with a nice lump sum, settle somewhere provincial, open a haberdasher's or a shop selling religious pictures and marry into the petty bourgeoisie. I know a couple like that: one in Vannes, the other at Colmar. Excellent mothers ... '

Jean felt Palfy was making fun of him.

'If you like, I'll introduce you to one,' Palfy said.

'When?'

'Not tonight, we have a dinner. But tomorrow if you like.'

Jean was ill at ease. He thought about Salah, whom he had not yet mentioned to Palfy. What pleasures had the prince's chauffeur been seeking in these unsavoury districts? Palfy's disclosures showed Salah in a disturbing light. A hundred questions occurred to Jean, to which it was getting interesting to find answers. Who were all those international Maries who had played the housemaid at Mademoiselle Geneviève's? Who was the blonde mulatto Marie whom he had met at Hampton Court, glimpsed later in the hall of the Chelsea house, then seen again in the brasserie in Via del Babuino? These were mysteries that needed solving. The Rolls was coming into the London suburbs. People here hardly gave the car a second glance, despite the fact that in all the crushing repetitive ugliness that surrounded it, it looked like a meteorite, an incomprehensible thing of grandiose beauty from another planet, which deigned to reflect in its silver bonnet and chrome radiator the fleeting, deformed images of a world of troglodytes.

Palfy drove his friend straight to Savile Row, where a tailor and his staff busied themselves about them. Palfy chose cloth for five suits and a dinner jacket for Jean, then led him to a shirtmaker and bootmaker.

'I don't want anyone to notice you,' he said. 'This evening I'll lend you a dinner jacket of my father's. He was about your height. Fortunately for you, it's old and very shabby and nearly antique, and therefore madly chic. It doesn't fit me, I regret to say. My father was tall and broad-shouldered.'

Palfy was living in Eaton Square, in a four-roomed flat that possessed a butler who wore a black suit and tie and white gloves.

'This is Price,' Palfy said. 'You'll notice that he's about my size. He's very good for breaking in my new shoes. Essential man, in every way. Of course he doesn't know French, but if you can say "yes" and "no", you'll got on very well with him.'

'Then – you've become rich?' Jean asked, dismayed, unable to believe that one could surround oneself with such comfort and pay for it all with bad cheques.

'Well, it's true that you haven't known me in my comfortable phase. But the wheel turns. Have a bath and get yourself ready. Dinner is at seven thirty. Price will bring you a tie and socks. Relax.'

History was repeating itself. This second arrival in London resembled, in its surprises, the first one five years earlier. Jean gave up trying to think and even drifted off to sleep for a few moments in his bath, exhausted by the night spent with Antoinette and the bad crossing. A discreet knock at the bathroom door woke him. Price's muffled voice was calling, 'Mr Arnaud, please.'

He dressed in a hurry. The dinner jacket fitted him well, despite being a little short in the sleeves. He had some difficulty buttoning the stiff collar and realised he had entirely forgotten how to tie a bow-tie. Price knocked at the door a second time. Jean opened it and, pointing at his neck, indicated his predicament. The butler understood immediately, pulled off his gloves, and tied the black tie. It was perfect.

But why go to such trouble? The Ascots were a couple of indeterminate age, rather hatchet-faced, who spoke absolutely incomprehensible English. Jane – despite her sharp features her face was pretty, her skin fresh – wore a lamé dress will all the grace of a coal sack. Her neckline gaped when she leant forward, revealing two fairly unappetising poached eggs. Both Ascots were very affable to Jean at the outset, and then, rapidly realising that he was not from their world, ignored him for the rest of the evening, talking only to Palfy, who gave up translating when he gauged Jean's total lack of interest in their extended personal conversation about a society in which he knew no one. To tell the truth, the dry Martini before dinner, the sherry with the turtle consommé, the claret with the roast, the Graves with the apple tart, the port with the Camembert (over which they went into raptures, gaining Jean a brief flicker of renewed interest) and the brandy with the coffee had all been too much for him to take. He was dropping from fatigue; his eyelids were drooping, his tongue was like cardboard, his mind wandering, mostly back to Antoinette, whom he would have liked to be caressing again tonight, after unbuttoning the stiff collar that had been digging into his neck without mercy. At ten thirty the Ascots stood up and left. Palfy saw them to their car. He returned to find Jean collapsed on the sofa.

'Not quite up to the mark yet, I see,' he said. 'My friends thought you were charming.'

'Charming? Me?'

'Utterly. They've invited you to the country next weekend.'

'You must be mistaken.'

'Well, obviously they're not particularly entertaining hosts, but it will amuse you to experience English country life for yourself.'

'Constantin, I didn't come here for that. I'm looking for work. Any work. You have to help me find something, not too mindless if at all possible. I dragged parcels around for nearly a year. I couldn't go on.'

'Work? Listen, my fine fellow. I've worked very little in my life and have no connections whatever among those who do. It's no good your relying on me to help you there.'

'But I can't just sponge off you, can I?'

'Why not? I live very well from sponging off other people. Let's make the most of it. Later on, you'll do your bit to help me if you get the chance.'

Dog-tired, Jean gave up arguing and went to bed to sleep and dream of Chantal de Malemort who, regarding him sadly, informed him that she knew about his affair with Antoinette and was giving him up.

'As a good Christian,' she said, 'I must sacrifice myself for that sinner's salvation. She loves you. Do not let her down. She is waiting for you in the barn with the abbé Le Couec, who will bless you.'

'What about you?'

'I am going to marry Michel. For his salvation.'

The revelation was so unpleasant that he awoke in the grip of nausea, and only just made it to the bathroom in time.

'You look positively green!' Palfy said to him at breakfast.

'I'm never going to touch another drop of alcohol.'

'You're absurd! You just need to get used to it, show your liver what's what. It's impossible to exist in society without drinking. Look at my complexion. I'm turning into a lemon, but I drink and I never suffer for it. It's a question of will.'

Price came in, wheeling a trolley. The poached eggs and bacon were still cooking beneath a silver dome. Jean ate while he listened to Palfy.

'You interest me, and you have every right to wonder why. First of all I assure you I have not the slightest interest in pinching your bottom. Do not for a moment imagine that I am a poof, even if I'm not all that wild about women. I know they find you attractive, and in time they'll find you more and more attractive. I noticed it only last night with Jane Ascot. On the way out she asked how she might meet you again.'

Jean looked at the poached eggs on his plate and remembered Mrs Ascot's gaping neckline.

'I know, I know,' Palfy went on, 'there's not much meat on her and she's not a wonderful example, but it's a sign: you're good-looking and, as they said in the eighteenth century, you have honesty written all over your face. What an advantage you have over me! Obviously you're raw material, shapeless, have not the slightest idea of how to keep a boring conversation going and possess none of the tools one needs to navigate one's way through a world of pretence. In short, it all remains to be done with you – apart from teaching you table manners. There someone has shown you what to do, and I've never seen you strike a false or vulgar note at dinner. One day we shall also get to the bottom of the mystery of your birth, though I personally don't set much store by genetics. You're the son of the people who brought you up.'

Jean, who had been considering wiping the yolk off his plate with a slice of bread, thought better of it. Price was standing behind him. He already felt badly enough about having let the servant see his striped cotton pyjamas, threadbare shirts and woolly slippers. Price had rummaged vainly in his case for a dressing gown.

'I am not motivated by fine feelings,' Palfy continued, 'if it helps you put away your scruples. My offer of an accelerated education is purely so that we can collaborate. I have big plans.'

'Aren't you going to tell me what they are?'

'No. Later.'

His refusal was terse. The matter was not for discussion. Jean wondered whether it would not be more prudent to leave there and then, the way he had left Mireille's. But what was he going to do with two thousand francs in his pocket? Get another job as a labourer? Scrub pans, deliver parcels, open doors? Watchful as a cat, Palfy sensed his hesitation.

'You can say no,' he said. 'I shan't hold it against you. I'll even drive you back to Newhaven.'

'I'm staying.'

'In that case, let's make a start.'

For a month Jean spent six hours a day following an intensive English course. He realised he had some basic knowledge, some ideas and even a vocabulary, without ever having established the connection between its constituent parts. The suits were finished. Palfy asked for the bill to be sent. The tailor exclaimed that there was all the time in the world. In the evenings Palfy hosted dinners at his club or at home. Never more than two guests, whom he chose carefully and whose background and what they represented he explained to Jean beforehand. Jean understood English better and better and was able to follow a conversation. No one paid much attention to him, and that left him free to observe as much as he wished. The following day Palfy would question him.

'What do you imagine Jonathan Sandow does for a living?'

'I've no idea, really. He didn't give a single clue.'

'For the very good reason that he doesn't do anything. He has a private income that is diminishing by the year. He's a complete fool and has a seat in the House of Lords. His wife left him for two years to go and live with a fisherman on Ischia. She came back last Christmas, and Jonathan pointed out to her that she was late for dinner.'

'I'll never understand anything about the English!'

Palfy was exultant: it was exactly what he was meant to say. Besides, there was nothing to understand. Jean was progressing by leaps and bounds. Palfy's own plans, however, remained secret. He regarded questions of money with as much contempt as ever. Suppliers, the garage, restaurants sent their bills to Eaton Square. Someone must have paid from time to time, otherwise Palfy would not have been able to disport himself like a lord for very long. Jean noticed how easily and quickly one picked up the habit of living without cares. He noted in his moleskin notebook,

> *f) Constantin is a perfect parasite. I should have nothing but contempt for his sort. But how, when I'm a parasite too? We live in a dream. It will be a rude awakening. Unless there is*

no awakening. In short, the moral is clear: living honestly is the surest way to wear yourself out. Society offers a thousand different solutions to enterprising spirits who want to leave drudgery behind. If I'd stayed at La Vigie, after twenty-five years of hard-working and loyal service I could have looked forward to taking Grosjean's place. By burning my bridges, taking a risk, I gave myself the chance to escape my misery.

g) Now the second question looms with more and more urgency. Who is Palfy? I'd give almost anything for him to tell me the truth about his financial situation. Am I the only one to know that he's a fraud?

Palfy declined several invitations to the country.

'We must think carefully,' he said to Jean. 'You're not quite ready yet. It would be a disaster.'

One day, instead of having lunch, Jean left his English lesson and found his way to the Chelsea street where he thought he might find Salah. The Hispano-Suiza was not in front of the house. He plucked up his courage and pressed the bell. A valet in a striped waistcoat, who was not the strange and obsequious Baptiste, opened the door.

'Mademoiselle du Courseau?'

'Oh, Mademoiselle isn't here,' the valet answered in French. 'Mademoiselle is in Scotland. She will be back on Monday next.'

'And Salah?'

'Salah is with Monseigneur on the French Riviera, at Cannes. If Monsieur would like to leave a message for Mademoiselle ... '

'Will you tell her that Jean Arnaud is in London? I'll telephone her when she comes back.'

'Very good, Monsieur.'

It had certainly been a mistake to have asked for news of the chauffeur too – a mistake that could have roused the new Baptiste's suspicions – but Jean noticed that for the first time a servant's prejudice had judged him favourably on his outward appearance.

That evening he mentioned this to Palfy, telling him the story of his first meeting with the prince, and he was surprised to see his friend paying close attention.

'How dramatic! Very few people know him. He's thought to be fabulously rich, and no one knows where his fortune comes from. As for her … mmm … '

'What do you mean?'

'I've missed her twice at weekends with friends. She is the darling of bohemian, super-rich London. Very pretty, I'm told. You *must* see her … *we* must see her … '

Palfy's eyes lit up, and Jean realised that in the situation in which he found himself he had just been slipped a trump card: Mademoiselle Geneviève. He would not disregard it.

The author has already regretted on several occasions not being able to speak at greater length about Geneviève du Courseau. We have seen her appear on the balcony outside her room when her father visited her just after the war. She was nineteen years old. Let us add up the years: she is thirty-six now and her beauty has grown and matured. But perhaps it is excessive to talk of beauty when one thinks of her face. Vivacity is more accurate. This young woman brushed by death, who carries a weakness that she carefully conceals, has been playing a wonderful part for fifteen years: she is the delight, the reason for living, the most admired object of a reserved and generous man who makes no demands and maintains her in splendour. She has freed herself completely from the milieu in which she was born, which is now no more than a distant memory. We have already noted this: she came back to La Sauveté only once, and then doubtless because it was on her way to Deauville. A visit that would have lasted ten minutes, if the Hispano-Suiza had not broken down on the hill up to Grangeville. In short, Geneviève has created herself from scratch.

Her French elegance is out of place in London, where she is always ahead of the latest trends in fashion, the theatre and film, and knows about all the budding actors, writers, painters and sculptors, to the point where people have started to take it as gospel that she is the true creator of new talents. She enchants by her intelligence, she surprises by the loyalty of her friendship, and no one can claim to have seen her make a mistake in love: her life contains only the prince. So no one can understand why that person, who shows (when he appears, which is becoming increasingly rare) an almost royal benevolence and total absence of prejudice, why that man does not marry the woman he loves. Geneviève herself never raises the question, and it is perfectly possible that she prefers being a kept woman to being a morganatic princess. The society in which she has elected to live has taken her side: Geneviève is untouchable. Whoever ventures a word against her will find themselves positively excluded from her circle. So, protected by some, ignored by others, she is one of the queens of London.

Jean telephoned the following week. She urged him to get in a taxi and come immediately, because she had guests for dinner shortly. Jean slipped out of the Eaton Square flat, leaving Price a message for the absent Palfy, jumped in a cab and, despite traffic jams, was at the house ten minutes later. The new Baptiste led him to the drawing room, whose decoration had been changed: there were seats now and a long sofa of black leather, and an entire wall panel lit by spotlights concealed in the ceiling was hollowed out with niches containing modern sculptures: serene ovoid forms, tormented abstract mechanisms. Was one of them his bicycle that Geneviève had given to John Dudley? Dudley had had no success with his crushed objects. He was twenty years ahead of his time, and while he waited for others to plagiarise him and be hailed as innovators by amnesiac critics, he was designing body shells for a large car maker. Jean walked around, studying the strange shapes on show. They surprised him, without his being able to analyse their meaning. When Geneviève came into the room, her knowing smile made him feel he had been caught out. She was dressed in an Indian sari, her hair held smoothly in place by a black headband that intensified her pallor. Shorter than he was, she put her hands up on his shoulders and gazed at him for a moment.

'I'm trying to see in you,' she said, 'what I remember about your dear maman, whom I love so much.'

'Maman died in June.'

'Oh goodness … it's happened … it's my fault. I didn't see enough of her.' Tears welled in her eyes, and she smiled a melancholy smile.

'How sad you must be! What about Albert?'

'Since they sold La Sauveté, Papa's been living with Uncle Cliquet.'

'La Sauveté has been sold?'

Jean reminded himself that nobody wrote many letters in her family, and that Geneviève had not even been told about his birth. He found her womanly open face beautiful, and so close that he leant forward impulsively to kiss her proffered cheek, fresh and without make-up.

'What are you doing in London?'

She possessed a rare gift: people who had known her for less than five minutes found themselves recounting their life story. Jean was startled to find himself almost telling her everything. The 'almost' is only to make clear that he did not recount Palfy's French villainies. He painted his friend as he presented himself in London: a fashionable man who seemed to know everyone. Geneviève interrupted him to ask him frankly, 'Dearest Jean, this … what do you call him … Balfy … or Malfy … isn't he a little bit homosexual around the edges?'

'It's odd you should say that about him. I hadn't thought of it, and then one day he assured me he wasn't.'

'Oh well … To tell the truth, I think I know something about him, but what? I've forgotten. Anyway, it doesn't matter … Bring him to dinner on Thursday. I'll be happy to meet him.'

*

Back at Eaton Square, Jean passed on the invitation to Palfy, who was exultant.

'Splendid! At a stroke you open a door that was closed, to a circle that admits practically none of the people I've introduced you to. You were born under a lucky star, Jean, dear boy. Well done. Soon London will be ours.'

'And what will we do with it?'

'Nothing, as you've guessed already. Absolutely nothing. Look down on it from a very high place.'

Jean did not entirely understand a plan that would end in scornful rejection of what had been conquered with such effort. The use Palfy made of his days also seemed singularly relaxed to him, in relation to their stated objective. In the morning his friend read the newspapers at length, walked in Hyde Park for an hour, had lunch at his club, went shopping or paid a visit to his tailor, returned home to change, went back to the club to play whist or bridge, and had dinner at home with friends or took Jean out to the houses of other wholly uninteresting friends. Apparently he was not short of money. In his garage he kept, in addition to the Rolls, a Morgan convertible, the cream of sports cars. If he had not had the means to pay from time to time the bills Price brought to him each morning on a silver tray, the existence of gilded idleness enjoyed by both of them would not have lasted very long. There was some mystery in this somewhere, but Palfy was not the sort of man you questioned with impunity. Jean approached him obliquely.

'I'm starting to ask myself how I'm going to pay you back for what you're providing me with so generously. I haven't got a penny to my name, or a single idea how to earn a living.'

'I am a philanthropist of the sublime sort. I'm getting ready for

315

a few personal shows of ingratitude, without which life would be a bed of roses.'

Dinner at Geneviève du Courseau's was not what Palfy had been hoping for. They were the only guests, as if it was a test. With all the instinct his large nose was capable of, Palfy realised it and deployed his resources intelligently. Jean was surprised to see his friend so well informed about the theatre and cinema, which he never went to, and about exhibitions of painting and sculpture for which he ordinarily professed substantial scorn. He even displayed a certain genius by stopping dead in front of an unusual object, a spade onto which the sculptor had welded two nails. It looked like a praying mantis.

'Admirable!' he said, leaning forward. 'The revenge of the world of things. The beginning of their animation. They will devour us all.'

'Do you know who it's by?'

'In principle I'd have said it was by Natalia, but don't laugh at me: I'm a complete ignoramus.'

'It is by her!' Geneviève said, surprised.

He had passed the test. He would be asked again. Walking back to Eaton Square on a delicious balmy night, Jean expressed astonishment at his knowledge.

'Why do you think I read the papers with such care every morning?' Palfy said. 'You can find everything there. No need to move.'

'But what about that sculpture you identified?'

'I'd seen a photo of it in a magazine. No more difficult than that. If you want to know what I think, we went down all right. It's very important. Next I would like to get to know the prince, about whom I am beginning to have my own theory.'

'What about her?'

'A marvellous person.'

Jean felt the same. His very limited experience of women was enlarging slowly. After Mireille, Antoinette and, on a platonic level, Chantal, he had discovered Geneviève, still clothed in the cachet of the du Courseaus, but freed from its bourgeois world. All evening long he had had the impression of meeting someone open, direct and without any false or naïve modesty. She was beautiful when she laughed, her laughter was genuine, and her fine blue eyes examined life with kindness, intelligence and lucidity.

A few days later Jean started to emulate Palfy and read the French daily papers. There was little mention of politics. The race for that year's literary prizes preoccupied a reading public that was happy to be addressed on any subject except war. For the Prix Goncourt, the name of Joseph Outen was mentioned nowhere. Did this oversight suggest a shock announcement of the prize being awarded to an outsider that Monday at Drouant's restaurant? When the name of Charles Plisnier was revealed – a forty-one-year-old Belgian novelist, author of a collection of short stories – Jean felt the scale of poor Joseph's disappointment. What had happened? He wrote to him. A reply came back by return.

> *Make no mistake about what happened. A conspiracy has taken place. My book, despite being finished in good time, was* not published. *Without any reason. For, all modesty aside, it is easily as good as Plisnier's* False Passports. *Put* very *simply: I'm still waiting for an answer from the NRF and Grasset, whom I offered it to simultaneously. My novel has been suppressed. Why? Because it* upsets people. *Yes, I upset people. Imagine! Someone who has something to say, and says it! That hasn't been seen since Zola's day. We are not permitted to impugn the honour of love or money. My novel*

317

will not be published. I have the bitter certainty of that now. If I want to continue writing, I shall have to confine myself to anodyne subjects: little birds, sunny days, and trips to the seaside. Count me out. You know me well enough. I'm leaving literature to the shopkeepers from now on. Even so, it hasn't been time completely wasted. Scribbling down my 300 pages, I discovered that I can draw. My manuscript is covered in doodles down the side of every page. There's no doubt that with patience and hard work I could have enough drawings for an exhibition in a year's time. I've sold a piece of my mother's jewellery that I'd held on to, which will be enough to keep me going until I start selling. You're invited to my show of course, which will take place in Paris in January 1939. Between now and then, don't count on me for much: I shall be a recluse for the duration. A single distraction: running. Yes, don't laugh. I'm a runner, and my lungs are improving every day. How many press-ups are you up to?

Jean was down to zero press-ups. He felt guilty, got up half an hour earlier, and resumed his exercises with pleasure. At the same time he realised that, as he counted each upward push of his body, he thought about Geneviève. He had never met anybody like her. Not only was she attractive and desirable, but after he had left her, her charm continued to work on him. He found himself trying to remember the tone of her voice, the sparkle of her eyes, the shapes made by her pink mouth. He could not even compare her to Chantal de Malemort. They belonged to two different species. Jean reassured himself: he loved both of them. It was his misfortune that they both seemed unattainable.

Unattainability was not a feature of the middle-aged English-women who invited him to the country with Palfy. Jean noticed that they were paying him more and more attention. He surrendered with a certain anxiety, not knowing where it would lead him.

'Nowhere, absolutely nowhere,' Palfy said repeatedly. 'Rosalind and Margaret would walk straight past you tomorrow if they met you anywhere in the least bit smart.'

Palfy encouraged Jean's pleasures of the moment. But why did he not sacrifice himself in the same way?

'I haven't talked much about myself,' he admitted. 'The truth is very simple: I'm neither homosexual nor impotent. Let's just say that I don't feel particularly strongly about "it". I need rather special conditions, which aren't very easy to bring together. To cut a long story short, I prefer professional women. It does no harm to anybody and actually enriches a sizeable group of idlers who look after the modest business it produces and keep it within the bounds of propriety. Having said that, the lovely Geneviève du Courseau has not called us. Many days have passed. Telephone that strange person, will you? I believe I have learnt how the prince who maintains her on such a lavish scale keeps his immense fortune topped up from day to day.'

'How?'

'That is a secret, dear boy.'

Jean felt he was groping his way through a world where he recognised nothing. Who were these society ladies who offered themselves to him in a bedroom adjoining their husband's and the next day looked straight through him? What goal was Palfy pursuing? As time went on it became impossible to doubt that he had, at least that particular year, sufficiently large means to live extravagantly. He slipped easily into that relatively closed society in which money counted as much as titles. He was at ease in it from his years at private school, then Oxford. How far that person was from the priest who stole from collection boxes and coaxed his old Mathis up the Nationale Sept! Jean occasionally had to do a double take, for he had only known people who were always the same and incapable of concealing a second or a third face behind the first. The abbé Le Couec was never anybody else but himself. The same was true of Monsieur Cliquet, Captain Duclou, Marie-Thérèse and Antoinette du Courseau. The only person who did not fit the mould was perhaps Michel. With him in mind Jean found an excuse to call Geneviève.

'I wondered what had become of you,' she said. 'I thought you had vanished. London is so big. Every day dozens of people go up in smoke here, leaving no trace. Yes, yes, I promise you, it's a bewildering city, where cannibals, serial killers and vampires prosper mightily. You wouldn't think so: everything's so gentle and subtle, and Londoners are so tactful that you never know whether the man who's so kindly giving you directions to the West End is really a murderer ... '

'I'm still alive.'

'Well, try and stay that way.'

'There's something I wanted to show you: an album of your brother's drawings.'

'Michel draws? It's the first I've heard of it. I should never have expected to find an artistic temperament in our family. What does he draw? Pigeons, the sea at Grangeville, the sailors' cemetery?'

'No. Portraits. He's already had several exhibitions.'

'Bring me the album. Tomorrow. At lunchtime. I imagine that your friend Calfy—'

'Palfy.'

'... your friend Palfy has lunch at his club. Come without him. We'll talk.'

When Jean told him about the invitation, Palfy smiled.

'I would happily have made an exception for that delicious creature, but it's better this way. Having said that, what an idea, inviting you to lunch at home! She's remained very French, from what I can see.'

*

We shall not recount Jean's lunch in detail, which he experienced as if in a trance. Geneviève was startled by her brother's talent and kept Jean's album to show it to a gallerist she knew. She smiled without comment when she saw that all the portraits were of Jean, as himself, as a cyclist, as an oarsman. She made him talk, laughed at their failed meetings in Grangeville, London and Rome, and let him know that the prince, whom she called Ibrahim, would be coming back with Salah in a few days' time. Oh yes, Salah was an extraordinary man: he knew and understood everything, and you could never give him orders because he anticipated them all. Then, passing quickly on, with a mischievousness that went unnoticed by Jean, she probed him about his girlfriends. He said nothing about Antoinette – out of respect for her – and regretfully too, because far away from her as he was, and knowing nothing of her actions, whenever he thought of her he was assailed by waves of tenderness – but he spoke at length about Mireille, who was roughly the same age as Geneviève. Her questions were spontaneous and subtle. He also confessed to his feelings for Chantal de Malemort, and by placing her on a high pedestal made Geneviève aware that he was capable of love. Later he became aware of her skill at questioning him; but I repeat, at this moment he felt that he was just opening his heart to her with all the impulsiveness of youth and no sense whatsoever of the risks he might be running. She questioned him about his successes since he had been in London, and he blushed. Palfy might have been happy to boast of his protégé's fleeting conquests; Jean would willingly have drawn a veil over them, but now he did not know how to stop, and mentioned some names. Geneviève reproved him mildly: this was not done. It was clumsy; if women found out he was indiscreet, they would not come near him. But he needn't worry: she would not say anything. He could trust her. By now Jean would happily have gone down

321

on his knees to speak to her. He had never met such an attractive woman. She kissed him on the cheek.

'Come and have dinner with your friend Palfy,' she said. 'He's an interesting man. Call me one morning.'

She rang for Baptiste, and as soon as he was outside Jean felt that he had been ejected. He was at such a loss that he went into a cinema and sat through a stupid film in which he thought he could spot a thousand allusions to the state he was in. That evening Palfy guessed everything.

'You are a billy goat, aren't you?' he said. 'I thought as much. That exquisite woman is just at the age when young flesh starts to seem tempting. Her feelings for you are twofold, sensual because she's ripe for something new and different, motherly because you could be her son. Having said that, she is upsetting my intentions. A good general never lets himself be taken by surprise. Let us therefore change our plans ... '

'Our plans? I don't even know what they are.'

Constantin thought for a moment, lit his pipe, and asked Price to bring the brandy decanter and leave them alone for the rest of the evening.

'In three months' time, I shall not have a penny to my name.'

This news landed on Jean like a ton of bricks, as he suddenly realised how, in a very short space of time, he had let himself fall into the trap of a life of ease. Even Price – whose judgement had turned out to be so sound – even Price considered him a gentleman, and had stopped laying out for him every morning his most worn-out shirt and saggy drawers and darned socks that brought back his hard year as an unskilled labourer at *La Vigie*. It all seemed very long ago. And how easily one got used to all this luxury and the well-timed provision of life's pleasures. Jean, who ordinarily drank very little, poured himself a large glass of brandy and downed it in one.

'You will no doubt point out to me,' Palfy went on, 'that I could reduce my expenses. For example, sell the Rolls and the Morgan and make do with an Austin, dismiss Price and take on a charwoman for two hours a day. An error, a profound error! We would merely be jumping out of the frying pan into the fire. No one would ever trust us afterwards. The only thing that counts in the world, believe me, is pure show. Yes, dear Jean, one must *appear*. Because if one fails to appear, one is scorned by fools.'

Jean thought about Geneviève. She didn't 'appear', she was exactly what she was: a woman whose face does not lie.

'Who are you thinking about?' Palfy asked.

'Geneviève du Courseau.'

'Do you believe in her?'

'Yes.'

'A little tedious! But … at your age … '

'I've never met anyone like her.'

'She isn't as rare as all that.'

'You don't know who you're talking about!'

'You're in love with her!'

'No, not yet, but if it happened it would be marvellous.'

'We're getting a long way from the matter in hand.'

'What matter?'

'Do you want to know?'

'I'll take a chance.'

The idea was ambitious. The plan was to sell, via interested amateurs, a new and extraordinary toothpaste. Different levels of vendors were planned, each purchasing their stock and reselling it to subcontractors who, in turn, would subcontract to others. From the outset, an unpaid capital was guaranteed by the first vendors. The company would launch without a penny in the bank and sell before manufacturing began.

'What is so extraordinary about your toothpaste?'

'Nothing, absolutely nothing. It will be a toothpaste just like the others, any old paste perfumed to taste like English sweets, a minty flavour or, I don't know, whatever works at the time.'

'Do you mean that you haven't got a product organised yet?'

Palfy made an irritable gesture.

'No. I've turned the problem around: first you sell, then you manufacture.'

'That's dangerous!'

'Yes, if it gets out of control it's fraud, pure and simple, and if succeed it'll be glory, profits and respect.'

'What's my job in all of this?'

'The initial subcontractors to bring me their money against amount of merchandise are Peter Ascot, Jonathan Sandow and Rory Afner.'

The truth began to dawn on Jean. On their country weekends he had slept with the wives of all three of these dupes.

'They've nearly signed up,' Palfy went on. 'A word from their wives will make sure they don't shillyshally too much.'

'If I understand you correctly, you took me on as your gigolo.'

'Oh, at your age you'd make love to a goat, wouldn't you?'

'Lily Sandow and Marina Afner are not goats.'

'No, but Jane Ascot—'

'She raped me. She threw herself at me and I didn't know how to say no. Palfy, you're a dreadful cynic.'

'Not at all, not at all. I'm enjoying myself.'

'And what's my share if I help you?'

'Nothing. I take all the risks, so I take all the profit. You've been living with me for six months. I'm presenting you with the bill.'

'I'll think about it.'

'Oh no you don't. You shit or you get off the pot, here and now.'

'And if I get off the pot—'

'Impossible. So we agree. It's late. I'm going to bed.'

He stood up, and Jean grasped his arm.

'One last question. Where did the money come from that you've been spending so lavishly for the last few months?'

Palfy affected the expression of a man grieving, lowering his dancing-girl's lashes over his dark eyes.

'I am going to disappoint you, dear Jean. I neither stole it nor fiddled it. It's my uncle Thomas's inheritance, my mother's brother. He worked for forty years to amass a decent lump sum to leave to me, and I've spent it in eighteen months. Quite moral of me, don't you think? I've always been against inheritance.'

Alone in his room, Jean opened the notebook he had started at Roquebrune, noting down reflections inspired by his life at that time. Months had passed without him having the urge to reflect on what he had discovered. He wrote:

> *h) I'm just a plaything in the hands of all those who possess a bit of personality: Antoinette, Mireille, Constantin. I may have succeeded in extricating myself without too much difficulty from the clutches of Antoinette and Mireille, but with Constantin the stakes are higher. Obviously I'm not going to run out on him. He's right. I shall help him as much as I can, despite the self-disgust I know I shall feel, but maybe you have to reach the point of self-disgust to start to know yourself at all.*
> *i) Despite the promise we exchanged, I haven't written to Chantal. It's not an omission, it's an admission. How dare I speak to her without embarrassment, after what's happening to me and my accepting it? The same feeling as after my return from Roquebrune, when I still felt 'dirty' from Mireille, and I avoided her.*

Inevitably, in the days that followed, he spoke to Lily Sandow, Marina Afner and Jane Ascot, and it was they who convinced their husbands. Constantin was exultant. He entrusted the devising of the toothpaste to a small East End chemist, found a laboratory and produced a batch of samples that made the business plausible. The start-up was stunning. The sales technique, which excluded wholesalers and resellers, attracted a large number of women. Before it had manufactured any product at all, the company had a million pounds of capital in the bank. Palfy operated skilfully. Jean scarcely saw him. He smoked cigars as long as his forearm and employed a chauffeur to drive the Rolls. Jean had lunch with Geneviève at a French restaurant in Soho. He felt that the intimacy between them had gone. She seemed cold, condescending and almost – the mortification! – charitable towards him. Prince Ibrahim and Salah were expected back in a few days. His room for manoeuvre was limited. As they were saying goodbye on the pavement, he decided to throw himself on her mercy.

'I'm very young. I don't know what I'm supposed to say … '

She stepped into her Bentley convertible and started the engine.

'I believe you're mistaken,' she said. 'Come and have dinner tomorrow with your friend Palfy.'

Palfy was anxious: would she have the nerve to invite them on their own? What an insult! She would have to answer for it. Jean shook with nerves and only calmed down as he counted the other guests: ten people who ignored them to begin with, as only artists know how, but by the time the dessert arrived Palfy, with his diabolical skill, had turned the situation around. All heads were turned to him, and Jean realised that everyone was wondering who this man with the long nose was, who was so good at making Geneviève laugh. After dinner, Jean found himself at her side for a moment and brushed her hand.

'No,' she said in a low voice. 'You're being indiscreet.'

His heart sank. For the rest of the evening he could not take his eyes off her, and he left the house with feet of lead. In the Rolls, as it glided silently along the Kings Road, Palfy sighed, 'You're feeling bad about something, aren't you?'

'Yes, very.'

'I would willingly warn you but—'

'But what?'

'It's difficult … just an impression … I've seen the two of you together … There is something—'

'You're not going to lecture me.'

'No, no, no. It's something else entirely … '

Jean could not get another word out of his friend, and so did not confess that he and Geneviève were going to the theatre the following day. When the time came, he had to lie, without knowing whether Palfy had been taken in. He met Geneviève outside the theatre. The play was uninteresting or hard to follow or both, but at one of its infrequent amusing moments Geneviève leant towards him to share her gaiety and he took her hand which he then refused to let go, despite her pretending to pull away at the start. As they left the auditorium she said simply, 'I don't like restaurants after the theatre. Come back to the house, there's bound to be something in the refrigerator.'

How simple everything would have been if she hadn't been French! She laid two places in the kitchen and served cold chicken with a bottle of Bordeaux. As if to avoid anything embarrassing being said, she did not let Jean get a word in. He for his part was not listening to her but counting the minutes as they slipped by, despairing of his indecision and his awkwardness, gazing at her animated, gracious, thoughtful and lovely face.

'Have you finished?'

He had not touched his chicken. She cleared his plate away and served him a Turkish coffee.

'Salah taught me how to make them, but I'll never do it as well as he does. What were you muttering?'

'Did my lips move?'

'Yes.'

'Then I must have been repeating to myself that I'm a fool.'

'No.'

'Why not?'

'Because things are the way they are, and I'm not going to change my life for anything in the world, and Ibrahim is arriving tomorrow. Goodnight, dear Jean. Go home and go to bed.'

On the doorstep her lips brushed his and she pushed him gently away from her.

'I'll telephone you.'

He walked home in pouring rain, soaked to the skin, his trouser bottoms splashed with mud as though he had crossed a ploughed field. Palfy was waiting for him in an armchair, reading a medical encyclopaedia.

'I'm improving my mind, as you can see,' he said. 'Looking for angles for our advertising.'

'Your toothpaste hasn't even been manufactured yet.'

'Therein lies a difficulty, it must be said. It appears to be impossible to find a single factory able to satisfy the fabulous growth in demand.'

'So?'

'So we are possibly looking at catastrophe within three weeks to a month. Let us give ourselves a moment's respite. Where have you come from, Don Juan?'

'From Geneviève du Courseau's.'

Palfy leapt up.

'You haven't slept together, have you?'

'Why are you asking me? Are you afraid that I'm going to let my charms go to waste, without being useful to your plans?'

'No, you fool … Answer me! You haven't slept together?'

Jean would happily have lied for the sake of boasting a little, but honesty won out.

'No. And it's not going to happen in the foreseeable future.'

Palfy fell back into his armchair.

'Oof! Pour me a brandy.'

'When you tell me why you said "oof"!'

'No conditions between us! Absolute rule.'

Jean, resigned, poured the brandy.

'So?'

'Well, dear boy, there are sometimes hypotheses that are better left untested. Geneviève and you are definitely related in some way.'

'Because of her sister, Antoinette?'

'No, double fool … The other evening I was watching you … But I'm telling you: it's only an impression. I may be mistaken.'

Jean grabbed Palfy by the silk lapels of his smoking jacket and forced him to his feet.

'Tell me, or I'll beat you to a pulp.'

'Let me go. You've lost your senses.'

'I want to know.'

'Do some calculations, work it out, dig around in your past. I'm suggesting, that's all. For my money, you're one of the du Courseau family. Perhaps you're Antoine's son or Marie-Thérèse's, in other words the half-brother of Antoinette and Geneviève and Michel. It needs to be gone into more deeply: in your position I'd go back to France and pump those who know. I'll pay for the trip. Incidentally, thanks so much for letting me go; I was about to knee you in the balls and put you out of action for a fortnight. A sad injury for a man of your calibre.'

'My calibre is as good as your calibre.'

'Thank you.'

'I'm sorry, Constantin, I don't know what I'm doing any more, or what I'm saying.'

'You are forgiven, my son.'

He vaguely sketched the sign of the cross and drank his brandy.

'Our lives are fragile. Let's not shatter them for reasons of vanity. In any case, quite sincerely, I'm very fond of you. I think of you as the younger brother I wanted and never had. Go. But you do need someone to shout at you sometimes. Price will pack a bag for you and the chauffeur will drive you to Newhaven tomorrow. Goodnight.'

Chantal was waiting for him in the rain at the landing stage. From the gangplank he recognised her slim outline, wearing a white hooded raincoat. She had answered his telegram, she would help him. With the hand she had pulled from her pocket she waved back. Six months had passed without altering their tacit agreement, even though Jean had not written. Would she guess everything, and would he be able to explain that certain things that had happened on a distant planet had nothing to do with their unconfessed feelings in any way? He felt, even at this distance, that he could already smell her fresh smell, awakened by the rain. She was flesh and blood too, and a disturbing oneness radiated from her body, her eyes, her voice, something he knew he would never find in his life again. His certainty of this was so acute that it was like a sharp, incurable pain in his chest. Everything would be spoilt if he opened his mouth. Where Chantal was concerned, a single truth mattered: that of their childhood, which they had to continue, protecting it from the compromises he had so easily accepted when he was away from her. His passport was stamped, after which he had to go through customs, where he was met by a suspicious official who demanded an explanation for his English suits. Their quality, and the Savile Row labels, roused all the spitefulness of a miserable mean-minded employee whose sartorial prospects would never rise higher than the Nouvelles Galeries' menswear department. Envy and stupidity are two ideas so powerful that, once they have established themselves in a man's head, they are impossible to get rid of. Jean was asked for a receipt. How could he explain that he had not paid for them? And that the tailor would probably never be paid by Palfy. Other passengers passed through unhindered, as a plump female customs officer with an impressive bosom, the seams of her uniform stretched to breaking point, inventoried his underwear. On the other side of the door Chantal must be getting tired of waiting, or perhaps she was beginning to worry. He asked if he could go through for a moment and come back. His request was refused, and he felt as if he was trapped in a net, in the corridor and box-rooms of the customs post, a grey maze that smelt of coarse damp blankets and unwashed feet. The last passengers were ushered out almost eagerly, as though they were attempting to distract the Republic's representatives from their true mission. The entire customs post was now savouring a victim. One from every ferry was the rule. This preoccupied young man, a little cocky, anxious to get away for a reason they were not aware of but felt they could easily guess, was hiding something he was unable or unwilling to admit to, some irregularity that their mediocrity immediately elevated to criminal status. Officers fell upon his two cases, counting his underwear, his trousers, jackets, drawing up a long inventory that seemed beneath contempt to Jean, so much did he feel that his one and only crime was to have been the agent of a diabolical Palfy. As a result he started to lie, to contradict himself, to get muddled, digging himself ever deeper, to the rabble's great delight. With such people there was no negotiation: the bill Jean was presented with swallowed every franc he had left. When he finally emerged, dispossessed and humiliated after six months away, he saw Chantal leaning against a pillar. The rain had soaked through the shoulders of her raincoat. She was shivering, despite it being May. Cars driving along the quay had already switched on their yellow headlamps, pairs of seeking eyes reflected in the shining asphalt. The sea smelt of fuel oil. Chantal smiled.

'I thought they were never going to let you out.'

'They discovered a major criminal: a Frenchman bringing back English suits. National pride was at stake. I had to pay. I don't have a franc to my name any more. I can't even take you out to dinner.'

'You're having dinner at Malemort. My father's waiting for us at the Café des Tribunaux. He's very intrigued about your journey to England.'

'I wanted to talk to you on your own.'

'You'll have to wait till this evening.'

They walked side by side along the main street, Jean carrying his heavy cases, careful not to bang into other pedestrians' legs.

'You didn't write,' Chantal said. 'I waited for a long time, then started to tell myself that you had good reasons.'

'My reasons weren't very good.'

'Well, in that case keep them to yourself.'

As they walked past *La Vigie*'s well-lit front window, the ghastly Grosjean was standing in the doorway, opening his umbrella. Jean's face reminded him of something, and he brought his fingers up to his cap. Jean shrugged his shoulders.

'Do you know him?' Chantal asked.

'I had him on my back for nearly a year. No one had treated me that way before, and no one will ever treat me like that again. He spoke to me as if I was a dog. Now I'm well dressed, and he raises his cap as I walk past. I've booked myself a seat in the front of the grandstand for the day they take him out and shoot him.'

Chantal did not answer. They reached the café, whose windows were misted up. The marquis, a curling pipe in the corner of his mouth, was reading a farming paper. He had not changed: sturdy, solid, his face weathered by country air, his broad hands used to driving his tractor, to fork and reins. He was bursting with robustness. Instead of lamenting an unsalvageable past, he seized life by the scruff of the neck and shook it with a gentleman's aloofness.

'*Hello, old boy*!' he said in English, folding up his paper. They were practically the only words he remembered, because, despite having been brought up by English nurses until he was ten, he had forgotten it all, as was proper. The smattering that remained so thrilled him that, whenever he chanced to string three words together, he nearly knocked down his interlocutor with the most enormous thump on the back. Jean was the recipient of the thump this time, and it affected him no less than the sudden attention he found himself receiving from the Marquis de Malemort. He would have sworn that this man, unsophisticated and elegant at the same time, had never noticed him before, had walked past a small boy named Jean Arnaud a hundred times without seeing him. Could it be the same as had happened with Grosjean, who now raised his cap at the sight of his former whipping boy? Jean did not yet appreciate that his journey to England had taken on, in the narrow milieu of Grangeville, the dimensions of an adventure to El Dorado. He had returned like the prodigal son, impecunious and wreathed in glory, full of experience. The marquis gave them a lift in his solid Peugeot 301, more often seen on potholed byroads than on Dieppe's macadamed streets. It gave off a smell of hay, flax and damp leather, belched like a pig at every gear change, but cantered up the hills in a clattering of old iron. It was a far cry from Palfy's Rolls! The marquise had cooked dinner. For a long time now, farm girls had ceased to consider it a sign of honour and promotion to empty the château's chamber pots. Jean faced a string of questions and sat up straighter: dinner at Malemort, served by the marquise and Chantal, seated opposite the marquis whose booted feet stuck out in front of him, was something he could never have dreamt of before his departure. He felt grateful to Palfy. Without him, nothing like this would have been possible. The dull resentment towards his friend that he had experienced since he left, lightened. Unfortunately conversation with the marquis turned out to be difficult. He was only interested in the English countryside, about which Jean had the most superficial idea, after spending several weekends in country houses set amidst romantic gardens, totally ignorant of external realities. However, he collected together his memories of conversations half listened to and realised that he could carry off a pretence of knowledge, that Chantal too was silent and listening to him with interest.

'Here it's all over!' the marquis broke in. 'In the space of a hundred and fifty years the Napoleonic Code has destroyed property ownership. The estates are disappearing one after another, parcelled up, subdivided and disposed of. We're condemned to having a single child. Since Napoleon, Paris has been governing France with its eyes closed. They see us as Chouans. There's not a single countryman in the government. Just professors, lawyers and mathematicians. Once every four years they notice us, in time for us to go out and vote for the conservatives.'

The marquis was happy to have an audience for his precious ideas. Jean listened to him, steeling himself to pay attention and trying to disregard the lovely figure of Chantal, who was busying herself around the table. In the farms nearby, Jean knew, women also served and kept quiet. The marquis began yawning. His day had started at dawn, he had ridden out for two hours with his daughter, and that afternoon had had several drinks while he waited for Jean and Chantal at the café.

'My boy, no standing on ceremony: you'll sleep here tonight. Monsieur Cliquet shares his only bedroom with your father. Captain Duclou goes to bed very early since he had his little attack, and the abbé is away at Lourdes with the young maids of Grangeville. Tomorrow you'll tell us your plans. *Goodnight*.'

He shook Jean's hand vigorously and left, shambling slightly from the effects of the pre-dinner pastis, red wine at table, and cognac warmed and cradled in his hand in a large snifter. Madame de Malemort put more logs on the fire and sat in an armchair next to the fireplace with a tapestry on her lap. She would not forget the proprieties: one did not leave a young woman of marriageable age and a young man alone together. Chantal sat on a sofa, making a place for Jean, and showed him photos taken during the summer at horse shows at which she had entered her mare. Having heard nothing from the English he had met but talk of lawns, rain, dogs and horses, Jean was able to answer with a few well-chosen words. Chantal was astonished.

'I thought you were only interested in cycling and rowing.'

'I've changed.'

'Very much?'

'Basically, no,' he said.

Chantal returned his gaze, paling a little. The marquise was dozing. Her days started early too. Her head rested on a wing of the armchair, stretching the folds of her neck. She was ageless; perhaps she had never even been young, just as she would never be old. With a face that was free of wrinkles but vacant too, her fine features expressed a distinguished absence of character.

'Don't stop talking,' Chantal whispered, 'if you stop she'll wake up.'

'Everything I want to say to you isn't ready to be said. I only started thinking about it today, on the ferry from Newhaven.'

'And before?'

'I was looking for you.'

'In other women?'

'Yes and no. No, because you're not in any of the ones I meet.'

'Why did you come back?'

'Is it a reproach?'

'No, but tell me the reason.'

Admit Geneviève? It was out of the question. Anyhow, that encounter had perhaps been no more than an illusion, mischief-making to throw him off his chosen path. He took a deep breath.

'An irresistible desire came over me, to find out who my mother is. To be clear – I don't care a damn about my father, who must be totally ignorant of my existence.'

Chantal lowered her head and was silent. Madame de Malemort

started, opened her eyes and picked up her tapestry with a limp hand.

'I must show you,' Chantal said in a normal voice, 'the filly and the colt that were both born on the same day last week. Papa is giving them to me.'

The marquise's eyelids gradually closed on her vacant stare, her head fell forward and her work-worn hands opened on her tapestry. She was not yet fifty. This family ate horrible reheated stews but did so from Limoges china, drank table wine but from crystal glasses, sliced their meat with chipped knives whose silver handles were engraved with their initials. They owned saddle horses and draught horses and arrived at mass in a trap, but drove to town in a 301 that was as old-fashioned as it was battered. They were lost between two worlds – the one they had come from and the one they were going to – that were entirely unalike. To forget that fatal contradiction, they shut themselves away in their mansion and accepted one invitation in ten. At no time had it ever crossed their minds that Chantal might break with tradition and marry someone other than a country gentleman.

'Why does it matter so much to you?' Chantal said with a sigh.

'I don't know: a physical need.'

'No. There must be a reason.'

Jean thought that she was more perceptive than she looked.

'Someone said to me, with great certainty … '

He stopped, embarrassed.

'Said what?'

'That I look physically as if I'm related to the du Courseaus.'

Chantal put her hand on his arm.

'It's true. And I'm not the only one to have noticed it.'

'Do they know?'

'No. They don't see themselves.'

'No one sees himself.'

Jean thought for a moment. In the du Courseau family one person had examined his features with extreme attentiveness. The album Michel had given him on the eve of his departure for

337

England was perhaps also an admission. And hadn't Marie-Thérèse du Courseau – before the unpleasant story at the cliff – shown a possessive generosity towards him that could not just be explained by her ostentatiously charitable behaviour? Finally, in the realm of the unsayable there was also the secret pact he had sealed with Antoine on the occasion of the punctured hosepipe, and then his alliance with Antoinette that had reached its culmination on the night he passed his baccalauréat, and lastly his attraction for Geneviève, and the way she had responded, holding him at arm's length.

'You know,' Chantal added, 'people talk without any self-restraint. Only one person could tell you: the abbé Le Couec. Even though he doesn't like you to raise subjects that embarrass him … '

The marquise raised her head.

'Children, it is getting late … Chantal, you ought to show Jean his room.'

She collected together her tapestry and wools and put both into a work-table, yawned unrestrainedly, kissed Jean on the cheek, stroked her daughter's face, and left the room after quenching the last of the blaze with a glass of water.

Chantal led Jean to a round room in the tower, the guest room, with an enormous bed swollen by a red quilt.

'I find all this strange,' he said. 'This morning I was still in London. Now I'm here with you. Where do you sleep?'

She did not answer, and began to unfasten her dress. Jean was afraid. An idea about what love should be was shattering in front of him as Chantal's body was exposed, white, slender, exquisite and fragile as a Dresden figurine. She kept her gaze fixed on him and, so as not to miss her looking at him, he hardly dared look at her. When she put her arms around his neck he was seized by a terrible anxiety.

He awoke at dawn, on his own in the great bed. A cock was crowing under his window. He patted the sheets with the flat of his hand to find a trace of the body that had vanished while he slept. No, he had not dreamt it. What an awful cheat life was! The one being he had respected endlessly had given herself to him without a word, and he had not ravished a virgin. Chantal knew as much about love as he did. He wanted to cry. He had never felt so lonely as he did for the two hours that preceded a discreet knock at the door and Chantal's voice calling, 'Jean, breakfast is ready.'

He stuck his head under the cold tap and went downstairs. The marquis was pushing away his soup plate before he sugared his bowl of coffee. Madame de Malemort was in her dressing gown, adjusting the toaster. Chantal, already dressed, looked down so as not to see Jean. A much more extraordinary thing than leaving London in the morning and going to bed the same night in a Norman château was being Chantal's lover now, and enjoying with her a confused pleasure in which were mingled images of Geneviève. The one, the girl, inspired all his desire; the other, the woman, inspired his admiration.

'*Good morning!*' the marquis roared in English. 'We're having a lazy start. Well, guests are allowed, but only on the first day.'

At eight in the morning he had already driven his cows out, fed the horses, cut down a tree and given the hens their grain. He had a full schedule for the day: to ride with his daughter, train a young Brittany spaniel, cut back the yews at the gates, get the churns ready for the milk collector, and that afternoon wait for the combine harvester hired for the week.

'I feel ashamed,' Jean said.

It was true, but for reasons that the Malemorts could not suspect. Standing behind them, Chantal looked at Jean. Nothing gave her away, except perhaps a faint shadow under her eyes. He no longer knew whether he loved her, now that she had given herself to him. The fallen veil had stripped of its attractions an old dream born in his childhood. He would have given everything to erase the night just past and go on living with his illusions.

'I need to go and see my father,' he said.

'How he will love that!' the marquise said, with the same conviction as if she had forecast that it would rain that afternoon. 'I saw him the day before yesterday at Marie-Thérèse's. He was watering.'

Yes, what else would he have been doing, dear Albert, but watering, planting, pruning trees and cutting back rose bushes? It was all he had left, now that he was without a home, a wife, a son. Life had been excessively unfair to him. And to rub salt into the wound, here was war looming once more, delivering a fatal blow to his life's hopes. On 11 March Hitler had invaded and annexed Austria. So Ernst had been right. You only had to read *Mein Kampf*. Jean had been expecting the usual litanies of life at Grangeville, but everything was changing. When, after seeing Chantal and her father off on their morning ride, he borrowed the marquis's old bike to cover the ten kilometres from Malemort to Grangeville, he was assailed by memories. He knew every bend, every farm, every spinney. On the hills he had paced himself on the way up, then thrown caution to the wind on the way down. He remembered a happy time that had posed few more challenging problems than that of keeping fit. Today his legs were like cotton wool, and he laboured half-heartedly along the road. A feeling of unease gripped him, something that would perhaps never leave him, a nausea he refused to identify. At last he saw Monsieur Cliquet's burr-stone cottage: a closed world, remote from the foolish drama that had taken him by surprise. Albert appeared on the doorstep; he was leaning on a walking stick, having for years refused to use one out of pride. A few steps from his adoptive father, Jean experienced a sudden lightening of spirit: this man was simple and good, narrow-minded but of a rectitude that nothing could break. There was a moment of uncertainty, a hesitation. Albert was not sure that the elegant young man in front of him, in a shirt and tie and wearing a cap of the same cloth as his jacket, was his son. They kissed each other, and Jean recognised the familiar prickle of his father's moustache and smell of cold caporal tobacco and coffee mixed with calvados that had been the smell of every morning of his childhood.

'Have you just arrived?'

'Yesterday evening.'

'Where did you sleep?'

'At the Malemorts'.'

Albert raised his eyebrows. He was not very happy about it. The classes ought not to mix, despite the marquis looking more and more like any other farmer. But how could he make Jean see it? Times were changing; the golden rules of twenty years ago meant nothing to the new generation. Jean saw his father's unhappy astonishment and tried to explain.

'They offered so kindly and naturally that I couldn't say no. And apparently the abbé is away on a pilgrimage.'

'Then you did the right thing. What about tonight?'

'I'm staying with them again, as long as you don't mind.'

'Me? You must be joking. Your uncle's still asleep. He's a late riser. You can say hello on the way back. Come to Madame du Courseau's with me. They'll be pleased to see you.'

They walked together to the new villa, completed at long last and standing in the middle of a garden in which Jean recognised his father's fixations: squares of lawn, ruthlessly symmetrical flower-beds, saplings in staggered rows, with none of the exuberant, romantic untidiness of English gardens.

'It'll be all right in two or three years' time,' Albert said, looking for Jean's approval. 'But will I see it? You've no idea how old I feel since your mother died.'

'I can imagine.'

They pushed open the gate with its painted plaque: 'La Michelière.' So Marie-Thérèse was clear about who she wanted this house to go to after Antoinette left home. The first person they saw was Michel. He was crouching with his hand extended over an ornamental pond, holding out birdseed to a pair of white pigeons that were flapping their wings on the far side, not daring to fly to him. Jean's appearance made him stand up.

'How did you get here? I wanted to write and thank you, but ask you to stop: I'm not ready.'

It took Jean a few seconds to remember that Geneviève had shown the album of drawings to a London gallerist, who had offered Michel a show in October.

'I can't do everything at once,' Michel went on. 'I'm still working on my engraving, but the most important thing I'm doing is practising for a recital at Pleyel in a year's time: nothing but Francis Poulenc. He's going to accompany me himself. You can't imagine how wonderful he is. From the first moment we met, we understood each other perfectly. He's writing two new songs for me based on poems by Cavafy ... you must know him, the Greek poet ... '

'No, I don't.'

Michel did not look disappointed. In fact he was not listening, as Jean noticed very quickly. He was only thinking about his recital, in which he had been encouraged by a music critic named Jean Vuillermoz. Vuillermoz was one of the two or three critics who understood modern music. The rest? Old buffoons and failures from the Conservatoire who understood nothing about anything, unless you slipped them an envelope ... Albert had moved away, and Jean was Michel's captive audience as Michel stood at the edge of the pond, looking taller than usual, dressed in beige corduroy trousers and a blue turtleneck sweater. The pair of pigeons flew upwards, circling high above them.

'They're lovely, aren't they?'

'Yes. I didn't know you were a pigeon fancier.'

'I'm learning. Have you ever dreamt you were flying?'

'Sometimes I do.'

'Do you know the psychoanalytic explanation of that dream?'

'No.'

Jean was inordinately relieved to be rescued from a long disquisition on pigeons and dreams by Antoinette's arrival. She was thinner, and from a distance her silhouette recalled Geneviève's, with a little less grace and lightness, her very short hair shaping a boy's face.

'You pig!' She ran towards him. 'You pig, you didn't tell me you were coming.'

She threw herself at his neck and kissed him on the cheeks with a vehemence that shocked Michel.

'What's got into you, Antoinette?'

'Nothing. I'm just happy to see him.'

'Me too. We're all happy … '

Crossly he turned his back on them and went into the house.

'Come inside. Maman would like to talk to you. I hear you've seen Geneviève. How is she? Tell me. Terrific, apparently. Do you know the man who keeps her?'

'Is that what your mother wants to know?'

'You idiot! Can you see her asking that question? Come on.'

Albert walked past, ignoring them, pushing a wheelbarrow with a box of petunias in it.

'I came to help my father.'

'He can spare you for a minute, and anyway you're not wearing gardening clothes. What beautiful tweed! Are you rich?'

'No, utterly broke.'

'Good. I like you better that way.'

Jean turned away, preferring not to see the lopsided figure of Albert pushing his wheelbarrow, and let himself be dragged towards the house.

'Where did you sleep?' Antoinette asked.

'At Malemort.'

'Ah!'

343

She squeezed his arm violently and was silent. Pigeons flew over their heads and landed at the edge of the pond.

'Filthy birds,' Antoinette said. 'Inedible too. I don't understand Michel. He spends hours every day taming them. Did you see Chantal?'

'Of course I did.'

'Did you sleep with her?'

'Why are you asking me?'

'No reason.'

Six months ago Antoinette would never have asked such a question. It made Jean feel uneasy. Piece by piece the edifice was crumbling. Inside the villa several pieces of furniture furtively bought back from the La Sauveté auction reminded him of the old house.

'Do you remember that chest?' Antoinette asked.

'It was in the hall.'

'I kept the chest of drawers from my bedroom and that low armchair. The rest is new. We had to make a very public show that we were changing our life, that Papa was never coming back.'

'Where is he?'

'We don't know.'

Alerted by the sound of a stranger's voice, Marie-Thérèse du Courseau was coming downstairs. Like the Marquise de Malemort, her face was unchanged. The absence of grace can work miracles. In a flash she assessed Jean's transformation, the new maturity of his features, the cut of his jacket and flannel trousers. Instinct warned her that he could no longer be spoken to as he once had been. She kissed him nevertheless, with dry, trembling lips.

'I'm so glad to see you again.'

Doubtless she genuinely was. Jean did not flinch at the sharp gaze that examined him.

'Did you see Geneviève in London?'

'Several times.'

344

'She wrote to Michel. She's terribly keen on his drawings and talked about organising a show for him. All thanks to you.'

Oh, I didn't do anything, apart from show her the album Michel gave me.'

He had, without being aware of it, touched a sensitive nerve. In return for his supposed admiration for Michel, Marie-Thérèse forgave Jean everything.

'It's a pity,' he said, 'that he's more interested in singing than engraving.'

'He's so good at both, he'll do both. Do you want to see his studio? Antoinette, will you take him? I must leave you, I have to go into Dieppe. You'll stay for lunch, won't you?'

'No, I'll have lunch with my father. But thank you.'

He was well aware that his father had lunch in Marie-Thérèse's kitchen, and in the evening made do with what Uncle Cliquet cooked up on his cheap portable gas stove while he leafed through that year's railways almanac.

They found Michel in his studio, with its glass walls that faced the soft north light. An unfinished canvas stood on the easel. Michel smiled in embarrassment.

'You've discovered a secret of mine. I've started doing oils. Nobody has seen it yet. It's *The Pilgrims at Emmaus*. What do you think of my head of Christ?'

'Very accomplished.'

The face was fine, that of a young man whose deep, calm blue eyes gazed out at them.

'It's the butcher's son from Grangeville,' Antoinette said.

'You can't imagine how serene he is. He can keep still without moving for hours on end in the studio. When I tell him he can stop, he stays here and asks me questions: his mind is still a *tabula rasa*, a fantastic uncultivated territory. He asks me how destiny chose him to be the very image of Christ. I say the same thing to him every time:

it was an intuition, a voice that told me to stop one day as I saw him leaving the boys' lycée in Dieppe. It could only be him.'

Outside in the corridor Antoinette winked at Jean.

'Do you know what's going on?'

'I think so.'

'So does Maman. A big shock to begin with. Then she accepted it, and now she prays for him, repeating that the ways of the Lord are not for us to know. You see ... religion everywhere.'

'What about the abbé Le Couec?'

'He sees absolutely zero. Michel takes communion two or three times a week. Even more elevated souls – and they do exist, forgive me, dear old Father,' she said, comically pressing her hands together, 'even more elevated souls would be taken in. Do you remember this bedroom?'

She opened the door into a small room that looked out over the garden.

'I only came here once.'

'We made love on the bare mattress.'

'Yes we did.'

She took him into the sitting room, patted the place beside her on the sofa, and took his hand.

'Is it really true that you haven't slept with Chantal?'

'Why are you asking me again? Chantal isn't the sort of girl you go to bed with just like that.'

'The way you can with me, for example.'

'I never said that.'

He did not recognise her completely any more. She had used make-up to give herself back some of the bloom she had lost so quickly. She was no longer the delicious ripe fruit from years gone by, the Antoinette of the barn, the Antoinette of the night he had passed his baccalauréat. Then he remembered another night, the night of his departure, at Dieppe, and her feverish and weary face touched him again.

'What have you come back for?'

'An idea that will seem stupid and and pointless to you. I'd like to know whose son I am.'

She looked down.

'I can't help you. I've never found out. The abbé would tell you if it weren't for the seal of the confessional. And it's likely that Maman knows too.'

'What about your father?'

Antoinette shrugged her shoulders.

'He never asked himself the question. You know him well enough. Why are you asking all of a sudden?'

'Someone said … '

He stopped; the words did not come easily. Would he ever be able to say it?

'What? Tell me.'

'It wasn't by accident that unknown hands placed me at the gates of La Sauveté nineteen years ago.'

Antoinette squeezed his hand.

'I've thought that too, but why?'

'Because I may be the son of your father or your mother?'

'Maman an adulteress? Be quiet, don't make me laugh. You've never looked at her properly. Papa? It's strange, I don't think so.'

'Nor me.'

'But you'd be my half-brother! In that case we've been gaily committing incest, just like they do in all the farms around here, with brothers and sisters sleeping in the same bed.'

'It wouldn't bother me very much, either,' he said.

Through the window he caught sight of Albert limping across the garden, a full flowerpot in each hand. Father and son still loved each other deeply, but their separation was almost complete. They could no longer play the same game they had played for so long. It would have been absurd. Albert never lied, never dissembled about anything. Jean felt an urge to be with him, to leave this pretend La Sauveté that possessed none of the charm of the old one.

'Who's living at La Sauveté now?'

'The delightful Longuets.'

'What about Gontran?'

'He's bought himself a Delahaye. Makes him irresistible. Apparently he wants to be a racing driver. All the girls are falling over themselves.'

'And you?'

'No, I'm finished with him since you know what. You know I can never have children?'

'Does it make you sad?'

'Yes.'

'What a bastard.'

Jean felt that Antoinette was about to say something, but she was silent and stood up.

'What are you going to do?' she asked.

'Wait for the abbé. He's my only hope.'

'And then?'

'I haven't any money. Find a job.'

'Why don't you go to Paris?'

'I don't have a sou.'

'I can lend you some. Papa sends me the occasional cheque behind Maman's back. I don't spend anything. What for? I'm dead and buried here already.'

He kissed her.

'It's not because I've just discovered you're a good person. I've always known it. But I need to take care of myself.'

'Will you tell me what you were doing in London?'

'Nothing exciting.'

She pouted.

'Were you being kept by a rich woman?'

348

He laughed.

'No. It's more complicated and simpler than that.'

At the door she kissed him back.

'Don't forget my offer of help.'

'You're really generous.'

'And stupid,' she laughed, with tears in her eyes.

Crouching at the edge of the pond, Michel was again stretching out his hand full of birdseed. Pigeons swirled around him. One pecked a seed from his open palm and another followed suit. He smiled with contentment.

'Did you see that?' he said to Antoinette. 'I'm going to Dieppe this afternoon to buy another pair.'

Jean walked towards his father.

'Papa, I'd like us to have lunch together. Do you want to go to Chez Émile? But I haven't got a sou. It'll be on you.'

'If you like, my boy, if you like.'

They said nothing to each other about peace. Albert no longer believed in it. He had carried his pacifism like a cross since the socialist Left had moved to warmongering and the Right to attempting to restrain its adventurism. Jean worried him too, reawakening his old anxiety that a man did not leave his class without shedding a few drops of blood along the way. He looked at him with a gruff tenderness that would not be fooled but was disarmed none the less by Jean's evasive answers to his questions. When the boy announced that he might go to Paris to look for work, Albert raised thick unruly eyebrows. Paris? Why Paris? There was no life better than country life, especially when it was next to the sea. There was nowhere and nothing more healthy. Jean made no attempt to reason with him, for fear of deepening their estrangement. Nor did he dare raise the question of his birth again, and by the time he returned to Malemort that afternoon he knew the answer would not be revealed so quickly. The abbé remained his only hope.

Chantal was at Dieppe with her father. The marquise offered him tea. He declined, saying he had letters to write that claimed his urgent attention. His notebook acquired a new page of reflections.

j) If I don't find out whose son I am one day, I'll end up spending my life as an invalid. Or rather – and only to my own eyes – a sort of monster of nature, a twentieth century offspring of the Virgin and the Holy Spirit. Albert is marvellous as Joseph, but who wants Joseph for a father?

k) What happened last night with Chantal is the first poisoned chalice of my life. I loved her face, loved to look at her. Now that image has been torn up and replaced by a body that is a complete lie. I need all my strength to struggle against the obsession that gnaws at me: who came to her before I did? I'll be the last to know, inevitably. Antoinette knows. She's dying to tell me, but she's scared of my reaction. There's only one way out: to leave. Two possibilities: London or Paris. In London I'll manage somehow. In Paris it will be harder. That means I'll be obliged to borrow the money that Antoinette offered me.

He closed the notebook and slipped it into his suitcase. Someone was knocking at the door. Chantal came in dressed in a soft wool skirt and polo-neck sweater. Leaning against the door panel, she refused to come any further.

'You've just hidden something,' she said.

'Yes. A notebook where I write down some very personal thoughts.'

'Do you write about me in it?'

'Yes. You see how I answer your questions very openly. Answer mine—'

She put out her arm, her hand up.

'No, don't ask it. What are we going to do?'

'Nothing. I intend to go either to Paris or to London.'

'Take me with you.'

'You're mad!'

'Perhaps.'

She slammed the door as she left. A tractor rumbled beneath the window. Jean saw the marquis at the wheel, wearing a cap and corduroy trousers, his shirt open on his athletic torso. Madame de Malemort was making her way to the kennel. It was time for her to exercise the Brittany spaniel and Braque d'Auvergne that her husband hunted with. Jean took out his notebook again.

> *l) The question in the last paragraph was badly put: I stand to suffer a lot less if the person who came to Chantal before me is someone I don't know. If, on the other hand, it's someone from Grangeville, I won't be able to bear it. It would send me mad. The wisest thing would be never to ask Chantal directly, but, strange as it may seem after my behaviour of recent months, I love her and only her, and last night has got me even more involved. I can't see any way out except* knowing.

Chantal again spent part of the night with him. They scarcely spoke to each other. At breakfast the marquis suggested to Jean that he might like to accompany him to the market at Dieppe. Chantal stayed behind to help her mother. The two men left in the 301, hauling a small trailer into which the marquis had loaded a couple of calves. While the marquis was in conversation with a livestock dealer, Jean took the opportunity to slip away to the last address he had for Joseph Outen. He found him in his attic, where two fanlights provided all the room's illumination. Joseph greeted him joyfully.

'You're not much of a pen pal, are you? Nor me, I must admit, though I have an excuse: I'm working like a slave ... '

'When's your exhibition?'

'My exhibition?'

'Of drawings.'

Joseph roared with laughter: he had given up all that nonsense months ago. He had encountered an impregnable wall of rejection. Every gallery, without exception. Jean had no idea how resistant dealers were towards new ideas, and artists themselves guarded the territory like wolves. You had to be utterly naïve to expect to make a breakthrough in times like these. Conditions were turning out to be the worst they had ever been: the big money was investing in Impressionists, the safe money in tinned food, for when war broke out. Joseph had destroyed his whole winter's work with a light heart.

'So what are you doing?'

'My dear chap, you know the words of Monsieur Homais: "One must move with the times." The idiocy of Flaubert's character is summed up in those words. We shouldn't be trailing behind the times or moving with them. We need to anticipate them. For what lies ahead of us? Nothing could be clearer. Hitler will soon annex the Sudetenland. France and Great Britain will declare war on him. Germany, whose military strength is nothing but a bluff, will be overrun by us within three weeks. Nothing very extraordinary there, except that we shall find ourselves face to face with the Soviet Union in a Europe dominated by Paris and London. Stalin will attack us. There will be a short and nasty war, and three months later Tartars and Kalmucks will be parading through Paris. That is the moment Chiang Kai-shek will choose to attack Siberia for supplying the Communist rebels. Eight hundred million Chinese will rush at the Soviet paradise. Why should they stop politely at the West's borders? They'll keep going until they reach Paris, Madrid, Lisbon and Rome. The future is Chinese, because the USA won't intervene. The two Americas will shut themselves up inside their Monroe doctrine. Can you imagine what our life will be like at that moment? Two hundred and fifty million Europeans wrestling with a Chinese army of occupation? Who will translate when General Chi Ho-li wants to order his *café au lait* each morning? There aren't twenty Frenchmen who speak and write Chinese. I intend to be the twentieth. For two months I have been learning Chinese.'

'In Dieppe?'

'Yes. Obviously I should be in Paris at the School of Oriental Languages, but our education system is completely fossilised. I'd be taught literary Chinese. Can you see me, armed with my literary Chinese, translating a peace treaty for Chiang Kai-shek or discussing his generals' requisition requirements line by line? They'd laugh in my face. But I've found an extraordinary chap here, Li Pou, who used to be a cook on a cargo ship, well read, a veteran of the civil war. He has taken me in hand. I work with him for two hours every day. Progress is slow for brains like ours, which have been trained by logic and generalisations. But I give you less than a year, no more than two, before you come and say to me, "Joseph, you were right." So why don't you make a start too? Just a second ... '

He drew back from Jean, startling him.

'What's the matter?'

'You're looking very swish. Have you made your fortune?'

'I only own what I'm wearing.'

'Good. You had me worried for a moment. Think hard about what I said, and come and see me this week. I'll introduce you to Li Pou. You're made to get on with one another.'

Jean thanked him. He would think about it. In the meantime he needed to find Monsieur de Malemort, who, having sold his two calves, had probably gone to ground in one of the cafés around the market and been doing himself no good. That was the gist of the mission with which the marquise had discreetly entrusted him that morning. Joseph smiled condescendingly: the aristos were jumping the gun a little. They would be better off drowning their sorrows when the Chinese came. He personally was very happy: he knew he was backing the right horse.

Jean left him sadly. He no longer saw Joseph the way he once had, as a big older brother whose life was a lesson in energy and adventure, but increasingly as a loser who laid every failure at the door of a general hostility to his talents. Jean felt that the world he had once lived in had not matured in the way he had. What had happened to turn the marquis into little more than a narrow-minded farmer, Chantal perhaps into a tart, to make Antoinette a has-been, Michel an ambiguous figure, and Albert – so decent and honest – an old quibbler? What had changed: them, or his own outlook on life? How he would love to have been left with his illusions intact. It was impossibly sad. He found Monsieur de Malemort at a café and managed to get him home, not without difficulty. Having put on an old pair of trousers and a wool shirt, he was about to go out into the fields with him on his tractor when the rain started, drowning the château and and its farm. Jean recognised the smell of Normandy: green and melancholy. The marquis pulled off his boots with an effort, changed into a sports jacket and grey trousers, and fell asleep in an armchair reading a farming paper. Chantal sat in silence next to her mother, who was knitting. From time to time Madame de Malemort glanced at the streaming window. Night was falling, buffeted by gusts of wind.

When Chantal came to Jean's bedroom after dinner, she was no longer the same defeated young woman.

'Do you understand now?' she said aggressively.

'Yes, I think I do.'

They appreciated each other better after this exchange, and their enjoyment was great. Too great for Jean to leave her behind.

'Living here is like dying,' she said. 'I don't want to die. When are we going to run away?'

'As soon as I've seen the abbé.'

'The abbé won't tell you anything.'

'I'm afraid you're right, but he's my last chance.'

Chantal's expression hardened.

'I won't wait another day.'

'Who will you go with if I don't take you tomorrow?'

'What'll it matter to you?'

'It will be unbearable.'

She threw herself into his arms. He undressed her slowly and let her misery overflow as he held her until dawn. The longest night of his life was ending in a defeat that he needed to turn into a victory, as Julien Sorel had done.

Chantal woke up. 'So?'

'We're catching the train to Paris this afternoon.'

Antoinette lent him the money, knowing what he intended it for. Timidly Albert reminded his son that war was looming and that no boy of twenty, sound in heart and mind, should take part in the madness to come.

'Desert!' he said in a choked voice. 'I'll help you.'

Monsieur Cliquet gave him the address of a former railway worker, a friend of his, retired for fifteen years but living on the top floor of a building that flanked the Gare de l'Est, from where he followed the movements of the trains. Jean could trust him: he was a man of great resource. Captain Duclou knew no one at the ministry but one of his cousins, a former navy carpenter, lived at Bezons, north-west of Paris. His advice was always good, and he had many connections in his locality.

Jean left first, quietly, carrying his suitcases. The butcher's car dropped him off at Grangeville, where he waited for the bus at the stop outside the grocer's. He was nearly knocked down as he stood there by a red Delahaye that swept out of La Sauveté like a whirlwind, driven by a young man in a white bandana. By the time he reached

Dieppe station Chantal was already settled in a compartment in one of the front carriages. He found a seat in an adjacent compartment until the train pulled out.

By dinner time, the two of them were standing on a platform at the Gare Saint-Lazare, clutching their suitcases, deafened by the capital's rumble and disconcerted, not knowing where to go. Their simplest plan was to cross Place du Havre and walk into the first hotel they came to. A station's presence was reassuring, they realised: it stopped them feeling like prisoners in the labyrinth of the enormous city.

The author feels that he ought to be interested here, if only fleetingly, in Chantal's parents, before he follows the young people in their first encounter with Paris. To do them justice he would have to describe at some length their reactions, their despair and fury, their dignity, and the lie in which they wrapped Chantal's departure. The day after her flight, the marquis did indeed make a genuine effort to find his daughter. Dressed in his town clothes, he caught the train to Paris with no specific intention in mind, relying on some miraculous accident to lead him to her, a mad idea whose futility became all too clear to him as he in turn alighted at Saint-Lazare. A few steps led to the station exit. The crowd was surging into the mouth of the Métro station; a long line of travellers was queuing for taxis. As he stood there, an old woman was knocked down by a bus in front of him. A spreading pool of blood reddened the road, and a circle quickly formed around her. The absurdity of his undertaking suddenly became apparent to the marquis. He bought a ticket and left for Dieppe again fifteen minutes later. Yet had he simply crossed Place du Havre he would have glimpsed his daughter and Jean sitting there on a brasserie terrace, eating a breakfast of *café au lait* and croissants served by a waiter in a white apron. Back at Malemort, he sold the two mares, the colt and the filly, and bought himself a new tractor. From then on he was seen only in his fields, working from dawn till dusk.

The summer of 1938 was fine and dry, the harvest far better than expected, but the state of alert that had settled on Europe was taking manpower away from the land. The army was on a war footing, retaining the younger age groups and calling for specialists. So when the prime minister, Édouard Daladier, returned from Munich after signing the agreement that would delay the conflict by a year, France breathed again. The marquis kept on working, not for his daughter's future any longer, but out of a sense of honour. He faced up to the devastation of his life, renouncing alcohol, which made the pain that tormented him worse. Madame de Malemort descended into silence and her needlework. The abbé Le Couec visited her several times, then gave up; she answered in monosyllables. Albert refrained from publicly blaming his son, though once again he felt the folly of social mobility. The possible war – inevitable in his eyes – preoccupied him far more, yet he too trusted Daladier because he was a countryman, despite being a history teacher, and a veteran of the last war. He had been in the trenches and would not consign new generations to that experience with a light heart. It was a feeling that was general in France. Daladier, with his felt hat pulled low over his eyes, his southern accent, his gravelly voice, the way he pronounced the word 'patrie',[17] reassured a population that was ready to entrust its fate to anyone. They called him 'the bull of Vaucluse' and failed to realise soon enough that he was a bull made of papier mâché, partial to his drink and society ladies. The English were also curious about him, and thought he possessed a rough charm that their prime minister, Neville Chamberlain, with his stiff collar and umbrella, lacked. Madame du Courseau refrained from commenting in public about Chantal's escapade, fearing the talk might turn to Geneviève and to Antoinette's past misconduct. She voiced her feelings to her son alone, whose clear-sightedness in having refused a planned marriage with the Malemort girl she admired all the more. What instinct! Jean was blamed, though mutedly, for at the slightest allusion Antoinette defended him like a fury. And what did Palfy think? Be patient. He is not far away. We shall see him reappear, very soon, in one of those reincarnations he is so lavish with. Let us instead resume our pursuit of Chantal and Jean after their breakfast on the brasserie terrace on Place du Havre. They saw the accident, the woman knocked down, the crowd gathering. Chantal felt sick, and the feeling stayed with her all day. Jean mistakenly thought that she regretted having run away. He told her she was free to go back if she wanted to; she refused. With Antoinette's money they had enough to live on for two months, but urgently needed to find work and somewhere to live. Since neither of them had any experience of Paris, they began by exploring it by bus, discovering its districts one by one. Chantal thought Neuilly was charming. At least you could still see pretty detached houses there, with gardens around them. She wondered how anyone could live in the other places they saw, full of dark apartments in big buildings blackened by smoke. Jean, wiser as a result of his stay in London, noticed that the Île Saint-Louis, in the sixth and seventh arrondissements, offered reasonable accommodation. Their resources unfortunately allowed them no such quality. Eventually they had to be content with an old building in Rue Lepic and two ill-furnished rooms in which you washed at the kitchen sink, although the bedroom window looked out spectacularly over Paris. They spent a week cleaning, polishing, and expelling blood-sucking insects left behind by the previous tenant. With an aluminium tub and the rose of a watering can purchased at the flea market, they felt they had made a bathroom. Chantal bought blue and white gingham at the Saint-Pierre market, ran up some curtains, and sewed a bedspread. On the same landing there lived a Spanish painter, Jesús Infante, who survived on nothing but red wine and peanuts, a handsome man in his thirties who wore his shirt unbuttoned on his hairy chest and had a constant five o'clock shadow and a dazzling smile. They heard him humming and yelling at his models, two or three girls of no great prettiness but sharp as tacks, who laughed back at him in their high treble voices. Jesús painted 'Montmartre nudes' for a tourists' shop on Place du Tertre: five pictures a month. They were absolutely horrible, but they were popular and he made a living from them, despite being exploited by the gallery. His daily labours done with, he closed his shutters, and by the light of a bare bulb worked on great collages of cut-outs that no dealer could be persuaded to show an interest in. It did not matter, he was happy, happier than he had been at Jaén in Andalusia, where his parents, ruined by the civil war, lived on a cup of chocolate a day.

Nor should we be sad at these frugal Parisian beginnings for Chantal and Jean: they had never been happier either. They loved each other and were at liberty. Jean sometimes thought of Geneviève and told himself that she would have approved of him. In any case it would have been impossible with her. Frankly impossible, for a reason that remained obscure but that Palfy had somehow detected. He forgot the awful disappointment of his first night with Chantal, and his euphoria swept away the terrible thoughts he had committed to his notebook: who had come before him? Perhaps it had only been a bad dream. He remembered their walks in the forest, their conversations with each other that had avoided all innuendo, their drawing closer with an agonising slowness that had so abruptly changed on his first night at Malemort. They made love often and with the passion of novices, especially during the day because they liked the daylight and because at night they still slept like babies, worn out by their domestic activities and Jean's lengthy journeys across Paris in his efforts to find work. No one, apparently, wanted anything to do with him before he had completed his military service. His baccalauréat did not improve his prospects. He was offered door-to-door selling. For three days he tried to sell a book of herbal remedies to the housewives of the twentieth arrondissement. Insults and threats made him stop. A single copy sold in three days was not enough to pay his travel costs. In the space of a month he gauged the immensity of Paris, how one could get lost there in an atmosphere that, when it was not hostile, was the soul of indifference. It was

Jesús who found him a job. When the painter had first arrived in France he had been a doorman and bouncer at a nightclub in Pigalle. The situation was once again vacant. Jean's build got him taken on. He spent an afternoon being taught how to restrain a difficult customer and eject him. As for opening car doors, any fool could do that. And holding out his hand – it was a question of habit. He put on the uniform belonging to his predecessor, reminding himself of the horrible doorman at the Adler in Rome, although his dislike of servants had been tempered slightly by the punctual, snobbish Price at Eaton Square. Satisifed on his first evening at having chucked out a drunken provincial quietly and without fuss, he was taken on full time by the manager. The nightclub was called Match and had become fashionable, particularly with a foreign clientele. At six in the morning Jean walked back up Rue Lepic – enlivened by concierges in slippers wheeling out their bins overflowing with rubbish, motorised street sweepers hosing down the cobblestones, and delivery vans tossing out packets of newspapers at still-closed kiosks – climbed up four floors, and let himself in to contemplate Chantal's exquisite face lying on the pillow, her black hair spread around it, the fine outline of her nose, her angel's eyelids fringed with long lashes, her slow breathing like that of a child, and her bare shoulders. When he lay down next to her she hardly moved. When he woke up around midday, lunch was ready, and they sat down together, talking as they had before, but at the same height this time, without him being on foot and her on horseback.

'You don't miss the forest of Arques too much, do you?'

'No. Apart from the days when you came with me, I thought it was a lonely place. I saw stags and hinds but no human beings. In Paris there are human beings.'

Jean was beginning to doubt that the beings of Paris were human. But they were beings, at least, and you approached them with curiosity. At Match he earned a decent wage, especially if he counted the obnoxious business of gratuities, and it enabled them to eat out in the evenings at restaurants that made Chantal's eyes shine with pleasure. One evening a drunken Italian, whose car he had been to fetch from its parking place at Pigalle, slipped a thousand-franc note into his hand to thank him. With it Jean bought Chantal a gold chain and a new coat that was very welcome at the end of autumn. She owned nothing, having left Malemort with what she stood up in and a practically empty suitcase. He was dressing her, piece by piece.

'You're wrong,' she said. 'I don't need it. I only go out to go to the market. In the morning, when you're asleep, I look out of the window and I say to myself: there is Paris, and there are millions of people who live the way we do, who don't know us, and whom we will never know. It's infinite, like space.'

Slowly he forgot that in his absence she had known another man, and not any other man but a decisive and demanding man. On the occasions when he allowed his thoughts to dwell on that fact, his fists clenched and he took out his anger on the first ill-mannered or drunken customer he was asked to eject from the club. In December he was cold, and kept warm by stamping his feet on the pavement under the illuminated sign. The bar girls came outside in their plunging necklines to bring him scalding hot toddies. There were three or four of them with their interchangeable assumed names, Suzy, Dolly, Fanny, pretty enough in the dark but already haggard and ravaged, despite their frequent nose-powderings and other restorations, by the time they left with an unsteady client. He could have slept with any of them, without consequences, but it did not occur to him. Chantal filled up his life. They were playing at husband and wife in a real world, where no one stood in their way to overwhelm them with sound advice or predict stormy days ahead as a result of their insouciance. They asked Jesús to lunch or dinner and he brought his peanuts with him, accepting only as an extra, with a startled tentativeness, a sardine in oil or an apple. He was dependably happy until the first of each month, which was the day he was due to deliver his five pictures to the gallery. Every time he returned humiliated. The owner, who knew about his collages and liked to mock him coarsely about them, greeted him with a 'Hello, Papiécasso'. Jesús would willingly have knocked him down, but he needed the monthly payments. To lose them would mean misery all over again, the way life had been when he first arrived in the city.

'You un'erstan',' he would say to his friends, 'I pu' up with it for my love of art. For my work! But I will smash him in his crooked face if he ask me to put a few mo' hairs in the bums of the girls if I wan' to sell them. Hairs in the bums, I say to him, hairs in the bums, Monsieur, my models don' have them! They are too poor to pay for some with the money zat I give them, an' you know wha' he say to me. "My boy, you only have to give them yours" … '

He opened his shirt to expose his well-muscled chest bristling with its thick, black curly growth. Chantal wept with laughter, and Jean loved to watch her listening to Jesús's obscenities without blushing.

Where was the future in all of this? A long way off, and the time to worry about it was when it came over the horizon. Sufficient unto the day were the pleasures of love and Paris which opened up to them when in the afternoons they came down from the Butte Montmartre to go to the cinema or the theatre, to walk in the Cité or on the Île Saint-Louis, to buy books from the booksellers along the *quais* and then go home and read them, lying together on the bed until it was time for Jean to leave for Match.

Apart from Jesús Infante, the building housed only shuffling, bad-tempered pensioners, two tarts who worked Rue Godot-de-Mauroy, and a dirty old man constantly on the lookout for skirts walking up the steep staircase. They were a long way from the Parisian society of which Balzac had made himself the chronicler. Chantal spoke to no one, except at the market from which she returned with their shopping twice a week. She waited for Jean, without impatience, because everything seemed new to her, putting up with the crudity of Jesús's conversations and the whiff of stewed meat that permeated the building, and had not even seen him dressed in his hireling's uniform because he changed when he got to the club. One day, when she was feeling particularly happy, she sent her mother the cruellest card imaginable in the circumstances. 'Am very happy. Warmest wishes.' To her father she sent nothing, not a word. The days passed, distancing her from Malemort and the massive boredom that seeped from its walls. She also thought about the one who had come before Jean and had rehearsed her so well in the drama of love. From that point of view she had no remorse, no regret. She had discovered the pleasure of living life in the instant, and there was no one there to reproach her for her failure to behave properly or her breaches of respectability. To tell the truth, she did not really care in the slightest what people had thought of her after she left.

And so she and Jean came through the dark and freezing winter that preceded, like an omen, the even darker and more freezing winters of the war and occupation. Jesús, frantically filling his coal-fired stove to keep his models warm as they posed in the mornings, nearly set fire to the building. Waking with a start, Jean refused to comply with the fire brigade's evacuation instruction and went back to sleep, watched over by an amazed and impressed Chantal. She feared nothing as long as he was there. A girl who had scampered from Jesús's apartment when the alarm was raised sat with them until it was over. She was naked underneath her robe. At Pigalle they called her Miranda. In private, far from her clients, she liked to be called by her real name, Madeleine. She began to come over after lunch to have coffee with them and tell the story of her night. Jean marvelled at the indulgent warmth Chantal displayed in listening to her. How could the Malemorts' daughter entertain such a friendship?

No two women could be more disparate. Jean pricked up his ears when he heard Miranda-Madeleine say a few words of English. She had spent two years in London around 1932, which put her there at the time of his first visit. He recounted the story of his meeting with Madame Germaine.

'Did I know Madame Germaine?' she said. 'Course I did! She taught "French" to masos; she was a funny old girl, needed no encouragement to get her whips out. She ended up with her throat cut but her stash wasn't touched, a nice little nest egg she left to her nephew, an invalid who went around in a little car. Her pimps found the bloke who did her in, a French waiter, a casual, jealous and nasty. He turned up a week later on a pavement in Soho, bleeding like a pig, his femoral artery cut, nice bit of specialist work. How old were you then?'

'Thirteen.'

'You're not telling me that at thirteen you were going round looking for tarts!'

'No, I was looking for my friend Salah.'

'Salah! You know Salah! The Negro with the Hispano.'

'What do you know about him?'

Madeleine's expression turned stony. She pulled her peignoir close across her drooping breasts and made her excuses to leave. It was impossible to get another word out of her, however circumspectly on subsequent occasions Jean brought up the subject of London and Salah. Only once did she talk to Chantal, one morning at the market when it was just the two of them.

'I'm saying nothing. I want to stay alive. Maybe Madame Germaine deserved the big grin. Not for me.'

She put her hand protectively up to her throat.

In March, walking past the Salle Pleyel, Chantal and Jean saw the poster announcing Michel's recital, accompanied on the piano by Francis Poulenc.

'I'd really like to go,' Jean said, 'if only to see him puff out his chest and purse those terribly red lips of his. Too bad! I'll be working. And of course all of civilised Dieppe and Grangeville will be there. It's not really the time or place to show ourselves off.'

A few days later Chantal suggested that she could go to the recital on her own.

'Of course you can go if you want to.'

Jean was upset that she had thought about it without talking to him, as though she were afraid of him.

'You will be seen. Antoinette will be there with her mother, and there'll be plenty of others you won't be able to avoid.'

'I'll keep away from them.'

'Not so easy as you think.'

'I'll wear dark glasses.'

'Do you really want to go?'

'Yes.'

'Then go.'

He woke her at six a.m., as he came in from work. Or rather he thought he had woken her up, because she was pretending to be asleep. Her eyelids opened to a terribly urgent and inquisitorial look. She did not ask him why he was looking at her that way, and she did not want him to ask her any questions either.

'What was it like?' he asked finally.

'Oh, it was very good … Michel is really talented. Apart from his friends and family, everyone had come for Poulenc. But at the end they were applauded the same.'

'Did anyone see you?'

'No, nobody.'

She turned towards the wall. Jean undressed, reflecting that he himself had met someone that evening, that everything had happened without a word, without a look, so that he could not even be certain that the moment could be real. An English car had stopped outside Match, and he had opened the door for Peter and Jane Ascot. Of course Peter had not recognised him, he never recognised anybody, but Jane had paused, and when they left two hours later she had looked straight at him, without registering any surprise. The encounter had lasted no more than a few seconds, but long enough to leave him feeling disconcerted. Jane had not counted in his life in London, even though she had played, thanks to him, a decisive role in Palfy's business plans. He could not remember having had the slightest feeling for her. Yet he had been flattered by her attention and the way she had been attracted to him. She had revealed to a young man still clumsy and unrefined, dazzled at the world he was discovering, that a woman of her background could show herself to be not just attainable but full of initiative. She had also unconsciously given him his revenge on Peter's snobbish disdain. That she was no Aphrodite was hardly important, for she more than compensated by her experience for her lack of beauty. What would she tell Palfy when she got back to London? If she said a word, he would either explode with fury or scorn Jean for ever more. Doorman and bouncer at a nightclub: that was all the use he had made of his initiation. He could already hear his friend's heavy sarcasm.

He thought he must have woken up earlier than usual. Chantal was not yet back from the market. Opening the curtains, he saw Paris gilded in a lovely mix of pastels, of blue roofs, grey smoke rising from their chimneys, and green spaces. His watch said one o'clock. He leant out to catch sight of Chantal, who would be coming back up Rue Lepic with her bag of shopping in her hand. She had probably got up later than usual after her evening at the Salle Pleyel. The breeze blew into the room, fresh and as if filled with a smell of spring. Jean walked to the sink and took his toothbrush from the glass in which it stood. His hand stopped in mid-air: there was only one brush. There was no tortoiseshell comb on the glass shelf, no make-up remover; the hand cream Chantal used when she had done the dishes was gone.

In the wardrobe there remained only English suits, an overcoat, his two cases. He began to tremble, then went through both rooms looking for a letter, anything scribbled on a piece of paper. Nothing. He had to stay very calm, not panic, examine carefully all possible clues, imagine the most simple and natural explanation, a telegram summoning her to Malemort to look after her sick father, something, anything serious and therefore comprehensible, that would explain everything. Above all he must not stay like this, his face stinging, hair tangled, in rumpled pyjamas. Must be a man, a real man, smile, laugh at himself. An intense fatigue was crushing his temples. His heart was thumping so hard he thought he could hear it. He experienced the most appalling difficulty in pulling himself together, then crossed the landing and knocked at Jesús's door. Jesús opened immediately. Jean realised straight away that he knew.

Jesús knew, so everyone knew. To the physical, almost intolerable suffering that Jean was feeling was added something he would perhaps be even less able to forgive Chantal for than her betrayal: the wound to his pride. But men have those foolish ways of behaving that save them from disaster. He spent several days completely shut off from life, out of time, registering neither darkness nor light. Madeleine came in around lunchtime, in her robe, without make-up, offering to an indifferent gaze a complexion eroded by years of powdered and rouged somnambulism. She made lunch, pulled back the curtains, opened the windows to let the sometimes cotton-cloudy, sometimes clear-skied city in, talked with a certainty that he wasn't listening to her but that the monotonous murmur of her voice would distract him from his fixation. Madeleine displayed seniority as well as authority the day she arrived and found, grouped around the table in their hats and with their hair done and looking very respectable, the three bar girls from Match who had come to find out what had happened to Jean. Needless to say, he had been sacked and a new doorman and bouncer now wore the menial uniform, an ex-wrestler named Bobby la Fleur.

'No style when he opens a car door,' Fanny said.

'Much too rough too,' Suzy added. 'The day before yesterday he chucked out a client who asked a married woman for a light.'

'He hasn't a mean bone in his body,' Dolly said. 'He's just very thick.'

Madeleine made it clear that their chitchat was out of place at a moment such as this. Fortunately Jesús took over in the afternoons and worked in Jean's apartment. Jean did not ask him how he knew, nor how long he had known. Some matters that cause too much pain need to remain in the dark, and that real friends, of however short a duration, will keep from each other.

'I like wha' I do,' Jesús said. 'One day they will lick my boots. I'm not a nasty man an' I keep my fee' nice an' clean so they don' feel too ashame'. Don' you think I'm righ'?'

Jean nodded. In a way his own situation was similar. Art and love both suffered ignominious defeats when they started out. When dealers began to recognise the genius that was in Jesús's collages, Chantal would realise her lover's feelings for her. Keeping one's feet clean? Yes, it was not a bad idea. At any rate Jean was aware that he was undergoing his first great disappointment in love, and hated it slightly less than he had expected. There would never be another one, and by its suddenness and depth this one even managed to seem quite noble, since he had survived Chantal's offence. He wrote to Antoinette.

> *Chantal has run off! Who with? That is the question. Or perhaps not. Not at all. The important thing is that she's no longer here. One day I'll recover, and you'll see me stronger than death itself.*
>
> *All my affection, Jean*

She wrote back by return.

> *Yes, she ran off with Gontran Longuet. She was sleeping with him at Grangeville before you came. What girl of her age could resist a red Delahaye convertible with a racing exhaust? Try to forgive her. The Malemorts, who thought you were the bee's knees (sorry!), are bitterly offended. I've had a bit of money from Papa, so I'm sending it to you. The stamp was franked at Saint-Tropez. He must be keeping himself warm at night*

somewhere around there. Finally, another bit of news: I've pumped the abbé so hard that he's given me a clue. But do you still really want to know? With love,
Antoinette

Jean felt that from this moment on, he no longer gave a damn. Chantal had gone off with that swine? She would soon regret it. Jesús confirmed it.

'I di'n' wan' to say to you, but I saw him. She has gone away in a red Delahaye what was waitin' ou'side the door. I saw the man: a very strange funny-lookin' face.'

Thus everything was illuminated. At the concert she had been unable to resist the little world of Grangeville, and Gontran had used the opportunity to reclaim his property. Disgust works like medicine. Jean got very drunk in Jesús's company and went out to look for work and new lodgings where the location of every missing object would not remind him of Chantal. He also wrote to Antoinette.

Is it really vital to know? I'm not so sure as I was before. Maybe it's not the right moment yet. Later, when I'm feeling a bit less shattered. I'll write to you.

He had just sealed the envelope when there was a knock at the door.

Palfy was there, his foot across the threshold so that Jean could not slam the door in his face.

'Hello, dear boy. You're not at all easy to track down. If not for Jane Ascot, we might have lost sight of each other for good. Fortunately I found your lovely girlfriends at Match. Delightful! Especially Fanny who more than deserves her name. I've always been rather partial to that sort of girl. Me and the women of the world … you know. Yes, quite true. Anyway, a little pillow talk and I got your address and discovered your lady love had ditched you.'

370

'Come in.'

Palfy inspected his lodgings.

'Perfect for a gay *grisette*. Alas, young ladies who grow up in châteaux quickly tire of the bohemian life.'

'I'm obliged to you for your sarcasm. I inflict more than enough of it on myself already. How are your affairs progressing?'

'What? Haven't you heard?'

Palfy sat down, pulled off his gloves, and calmly filled his pipe and lit it, imbuing the room with a comforting smell.

'Bust!' he said, smiling. 'One fool took fright and immediately found plenty of other fools to follow his example. Front-page news for a week. Worth at least a hundred thousand sterling, publicity like that. My picture splashed all over the papers. They even published pictures of the Rolls, which I sold straight away to Lord Donovan, and the Morgan – Lady Quarry bought that. Price took a job with the Ascots. Ruin, dear boy, magnificent ruin. In the eyes of the law anyway, because you'll remember that the idea was spectacular … The only problem was that it was unusable in Europe. So …'

He raised his right hand, pointing his finger.

'… so I sold it to an American consortium. Three of them came over from New York, and I spent a week explaining my system to them. In their opinion it ought to be workable in New York. They offered me a percentage, but I went for ten thousand dollars deposited at a bank in Paris instead. Enough to live like a prince for six months. And when it runs out I'll get a job digging roads … '

'What about England?'

'I am the subject of an arrest warrant. So why don't we head south instead, both of us? My treat.'

'I couldn't possibly.'

'Why not?'

In reality there was no serious reason not to. By the time they had finished lunch at a restaurant in the Place du Tertre, Palfy had his way. Afterwards, as they walked past the gallery that Jesús

371

supplied with his vulgar daubs, Jean stopped. In the middle of th
window stood a canvas of a naked young woman, standing in a tu
and showering herself with the rose of a watering can. It was nc
Chantal's face, but it was her body without a shadow of doubt: th
pretty buds of her hardly ripe breasts, the downy hair of her belly
her long, slender horsewoman's legs: and behind her the curtains c
blue and white gingham.

'Jesús too!' Jean said.

Palfy put on his most compassionate expression.

'Do I guess correctly?'

'Yes. It's getting comical.'

'Let's not delay, in that case. This district is bad for your health.
was intending to buy a car –'

'You don't steal them any more?'

'It's been a bit dangerous for the past six months. No. Let's catc
the Blue Train. At Cannes we'll be able to pick up something nice an
inconspicuous. We'll go and fetch your case now. On one condition

'Which is?'

'No punch-ups with the aforesaid Jesús. I caught a glimpse c
him. He's built like a fairground wrestler. Anyhow, I cannot stan
brawling.'

They met him on the stairs, carrying a canvas under his arm.

'I'm leaving,' Jean said. 'No regrets.'

'Ah, I un'erstan'. You're right. Forget 'er.'

'You too. Forget her. She made you suffer, didn't she?'

'Yes, listen, Zean, I'm a bastar'. Your Santal, I –'

'No explanations. She cheated on us both, and now that there ar
two of us it should make us less sad.'

'S'e enjoy' posin' nude—'

'Let's not talk any more. Goodbye, Jesús.'

He stopped at the second floor to kiss Madeleine.

'You're looking better,' she said. 'I'm glad to see it. You see, th
sorrows of love, you get over them faster than you think. I've live

through all sorts, for blokes who weren't worth my little finger, and I'm no worse off today. What are you doing with your two rooms up there?'

'Nothing. Take anything you want. Here's the key.'

'I'm going to ask the landlord if I can swap. I'm fed up with my window overlooking the courtyard, and you arranged your place so nicely. It's just my style. But take your stuff with you.'

'No. There's nothing I want to see again. Not even the books.'

'Books? Now there's an idea. I've been telling myself I ought to start reading. I'll give it a go, it might be fun. But send me some postcards.'

Jean kissed her, and in the commotion Palfy followed suit. He thought she was charming and would willingly have delayed their departure to spend some time with her.

And so Jesús Infante drops out of our story for a few years. The author would not like to spoil the story's suspense by relating too soon how and in what circumstances Jean will see him again, or what will have become of him. His appearance here is fleeting and of minor significance at this moment, but he is still young: thirty at the most. His fate is not yet sealed. As for Madeleine, she will not stay far away.

That evening on the train Palfy and Jean went to the dining car and drank champagne. Nothing, clearly, would ever stop Palfy leading a life of delights and comforts. He loved himself with a candour stripped of all artifice, and not for a second did the idea of the ruin he was piling up in his wake disturb him. Jean nevertheless found his mood tinged with melancholy, for the most unexpected reason.

'Delightful, your Madeleine,' he said as he raised his glass. 'Let us drink to her. Deep down, it's a woman like that I'm in need of. Where can one find tenderness, except with creatures whose profession it is? Hello, goodnight, no regrets. Life's too short, there are too many things to do, and anyhow no one could love my little manias. Oh, we are going to have fun, dear boy. I've had a splendid idea. It will need some sun to ripen it. Hooray for Cannes!'

Jean felt that he had been taken captive once more, having thought he had escaped Palfy for good, but in the distress that still held him in its grip he accepted that it was the only way out. In Paris he would have been miserable. At Cannes he would find a job, any job. The night in the sleeping car seemed endless to him. The rhythmic panting of the train paused only for a few minutes when they stopped at stations where announcers with robot-like voices chanted their names. From Montélimar onwards these voices spoke with southern accents, and his mind went back to Mireille and Tomate and the waitresses at Roquebrune. A different suffering had had him in its grip then, and he had escaped it by running away. Would it be the same with Chantal? ? But his affair with Mireille had been nothing like the love he had just lost. She had been a terrible habit that could eventually be shaken off. Chantal had encompassed the memories of childhood and the promises of womanhood. He had overcome the pain of his first night at Malemort, and afterwards they had been happy. She would never be happy the way she had been with him. There, at least, was a comforting thought he could stir up like a sort of curse on Chantal.

Once they were past Marseille, Palfy knocked on his door.

'Get up, you idler, and have some breakfast.'

From the window of the dining car they could see the Mediterranean, pale blue in the morning sun, and the palm trees of Hyères and the lazy coast.

'However you look at it, it's easier to be happy here,' Palfy said. 'Obviously it's a little soporific, but we shall triumph over our laziness.'

'I'm not lazy.'

'And how wrong you are not to be.'

At Cannes they booked into the Carlton, where Palfy filled out his registration form without hesitation: 'Baron Constantin Palfy'.

Jean performed a rapid calculation: the money Antoinette had sent him would pay for his room for a week.

'Don't worry,' Palfy said, 'we're using my seed capital. Now we have to find ourselves a vehicle worthy of our talents.'

They spent the day doing the rounds of the town's garages. All they could find were mass-produced French saloons or Cadillacs that looked like hearses. Palfy wanted a convertible.

'We shall be spending the summer here, remember. We may as well make the most of the fresh air. You need sun and wind, your face makes you look like a man who was recently exhumed. You don't imagine we're going to be nightclub doormen, do you?'

At the last garage, Palfy took a step back in admiration of an undeniable monster: an Austro-Daimler roadster, forty horsepower, garnet-red, and six metres long. The endless bonnet and enormous boot left barely enough space in between for two or three passengers to squeeze onto a bench seat of white leather. The salesman opened the bonnet to reveal an engine big enough to power a ferry: eight cylinders in line and quadruple carburettors. Palfy fell instantly in love with this behemoth, which had languished for a year at a knock-down price: no one wanted a car that did nine miles to the gallon. What tipped the balance for him was that the Austro-Daimler had belonged to a grand duke who had married a Texan and gone to live in the USA. It was a one-off that would never be built again, an absurd, pointless folly, the sort of car that had already earned its place in a museum. Although he was of average height, Palfy looked like a dwarf behind the steering wheel. Despite the power of its eight cylinders, its chassis and coachwork were so heavy that it could only reach 100 kilometres an hour, then 120 and finally 140 on very long stretches of road where it could be pointed straight ahead. In other words, in the Alpes-Maritimes and through the Esterel the best that could be said for it was that it would be stately. Palfy could not care less. He loved cars for their looks – as he had his elderly Mathis and his Rolls in London – not for their engineering.

They took delivery there and then, drove up and down the Croisette, and parked outside the Carlton, where they went straight up to Jean's room to admire from above the garnet-red roadster, its white leather seat and the glittering chrome of its headlights and bumpers. They were standing on his balcony, Palfy as excited as a child with a new toy, when a yellow Hispano-Suiza, old-fashioned but with an immutable elegance and majesty, parked behind the Austro-Daimler, driven by a white chauffeur in a blue uniform who opened the door for a dark-skinned man in a plain grey flannel suit. Salah, for he it was, vanished with a rapid step into the hotel.

'Fantastic!' Palfy said. 'I've always thought that when a black man prospers he ought to take on a white chauffeur.'

'It's Salah, the prince's old chauffeur! I mean, old because he looks as if he's been promoted. A wonderful man. The prince must be staying at the Carlton. He always comes to the Riviera in spring!'

'Luck smiles on us, does she not, dear boy? I know now why I came to prise you from your garret in Rue Lepic. You were the very man I needed. You can't believe how much you were … You must introduce me to the prince.'

Jean did not reply. He now knew that he would not escape Palfy and his grand schemes as easily as he had thought. He was a devil incarnate, and for the moment also a saviour without whom he, Jean, might well have drowned. He nevertheless promised himself to be more circumspect this time, and not end up having to pay with his body for Palfy's squalid enterprises.

The concierge gave them the required information. Yes, the prince was living at the Carlton, as he did every year at this time. He was one of their longest-standing customers. The Côte d'Azur air calmed his asthma. Well, usually … although this year he had not left his room for two weeks, and a doctor, plus nurse, was in permanent attendance. His was telephone was never answered, apart from once a day, in the evening, always at the same time, when it took a call

376

from London. A black secretary, an Egyptian, took care of all the practical details.

Jean immediately had a note sent to Salah, whom he met at the bar an hour later, before dinner. Salah had not changed, apart from a few grey hairs at his temples and early wrinkles that betokened a face of deep creases in old age. The last time they had seen each other was the evening they had spent at Via del Babuino.

'I greatly regretted leaving in such a hurry the next morning,' Salah said. 'The prince wanted to go to Venice. The doorman at the Adler was meant to give you an envelope with 500 lira from the prince that I left in your name.'

'Not only did he not give me the money, but he was also vile to me. Because of him I conceived a deep hatred for doormen, and have been punished for it. For six months I had to work as a doorman myself.'

He told Salah the story of his return from Italy, the year he had spent portering at *La Vigie*, his winter in London.

'Yes, I knew you were there. The prince was not well. He couldn't cope with the fog and cold. Afterwards he was in remission, but at the moment we are going through a difficult period: acute shortness of breath and neurasthenia. Madame is to come in the next few days, although every evening he does his best to reassure her ... '

Salah stopped talking. Palfy was standing at Jean's side in such a way that it was impossible not to introduce him. Salah's expression changed barely perceptibly, as if he felt a secret aversion for this figure deliberately imposing himself on them, this man in blue blazer and white flannel trousers with a cravate tucked into his open shirt and an ironic smirk on his lips. In common with other former servants, Salah had learnt to judge at a glance those who belonged to the owning classes. Rich or broke, Palfy was one of them.

'I must go back,' Salah said. 'We shall meet tomorrow.'

'Won't you stay and have a glass of something?' Palfy asked.

'I don't drink alcohol. Two orangeades is one too many.'

Alone with Jean, Palfy rubbed his hands.

'A quite remarkable fellow!'

'What makes you say that?'

'His instinctive wariness. I much prefer that to the dupes who say yes immediately. This one is no dupe, I guarantee. Nor his prince … Nothing could be more promising for what I have in mind.'

'Constantin, I've had enough of your mysteries.'

'Never mind! Mysteries they must remain a little longer, then you'll understand. But do me a favour this minute, will you? Write to your friend Madeleine, ask her to join us. I'll write her a little cheque so that she can buy herself some respectable clothes and book a sleeper.'

'You must be mad! You saw her for all of five minutes. Don't try to tell me you've fallen in love!'

'Me in love? I should not dream of being so vulgar, dear boy. No. But I think she may be just the woman I need to manage my business.'

'Listen, Madeleine earns her living by turning tricks. That's bad enough for her. Do not get her involved in one of your rackets. She was kind to Chantal and me. I like her. Leave her out of it.'

'Fool! These are her last years. In a year or two she'll be picking up Arab labourers at the factory gates. So let us rescue her.'

'I didn't know you belonged to the Salvation Army.'

'A brand-new side to me, eh? Just do as I ask. You have no right to spoil her chance of a lifetime.'

Jean wrote to Madeleine, enclosing Palfy's cheque. Three days later they waited at the station for her to step off the train. Her transformation into a respectable woman had not been entirely successful. Palfy took her in hand, booked her into a modest hotel and reassured her that he would soon find her an apartment worthy of her. With a telephone.

'A telephone? What for?' she asked, suddenly anxious. 'I don't know anyone here who will call me.'

'But I know plenty.'

She confided her anxiety to Jean.

'Your chap is strange. He's got to be a pimp. And if he thinks he's going to drop in and read my meter for me, he's wrong. I work for myself.'

'I don't think he is a pimp. If he turns into one, you can drop him like a shot.'

Jean met Salah again, to ask if he would help him find a job. He waited less than a week before a travel agency engaged him to organise the leisure activities of groups of English tourists who had come to the Riviera to rest. How was he to organise leisure activities for English people on holiday? He had no idea at all. He moved out of the Carlton and took a room in the same hotel as Madeleine. The agency's office looked out onto the Croisette. Several times a day he saw through the window the garnet-red Austro-Daimler driving past with Madeleine at Palfy's side. He had persuaded her to dye her hair black. She wore very little make-up and smoked with a tortoiseshell cigarette-holder. From time to time the Hispano-Suiza also stopped outside the office, and Salah came in to talk to Jean.

'Are you all right?'

'Yes, it's not boring, and I'm earning my keep; I'm not dependent on Palfy. How is the prince?'

'No better nor worse. He's still in his room. I talked to him about you. He would like to see you as soon as he is better. Madame spoke very highly of you to him. Although she also spoke highly of your unusual friend … '

Jean did not dare ask if she was going to come to Cannes. He dreaded her coming, and longed for it. Dreaded because of the unspeakable confusion she had thrown him into, longed for her to come because she had been a revelation, a dazzling revelation, to

379

him. Alone again, he found it hard to bear the lack of a woman's company that left him facing the first genuine failure of his life so far. From the nights spent in anguish and distress he assessed the appetite and needs created in him by Chantal. He went to see Madeleine, in her room above his, and unburdened himself to her.

'I've picked up a really bad habit, a very lazy streak. I need to be with a good woman. Do you think I'll get over it?'

She kissed his forehead.

'You're a very nice boy. For a little while you two made me believe in love. But there's always disappointment waiting. I need to thank Chantal for reminding me. Don't fall in love any more, sweetheart. It hurts, and it's stupid.'

He realised quickly that Madeleine was changing from one day to the next. Supposing Palfy was Pygmalion? Madeleine was working on her English, which she had spoken fairly fluently when she lived in London, and he found out she was also taking elocution lessons. Her Parisian drawl was fading. She started expressing herself more clearly, in a calm voice.

'Your friend will end up making me sit my school certificate. He's a strange chap all right. He ain't even – I mean he *has not* even asked to sleep with me. You see how I use negatives now? I didn't think about it before. Apparently it's very fashionable.'

Palfy's ultimate goal still remained a mystery. With his aplomb, psychological acuity and, even more, his phoney barony, address at the Carlton and Austro-Daimler, he had not dragged his heels about meeting Cannes high society. The *Éclaireur de Nice et du Sud-Est* published a picture of Baron Palfy dining at the same table as the Aga Khan and the Begum, hugely distinguished company in the eyes of idiots. Like Salah he frequently paused at the agency to talk to Jean.

'You're looking well! Makes me feel good! What about your work?'

'It's very interesting.'

'I'll end up thinking that work is what makes all of us healthy. You see what kind of an influence you have on me.'

He would take Jean for dinner at a restaurant at the old port, and sometimes even seemed to want to be sincere.

'I don't know why I like you, but I do like you, Jean, for sure. If I think about it, I could have been a boy like you ten years ago. But I got thrown in at the deep end. I kept my head above water, sometimes in a good way, sometimes not. And then I suffer from this curious absence of scruples, almost an illness. Everything is too slow for me; the result is that I push things, events, people. I liked the way you didn't come back to London, where life was easy. I was disappointed, but I felt it was the right thing. It's the same here. You've got yourself a job. Fine by me. You're not an easy boy to ruin. I sometimes think I've cracked it, and then you rebel, you're off. That's good. You're a decent fellow, someone who won't ever betray me. Am I right?'

'Yes, you are. I wouldn't. But why don't you give up this life, Palfy? How can you live constantly with the prospect of being arrested or going to prison? It would drive me mad.'

'They haven't caught me yet. My star is still protecting me. Luck is the only bitch. She puts all the trumps in my hand and at the last minute she folds, and I fall from a great height. Which is not to say that I don't love the fall. It's intoxicating. Every time I tell myself: perhaps there is some great innate Justice, some playful God who's protecting me from myself. Obviously one shouldn't examine one's surroundings too much at a moment like that, it's too depressing, that meanness triumphing over the world. But I drool over it. Anyway, even so Justice moves me, as she did when I was a little boy and I thought she was very beautiful, despite her big tits.'

'You won't hurt Madeleine, will you? She's a really kind woman.'

'Don't worry. She has nothing to worry about, except earning her living without using her body to pay for it.'

He paused and seemed to reflect briefly before offering his next confession.

'Do you want to know part of my secret?'

'Yes.'

'I'm enormously amused by human stupidity. It's a rolling performance, no breaks, no intervals. In a few weeks, a few months, you'll see it unleashed when war is declared … '

War? Jean heard people around him talking about it and listened with half an ear. In his childhood he had heard them keep bringing up the same stories, and he scarcely believed in them any more. Albert had protested too much to be credible. But the rumble of war talk amplified and began to weigh upon even the most careless and egotistical, closing down people's enthusiasms and facial expressions and drawing a blood-red line through the future.

Jean's task was to escort groups of British visitors on holiday in Cannes. He accompanied them to the Îles de Lérins and to the perfumeries of Grasse, to the lavender fields and the fortified villages at Èze and Cagnes. His charges, elderly couples for the most part, pink and pale-skinned, found it very beautiful and marvelled at the slightest thing. They never talked about war, even though there were often old soldiers among them. They had come to soak up the sun and enjoy the still-fresh air of the last of springtime, and were indifferent to the rest of the world's affairs. They were either reassuring or ridiculous, depending on your point of view, but Jean liked them and, if only for the pleasure of hearing them say, 'How lovely!' he did his best to widen the scope of their sightseeing. Remembering the unbounded delight of the old ladies on the boat up the Thames to Hampton Court, he suggested to the owner of the agency that they should hire a small yacht to explore the inlets of the Esterel as far as Saint-Raphaël. The idea met with approval, and he was given the name of a skipper from Saint-Tropez who rented out a motor yacht, the *Toinette*. The owner himself came to the agency to introduce himself to Jean. At forty-five he still had the figure of a young man, and the odd crease in his suntanned face added the merest hint of weariness to his rough charm. As he kept his skipper's cap on, his baldness went largely unnoticed: to greet female passengers he simply raised two fingers to the peak of his cap. His accent, nonchalance and affected coolness charmed Jean. They quickly came to terms: the *Toinette* would anchor at Cannes twice a week to take his tourists out for the day.

'British?' he said. 'They'll be fine. They know the sea. I wouldn't be so keen if you'd said some other nationality. Me, I go out whatever the weather. No excuses!'

He was exaggerating. The first two or three times the *Toinette* stayed at her moorings; the mistral was blowing, and the skipper claimed there was a problem with the engines. Finally they got out to sea, where he told Jean his story. He had racketed across all the oceans of the world before finally coming home to settle at Saint-Tropez with a wife who owned a hotel there, Chez Antoine – it was known all over the region – a proper museum, full of Picassos, Derains, Segonzacs, Braques, Frieszs, Tanguys, Dalís, Ernsts. With a gesture he indicated that the quantity was such, no one knew exactly how many. It would all go to the little girl, Antoinette, 'Toinette' for short, who looked like an angel and was the apple of her uncle's eye, the uncle who lived with them. As the weeks went by, his accounts varied sufficiently for Jean to entertain doubts. But people nodded and assured him that the hotel existed, and its walls were covered with beautiful pictures. Théo, the skipper, was perhaps not a complete liar, except when he was recounting his round-the-world voyages, for clearly he had only ever navigated in coastal waters and always made for port at high speed the moment he glimpsed the slightest hint of fleecy clouds on the horizon. Rashly Jean mentioned to him that his uncle, Captain Duclou, had rounded Cape Horn several times. Théo made a derisively dismissive gesture.

'Cape Horn! Know it by heart. And I tell you: there's no love lost between us.'

Jean was enchanted by it all: the politeness of the tourists he accompanied, the Côte d'Azur's beauty before the July and August crowds, the inconsequential singsong charm of the accents he heard. He forgot his sorrow, and the sharp memory of Chantal's disappearance, even though he would have liked to have her beside him to share the new, wild beauties of this coast. Unthinkingly, he went on wishing that Geneviève would come. Salah told him that the prince, who was feeling stronger, had dissuaded her from joining him. The former chauffeur frequently came to fetch Jean for lunch. One day brought up the subject of Palfy.

'I know he is your friend, but I don't understand him. What is he doing here? One sees him everywhere. One sees him too much. If the scheme he is setting up here is as shady as the one he set up in England, he'll have problems.'

'Salah, I don't know. I like Palfy. He's a happy rogue. He makes genuinely grand gestures. I shall never be like him, and perhaps I ought to regret that.'

'No. Don't regret anything. One needs to be better armed than you are to ward off his wiles.'

Jean closed his eyes in vain, he could not ignore everything. Madeleine moved out of the hotel and up to a studio on the hillside, which she would have liked to decorate with prints and pompoms on the lampshades. Palfy forbade it. He chose the furniture, the curtains, the carpets, the prints. She understood none of it, and acquiesced with a humility learnt from years in men's company. She was his creature now.

The reader, better informed than the hero of this story, will be surprised that Jean has not made the connection between Théo's hotel and Antoine du Courseau, especially after the information Antoinette had given him. Antoinette, *Toinette*, Chez Antoine – Mireille Cece's as well as its Saint-Tropez counterpart, not to mention the garage at Aix – there were enough clues there to put any detective wise about Antoine's whereabouts. But Jean had loved that good, generous, absent man. The idea of pursuing him to his hideaway did not even cross his mind. He would have considered it a betrayal of their ancient, secret pact, and of that last night spent together at an empty, echoing La Sauveté. At the beginning of July, nevertheless, the Toinette arrived at Cannes with an extra crew member on board: a slim girl of fifteen with light-coloured eyes and chestnut hair. She spoke with the same appealing singsong accent as her father. To be fifteen in 1939 was still to be a young girl, to lower one's eyes without shame, not to speak until one was spoken to. She looked after the bar, the picnic on board, the children and the old ladies. When she was there Théo stopped swearing and telling tales of round-the-world voyages.

'Have you seen many as beautiful as her?' he asked, over and over again.

Business remained good until the beginning of August, and then there was something in the air that was not yet anxiety, nor simple worry, but more a sort of instinctive, animal-like drawing back. Only the British seemed not to share it. They came in organised groups, got themselves sunburnt and drunk on rosé wine from the Var, were enraptured at the slightest treats offered by the agency – the bus excursions, boat trips, evenings out at the Palm Beach casino – and had a flutter at boules. Jean, who had not had any news from Ernst for a long time, opened a letter one morning in which his friend imparted some disturbing information.

> *Dear old Hans, I'm writing to you on a Sunday afternoon, during our six hours of weekly rest. There's a thousand of us, boys my age, in a wonderful camp in the Black Forest, living close to nature while we undergo intensive training. Yes, these are university holidays, and I'm using them to do basic military training. It's very exciting and we all feel it gives our life a meaning when our country is so threatened by Poland's constantly aggressive stance. We turn our thoughts towards our German-speaking brothers living beyond our frontier under the insolent tyranny of Colonel Beck. For now it's just humiliations and skirmishes. Tomorrow there could be a massacre. Poland must know that the Reich will not sit idly by while genocide is committed. Our Führer has warned the Poles. Dantzig is German at heart and in spirit. The present injustice is too blatant for our young hearts to accept it. Do not let any of this disturb you! The new Germany only wishes France well ... And even Great Britain. There will be no war in the West. The Munich agreement is signed and sealed, on the honour of two veterans of the last war, who knew the horror of the trenches: Daladier and our Führer. Send me your news. How are your studies going?*

Jean showed the letter to Salah when he came to the agency later that day. He read it, handed it back and said, 'It confirms everything the prince has predicted. In any case, we are leaving for Lebanon tomorrow. Madame is arriving this evening.'

Geneviève in Cannes! Jean felt his legs turn to jelly. At a distance Geneviève was an abstraction, a practically imaginary person who spoke into telephones and only appeared trailing a shimmering, mocking light in her wake. Close to, she would really exist again, and despite holding out no hope that temptation would spark off its simultaneous awkwardness and pleasure between them, he had had a febrile fear of it, ever since Palfy's whispered warning.

'I won't manage to see the prince, after all,' Jean said.

'You'll see him this very evening. That's why I came to the agency. I'll take you to him.'

At the Carlton Jean looked anxiously for Palfy, but the Austro-Daimler was missing from its usual parking space. They went up to the fourth floor, and Salah asked Jean to wait in a small anteroom. Five minutes later he reappeared, standing back from a door that opened into a bedroom with half-drawn curtains that let in the ochre light of late afternoon. An indefinable scent permeated the room. Was it medicine, or some subtle, oriental perfume? He could not tell. Sitting at a small desk by the window, the prince closed a folder. The transparent and waxy skin of his face was attached to a death mask in which there lived, velvety and shining, two heavily lashed eyes which seemed enormous beneath the broad, low projection of his brow, crowned with grey hair full of blue glints. All Jean could see of the rest of him was a torso enveloped in a garnet-coloured silk jacket and a neck delicately protected by a white scarf knotted like a hunting tie.

'So here is Jean, my friend Jean from the hill at Grangeville, from Rome and London and Cannes … a boy who has grown up greatly, seen many things, and works valiantly.'

He held out a cool, thin hand that felt weary and that Jean merely brushed for fear of breaking it.

'I have wanted to see you for a long time, Monseigneur, but Salah told me you have been too tired. I'm happy you're feeling better.'

'I'm not better, but we must leave. War will be declared within a month. I do not get involved in such quarrels. But you? It worries me. You will be sucked into this great machine. You will have to survive, Jean. It's too ridiculous to die at twenty. For nothing, so that the world of tomorrow can be worse still than that of today. I cannot take you with me, you would be a deserter, but I want to do something for you. Here is a sealed white envelope. You are to open it only in case of extreme need. Inside it there is a second envelope, with a name and address. You can at any time present yourself to the addressee and give him the second, *sealed* envelope. If, at the end of the war, you have not needed it, destroy it in its entirety, without ever seeking to know to whom I was directing you. I have been glad to see you, Jean. There is a good chance that it may be for the last time. You cannot imagine how cruel it is to say farewell to objects and people and to repeat to yourself: this is the last time. There are so many pictures of which one would like to preserve a memory … But I am very calm and I am ready. The war will seem long to a man who is weary, very weary.'

'Monseigneur … '

'Goodbye, Jean.'

He extended his hand, which Jean pressed gently, trying to convey his emotion. Salah made a sign, beckoning him to the door. The prince was already opening his folder again.

In the Carlton's lobby Salah took hold of Jean's arm.

'Come over here. I have something to say to you.'

They sat on a sofa next to a window, through which cars could be seen stopping and guests coming and going. The luxury hotel resembled an anthill, animated by unceasing movement: the ants arrived with their suitcases and left again with their hands free, while doormen channelled this ebb and flow of motion, running to the cars, opening doors. Dusk was falling red upon the sea. In the middle of the bay a cruise ship was switching on its deck lights.

'Never speak about that envelope,' Salah said. 'I say that in deadly earnest. It's your secret, your talisman. Even your best friend must know nothing about it.'

Jean realised that 'best friend' meant Palfy, the very person whom he feared might materialise at any moment and swoop down on them.

'We don't know if Monseigneur can survive the voyage. I hope he can. Madame's arrival will help him, but it will be a great shock for her. He has hidden his state of health from her.'

'Does he love her?'

'Immensely.'

Jean felt profoundly uncomfortable. In his appetite for life, and in the muddle of his feelings, he had, in his imagination, betrayed the prince, a singular man who had shown him nothing but goodness. Was every life subject to this series of temptations that couldn't be kept in check, from which only happenstance or some ruthless decision could save you? He felt ashamed and promised himself that he would spell out his resolve to do better, in black and white, that evening in his notebook.

'Lastly, there is another thing,' Salah said in a different voice, as if he wanted to inject a more serious note of warning into his words. 'Yes, one other … I doubt you will understand, but you'll pass on the message, I'm sure. You are to warn your friend, "Baron" Palfy, that he is involved in a much more dangerous game than a person of his sort should be. If he weren't your friend, he would already have found himself in serious trouble. Some well-informed people have granted him a reprieve. But it is only a reprieve.'

Salah saw that his words had disturbed Jean, and he placed his hand on his arm to reassure him.

'Don't worry, it's nothing to do with you. Now let us talk about something else. When this war is over and Monseigneur and I come back to Europe – or perhaps I alone – I should like to see you. Paris and London are both enormous. We could pass each other a hundred times without seeing each other.'

Jean thought hard. The only lasting affections that he could count on were those of the abbé Le Couec and Antoinette. Albert would not survive a war that had insulted his only article of faith: peace at any price.

'I think you could always write to Antoinette du Courseau, Geneviève's sister. She will know where I am.'

Salah wrote the address in a notebook.

'Do not let us lose sight of each other, my dear Jean. How the time here has flown past! I've hardly seen you. We haven't talked about anything. I would have liked to share my admiration for a marvellous poet with you ... You must have heard of him, and you must not make fun of me because I am completely self-taught. I have had to go a long way on my own down a path along which you were guided at a very young age.'

'Who do you mean?'

'Paul-Jean Toulet.'

'I've never read him.'

Salah raised his arms.

'You fortunate man! You have a delightful writer to discover. I envy you. Tomorrow I'll send a copy of his *Counter-rhymes* to you at the agency. I'll leave you the joy of hunting through bookshops for the rest: *The Stripling Girl*, *The Misses La Mortagne*, *Monsieur du Paur*, *Public Figure*. Reading him, you will think of me, and above the fray we shall maintain a Touletian friendship.'

A bellhop appeared in front of Salah.

'Monsieur ... The prince is asking for you. Urgently.'

Their goodbye was brief. Salah disappeared into the lift and Jean walked out of the hotel. Night was falling. He did not know where to go in this elegant and handsome town that was so cold in the evening, without secrets and so aloof that to encounter it in the darkness was to feel immediately uneasy. His solitary evenings usually ended in a small restaurant at the port where Palfy sometimes joined him, but mostly he returned to his hotel room to read. He had started on a reading list of epic proportions: Proust's *In Search of Lost Time*, Roger Martin du Gard's *The Thibaults*, Jules Romains' *Men of Goodwill*. Many of his nights were now spent with his nose in a book, and whether excited or disappointed, he felt that his life was gaining a new dimension as his curiosity was awakened and he measured the narrowness of his own experiences against other destinies of so many different stamps. At twenty, he felt he had seen nothing. His work at *La Vigie*, his six months in London, his job at the agency were dead ends. He would have given anything to go to Lebanon with the prince, and then maybe to Egypt. At least war – if there was going to be war – would make some space and movement. For a short time that evening he wished it would come, in the form in which it is often imagined by naïve eyes: a masculine adventure that disrupts the monotony of a cowardly and gloomy world in which boys of his age encountered only brick walls to bang their heads against.

Palfy did not turn up at the restaurant, and when Jean called Madeleine the telephone rang vainly in an empty apartment. He left a message at the Carlton, went to bed, read, and slept. The next day Palfy remained untraceable, but when he called Madeleine again she answered immediately.

'Yesterday night? I must have gone out for five minutes to get cigarettes. I don't leave the apartment for anything else, as you know. It must have been you I heard – around nine? – as I had my key in the door. I ran, but I was too late. I was afraid it might be Palfy. He would have been furious.'

'Why?'

'He likes me to be at home then.'

'Oh. Okay … Listen, I need to see him, the sooner the better. Tell him, will you?'

'Mm. Jean … do you think he's really a baron?'

'He's as much a baron as I am.'

'You're a baron too! I thought so.'

He did not have the heart to disillusion her. That evening, before dinner, he went for a walk by the port. A new liner was waiting out to sea, and launches were leaving, loaded with passengers. The exodus was under way, still hardly perceptible but clear enough for it to be unmistakable nevertheless. Jean mingled with the other onlookers and friends of travellers gathering on the quay. The yellow Hispano-Suiza appeared, driven by a white chauffeur with Salah seated beside him. It stopped in front of the customs building. A nurse came forwards, pushing a wheelchair. Salah and the chauffeur sat the prince carefully in it. Geneviève followed, wearing a light-coloured dress and a beret, with a travelling coat over one arm and a jewellery bag in her other hand. Jean had time to register her lightly made-up face and see its sadness and disarray. How would she survive so far from London and her friends? The group moved towards the police and customs building. They emerged again on the other side of the barrier, and two porters lifted the chair into a launch at whose bow there stood a black sailor in a white turban and uniform. Geneviève turned round to look at the crowd gathered on the quay. If she had known he was there, she would have been able to make him out among the other anxious and curious faces. The launch cast off and pushed back, helped by the sailor at the bow with his gaff. Salah stood next to the prince, one hand resting on the back of the wheelchair, contemplating the diminishing quay, the town switching on its first lights, France and Europe in their last days of peace.

'The rats are leaving the sinking ship,' someone said behind Jean.

Other cars were arriving, bringing their passengers: a Cadillac, a Rolls-Royce, a Mercedes, a Bentley. The yellow Hispano-Suiza started up. The chauffeur had taken off his jacket and was smoking a cigarette.

Jean called Madeleine. She sounded anxious. No, the 'baron' was not in Cannes. In the society column of the *Éclaireur du Soir* she had seen a photo of him in a dinner jacket at a reception at the Casino de la Méditerranée at Nice. Perhaps he had stayed on to spend the day there. She also needed to see him urgently. Jean walked the streets of Cannes for a while, alone and lost. He was reluctant to return to his hotel room, for he knew that reading would not banish the two images that had suddenly forced their way back to disturb the peace of mind he thought he had found: Geneviève going away from him towards the Middle East, and Chantal, her long hair tumbling across the pillow, framing her sleeping face. Running away had made no difference. Everything was still there within him, and the one person he would have liked to confide in lived cooped up in Grangeville. Writing to her might alleviate the obscure, nameless pain that he felt.

Dear Antoinette,
Midnight. I have no one to talk to. I wish you were here. I want mussels, cider and apples. I dream of a green field. I saw your sister just now, boarding a ship for Lebanon. It hurt to see her go, as if I had lost someone dear to me. It seems impossible to deny that I'm as attached to the du Courseaus (not all of them!) as I am to my own family. A question I hardly dare ask: where is Chantal? Do you know? With love, Jean

In his notebook he wrote:

m) Writing is a wonderful exorcism. A letter to Antoinette and I feel better. And often — not often enough — this notebook has served to show me things more clearly in the muddle of every day. Everything's so complicated! And no one warned me. All I was told were platitudes. Geneviève could have talked to me. It didn't happen, and doubtless Palfy was right to put me on my guard. Now there she is, disappearing. I shan't forget the real heartbreak there was for me in her last fleeting appearance. Where did I read, 'The heart must either break or turn to lead'? Mine will have to turn to lead, or I'll be no good for anything.
n) We know nothing about other people. Or rather, others know everything about me and I know nothing of them. On my

list of questions that I need to resolve, one of the most important is about the prince and Salah. After the message Salah gave me to pass on, I no longer see him in the same light. Palfy has to clear up this mystery, as he also needs to tell me what he is up to with Madeleine.

o) I have placed the prince's envelope on the table in front of me. It is the apple of the tree of knowledge. Am I Adam or am I Eve?

Next morning the *Toinette* docked at the marina and Jean had to give Théo some bad news. The group of English tourists booked for that day had just cancelled. The agency was sinking under the weight of telegrams from holidaymakers announcing that they would rather not come just now. Théo took it badly.

'What are they worried about, these *Angliches*? That we'll make corned beef out of their suckling-pig hides? The war? But there isn't going to be any war in Cannes. Two weeks, two weeks I tell you, my fine friend, is all it will take General Gamelin to drive those Germans straight back to Berlin with a marching band to lead the way. I tell you … the Saint-Tropez brass band is ready to go. Right out in front!'

Jean stayed on board for lunch. He enjoyed Théo's posturing and unflagging swagger, and for once Toinette was not unreachable. She had no one to serve and she stayed sitting at her father's side, leafing distractedly through a fashion magazine. She was listening, without appearing to, and refilling their glasses. Jean watched her lovely fifteen-year-old face, her beautiful light eyes, from her mother almost certainly, her long chestnut-coloured hair and her bare arm as she poured, with its still-childlike hand. Who would be the first to capture this sweet being, so lovely in her simplicity and natural beauty? The first Gontran Longuet who appeared on a motorbike or at the wheel of a red Delahaye, most likely, if all women were the same.

There was a moment when he mentioned he was from Normandy. Toinette looked up and stared at him. Théo noticed.

'That always sets her off. Her uncle's Norman. He talks to her about Normandy sometimes, how it rains there and the light, when there is any, it's very pretty.'

'Does he often come to see you?' Jean asked.

'Does ... He lives with us! He only likes the Midi now. He's a funny bloke, I can tell you. He owns a Bugatti.'

Jean no longer had any doubts. Antoine du Courseau was alive and well at Saint-Tropez, unbeknown to his family, and this shy, graceful child was not his niece but his daughter. If you looked carefully you could see straight away some of Geneviève's features, and that look Antoinette had had at the same age, as if butter wouldn't melt in her mouth. And her name! Toinette. The boat. The hotel and its sign: Chez Antoine. Everything was becoming clear.

'What are you thinking about?' Théo asked.

'About Normandy.'

Théo had drunk so much pastis that he began casting glances at his cabin, eager to have a siesta before putting to sea again.

'Well?' he said. 'Is that it for this summer? He might apologise, Herr Hitler, for spoiling our lives. Anyway ... if it works out again, send me word and I'll come.'

He yawned and moved towards the bridge. Jean caught Toinette's eye and she smiled shyly. He leaned towards her and murmured, 'Tell your uncle that Jean Arnaud sends his very best wishes. Promise?'

'I promise.'

Théo whipped around anxiously, as though Jean had made the most of his few seconds of inattention to show his daughter his private parts. Their smiles reassured him. At the gangway he said, 'All the best ... bye. The little one's sweet, isn't she?'

'More than sweet. Bye, Théo. I'll phone you.'

The afternoon was undemanding. He was the only one in the office when the postman arrived with a parcel for him: Toulet's *Counter-rhymes*, which Salah had promised him. Two of his colleagues had received their call-up papers. The owner of the agency was wearing a suitably serious expression. He could already see himself walking behind a hearse, having placed a notice in the window: 'Closed for reasons of general heroism'. At last Palfy appeared, wearing a shantung suit, a blue silk handkerchief spilling out of his breast pocket.

'Come. I'm taking you out. I've found a delicious bistro at Mougins where we shall taste kid *aux herbes* courtesy of Madame Victoire. A highly indicative name for an era such as ours.'

The Austro-Daimler was outside. Palfy hummed all the way to Mougins. When they were seated he ordered pastis and tomato juice. They seemed to know him, and Madame Victoire kissed him.

'You are unfaithful to me, Baron.'

'Me?' he exclaimed with indignation.

'Yes, you!'

'All right, I admit it!'

'Your cynicism is shocking!'

Jean did not know where to begin. Palfy looked so happy. Did he have any right to curtail the happiness of a man so sure of himself? He let him keep talking, and as Palfy did so he pulled a packet of visiting cards out of his pocket and handed one to Jean.

>At Cannes ...
>Mme Miranda
>Tel: 28-32

'Simple, elegant, discreet. Don't you think? I adore the name Miranda. Where did Madeleine get the idea to call herself that? Can you see me having her answer the telephone as ... Mme Madeleine? But Miranda's almost a fairytale name for the French, for the English too come to that, they all have a little niece called Miranda, an aunt

Miranda, a sister Miranda. Can't you see the attraction?'

With horror, Jean thought he understood.

'Constantin, for heaven's sake, don't tell me you've become Madeleine's pimp.'

'No, you fool. Madeleine's past all that. Instead I have appointed her the head of a charming, and entirely frivolous, network of pretty girls and women who have difficulty making ends meet. A telephone call, a little disclosure of one's tastes, and she finds just the right match from her card-file index. Obviously the card files need expanding. We're recruiting – Madeleine mainly – nice little wives whose husbands are looking the other way. Professionals are out, of course. Somehow they always strike the wrong note. Now, you can help ... no no, I beg you ... none of your sensitivity ... you're in constant contact with English visitors. Here's a packet of visiting cards. All you have to do is distribute them intelligently. No need for explanations, clients will understand at once. My system is completely new. A great pity I'm not able to patent it. I've already got a name: "Call Girls & Co". All right?'

Jean hesitated. There were only the two of them in the small restaurant, which in August should have been full to the doors, with customers crushed together at long tables and busy waitresses nagging them. The rats really were leaving the sinking ship. Soon there would be only Palfy and himself left in France to face the coming war.

'I should hate to think I was forcing you,' Palfy said, annoyed by his silence.

'You're not forcing me, but I've got a message for you. I'm afraid that in your scurrilous scheme you've treated the competition much too lightly. Apparently if you hadn't been my friend you wouldn't have been given a second chance.'

Palfy put down his glass without flinching. He knew how to take such shocks.

'I see,' he said. 'I would be awfully grateful if you would reveal who asked you to convey this message.'

'Is that absolutely necessary?'

'Absolutely. If it's the owner of some crappy little brothel, I am not scared in the slightest. But someone highly placed would definitely worry me.'

Jean did not hesitate. If he failed to reveal Salah's role, Palfy would treat the matter as a joke. It was far better to really put him on his guard.

'Salah.'

Palfy picked up his glass and drank its contents in a single gulp. The roast kid was served.

'I'm not very hungry any more.'

'Why do you think Salah's warning is so serious?'

Palfy shrugged.

'The reason is slightly delicate to explain.'

'Do tell me.'

'Your friend, the prince, is a real prince. An Egyptian title, I think, and fairly authentic, at least more so than mine. Clean hands, doubtless transparently so, though I have not seen them. Educated at a French college, then Oxford, has travelled all over the world, high society, considerable fortune. If you haven't lived such a life, you have no idea how boring it is. So how do you distract yourself? Exploiting the stupidity and vices of men is one temptation. Sex has been an investment of his. Oh, not directly, of course … One must keep one's hands clean, always! But through the agency of devoted aides. Salah, among others. Even that Longuet fellow from Grangeville. Do you remember telling me how surprised you were that he mentioned his name to you in his car in Rome one evening? The centre of the organisation, and his headquarters, are in Lebanon.'

In Lebanon? That explained everything: the reason for their departure, their destination.

'How do you know?' Jean asked.

'Oh, little by little … In London people talked and, you know … in my free time I keep bad company … The girls sometimes talk … I've built up a picture of a very small part of a large network that covers several countries. Unwittingly you helped me. For example, that house in Chelsea is a cover—'

'Does Geneviève know?'

'No. Definitely not! But you can see that the facts prove it: the dubious butler, the different chambermaids every morning. They have work permits, "regular" employment. The famous Madame Germaine, who whipped half the masochists in London, worked under their protection. You found Salah there.'

Two American couples came into the restaurant after hesitating at the sight of its interior, which, apart from Jean and Palfy's table, remained empty. Victoire took possession of them, lit some candles and was translating the menu into irresistible English until one of the men interrupted her in perfect French and pointed out that there was an essential difference between a rock lobster and a lobster and that only dullards would confuse one with the other, and would she please not consider them as such because it irritated them, especially as they were, all four of them, great friends of France.

'Something of a misjudgement on her part,' Palfy murmured. 'A very French error that is the result of your preconceived ideas and lack of curiosity. You're a whisker away from treating the rest of the world as fools, which is your way of reassuring yourselves about who you are. But what a letdown it will be for you when you lose the war!'

'Do you think we're going to lose it?'

'Who can doubt it?'

Palfy drove slowly back down to Cannes. The cool night air,

the engine turning over in near silence, the Austro-Daimler's overpowering majesty, produced a heady sense of freedom. It would have been so pleasant just to go on living like this, not to see the clouds massing on the horizon. They stopped outside the building where Madeleine lived. There was no light at her window.

'She can't be asleep already,' Palfy said.

They walked up two floors and rang her bell, but there was no answer. Palfy had a key. The apartment was in disarray, the bed unmade, the cupboards and drawers empty and wide open. A light had been left on in the bathroom. They looked at each other. Did they have to find out what had happened?

'We risk coming across a truly revolting spectacle,' Palfy murmured.

He was pale and calm, concentrating on how best to conduct himself, and Jean realised that this time the age of fun, the age of carelessness and excess, was over. A terrible shadow passed over them both, all the more threatening for remaining secret and invisible, for only having been hinted at. They still had time to wipe their fingerprints off everything they had touched and silently tiptoe away.

'A little courage!' Palfy said, his voice shaking.

He opened the bathroom door. Empty. The bath still full of water. On the glass shelf above the washbasin some perfume bottles still stood unstopped.

'Phew!' Jean said.

They went back to the bedroom, and on a corner table found a sheet of paper folded in four, in Madeleine's large round handwriting.

> *Constantin, I like my life. My little place in Rue Lepic's worth more than your big place in Cannes. 'They' warned me. They was nicer than I expected. Usually its curtains straight away. If I was you, I'd get out fast. No hard feelings*
> *Madeleine*

'They have been quick,' Palfy said, a trace of admiration in his voice.

The telephone rang. It was a 'customer'. He sent him packing.

'The annoying thing,' he said, as the car wound down towards the port, 'is that I put money into the idea. The car? I won't get a penny for it. All those panic-stricken millionaires have gone off and left dozens of unsaleable monsters behind. I settled my bill at the Carlton yesterday. I should be able to stay there another couple of weeks if I leave the weekly bill unpaid for a while, and thenmake myself scarce. A real shame that I couldn't patent my little invention and sell it to the Americans. More difficult than the last time around. A question of morals. Very punctilious, you know, the Americans, about morality. In ten years' time you'll see I was right. One should never be ahead of the morals of one's time, whether one's selling toothpaste or pleasure. That will be my consolation: to have been a pioneer. What about you? Are you happy with your job at the agency?'

Jean agreed that it was bearable, that he had known worse and that, going out nearly every day with the tourists he looked after, he was less bored than he would be sitting behind a desk. Even so, the future seemed limited. He had no chance of getting a better job until he had done his military service, and actually the necessity for that seemed to be fast approaching. He was twenty and he could go early, before he was called up.

'Dammit!' Palfy said. 'That could be a way out.'

They stopped beside one of the quays. Both French and foreign yachts were moored there. Crews were sitting drinking and eating in their cockpits, by the light of storm lanterns.

'Usually there are ten times as many foreigners,' Jean remarked. 'Have they all gone? Yesterday I heard a man in the crowd say, "The rats are leaving the sinking ship!"'

'They're fools! A lightning war, and Europe will be German, or French. Great business opportunities are coming. It's a good sign that the rats are leaving. Let us stay, and swear that if, in two weeks' time, I have failed to come up with a new scheme, we shall enlist in the French army.'

'My father won't be able to bear it.'

'Oh come on … he'd be ashamed if you wriggled out of it. One military march, and the most hardened onlookers have tears in their eyes.'

The next fortnight flashed past. The agency closed. Cannes was emptying. The fine summer was dying gently away, indifferent to the preparations for the great upheaval. Jewellers were selling off diamonds, banks dollars. From the horizon in the early morning came the dull, rhythmic *crump* of artillery. The French navy was exercising out at sea. A regiment from Marseille marched through the town. Troops were taking up defensive positions on the Italian frontier. Mules pulling mountain cannons followed. A regiment of Senegalese garrisoned at Fréjus left for the north. At the harbour master's a queue formed of foreign yacht owners waiting to have their papers stamped to leave for Spain or Gibraltar. Shops began to run out of sugar, coffee, tea and jam. Jean and Palfy went for drives in the country behind Cannes, where a soothing indifference reigned, sampling the last of a summer that had been heartbreakingly tranquil and delightful. In the cafés, between games of cards and boules, people listened to the wireless as it broadcast with undeniable and vindictive skill its news digest preparing the population for war. Jean was tempted several times to go as far as Saint-Tropez to see Théo and Toinette and confirm that the Norman uncle was really the man he thought he was. He made do with calling Théo on the telephone on his last day to tell him that he was enlisting.

'In the Train des Équipages?'[18] Théo asked with a trace of anxiety.

'No, no. Infantry.'

'But you'll be on foot, and Berlin's a bit far for marching.'

'I'll hitchhike.'

'All right then. You're a brave one. I'm just in the GVC.'[19]

'The GVC.?'

'Guarding the lines of communication. When you're past forty they don't let you go to war, especially when you're a father. Anyhow, it'll be short, I'm telling you ... Théo is telling you. We'll expect you back at Christmas to slosh down some champagne with us. And come back with a Croix de Guerre. That'll please Toinette.'

'Send her a kiss from me.'

'Send her a kiss!'

Jean felt Théo was taking himself a little too seriously as a father, and being excessively strait-laced. Of course he wished Toinette nothing but well. Come to think of it, why shouldn't she be his wartime godmother? Théo said he would have to think about it.

'I don't want her to get any ideas. At her age, for heaven's sake!'

'Ask her uncle Antoine what he thinks. Tell him it's for Jean Arnaud.'

'Why? He hasn't got a clue who you are!'

'Yes he has, I promise he has. I'm a friend.'

The second week's bill from the Carlton resembled, as foreseen, one of those ultimatums that had been echoing around Europe for the past three years. It was impossible to misread its tone. Palfy had already safely hidden several suits and some underwear, basic necessities for a future hoax that he was already applying his mind to. In the meantime he needed to disappear as fast as he could. Posters on town-hall doors were inviting him to do just that: 'Enlist. Re-enlist. Beat the call-up.' Despite having been discharged at twenty, he requested to take a new medical board. The medical officer noted his hollow chest, but in the face of his intense feigned patriotism passed him 'fit for active service'. Jean was passed fit without reservation.

A fifty-franc note slipped to the orderly secretary in charge of the allocation of recruits to training depots got them onto the same list. They were each issued with directions, but Palfy tore up their travel warrants. After a final tour of the town's nightclubs, where age-exempt saxophonists blew up a storm on empty dance floors, they climbed into the Austro-Daimler and headed west and north, towards the Auvergne.

Palfy was in raptures at the thought of the magnificent bill left behind at the hotel. At every stop he took the account out of his wallet and grieved at not having ordered caviar and champagne every night.

'One day I shall regret it bitterly. But the truth compels me to say that at this moment I am sick of champagne, caviar, lobster *à l'américaine*, and *foie gras*. One must take care of oneself. The MO was right, apart from the fact that he needs new glasses: it's not my chest that's hollow, it's my stomach that's ballooning.'

Three days later, after numerous stops at restaurants and country hotels, the all-consuming Austro-Daimler pulled up outside high gates at the entrance to a field at Yssingeaux in the upper Loire. On a washed-out banner they read: 'Military Training Centre. No entry.' A huge sergeant was on guard duty, his helmet and boots greased, his thumbs tucked into his belt.

'Move along!' he shouted mechanically.

It took him some time to realise that the two men alighting from the monstrous dimensions of the vehicle in front of him were recruits. And recruits liable to a week's confinement to barracks for arriving two hours late.

'What – what about your car?' he asked, shocked that they should abandon their fabulous conveyance so blithely, in the middle of nowhere.

'My chauffeur, who is following behind on his bicycle, should be here in a moment. He will drive it to the garage. And if by some chance he should fail to appear, it's yours. An extraordinary vehicle, whose like we shall not see again. It was built especially for a Russian grand duke.'

The sergeant judged that this strange recruit was in urgent need of basic discipline and the full rigour of the regulations that constitute the strength of all armies. He sentenced both men to a week's confinement. Across open fields – they would be given a key when they had earned the colonel's trust, as the orderly subtly put it – they were led to a barn where several men, all completely drunk, were snoring in the straw. Palfy changed into his silk pyjamas, quite unbothered by the strong smell of rats.

'You see,' he said to Jean, who was still angry at their reception, 'we are about to learn the hard way. They are going to temper us in the steel from which victories are forged. *Vive la France!*'

Their neighbour, a hirsute ginger-haired man bristling with stalks of straw, sat up.

'*Vive la France?* Shut your gob. Demob is all we give a shit about!'

And lay down again. For the record, let us note that this rebel's name was Boucharon, that, slowed down by his flat feet which prevented him from running, he was, in June 1940, taken prisoner by the enemy and sent to Silesia, where he had to wait another five years to be demobilised. Poor Boucharon, a victim of society, the state and himself. There were hundreds, thousands of Boucharons whose fates were sealed that night of 31 August. The following day, emerging from the aftereffects of their overindulgence in red wine, these warriors took a moderate interest in the news of the day: the Germans were invading Poland. A captain explained to them that the Polish cavalry were accomplishing marvels and that the Nazis' armoured divisions were staring death in the face. With their lances the Poles were aiming at the firing slits and putting out the eyes of the German tank crews.

The whole troop having been confined to barracks, Palfy and Jean hardly minded their week's punishment. As the depot lacked new kit, the men were issued with blue-grey uniforms from the last war. An orderly appeared with clippers. In an excess of enthusiasm that had more than a whiff of insolence to it – the high command did not require such zeal – the friends had their heads shaved. They had to ask for new forage caps which did not slip down to their ears. Throughout the first week the Austro-Daimler remained parked outside the gate where they had left it. The colonel summoned Palfy.

'Private Palfy,' he said nervously, 'I have decided to speak to you myself. You have arrived at this training depot in a car that demands financial resources well beyond the means of a private soldier, second-class. At such a moment as this, that represents something of a scandal. It must cease. Remove that Austro-Daimler, which offends the patriotic gaze of all of us, and let us see it no more. On another matter, having received a report from the officer in charge of mail, I must warn you that you do not have the right to receive letters addressed to you as "Private Baron Palfy, second class, Yssingeaux". The use of titles, be they real or false, is forbidden in military correspondence below the rank of lieutenant. I could have had the duty sergeant inform you of these matters. I preferred to take them up with you myself. I trust that you understand the seriousness of my warning. You may go … '

Palfy sensed that the colonel had been on the point of saying 'my dear baron', but had stopped himself in time. He saluted, replaced his cap and, after a sparkling about-turn, went out. The Austro-Daimler was sold, piece by piece, to Yssingeaux's three garages. A scrap merchant bought the chassis. Crushed, it would be used to make artillery shells, an excellent way to return the steel to its country of origin. With the rest of the army watching France's borders, the training of new recruits and reservists continued in the serenity and calm of an imperturbable, determined Auvergne. A warrant officer taught two hundred fighters the unbeatable way to win a battle: as soon as tanks were sighted on the horizon, all they had to do was dig a hole fifty centimetres wide and one and a half metres deep. When the tank reached the infantryman, he crouched down, waited for it to pass over him, then straightened up and shot the tank from behind. This clever tactic was known as the 'Gamelin hole' after the general who, from his operational headquarters at Vincennes, was commanding the Allies. Simple, but someone had to come up with it.

Palfy, with his good humour and sarcastic comments, helped Jean put up with this idiotic life. Their evenings were spent writing enthusiastic letters, hoping that they would be read by the censors. Madeleine was the first to reply to Palfy. Jean received half a page from Albert.

> *I have no right to judge you. Freedom is one and indivisible. My faith remains intact and I shall stick by it. I swore to myself that you would never be a soldier. My disappointment is very great. I expect it will finish me off. I'm an old man. Don't ever turn up at my house in uniform, I shall shut the door in your face.*
>
> *Albert*

In mid-September Jean was summoned to the guardhouse. A lady was asking for him. It was Antoinette, in a grey dress and little provincial hat, her features drawn from two nights spent on trains. She started when she saw him with his head shaved, then smiled when he told her he had done it as an act of defiance. A good-natured lieutenant granted him a pass till midnight. Jean accompanied Antoinette to the Hôtel d'Auvergne, where she had booked a room. They had dinner in the low-ceilinged restaurant, not far from where the colonel was eating and watching them out of the corner of his eye, mildly disconcerted at this intake that contained barons and privates, second-class, their heads shaved like billiard balls, who held hands with elegant young women clearly of good family. Jean did not hide his pleasure at seeing Antoinette again. She was a link to a time in his life that it felt good to cling to, to remember what happiness had been. He did not look at her as he once had. Faded already, she was no longer the heady flower of their trysts beneath the cliff and in the barn, the sad lover of his last night at Dieppe before his departure for England. He found her gauche in comparison to Geneviève, and even to those worldly English wives who had slipped into his room at night during his weekends in the country. She lacked Chantal's freshness. But she was Antoinette, his friend from the beginning, the first girl who had known how to make him happy and make him suffer. She had also braved two nights on a train to see him and bring him socks she had knitted herself, chocolate, books, and money. All pretexts that failed to hide the feelings that she no longer dared show him directly. She also brought him something even better than these presents: news from Grangeville. Chantal had returned to Malemort and taken over the farm from her father, who had been mobilised. Her mother refused to speak to her. In the evenings she rode to Grangeville on her bicycle to meet Antoinette. They spoke a great deal about Jean. Gontran Longuet, a corporal in the Train des Équipages, had turned up for two days' leave dressed in a comic-opera uniform and brandishing a stick. Chantal had refused to meet him. Michel had been enlisted in a signals company in which, along with other pigeon fanciers, he helped train carrier pigeons that, whenever the handle on the field telephone broke, connected the headquarters at Vincennes to General George's forward command post fifty kilometres away. Marie-Thérèse du Courseau, settled into a hotel at Compiègne very close to her son's unit, had the great joy, thanks to the influence of her brother, deputy and member of the commission on the uses of tobacco in the Assembly, of dining with her son every evening. There was not a soldier in the French army more mollycoddled than he was. Joseph Outen, an officer cadet in a fortress regiment, was standing guard somewhere on the Maginot line, where he filled his spare time with the study of Zen Buddhism. The abbé Le Couec had got himself into serious trouble. Three days after war had been declared, a pious bigot had reported to the gendarmes that in knocking at the door of his rectory she had heard the abbé speaking German to two men who had hidden themselves in a bedroom before the abbé answered her knock. Monsieur Le Couec had been questioned for forty-eight hours by the military police before being released. He insisted that he did not know more than three words of German and had been speaking Breton to his friends. Now, every morning, he had to register at the gendarmerie. (Jean did not interrupt Antoinette, but the memory of Yann and Monsieur Carnac came back to him. What had become of those two strange figures?? Let us not spoil the suspense by revealing too soon how they will surface once again.) Albert, likewise, had been arrested in Dieppe for insulting a deputy in the street. The deputy in question had voted for war in the Assembly. Having learnt that his attacker was a disabled veteran, highly decorated and mentioned five times in dispatches, the politician decided not to press charges. But Albert was under surveillance by the gendarmes and forbidden to leave Grangeville.

After dinner, under the envious gaze of the colonel and a major, they went upstairs to Antoinette's room. Jean made to kiss her. She pushed him gently away.

'No, my darling. Just on the cheek, please.'

'Is there someone in your life?'

'Absolutely nobody. I'm twenty-five and an old maid, I promise you, for the rest of my life.'

'So?'

'Sit down, dearest Jean. Do I always tell you the truth?'

He lowered his gaze. This time there was no escape. His heart was racing, and he turned so pale that Antoinette hesitated.

'I could still say nothing.'

Jean breathed deeply. He needed his strength and courage to start out on this new stage of his existence, in which he would know whose son he was.

'Go on,' he said, closing his eyes.

She stroked the shaved nape of his neck, as if she were stroking a large, sad cat.

'I love you,' she murmured.

Her hand was soft, the light, gentle brush of a mother putting her child to bed. He would have liked to sink into sleep, his face buried in Antoinette's thighs, lulled by her touch and smell.

'Have you ever had any idea?' she asked.

'No.'

'Not the slightest?'

'Maybe.'

'In that case, you're right.'

'You mean I am Geneviève's son?'

He opened his eyes and saw her nodding, a serious smile on her unmade-up lips.

'And of whom?'

Antoinette shrugged.

'She probably doesn't know herself. A doctor at the clinic, or another patient, one evening when she was bored. It was Maman who gathered you up and put you on Albert and Jeanne's doorstep. I don't know any more than that.'

Now he understood: everything was becoming clear. He would have liked to make love with Antoinette one last time, to roll on the bed, stroke her breasts and stomach. He put his arms around her.

'No,' she said. 'Don't tempt me. It's become impossible since I found out, yet the only reasons I can find to refuse you are awfully bourgeois. I'm scared. There you are: as if it was an ancient curse. Before, I didn't know. Let me go.'

She pulled away and kissed him on both cheeks.

'Don't be scared,' she said, laughing, with tears welling up, 'don't be scared, I shan't ask you to call me Aunt Antoinette. Goodnight, darling, go back to your barn. I need to sleep. I have a train to catch at five o'clock tomorrow morning.'

*

As he was making his way back to the depot on foot, the black Citroën belonging to the colonel stopped level with him. Lowering his window, this very superior officer invited him to get in.

'It's dark and cold. A colonel is father to his regiment.'

'I could definitely do with a father,' Jean said.

'I understand: it's not a bad figure of speech. You mustn't let the news get the better of you … '

'What news?'

'The Soviets have invaded Poland in their turn. Tomorrow we will know officially. The information has been censored until we know exactly what to make of it. Friends or foes? We'll soon find out. Anti-communist propaganda is already rearing its ugly head. Who can predict the future, especially what happens next? No one. Appearances suggest that the two nations, German and Soviet, have officially partitioned Poland between them, but just imagine the moment when the two armies, Nazi and Communist, find themselves face to face. The guns will start firing by themselves. Then we shall intervene, and cut through Germany like a knife through butter … '

'I thought Germany had no butter, but plenty of cannons.'

The colonel laughed good-humouredly.

'You've got a quick wit, like your friend Palfy.'

Then, sauvely: 'You were with a very pretty young woman this evening.'

'She's my aunt.'

'Hell! If I'd had aunts like that , my life would have been a lot less gloomy. And how long is she staying?'

'She's leaving tomorrow morning at five o'clock.'

The colonel, visibly chagrined, was silent. Five hundred metres before the depot he asked his driver to stop.

'You'll understand that for discipline generally it would be disastrous for the colonel to be seen giving a recruit a lift back to camp. Goodnight, my friend.'

Jean walked on, immediately forgetting the colonel, overcome again by the whirlwind of thoughts that assailed him. Poland occupied an infinitesimally small part of them. In the barn he woke Palfy, who had been asleep on his straw mattress.

'The Russians have gone into Poland,' he told him.

'Mmm, that is bad news! I fear we'll soon be overtaken by events.'

'That's not all ... '

He reported what Antoinette had told him.

'Marvellous!' Palfy said. 'We shall be invincible, with your uncle Michel in a pigeon-fanciers' unit and Gontran Longuet as a brilliant corporal in the Train des Équipages, Théo guarding our lines of communication, the abbé Le Couec and your father being watched by the gendarmes, and the two of us at the bottom of our Gamelin holes. Long live the French army!'

'Ye gods! Can'y you just shut up at this time of night? Demob!' Boucharon grumbled.

'Go back to sleep, old thing. Tomorrow France will have need of men like you.'

Boucharon turned over on his straw mattress and immediately started snoring.

'So,' Jean said in a low voice, 'you don't give a damn that I'm Geneviève's son.'

'Absolutely! But remember one thing: I stopped you on the edge of the precipice. One step further and you would have been sleeping with your Ma-a-man ... Greek tragedy in all its horror!'

It was true: without Palfy's intuition, irreparable damage might have been done.

'Get undressed and go to sleep. I'll bet you need it. Would you like me to tuck you in?'

'No thanks,' Jean said.

He took a long time to fall asleep. Images swarmed in his head:

Antoinette's pale body, lost for ever, Chantal refusing to see Gontran Longuet, Geneviève leaving for Lebanon, and tomorrow the war that would affirm the manhood he had at last attained. He had got there empty-handed, disowned by Albert, alone and with a heart of lead, his only talismans the prince's white envelope, the volume of *Counter-rhymes* given to him by Salah, and his notebook as a witness to his past. What, or whom, was he going to believe in?

Next morning the officer in charge of the mail brought him a letter, to which he knew that from now on he would not dare to reply.

> *Dear godson, I send you my best warm wishes and a muffler. I hope it isn't dangerous there, where you are. Don't catch cold. Uncle Antoine sends you a thousand affectionate thoughts. He says you are his only friend. He kisses you, and I shake your hand.*
>
> *Toinette*

That is not an ending, the reader will say, irritated not to know what is in the sealed envelope given to Jean by the prince, or what role Yann and Monsieur Carnac have yet to play, or how Palfy's war will turn out. Jean Arnaud's life is full of promise, and it has hardly begun. He was a foundling boy. We shall tell in another book how he becomes a man.

Notes

1 The allied Army of the Orient, based in northern Greece in the last year of the First World War.

2. Royalist insurgents from western France during the French Revolution.

3 '*Mirobolant*'.

4 Route Nationale 7, the main road between Paris and the Italian border.

5 'Mirelingues' means 'of a thousand tongues' and refers to Lyon's status as a commercial centre, especially in the Middle Ages. 'Mirelingue-la-brumeuse ' = 'foggy town of a thousand tongues'

6 A nationalist and monarchist daily newspaper.

7 In France's general election of 1919 several new deputies were war veterans, and the Chamber of Deputies was nicknamed the *Chambre Bleu Horizon* in an allusion to the blue-grey colour of French uniforms.

8 Édouard Herriot served three terms as Prime Minister in the Third Republic and for many years as president of the Chamber of Deputies.

9 The nickname of a Genoese boy, Giovan Battista Perasso, who started a revolt in 1746 against the Habsburg forces occupying the city. Two hundred years later Italy's Fascist government named the Opera Nazionale Balilla, a paramilitary youth organisation, after him.

10 A youth movement aligned with the aims of the *Parti Radical*, France's oldest political party.

11 Leopoldo Fregoli, a famous Italian impersonator and quick-change artist of the early 20th century.

12 The 'Norman hole': a measure of calvados drunk between courses that is intended to refresh the palate and reawaken the appetite.

13 On the east side of the port.

14 Émile Littré's *Dictionnaire de la Langue Française* is a four-volume dictionary originally published in Paris in 1863–72.

15 *La Nouvelle Revue Française*, a literary magazine founded in 1909 that was the precursor of the publishing house, Éditions Gallimard.

16 Le Prix Goncourt, France's most prestigious literary prize, first awarded by the Académie Goncourt in 1903 after its foundation by Edmond de Goncourt in memory of his brother Jules.

17 'Motherland'.

18 The logistics and supply corps of the French army, created by Napoleon in 1807.

19 Service de Garde des Voies de Communication.